Arthur

Flint

BY CHARLES G. NORRIS

Doubleday, Doran and Company, Inc.

GARDEN CITY, NEW YORK

1944

PRINTED IN THE UNITED STATES
AT
THE COUNTRY LIFE PRESS, GARDEN CITY, N. Y.

To my long-suffering, patient, and loyal friend,
D. WALTER McLELLAN

This book is a work of fiction. It is neither history
nor biography. Some readers may overlook this fact,
since the story deals with social and economic questions which are not only real, but contemporary and
controversial. So it may be well to emphasize that
this is a novel and does not describe actual happenings or portray real people, living or dead. The story
and its characters are the creation of the author's
imagination.

An emerald is as green as grass;
A ruby red as blood;
A sapphire shines as blue as heaven;
A flint lies in the mud.

A diamond is a brilliant stone,
To catch the world's desire;
An opal holds a fiery spark;
But a flint holds fire.

CHRISTINA ROSSETTI

Flint

CHAPTER I

A LOWERING FOG hung menacingly over San Francisco. On this bleak December day in 1933, it looked like a giant's hand with claw-shaped fingers poised above the town as if to clutch it in a strangling grip.

The thought occurred to J. O. B. Rutherford, standing between the heavy brocade curtains in his mother's lavishly furnished parlor and looking out through the window. The buildings on the next rise of hill were blocks of pale gray and darker gray superimposed upon each other like a Cubist's painting, their tops and chimneys lost to view in the thick overhanging murk. A fine drizzle was falling, turning the asphalt of the streets black, the sidewalks a shiny inky lacquer.

"Hell of a day for Christmas," a strong young voice said at his shoulder.

It was his son Stan who spoke. Aware that he was there, J.O.B. did not turn.

The two men stood beside each other silently regarding the dismal prospect, each thinking his own thoughts. Stan was glad that he and his family had had only to walk across the street to reach his grandmother's house, whereas the Baxters—his uncle, aunt, and his cousin Chris—who had driven in from Visalia the day before and had stayed the previous night at the Mark Hopkins Hotel, would have to come to the Christmas breakfast by taxi. Meanwhile his father with an inward smile of satisfaction reflected on the pleasure his daughter was certain to have when she opened the box marked "Revillon's, New York."

From the Bay came the prolonged muffled growlings of ferryboats plying their courses across the water, their bass warnings punctuated now and then by sharp barks of smaller craft.

"When's the *San Fernando* due?" the older man asked. "I'm glad she isn't trying to make port in this soup."

Before Stan could answer there was an interruption—the approaching murmur of feminine voices, laughter, and the tread of light feet coming down the stairs. Two women entered—lovely Daisy, J.O.B.'s blue-eyed, golden-headed daughter and her cousin, Eleanor—tall, beautiful, imperious, who even now, as she greeted her uncle and her cousin, did so in a condescending manner. She was twenty-eight, a stately creature, needing only a crown upon her carefully dressed brown hair to complete the picture of a princess.

"You're the living embodiment of Grandmère's spirit," Stan told her, kissing the cheek she presented. "You're what they'd call in the 'nineties a Gibson girl, but I swear I don't think they were as beautiful. Merry Christmas to you, my dear!"

"Thanks—and a merry one to you, and to you, Uncle."

"My dear, as usual you look . . . Where's your aunt Fran?"

"With Grandmère. She'll be down directly. Daisy's been telling me about the launching. She says the bottle wouldn't smash and she forgot the name of the boat. Was it awful?"

"No, no; she acquitted herself handsomely—although the bottle was a bit stubborn."

"You christened her—what?"

"Well, she'll belong to the Mission Fleet. We named her the *San Gregorio.*"

"Why not the *San Juan Bautista?*"

"Too hard to pronounce, isn't it?"

"San Gregorio wasn't a mission!"

"What difference does it make? We operate the Mission Fleet whether or not the boats are named after actual missions."

They talked of the new ship that had been launched the day before at the Morse shipbuilding yards in Alameda for Wickwire, Rutherford & Company, at which ceremony pretty little Daisy had officiated.

This young lady now came to stand beside her father, slipped a small hand beneath his arm and leaned her head against his sleeve. J.O.B. looked down at her with pride and affection, patting the hand.

She was a darling girl, he thought, with china-blue eyes that had a way of staring in a surprised way at people, and she had finely spun golden hair which curled prettily about her ears and at her temples.

"Puss," he said, tenderly, hugging her small hand against his side. He thought again how pleased she was going to be with the mink coat. Smiling affectionately, she returned his look but did not speak.

Stan and Eleanor had sauntered toward the other end of the long room where in the bay window stood the resplendent Christmas tree, glittering with brilliant colored balls and silver tinsel. J.O.B. heard his niece telling his son:

"She kept them up until past midnight, changing this and changing that; she was perfectly ridiculous about it. 'This red ball up here on this branch tip must be lowered two feet or moved to the other side so's to balance.' She wouldn't be satisfied until the last detail suited her. However, you'll have to admit she's made them trim a perfect tree."

They spoke of his mother, of course, Grandmère, and of the servants, who besides Wilbur, the butler, included the Chinese cook, little Kay, his helper, Annabel, the housemaid, Susie, Grandmère's personal maid, and Greenwood, the chauffeur. Idly J.O.B. wondered who among the six she had chosen to carry out her mandates, suspecting their resentment, and suspecting, too, how they must all dislike her. His mother was of the old school and a servant was a servant to her, to do her bidding no matter how unreasonable her whim; waiting upon her or any Rutherford, she considered, was a privilege.

§2

It was the annual custom of the Rutherfords to gather on Christmas morning at Lloyd's house for a bounteous Christmas breakfast, after which followed the distribution of presents piled in gay confusion around the base of the tree.

The house, with its old-fashioned big rooms on either side of long halls bisecting lower and upper floors, still belonged to Grandmère, although her son Lloyd, his wife, and daughter lived with her and Lloyd paid all the bills. Grandmère was a woman approaching her eighties now, a wrinkled, arrogant old dowager who wore carefully marcelled wigs of dazzling white upon her head, and about her lean throat dog collars consisting of rhinestones by day and diamonds by night.

Lloyd, J.O.B.'s brother and the elder of the Rutherford sons, was a man of almost sixty, with a crown of tight curling white hair which he kept closely cropped. He was dignity personified—conservative, austere, his manner judicial—a leading attorney in the city, a corporation lawyer, was influential, wealthy, respected, and had been offered the Republican nomination for United States senator, had declined it though knowing his election was more or less a foregone conclusion. His wife, who had been Bessie Farthingale, was a plump, crinkly haired, amiable lady—a good deal cleverer than she looked. Their daughter was the stately Eleanor. There was a son, too, three years older than Eleanor, an odd, unbalanced boy, Frank, but of this scapegrace his father never spoke. Frank had a dark and unsavory history, had been mixed up with an unscrupulous woman, a scheming nursemaid, had quarreled with his father and long ago run away to sea. No word had been had of him in years.

Next to dignified Lloyd came his brother, the portly J.O.B.— large-stomached, heavy-jowled, with a flowing mustache and goatee like Louis Napoleon's—whose full name was John Ogden Breckenridge Rutherford and who was universally called by his initials, not only by his family and intimates, but by subordinates in his large and active shipping and trading company. J.O.B., president of Wickwire, Rutherford & Company, was a man whose name was one with which to conjure from Seattle to New Orleans. He and his wife, Frances, who had been sole heiress to the old Wickwire Steamship Company, had two children, Stanley, now twenty-eight, and Daisy, the golden-haired Dresden beauty, just turned twenty-three.

There was still another Rutherford, an only daughter, Charmion by name, who had married a prosperous farmer, Reginald Baxter, of the San Joaquin Valley, an amiable, inhibited, and rather stupid man who had unbounded faith in the fruits of his orchards and in the produce of his broad acres. One son had been vouchsafed this couple—a youth now some twenty-five years old, Chris—Grandmère's spoiled darling —a dissolute young man, artistically inclined and gifted as well. This gay troubadour had a mop of yellow hair which he wore long and had a way of tossing carelessly from his forehead, and though slight of build, he was undeniably handsome, with a girl's complexion, a clean-cut profile, a hard mouth, thin lips, and flashing even teeth. He could play the piano acceptably, paint, act, write jingly and amusing poetry, and now and then an article authored by him—an account of some adventure which may or may not have happened on one of his cruises aboard the *Jabberwock*—would appear in an eastern yachting magazine.

Chris was the apple of his grandmother's eye. As a young woman she too had been talented. It was easy today to believe that once she had been beautiful, and she was fond of telling her children and her children's children of days when she had played leading roles in amateur theatricals. That she had been a Breckenridge, she was ready to remind any listener—Caroline Emitt Breckenridge of Savannah, Georgia, direct descendant of Lord James Edward Oglethorpe. She had a way of lifting her head when proclaiming her genealogy, defiantly looking down her nose from under lowered lids as if inviting challenge. However successful she had become socially in San Francisco as Mrs. J. Ogden Rutherford, Sr., it was the fact she had been a Breckenridge of Savannah of which she was proud. Ambitions of earlier years doubtless had been thwarted, outlets for self-expression blocked; what these may have been she was unable to say today, but she recognized them again in her grandson Chris, and she showered him with favors and affection. Grandmère was a wealthy woman— she had never known anything but wealth since the day she had been born—and it had been she who at some teasing suggestion from Chris had given him the money on his twenty-first birthday to purchase the *Jabberwock,* a twin-screw Diesel cruiser on sale for a song at the moment in the port of San Pedro. The boat unquestionably had been cheap, but her upkeep was another matter, and Grandmère was continually handing out checks to her beloved harum-scarum grandson in order to pay operating costs. Chris needed a captain and a crew of six. Once or twice a year, accompanied by congenial friends, he made a run to the Hawaiian Islands or Tahiti or even farther, and was gone a month or more. His cousin Eleanor resented her grandmother's rank favoritism and treated Chris coolly; Stan had small respect for him, but to Daisy, Chris was an attractive, romantic figure, and hardly an acquaintance among her girl intimates did not confess unashamedly that she was in love with him.

§3

Christmas breakfast, as the Rutherfords observed it, was a feast. It started with various kinds of fruit; then came cereal, which it was considered obligatory to eat or at least sample, as Lloyd, J.O.B., and Charmion, when children, had always clamored for it. After the cereal appeared eggs and then fish—kippered herring, mackerel, and bloater—and finally waffles and hot cakes. There was coffee of course —tea for Grandmère—and numerous kinds of bread: hot rolls, toast, coffeecake, crullers, corn bread, and popovers.

As usual, Grandmère presided, her older son on her right, Charmion on her left. Every now and then she would put out one of her thin, bony claws—her fingers loaded with rings—and pat their hands, smiling a wrinkled smile of approval and affection. She could not reach J.O.B., her favorite child, who sat on the other side of his sister, but whenever she caught his eye she would nod at him and make the same kind of fond grimace.

Around the table, eleven strong, the family gathered. Placid and good-natured Bessie was on J.O.B.'s left, then came Stan and Eleanor, while opposite his grandmother lounged the amusing and attractive Chris, talking animatedly, as he always did when near her, to admiring Daisy. Next to her sat Reggie Baxter, owlishly regarding the company, silently and methodically eating his food, emptying his plate, thinking his own thoughts, which presumably were concerned with smudge pots, pruning, and spraying. Frances with her thick spectacles and honest face completed the circle.

This lady never quite comprehended her husband's family. Married for thirty years to J.O.B., she still felt herself to be Frances Wickwire —"Frannie," as her mother had called her in the days of her Boston girlhood. Long ago her parents had died and two older brothers as well, and today she was an entrenched Rutherford. She lived in an enormous turreted, gable house across the street, surrounded by a pretentious garden, a stable—now transformed into a commodious garage large enough to hold four cars—servants, and all the money she could ever spend. Money, money, money—she could give it away with both hands if she wanted to. But Grandmère, her son, the sedate and pontifical Lloyd, and his heavy-going and cumbersome sister— so ineptly named "Charmion"—these and their mixed and curious progeny were an alien people to her. Even her husband was alien. She looked at him across the breakfast table this morning, wondering, studying his solid, florid face with its heavy jowls, the puffed sockets beneath heavy-lidded eyes, his well-cared-for mustache and neatly trimmed goatee. She knew where the hairy mole was between his shoulder blades, she knew he wore a false upper plate, that he was troubled with hemorrhoids, and that an abdominal corset supported his protuberant stomach, but she asked herself as she examined him if she had really ever known him—known him as his mother knew him, as his brother and his sister did. Her gaze turned comfortably to her handsome son Stan with his clean-shaven, square jaw, his fine eyes and strong features—self-reliant, purposeful, determined— and to her delicate flowerlike Daisy, with her sparkling china-blue eyes alight now with enjoyment of some idle chatter from Chris. Her children she knew; they were her own, part of her life, her home, herself. The others . . . ? She drew a deep breath, straightened herself, suddenly uncomfortably aware that already she had eaten too much.

Grandmère was rattling her ringed knuckles against the rim of a plate.

"Well, children—what say? Presents now?" And then to Lloyd as she rose and took his arm: "What a lovely custom it is to have all of us together for Christmas breakfast year after year!"

Lloyd, leading her across the hall to the parlor, heard her sigh. He suspected she was thinking of his wayward Frank—the one person missing from her happy circle—and he hoped she would not speak of him. He frowned and piloted her to a gilt upholstered armchair. The rest of the family found seats about the sides of the room, composing themselves with affected indifference, Lloyd and his brother opening cigar cases, exchanging brands, snipping off the tips of their weeds, lighting them with care. Chris threw himself on the floor at his grandmother's feet, resting his back against her chair, his head at her knee where her knuckly old fingers could play with his loose wavy hair.

Ever since she had been old enough to manage it herself, it had been Daisy's duty to distribute the gifts. This she did very prettily and charmingly, pausing a moment as she stooped and seized a package or a box from beneath the tree, to read the name, then fluttering forward to present it, uttering now and then a little cry of pleased surprise when she discovered one inscribed to herself:

"For Grandmère with love from . . . Stan. Uncle Lloyd from . . . oh yes . . . from me! [A kiss.] Aunt Frances from Eleanor—with love, of course. For Mother from . . . from Chris. Oh, I guess that's for you, Aunt Charmion. Bessie with Christmas love from her husband. Oh, and here's another for me! My goodness!"

In a short time the floor of the big room was littered with torn wrappings, striped papers, colored string and lengths of ribbon. Stan was showing with satisfaction a pair of pearl studs, Chris admiring a new Purdy shotgun in its green plush case—imported directly from London, so his fond grandmother whispered; Eleanor exulted over a glittering diamond necklace—a gift from her father and mother— sixteen beautifully selected and graded stones on a chain which just spanned her slim white throat, but most excited of all and most charming to watch was Daisy in her voluminous mink of finely matched skins. Oh, my, it was superb . . . oh, my, was there anything so scrumptious! . . . "Oh, Daddy, you're just a dar-dar-dar-ling!" And there were checks, checks, checks from the two elder Rutherfords and even larger ones—some of four figures—from the old lady! The young men kissed their mothers, their sisters and cousins, and the withered cheek of generous Grandmère; the girls embraced each other and everyone in the room; there was much confusion, milling back and forth, shrill exclamations and gruff laughter, a mounting and dimin- ishing hubbub, lessening by degrees to a more seemly decorum as the younger generation gathered about Grandmère's chair to repeat its thanks, to compliment and cajole her, to make pretty speeches. In the meantime the Rutherford brothers conferred from armchair to armchair through the smoke of their cigars, while the matrons, their heads together, murmured confidentially, and Reggie, seated by him- self on the piano bench, studied the carpet silently.

"Come, Lloyd, it's time for the servants!" Grandmère stretched her lean neck to address her older son above the heads of her admiring grandchildren. "Stan, dear, call them, will you?"

At this stage of the festivities it was part of the Christmas program for the servants to file into the room, admire the spectacle of the brilliantly lighted tree, share in the family rejoicing, and receive their Yuletide remembrances.

"Everybody be seated," Grandmère commanded, "and Lloyd, you'd better find your Bible."

A reading of the story of the Nativity according to St. Luke was an integral part of the morning's order. With all the hustle and bustle that went on at Christmastime, it was highly likely—so Grandmère observed—that the "help" might easily forget the reason for all the rejoicing. It wasn't amiss to remind them, she would add with a knowing nod. The family acquiesced to this, as it had been part of the Christmas ritual for as many years as the oldest among them could remember.

Obedient to her wishes, the family found its seats again, Lloyd regretfully extinguishing his cigar, thumbing the pages of a Bible, searching for the passage, while Chris re-established himself at his grandmother's knee. The room quieted; a pause ensued—but there was no sound of an approaching company.

"Goodness sakes alive!" rasped the old lady; "what's keeping them?"

Presently Stan entered, announced that the staff was on its way, and within a moment or two, with downcast eyes, the six servants filed in—looking a bit sheepish and very solemn, Daisy thought—the tall austere figure of Wilbur, the butler, heading the line.

"And there were in the same country shepherds abiding in the field, keeping watch over their flocks by night . . ."

Lloyd read very well, his mother thought. Why shouldn't he, she reflected, with all his law practice—addressing meetings, haranguing juries and the like?

She glanced at the domestics, at the family ranged about the room, noting all were dutifully attentive.

Bessie, as a matter of fact, was the real mistress of the house. It was she who gave the orders, made the arrangements, engaged and discharged the servants, but her mother-in-law never for a moment conceded her any authority superior to her own. She, Grandmère, was head of the house of Rutherford, had been so ever since, as the bride of the late J. Ogden Rutherford, she had opened the Rutherford home, and she would remain head of the clan until the end of her days.

It reflected creditably upon Bessie that she could run the household, its servants, and its routine so effectively without ruffling the temper of her irascible old mother-in-law. It required tact and crafty circumvention at times, but easygoing Bessie liked her job. Sometimes Eleanor accused her mother of being hardly more than a housekeeper to the old lady, but to this Bessie usually smiled cryptically, nodding amiably. Quietly and unobtrusively she went about her business and usually did as she liked.

When Lloyd had finished the scriptural reading, Grandmère nodded approvingly, said to the listening staff: "We wish you all a very Merry Christmas," and to Bessie immediately: "You have their envelopes? . . . Give them out, won't you, dear Chris, and tell them again we wish them all a very Merry Christmas and a Happy New Year."

Each envelope bore a servant's name; there was a seal of a Christmas wreath and another of the head of a Santa Claus pasted on its outside and, within, an appropriate Christmas card and a folded ten-dollar bill. Chris obligingly handed them out, presented each with a wry, good-natured smile, friendly and engaging, murmuring some comment as he did so which brought a smirk to several faces.

"And now, my angel boy," Grandmère said as the ceremony was completed and the servants with silent nods of appreciation left the room, "be a darling and play 'Nazareth'; we want to sing it all together as we always do each Christmas."

§ 4

J.O.B.'s house was on a corner and stood diagonally across the street from Grandmère's. Both homes were old-fashioned, comfortable residences, products of the 'eighties. J.O.B.'s was the larger, was turreted and gabled, and pretentiously reared itself in an overgrown garden of arbors, walks, fish ponds, and artificial grottoes. Miraculously both buildings had escaped the conflagration of 1906; the fire, after having wiped out the lower half of the city, had been stopped almost at their doorsteps. J.O.B. had purchased the property a few years prior to the holocaust, and while the earthquake had sent two of its brick chimneys crashing into the garden, the house itself had not been seriously damaged. He had purchased it from Willard Hughes, who had made and lost several fortunes in mining speculation, and J.O.B. had acquired it for half its worth during one of its original owner's financial straits which proved indeed to be his last. Out of date, in constant need of repairs, it still presented a handsome front, and J.O.B. was inordinately proud of it. The stables where old Hughes had kept his carriages and horses were at the rear and faced a side street, but J.O.B. had made the ramshackle building into a commodious and up-to-date garage, and now a curving driveway, well shaded by tall shrubbery and overhanging foliage, led from it to the front steps and thence to the imposing entrance gates of wrought iron connected by an arch of gilded iron scrollwork. His house! The palatial residence of J. O. B. Rutherford, president of Wickwire, Rutherford & Company! A mansion the people of San Francisco might well admire!

Here Stan and Daisy had spent most of their childhood days with faithful Carrie, part nurse, part governess, part housekeeper, watching over them during the time when their mother had been an invalid. Frances had lain abed for the better part of a decade. Neither Stan nor his sister had ever known just what had been the matter with her, but years ago, while he had been away at boarding school, the boy had been told his mother had gone to a hospital, and a very serious operation had been performed. Now she was so well, so bounding in health and energy, it was hard to believe there had ever been dark days when he and his small sister had been cautioned every time they entered the house to be "very, very quiet."

Part of the Rutherford observance of the Christmas holidays was an eight-o'clock dinner at this, the younger brother's house. All the family looked forward to this banquet, for Frances set an excellent table, J.O.B. dispensed cocktails and sherry, served various kinds of wines and vintage champagne with an unsparing hand, and the atmosphere of the house was freer, less stilted than that of Lloyd's, where Grandmère dominated the scene and was querulous and critical. At J.O.B.'s the old lady regarded herself as a guest and behaved accordingly. Then too there was an airiness about his home—the rooms were larger, more open, there were easy exits and convenient corners into which to slip. Elegance predominated—from mammoth electroliers, dangling with hundreds of glass-prismed pendants, to enormous white skins of polar bears on the floors and tall Chinese cabinets whose doors were beautifully inlaid with mother-of-pearl.

Stan, coming downstairs in his tuxedo somewhat in advance of the rest of his family, glanced in through the folding doors at the dinner table glittering with sparkling glassware and shining cutlery, a tall silver vase, gushing an armful of long-stemmed red roses, resplendent in its center. There were candelabra at either end holding tapering red candles, and sprays of holly and redberries arranged in pleasing patterns on the snow-white embroidered cloth. The whole house was redolent with the spicy fragrance of Christmas wreaths and garlands.

To his mild surprise, as he counted the places at the board, he noted their number came to twelve. He was at a loss for a moment to account for the extra guest. Then he remembered hearing his mother at breakfast a fortnight ago asking his father whether or not she should invite Syd Watterbury, the company's general manager, to dinner on Christmas Day. Syd was a bachelor, had no family, was good-looking, a conscientious if not a fluent talker.

"For Eleanor, you know," his mother had explained; "anyway, he'll balance the table, and it would be nice to have him, don't you think?"

"Sure, go ahead; Syd's all right," J.O.B. had approved.

The conversation came back now. Yes, Syd was a fine fellow and he'd be all right for Eleanor, only Eleanor frightened most eligible bachelors away with her hoity-toity airs and supercilious manner.

He shrugged indifferently and crossed the hall to the front room, where the company would assemble. It was an oddly proportioned room, octagonally shaped, with a small conservatory opening off one side where ferns and potted plants flourished and a couple of canaries in gilded cages cheeped and twittered through the day. Stan found Daisy here, standing before the fireplace, a slippered foot resting upon the steel rods in front of the hearth, her hands holding to the mantel at the level of her head, silently regarding the unlit logs. She wore a balloony dress of taffeta—pale blue flowers on a creamy background—and there were cornflowers in her hair.

He stood looking at her with admiration and some concern—radiant she was, lovely and girlish!—but was there something troubling her?

"Dais?"

She turned at once, her red lips breaking, her blue eyes alight with their usual sparkle.

"Anything the matter?"

"*No-o!* I came down a bit early so's to be on hand in case anybody came. Mother's got a headache."

"Oh, too bad!"

"Nothing serious. Says she ate too much at Grandmère's. . . . It was pretty awful, wasn't it?"

"Christmas breakfast is the old lady's idea, not Uncle Lloyd's or Aunt Bessie's. Grandmère insists everybody must stuff themselves out of shape. We're all afraid of her; do just what she says. . . . I suppose it's her money."

"Nonsense. We'd be just as kind and as fond of her if she didn't have a cent."

"Don't you believe it! It's her dough that makes us all do her bidding."

"I suppose Chris will get most of it."

"Shouldn't wonder. He isn't worth a damn; I mean he couldn't do a day's honest work if he had to, so he might as well inherit a sockful."

"You're the only other one—grandson, I mean—who might, aren't you?"

As they talked, she fitted a small white rosebud into the lapel of his dinner jacket.

"Huh, I want none of her money," he said gruffly.

"What happened to—to Frank? I never *did* know the ins and outs of his story. What did he do?"

Stan gave her a quick appraising glance, lit a cigarette with deliberation.

"How old were you when they had the row?"

" 'Bout thirteen."

"He was twenty-two or twenty-three then. It's a long time ago. Must be . . . let's see; he's four years older than I, so he's thirty-two or -three now."

"What happened?"

"He got mixed up with a nursemaid."

"How? Tell me, Stan. I'm not a child any more, and I might as well know what sort of skeleton's concealed in our family closet."

"Oh, he's no skeleton; he's very much alive and kicking; ran away to sea, you know; I don't know where I got the impression, but I understand he's sort of a bum now—hangs round the docks and picks up a living as best he can."

"But what did he *do?*"

"You know where the Stovals live in the next block? They had a nurse who took care of their baby; the baby is that girl they call Babbie now. At any rate, the nursemaid was attractive, pretty and all that, about the same age as Frank, at any rate old enough to know what she was doing. He thought he was in love with her, wanted to marry her and so on. Uncle Lloyd put his foot down. Then she claimed she was going to have a child; wanted money, I guess. He threatened to have her arrested for blackmail, planned to get Frank out of the country, send him to Europe, China, anywhere so long as he was out of the way, but before he could move, Frank declared he was going to marry the girl and told Uncle Lloyd where to get off. There was an awful fight. Frank said some pretty savage things, walked out of the house, and nobody's seen or heard from him since. . . . He was a queer one, anyhow, not a bit like the rest of us, always had a lot of nutty ideas."

"I don't call it queer or having nutty ideas to want to marry the girl he loved and who was to become the mother of his child!"

"Oh, he ruined his life, just chucked it away."

"I don't see why."

"Can't you imagine what a fit they all had?"

Daisy remained silent for a time, stroking her small chin.

"I still don't see," she said.

"See what?"

"What he did that was so awfully wrong."

"Well," Stan told her with a touch of impatience, "good sons don't do that sort of thing. In the first place they don't get servant girls into trouble, and in the second, they don't want to marry them."

Daisy shook her head.

"I don't see——" she began again and paused; Martha, the maid, was hurrying down the hall to open the front door for the first of the dinner guests.

§ 5

Chris was late. By half past eight he had not appeared nor had any word come from him. The sherry and cocktails were passed and re-passed, the canapés—cold smoked salmon, and savory morsels of chicken wrapped in thin slices of bacon speared by a toothpick—made their rounds a second, a third time. It grew to be quarter of nine, ten minutes to—the hour struck.

"I wouldn't wait for him another minute," Grandmère declared.

"He was in his room at the hotel getting dressed at seven o'clock," his mother said, with an uneasy glance at her husband.

"Maybe he lay down on his bed and went to sleep," Reggie hazarded. "Shall I phone and find out?"

"If he's gone to sleep like that, let's let him be, don't you think?" Frances asked with an inquiring look around the circle of her guests. "When he wakes up, he'll come along. Let's go in."

Daisy was interested in observing Syd Watterbury, who was opposite to her and sat next to Eleanor. Her cousin wore her diamond necklace tonight, other diamonds in her ears, and on her head, half hidden by her fluffy mouse-colored hair, a shallow crown of silver filigree. She looked more stately and princesslike than ever, Daisy thought. Her gown was a plain ivory satin with a train; it clung closely to her figure, and it was obvious there was very little if anything beneath it; her arms were bare to the shoulder, and the dress was cut fairly low in front and almost to the waistline in back.

Daisy knew perfectly well that her cousin had no desire to dazzle Mr. Watterbury; his existence was a matter of no concern to her, as indeed was that of most men. It was Eleanor's mood to dress up in all her finery tonight to please herself first, and next to impress the fam-

ily. Daisy and Stan were fulsome in their praises, but the older generation merely eyed her critically and said nothing. It was the Rutherford way. Only Grandmère unbent so far as to tap her granddaughter's bare arm with her lorgnette and nod approvingly.

Syd Watterbury, however, made small progress with Eleanor, and
the girl showed no interest in helping him. He floundered from one
subject to another, and his observations she acknowledged only by
monosyllables or polite smiles and inclinations of her head. Daisy felt
sorry for him. He was a nice-appearing man, about forty, with dark,
handsome eyes, and a slightly turned-up nose which oddly made him
attractive. He seemed anxious to please, and Daisy would have liked
to change places with her cousin. Eleanor was behaving abominably.
Once Syd caught her blue eyes fixed on him, and before she could
avert them she smiled involuntarily. Promptly she gave her attention
to Aunt Charmion and pretended to be absorbed in her conversation
with Uncle Lloyd.

It was all very dull. The place next to her where Chris was to have
sat was vacant. She tried to listen to some of the talk ranging up and
down the board and wondered vaguely why so many insipid and un-
interesting things should be said and why these should be accepted
with such grave consideration.

Her father to Aunt Bessie:

"The port of San Francisco has seventeen miles of berthing space
and eighty-two docks with a cargo capacity of nearly two million
tons, and it is also capable of accommodating two hundred and fifty
vessels at one time."

"My goodness, is that so? I had no idea."

Grandmère: "There's a terrible blizzard raging in the East. I happened to hear it over the radio while I was dressing this afternoon.
As I said to Susie, we don't have anything like such things out
here—and we had very few storms that I can remember in Savannah.
I declare I think most Californians just take their good weather for
granted—don't you think so, Stan?"

"Beg pardon, Grandmère? . . ."

Aunt Charmion to Uncle Lloyd: "We've had only eight and a half
inches of rain so far this year, and Reggie's really worried."

Uncle Lloyd: "The Hoover Dam when completed will impound

the surplus waters of the Colorado and will serve to irrigate the entire Imperial Valley. Why don't you move down there?"

Her mother to Reggie: "You must have some more of the goose, Reggie. Oh, I insist! Just wait a minute and I'll ring. She'll bring the platter back; she knows my signal. I always press the button twice when I want a second helping of anything."

Syd Watterbury to Eleanor: "I hope we're going to have some international polo this year. We beat England, you know, in 1930, and we haven't had a try at them since. . . . You're not interested in polo?"

Eleanor: "No."

Syd: "Well, I remember seeing Eric Pedley play years ago at Del Monte . . ."

Stan, mercifully interrupting: "I wonder what the deuce happened to Chris."

At his very words there was a ring at the front door.

"There he is," everybody said.

It was at once apparent that Chris was not alone. There was his voice, and then another's—a man's voice.

He came in a moment later, flushed and a trifle rumpled. Daisy saw he was tipsy.

"Oh, I'm terribly sorry, everybody! Terribly—terribly sorry. You'll forgive me, Aunt Fran? And please, Unc? I got into a frightful jam! Explain later. . . . I know, I know, I know! This is Christmas dinner and everything—and I'm just as sorry as can be! Please, Mom." He kissed his mother and then Aunt Frances and ran around the table to embrace Grandmère. All the while his companion, a young man in faultless evening dress, white tie and waistcoat, stood between the curtains of the folding doors, smiling pleasantly.

"And look, everybody," continued Chris, gulping and on a great rush of breath. "I found a buddy of mine and brought him along with me. He didn't have any place to eat his Christmas dinner, and I insisted he come with me. You don't mind, Aunt Fran, do you? That all right, huh? . . . Listen, folks, this is Mr. Lester Armitage of Hollywood and all points south. You've all heard of Lester Armitage, I'm sure. 'Member him, Dais? He was the star in *Gates of Paradise, Haunting Melody,* an' *Skyrocket*—weren't you, Les? Take a

bow, boy, take a bow. Folks, meet Mr. Lester Armitage of pictures.
. . . Come on over here, Les; take my chair next to Daisy. She's my
cousin and she's a sweetheart. You sit down, Les; don't mind me. An'
lissen, Aunt Fran, we don't want any of the first courses; we'll start
in just where you are. Isn't that right, Les—isn't that right? We don't
want anything, you know, that's been served already. Truly, Aunt
Fran. Honest to God!"

Chris carried everybody before him. The company bowed, accepted the stranger, J.O.B. rose, as did his son, who came forward,
extending a hand.

"I'm Stanley Rutherford," the latter said; "glad to know you, sir.
This is my sister, Daisy—Miss Daisy Rutherford—and on your other
side, my grandmother, Mrs. Ogden Rutherford. Please be seated; my
sister will look after you."

Charmingly, graciously done, thought Daisy, smiling up at the
newcomer as he took the seat beside her.

In the confusion of the moment she could not tell whether she had
ever hear of Lester Armitage or not, but at first glance she recognized the movie type. He was one of those dark-haired, dark-eyed
young men, with a perfect profile, handsome teeth, expressive mouth,
and an engaging smile.

He began to talk easily and comfortably.

"I think it's perfectly disgraceful for Chris to bring me here into an
intimate family gathering like this on Christmas Day. I feel just—I
feel like such an interloper! I had no idea. Chris didn't explain. I
met him tonight in the bar at the Mark. I'd known him before; he
was down at Catalina with his yacht once; I went on board. Then in
Santa Monica we were together at a week-end party. Tonight, over
a couple of drinks, I happened to mention that my date for the evening had gone haywire and I was on the loose; he insisted then on
my coming with him and having dinner with his family. It's an in-
trusion, inexcusable——"

"Oh well," said Daisy, rapidly regaining her composure, "now that
you're here we'll all have to make the best of it—you as well as we.
What say?"

He laughed at this, showing his fine white teeth.

"Grand," he said. "Now you make me feel at home. Tell me about the family; who's who around the table—and in particular, that goddess sitting directly opposite us?"

"My cousin Eleanor. She's quite stunning, isn't she? I'll see you meet her again after dinner."

The conversation moved along. Daisy decided—movie actor or no movie actor—Mr. Armitage was an entertaining gentleman. She began to enjoy herself. Chris was up to his usual monkeyshines. He had wedged himself in between her mother and Uncle Lloyd and had everyone within earshot convulsed with laughter. Uncle Lloyd's face was red and congested as he laughed, its flaming color in marked contrast with his white, close-cropped hair.

"Well, that's right, isn't it, Uncle? That's right, isn't it? You can't make any money that way."

Again the laughter pealed forth, Chris the while maintaining a stony expression as though he spoke of a most serious matter.

"Oh, you bad, *bad* boy!" Daisy heard her mother expostulate; "you'll be the death of me!"

The evening, the girl noted with rising spirits, had begun to be gay. The conversation grew noisy, laughter echoed laughter, everyone seemed to be trying to say something at once. She could hear her grandmother complaining now and then:

"Oh, I *wish* I knew what they were laughing at! Why doesn't that scamp come up and sit by me!"

"I see Roosevelt's going to step up Henry Morgenthau to fill Woodin's place."

"D'y'u read the editorial in the *Chronicle* yesterday morning? Fine stuff."

"It's Scharlachberger Spatlese, 1921. I get it direct from Germany. Through a friend. Don't pay a cent of duty."

"Mr. Shuey of the Emporium tells me they did a splendid business these holidays."

"I'm going to have the whole front lawn dug up this spring."

"You can't get more than four or five cents a pound for prunes now. Before the war . . ."

"Those waterfront bums ought to be jailed. We haven't had a bit of trouble with the longshoremen since 1919."

"Of course, *I* think Greta Garbo is the loveliest of them all."

"I liked her so much in . . ."

"And did you see Elizabeth Bergner in *Catherine the Great?* Wasn't she *won*-derful? And I like young Doug in that, too."

"You know what I'm going to do with my check, Grandmère?"

"Have some more of the Bar-le-Duc and cheese, Reggie. It's good, don't you think? You can't get things like that in that awful out-of-the-way place where you and Charmion live, can you?"

". . . we'll sail in about three weeks, soon's I can get the *Jabberwock* ready. We'll make San Diego first, then Ensenada, do some fishing off Cape San Lucas, stop at Mazatlan for fuel and provisions, keep on south and touch at Colima and Acapulco; the tuna and sailfish ought to be running at their best then. Les Armitage says he can go, and I can get Johnny Williams, Griffith Adams, and maybe Phil Baldwin. . . . No chance of you, Stan, is there?" Chris asked in the silence to which the table had quieted.

Stan shook his head. All turned their eyes on Chris.

"Lester says he thinks maybe he can persuade Carey Douglas to join us. Wouldn't that be swell!"

There was a pause while the young man drained his wineglass.

"When would you expect to leave?" his mother asked in her heavy, lifeless voice.

"Oh, I don't know. Soon's Cap can get her ready. She'll have to go into dry dock and have her bottom scraped, and there'll be supplies and equipment and fuel to order. Maybe we'll get as far south as Panama. We may fly home and leave the *Jabberwock* to work her way back. It's going to be a *swell* trip!"

"And you'll be gone . . . for how long?"

"A couple of months, maybe three. All depends on Mr. Armitage, whether the pictures can spare him that long. . . ."

The talk continued, now centering on the trip Chris proposed. They discussed the correct tackle for tuna and sailfish. Somebody said something about "laminated," and Chris advocated a "Montague" while Armitage thought a "Tycoon" would be better.

"And gee, Grandmère," the young man called across the table, "I'll have a chance to try out my new Purdy at Ensenada. The quail are so thick down there, they say you almost step on them."

Daisy busied herself with cracking walnuts, her small face contorting as she broke the shells in a nutcracker. As she did so she wondered how it was that Chris, just because he had a rich and doting grandmother, could blithely and lightheartedly go off on a fishing trip, inviting other rich and favored young men to go with him, when as Stan said he "wasn't worth a damn" and couldn't do an honest day's work if he had to.

CHAPTER II

THE "JABBERWOCK" WAS TO SAIL with the tide promptly at six in the evening, but Daisy arrived at the yacht club fully an hour earlier. Already a crowd of idlers had gathered on the dock next to the cruiser's berth and stood curiously inspecting her. The trig craft seemed especially beautiful to Daisy this late afternoon, and the girl paused a moment to admire her long, tapering water lines, her squat, sawed-off funnel poking its head above the forward cabin, her polished mahogany and white trimmings, her radio mast draped now with brightly colored signal flags. Despite the corded crates piled high and covered with tarpaulins on her forward deck, there was a smartness and completeness about the little cruiser which caught at Daisy's heart.

Even as the girl made her way along the pontoons to where the *Jabberwock* lay, she was aware of an excitement. She saw it in the faces of the onlookers, felt it in the sleekness and the neatness and preparedness of the yacht itself, and sensed it in the knot of men gathered in the cockpit where Chris—smartly turned out in yachting cap, brass-buttoned blue coat, and white trousers—was filling glasses of champagne, while Jimmy, the Filipino cabin boy, stood by holding a tray. Among the men she recognized Armitage, attired similarly to Chris, and identified Johnny Williams, whom she had never liked since the day at the Burlingame Country Club when, far gone with liquor, he had lurched drunkenly against her. In their midst, too, she spied her grandmother, royally established on one of the cushioned seats, holding out her glass for Chris to fill.

Fore and aft there were others, strange men and women in shore clothes, whose presence bewildered her a little until she remembered that Chris had told her that friends and families of the officers and crew would be on hand to say good-by to them.

As she was about to step aboard, a strong hand caught her elbow to steady her and a man said: "How do you do, Miss Rutherford?"

The face her eyes encountered stopped her, and she stared at it, frankly puzzled. It was a face she knew well—familiar, very familiar —but yet, in the white starched uniform of a ship's officer, she could not place its owner. She looked her bewilderment, aware the while of some pleasant association. He was a handsome young man, some twenty-six or -seven years of age, with a skin as dark as an Indian's —smooth and copper-hued—hair wavy and coal-black, and eyes that were brown, agate brown, warm and humorous with flecks of gold like specks of mica in them. They were alight now with amusement as he smiled at her.

"Guess you've forgotten me," he said, his teeth very white between his parted lips. His speech was a pleasant drawl, slow but not halting, and that too was familiar.

"No, no," she answered hurriedly, her hand half raised to prevent him enlightening her. "Wait . . . wait . . ."

Oh, she knew this man—had known him *well* somewhere, years ago . . . and she had liked him, admired him enormously.

"Vincent Oliver; 'member now?" he prompted.

One white gloved hand flew to her mouth; with the other she caught at his sleeve.

"Of c-c-course!" The exclamation was half muffled by her fingers as her thoughts carried her back and back—five, six, seven years ago —when as a fluffy-haired girl in her teens, a boarder at Miss Carlton's Select School for Young Ladies in Palo Alto, she had cheered and screamed frantically for the star and captain of the Stanford football team. She had met him later at Miss Carlton's Senior Dance—some kind genius had inveigled him there!—and a week or two afterwards she had encountered him on a Saturday night at the Mark Hopkins and they had danced and danced. Next day he had telephoned and she had thrilled and glowed, her heart hammering . . . and then abruptly there had been silence. The next fall she had gone east to Sarah Lawrence College, had lost track of him, ceased to think about him.

"Pl-*ease* explain," she began somewhat incoherently. "What in the name of everything queer and unaccountable brings you on board the—the *Jabberwock!*"

"I'm assistant engineer." His teeth flashed.

"You're what? . . ." *Oh, my goodness, it isn't right for any man to be as handsome as you are!* she thought.

"Assistant engineer," he repeated. "I studied marine engineering after Stanford," he pursued. "Been at sea for five years now. Got my license last fall. And you? What're you doing here?"

"Why . . . Chris, Chris is the owner."

"Mr. Baxter?"

"Certainly. He's my cousin."

Young Oliver's face underwent a quick change.

"Well, this *is* a coincidence," he said lamely, working his jaw in embarrassment. "How was *I* to know?"

"How *were* you?" she echoed, laughing companionably.

"Hey, Daisy, come on! What're you doin' there? Come on and have some champagne!" Chris called imperiously.

"I'll see you again before I go," she smiled, fluttering a white gloved hand at him as she departed.

Chris and his friends immediately claimed her. He kissed her soundly, and Grandmère beckoned her to stoop, offered her her cold, withered cheek, croaked cheerfully. Here were Lester Armitage, Johnny Williams, Syd Watterbury, and half a dozen others; presently Mother, Aunt Charmion, and Aunt Bessie descended upon them, accompanied by her ponderous father, whose bulk prevented him from coming any farther than the narrow deck outside the cockpit. Stan put his arm about her, gave her an affectionate hug; with him were Uncle Lloyd and Eleanor. And then there were dozens and dozens of friends: the Percy Grants, Jim Ahearn, the Trowbridge girls, Horatio Nickel and his daughter Laura, more and more and more—apparently everybody the Rutherfords knew in San Francisco! The yacht swarmed with people; the cockpit was jammed; the Filipino boy stood helplessly in the doorway of the galley, balancing a tray of champagne glasses, unable to pass them. People shouted, pushed one another, called greetings across shoulders, laughed, expostulated. Somewhere Daisy thought she heard the strains of a band, and Stan explained it was a record playing on Chris's Victrola in the cabin. Chris himself was laughing violently, red of face and flushed with excitement, his wavy yellow hair falling in loose disorder across his forehead. Daisy saw Lester Armitage again and suddenly realized she did not like him. He had backed Eleanor into a corner—perhaps the crowd forced him to be so close to her—and was talking rapidly and gesturing dramatically; his manner was too smooth, too professional. He challenged comparison with Vincent Oliver, who was far, far handsomer, and so much more honest-looking. That was it, she thought—honest. He was honest and—and unspoiled. He was a *real* man! She looked for him above the heads of the crowd, but there was no sign of him.

"Daisy! Daisy! Get me out of here!" An angry wail from Grandmère. "They're pushing me! They're *hurting* me!"

One glance at the old lady showed that as a matter of fact she indeed was in distress. Still in a corner where Daisy had first seen her; the crowd had turned its back upon her, and people were slowly and somewhat roughly being jammed against her knees.

"Stan!" the girl called; "Grandmère!"

Her brother instantly came to the rescue, elbowed a passage to the old lady's side, forcing the crowd to the right and left, and at once everyone was solicitous, making an aisle through which he could safely pilot her; Daisy saw Vincent Oliver offering her his hand. She jerked Chris's sleeve.

"Is Carey Douglas going along?"

"No, he can't; got to work. . . . 'Re you going to miss me?"

"Of course; hope you get a whopping big tuna."

"Oh, we'll have fun all right."

"You *ought* to. Chris, how many are there of you—all told, I mean? How many will there be on board?"

"Well, Phil Baldwin can't join us till we get to San Diego. Now, there's just three of us—Lester Armitage, Johnny, and me. Damn it! We won't have any bridge until we pick up Phil."

"And the crew?"

"Fine lot of hearties. Cap Dillon found 'em. Mate's sailed with me before, when we went down to Tahiti a year ago. 'Member? And you know Jimmy—and then we've got a new cook, a Dutchman, an' Cap says he's a wow."

"And the rest?"

"That's about all. There's the chief, of course, and his assistant and —and one A.B. We ought to have two, but it makes it pretty crowded in the fo'c'sle."

"You mean by 'chief' the chief engineer?"

"Sure, Abner. Don't know his other name. Good man, I guess."

"And his assistant—that nice-looking fellow? Who's he?"

"How the hell should I know! . . . All right, Cap. Everybody ashore. We got to catch this tide, y'know, Dais. God, what a mob! Why didn't some of 'em stay home? Come on, kid, let's you and me have a quick one before we shove off."

He reached for two glasses from Jimmy's tray, handed one to her and emptied the other in two swift gulps. Then, flourishing the goblet, he turned to his guests, who for the most part had now gathered on the dock above the cruiser's berth.

"So long, everybody. So long, Mom. I'll wire you from San Diego, and you can always get me by wireless, 'member, if anything should happen. Tell Pop to take good care of himself and keep the canker-worms out of the banana vines. Sorry he couldn't get here, but it isn't as if we were sailing for China! Ought to be home by Easter; try to anyway, and if I get a three-hundred-pounder, I'll fly back and char-ter a plane to bring the bozo with me. . . . Good-by, Uncle Lloyd; keep the shysters out of the legal profession. More money, y'know— for *us!* . . . So long, Uncle J.O.B. Don't let the girls along the water-front sing songs to your sailors. Keep 'em clean and healthy, I say, and don't let 'em taste a drop of grog! . . . Good-by, Tante, don't let Eleanor go into the trapeze business. . . . And good-by, Grand-mère; you've given me everything, you know. I'll write you love let-ters every day and bring you home the sword of the biggest sailfish in Mexican waters. With my sword or on it! How's that? Ha-ha!"

Daisy, moving slowly in the wake of the disembarking crowd, saw Vincent Oliver waiting for her, and her heart leaped in a way she had never experienced before.

"I'm sorry I'm sailing just as we've met again," he said. His smile was the most engaging she'd ever seen. Nothing could be bad about a man with a smile like that!

She looked at him, studying his face, and the swift thought followed that so handsome a man would never be faithful to any one girl. He might be a ship's officer—assistant engineer and all that—but he was a sailor too! No, it couldn't be. . . .

"Perhaps I'll see you when you get back," she said without enthusiasm.

"Oh, you bet. I'll give you a ring—but you'll be hearing from Mr Baxter when we'll be getting home. He has the say of it, you know." He smiled again and, suddenly sobering, observed, "I wish I weren't going."

She met his eyes coolly.

"You'll have a splendid time," she said evenly, "fishing and hunting and cruising about in tropical waters. It must be fun to be an officer on board a yacht."

"Oh, I'm lucky all right to land this job. The last trip I made was on board a Norwegian tramp, and it took us twenty-eight days to get to Sydney."

"Like the sea?"

"Oh, you bet. I've always wanted to be a sailor."

"But you went to college?"

"Sure. Stanford. The coach persuaded me. We lived in Redwood City; I went to high school there, and when my father died, that left just my mother and me. She's been an invalid for years. I had to get a part-time job, but I managed to work my way through school and then college; they were very good to me because I could play football. After I graduated I thought I'd take up marine engineering. It's interesting and's got a good future—I think."

"Where did you go to study for that? I mean what college did you attend after Stanford?"

"Oh, not any. Just got some books and studied at home for a while and then went to sea. That's where you learn. Begin as a wiper, you know, and work up to be an oiler—that way. Then when you think you know enough you take an examination."

"I see."

"All ashore that's going ashore," somebody cried, imitating the call on ocean liners.

"You'll let me come to see you or ring you up or something, soon's we get back?" Vincent asked, awkwardly touching his visored cap.

"Oh yes—surely." She said it lightly, determined to appear indifferent, but her heart was saying: *He never will; he'll never think of it again.*

"Good-by, Dais. Good-by, Miss Dresden Princess. Good-by, Miss Rutherford. Wish you were coming along."

"Wish I were, too."

"Good-by, Grandmère. I'll be seein' ya. . . . Good-by, everybody. So long, Stan. . . . All right, Cap! That's the last of 'em. Soon's you're ready. . . ."

From deep inside the bowels of the cruiser the engines sounded a deep rumble. More than ever the yacht suggested a bulldog—teeth bared, underjaw thrust forward, ready to fight, growlingly awaiting the buffeting of waves. There was a quick tread of feet on the deck —men running in tennis shoes—Captain Dillon stood by the wheel, the mate clung to a forward stay, directing a bystander on the pontoon to cast off a rope, then came a fresh and faster rumble, a turmoil of water gushed up from beneath the boat's stern, and the *Jabberwock* began to back slowly out into the yacht basin.

"They're off. Good luck!"

Chris and his companions in the cockpit lifted their glasses and toasted the crowd of waving friends. Jimmy refilled the goblets, and again they drained them.

"Lord, they ought to have fun!" someone said in the watching group, and then at Daisy's elbow, with a savage sneer, a man growled:

"Fun? The lousy bums! I hope they all drown."

The tone was so unpleasant that the girl turned instinctively. A rough-looking man was there with hatred in his eyes—at least in one eye, for the other was sunken and closed. She turned her back. A loafer—probably one of those waterfront toughs of whom she had heard her father speak so disparagingly. She straightened her shoulders, lifting her head.

The *Jabberwock* had pulled well out into the tiny harbor. She

could see the captain anxiously watching prow and stern, spinning
the wheel, noting the position of piles marking the channel and of
other boats moored to their buoys. The assistant engineer was nowhere in sight.

A short blast sounded—the bark of a dog! The water churned violently beneath the boat's stern, and the yacht began to make headway. The three men standing in the cockpit cheered, waved their
caps, once more raised their glasses. There was a final exchange of
shouts.

"There she goes," Stan said. "Thank God, I'm not going along."

Daisy, beside him, looked up in surprise.

"Why?"

"O-oh," he said, prolonging the syllable, "I wouldn't have any fun.
Too much bulling and chewing the rag and talking of things about
which none of them know anything. Oh, not about yachting and
fishing, Parkers and Purdys and Greeners; they know all about them
all right. I'd enjoy the fishing, but that kind of do-nothingness gets
on my nerves. I'd go nuts."

"Well," said his sister wistfully, "I think I'd give everything I own
or expect to own for the rest of my life if I were on board."

§ 2

Fifteen minutes later the *Jabberwock* was passing through the
Golden Gate over which a mighty bridge was presently to rise. Already there was evidence that the massive concrete blocks were being
poured.

Ocean groundswells were beginning to be met, and the yacht
dipped her nose courteously at their approach and then lifted herself
somewhat disdainfully over them. A big red-hulled freighter was
coming in on the starboard bow, riding high and wearily, rolling a
bit, as if glad to be making port. The March evening was turning
cold, and the wind had stiffened, but there was no fog, and the dying
sun was lost behind a heavy bank of murk obliterating the horizon.
To the rear, myriads of lights were beginning to twinkle, and near
at hand a bugle sounded clear and sweet from the Presidio.

"You get a sense of leaving behind you millions and millions of people all crowded together in rabbit warrens, fighting and quarreling about how to make their livings, but out there, there's nobody—just open water, sea and sky, and a few ships," Johnny Williams observed.

Neither Chris nor Lester made any comment. The latter's thoughts were far away; he was thinking about his agent in Hollywood who, he believed, had double-crossed him; Chris was pleasantly somnolent, feeling the effects of the champagne he had drunk, aware mildly that he was getting cold and ought to put on his reefer.

"It may be a bit choppy tonight," he drawled sleepily, and then, lifting his voice, he called: "Jimmy, let's have some old-fashioneds."

To his surprise he found Captain Dillon confronting him.

"Pardon, sir," said the officer; "we seem to be having some trouble."

"Trouble?" Chris demanded sharply.

"She don't seem to be acting right. The rudder doesn't answer properly."

"What you mean?"

"Well, sir, I dunno. Noticed it first when we pulled out; she don't behave right. Was okay during the test on Thursday. Ran her up to Paradise Cove, and we were making fifteen knots and her engines were turning over nicely. There was nothing the matter with her. My guess is the pintle's come loose in the gudgeon. Unwise to take her out tonight."

Chris stared at him with frowning eyes.

"You mean—put back?"

"Well, sir, I don't think it would be safe. She just won't answer the wheel the way she ought."

"But that would be so—so damn stupid, such an anticlimax to the hullabaloo and hurrah of our getting away . . ."

Dillon bent his head.

"What do you propose? Try to steer her back to her berth and lay up at the yacht club till we can get her fixed?"

Again the captain bent his head, this time twisting it to one side doubtfully.

"That's a hell of a note," Chris exclaimed disgustedly.

Armitage started to interrupt, but Chris sharply cut him off.

"Well, for Christ sake," he shouted; "what do you propose to do?"

"She'll have to be put in dry dock——"

"In *dry dock!*"

"If the pintle's loose, there's no other way——"

"Oh, for God's sake!" the young owner cried angrily.

Silence. The *Jabberwock* dipped her nose into a larger swell, and a shower of spray splattered them.

"Come below."

The four men found seats in the cabin. With an imperative gesture of a forefinger, Chris directed Dillon to take a chair and yelled loudly to Jimmy for old-fashioneds.

Rapid exchanges followed, Chris slowly coming to appreciate the seriousness of their predicament.

"I think we ought to turn back and make port while there's still light," the captain urged.

"All right," Chris conceded, after final thought. "And then what?"

"If we can't make the yacht harbor, we can lay outside and get one of Tom Sharkey's tugs to tow us in. Reach him by radio, I reckon."

"And next?"

"Then tomorrow we'll have to make arrangements with the Morse Dry Dock Company to have her hauled out of the water and see what's the matter."

Scowling, Chris considered this, slowly sipping his drink.

"Why do we have to wait *that* long?" he demanded. Then briskly his tone quickened. "Say, lissen, Cap, I tell you what we'll do: bring her about, take her back to the yacht harbor, get her alongside if you can, and if you can't, send me ashore in the Cris-craft. I'll get the Morse shipyards on the telephone and by God we'll have the boat in dry dock tonight, get her damn rudder fixed, and catch the morning tide at six o'clock. I'll bet the tide's no more than an hour earlier in the Estuary than down the Bay. . . . Got your docking plan on board?"

"Yes, sir."

"That's luck, and if more luck holds, we'll find an empty dry dock waiting, we'll get a tow across the Bay, and you, Johnny, can hop a taxi, catch the first ferryboat across, and take that docking plan with you; they'll be all set for us as soon as we get there. All I want is a telephone. We're going to catch the six-o'clock tide tomorrow morning or I'll know the reason why!"

§ 3

"That young scalawag of a nephew of ours has got himself—and us!—into trouble."

"Who do you mean?"

"Chris."

"What's he done now? I thought he sailed for Mexico."

"He did, but he had to put back. I think I'd better come up and see you. Going to be busy?"

"No, come ahead."

J.O.B. hung up the receiver, leaned back in his swivel armchair, sat staring out of the window, pulling slowly and thoughtfully at his goatee. In his mind's eye he could see the close-cropped curly white head of his brother Lloyd, see him sitting in his office with the telephone receiver at his ear—and he thought of him with both pleasure and satisfaction. Lloyd was always calmly judicious, never got excited, was always willing to listen with sympathy to others' troubles.

J.O.B.'s big office on the ninth floor of the Wickwire, Rutherford Building was filled with pleasant light this morning. It filtered in with golden luster through the Venetian blinds that screened the three eastern windows. The room was handsomely furnished, with the president's big desk a little off center and facing the door, several commodious chairs placed advantageously before it for easy use, a low davenport along one side of the room—all of polished mahogany. The walls, papered in gray with an almost indistinguishable pattern of sailing ships in soft gray tones, were covered with many framed photographs, most of them of more ships, old-fashioned types, clippers under full sail, and long, lean-looking steamers with tall smokestacks and bare spars: "The *San Francisco*—built by the Scott Shipbuilding Company, Bethlehem, Pa., 1903." There were a great many of these, and arranged on stands about the room were wooden models of more ships and steamers, beautifully executed, with small brass plates beneath each one giving the vessel's name, the builder, and date. In addition to the ship photographs, there were photographs of several men. One prominently displayed was of old Francis Wickwire and, flanking this, photographs of his two sons, Joshua F. and Waldo E.—both of whom had once been J.O.B.'s partners. There were pictures, too, of J.O.B. himself—a younger J.O.B., taken in company with the last two—at a dinner at the Palace Hotel on the night following the launching of the *San Mateo* where Mayor Rolph had been guest of honor, and another of the three men at the opening of the Panama Pacific Exposition in 1915.

One particular photograph, now a little faded, was especially prized by the present president of the line; this was of the old Wickwire offices in Boston, where the founder of the company had ruled the destinies of men and ships for many successful years. The date was uncertain, but J.O.B. insisted it had been taken in '75. The building had burned to the ground long ago—J.O.B. had never seen the structure itself, but to him it represented history, sound business methods, integrity, square dealings. At the top of the company's letterheads today appeared a diminutive engraving of this same building, showing the old original offices and the date of 1868, when Francis Wickwire was supposed to have founded the business.

There were still other photographs—these in handsome silver frames on J.O.B.'s desk; a lovely one of Daisy in the dress she had worn at her debutante dance, one of his wife looking very militant and not in the least like her, and a third, a studio study of the two children presented to him by them on his birthday some years ago. Once, balancing Daisy's, there had been a picture of Stan, taken just after he had graduated from Harvard and before he had gone east again to enter its Business School, but after becoming an employee of the company, Stan had objected strenuously to having it displayed so prominently on the president's desk, and his father regretfully had substituted the one of the two children.

Today, however, J.O.B. was not thinking of any of the furnishings of his big office which he liked so much. He sat with frowning eyes and still stroked his goatee. Minutes passed. At last with a sigh as if he assumed a heavy burden, he straightened his chair, flipped up a switch of the interoffice communicating telephone, said without looking at the instrument:

"I'm going up to see my brother at his office. Call me there if you want me. Tell Mr. Stanley I'm going to the club for luncheon and for him to join me if he's free."

Then he rose with effort, shoving his big bulk upright with one hand on the chairback, the other on his desk, hunched himself into his overcoat, which he took down from a hanger in a closet, fitted on his derby hat with care, and stepped into the corridor through a private door.

It was some six or seven blocks to his brother's law offices, and ordinarily he would have walked them for the exercise, but today he was too perturbed; he decided to taxi.

Poltney, Campbell, Rutherford & Hart occupied the three top floors of the Edison Bank Building on Montgomery Street. The atmosphere of these offices was very different from the hustle and bustle, the hurrying feet and clanging elevator doors which pervaded the premises of Wickwire, Rutherford & Company. Here decorum reigned, voices were hushed, soft carpets deadened footfalls; the furniture was solid, substantial, the windows curtained. J.O.B. claimed that calling on his brother was like visiting the Chief Justice of the United States.

Skipping the other offices of the firm on the thirteenth, fourteenth floors, he got out at the fifteenth, nodded to the girl at the reception desk. As usual he had to wait. Sometimes he thought Lloyd kept visitors waiting just to make them realize how busy he was, yet he knew his brother was probably the hardest-working and certainly the most important attorney in the city. Frequently Lloyd had to telephone to Sacramento, Los Angeles, New York, and even Washington, and was on the wire sometimes as long as half an hour.

"Well," J.O.B. said when finally he reached his brother's sanctum, "it seems to me I never come to see you except when I have some unpleasant business on my mind. The last time, I think, was that salvage case."

"What sort of a mess has our Gilded Youth got himself into now?" asked Lloyd. "I thought he was safely on the high seas."

J.O.B. struggled free of his overcoat, placed it and his derby hat on a chair, seated himself heavily in another. Lloyd's office was somber and dark and filled with books whose leather bindings gave off a musty smell. It was a room suggestive of profound thought, judicial conferences. Here learned briefs were written, documents examined, political campaigns mapped out, candidates for the office of governor discussed, new laws conceived, plans formulated to amend old ones.

"He's on the high seas all right, and safe enough, but he's left the rest of us to face a very unpleasant situation," J.O.B. observed.

Lloyd picked his pince-nez from the bridge of his nose, let them fall to dangle from the ribbon about his neck, tilted back in his chair, and neatly fitted his finger tips together.

"Well," he said, "let's have it."

"It appears he had some steering trouble soon after he had cleared the yacht harbor. His captain reported it before they had passed the Heads. They returned under their own power to the yacht club and engaged a tug to tow them over to Bill Morse's shipyards; there they put the *Jabberwock* in dry dock and went to work on her. I don't know yet what was wrong, but Bill Morse is, as you know, a very close friend of mine; his superintendent and all his men know it, and they'd do anything in the world for a nephew of ours. As I get the story, they pulled the boat out of the water on the marine railway and sent for a gang of machinists and helpers. By that time it must have been past midnight. I have no idea how much of a job was involved or how long it took, but while the men were whanging and banging at their work, our precious nephew and his roistering companions were making merry on deck. You will recall that Chris was liberally pouring champagne just before the *Jabberwock* sailed, and I have no doubt that he and his Hollywood friend and that other undisciplined boy—Williams his name is, isn't it?—kept up their swilling and drinking until they all got drunk. There was some singing and loud laughter, and finally one of the roisterers flung an empty champagne bottle over the side—not one but *two!*—and the second bottle struck a machinist's helper, laid open his head, cut his eye, and—so an impertinent shyster would have me believe—injured the optic nerve."

Lloyd's frown deepened as he listened, and the slow, rhythmical motion of his finger tips as they parted and came together again ceased for a moment.

"What happened next, I don't know," J.O.B. continued; "the men working on the boat wanted to climb aboard and make trouble. Someone quieted them. However, they called an ambulance, and the injured mechanic was driven to the Flower Hospital, where his wound was dressed. The *Jabberwock* sailed, and the next thing is that the union's business agent gets wind of the affair. There it is—a perfect setup! Rutherford nephew gets drunk—drunk on champagne, mind you!—throws empty bottle over side of pleasure yacht, hits young union machinist in the head, injures him—and, according to their reports, endangers the sight of one eye. Man must be compensated. Union business agent sees union lawyer—a horrible, vituperative Italian person who stinks of onions and garlic!—Mr. Giuseppe Paulini. Promptly this odious person comes to see me, demanding damages.

"I tell him I'm only the young fool's uncle and he has a perfectly good father down at Visalia who is well qualified to settle the case, but Mr. Paulini is smart and knows I don't want this story to appear in the newspapers; I don't want my name mentioned, nor that of Wickwire, Rutherford & Company. He says pay—and what the devil am I to do?"

Lloyd smiled good-naturedly and repeated: "Pay."

"I was afraid you'd say so."

"I don't see what else you can do if you don't relish the publicity. It smacks of blackmail, of course, but if it is sufficiently important to you not to have the affair aired, I think you'd better satisfy Mr. Paulini."

"Damned little jackanapes!"

"Who, Paulini?"

"No! *Chris!*"

"I'm afraid so."

"And happening just now, when there's so much trouble on the waterfront! He couldn't have chosen a worse time."

"What do you suppose he'll settle for?"

"As much as he can get. That's what I came to see you about. You'll have to talk to him."

"Ah, you can get someone much better than I. After all, I'm the boy's uncle, too. I don't want to get mixed up with any of his foolish escapades any more than you do. . . . There's a smart young attorney I know, named Nathaniel Jacobs, and he'll be glad to represent you. I'll send him round to see you in the morning. Better still . . . wait! See if I can get him now. His office is just around the corner."

He reached for his telephone; in a moment he had the young lawyer on the wire. Mr. Jacobs would be glad to come over immediately.

"It is *most* unfortunate," J.O.B. said with exasperation as the two brothers waited, "that this incident should come up just at this time. I'm afraid we're in for trouble with the longshoremen. They seem to be determined on striking. We haven't had any disagreements with them since we broke their union in 1919. Now the Communists have been spreading their propaganda and taking advantage of the National Recovery Act——"

"A mare's nest for trouble," Lloyd broke in. "It may have been conceived with the best intentions in the world, but it is bound to foment unrest, lawlessness, class warfare. A grave mistake, I fear, which our President will live to regret."

"We haven't been able to comply with the regulations of the NRA. The shipping interests haven't formulated a code."

"Why not?"

"Well, you see vessels of all nations call here, and all would be subject to the provisions of a code, and so far it has been impossible to secure a complete agreement among them. We've done our best to satisfy the longshoremen. Only last December we raised their wages from seventy-five to eighty-five cents an hour and agreed to fix overtime at a dollar and a quarter."

"I thought you said you hadn't been having any trouble with them?"

"True, but the NRA, last June, started it. It began with the Nickel Line when they—for damn good reasons—fired four stevedores. These fellows appealed to the Regional Labor Board, who supported their contention that they had been discriminated against for belonging to an unfriendly union."

"I understand. You reported the case to me at the time."

"As soon as the International Longshoremen's Association was okayed by the board, members of Blue Book Union——"

"That was the longshoremen's organization supposed to be controlled by the shipowners, wasn't it?"

"Nonsense! We never came in contact with the men—only with their representatives—and, as I say, we voluntarily raised their wages."

"Didn't that satisfy them?"

"It satisfied the men belonging to the old association, but the new organization, inspired, I am convinced, by Communists, is bent on making trouble. They began organizing and last month held a convention here, which they claimed was attended by delegates representing longshoremen from every port on the Pacific Coast. I doubt it very much."

"Doubt what?"

"That the convention represented all the longshoremen they claimed. It was whipped together by radicals. They sent a delegation to see me; I refused to meet them. Now they threaten to call a strike on the twenty-third of this month. By God, Lloyd, if they want a fight, we'll give 'em one! We'll fight 'em just as we did in 1919, bring in a bunch of strikebreakers and run 'em off the waterfront!"

The announcer buzzed, and Lloyd picked up his receiver.

"Yes, show him in," he said.

The man who entered was an odd-looking individual. His youth impressed J.O.B. at once. He had bright red hair, pinkish eyebrows and lashes, a ruddy face; with all this singular coloring, he had blue eyes that twinkled, an ingratiating smile, a pleasant expression. Lloyd greeted him familiarly, introduced him to J.O.B.

Jacobs listened as the elder Rutherford outlined Chris's scandalous behavior and described the predicament in which both his uncles now found themselves.

"We admit the injured man's contention," Lloyd finished; "we admit that our nephew or his companions were to blame, and I am sure my brother would want—for the sake of the family—to make some sort of restitution which would be satisfactory. We thought you'd be just the person to see this union business agent and arrange a satisfactory settlement."

Nathaniel Jacobs smiled pleasantly, screwed his head to one side, shook it in an apologetic negative.

"Fraid I can't be of help, Mr. Rutherford. You've been very kind to me and sent me a lot of business, but I'm on the other side."

"You mean?"

"I've sort of thrown in my lot with the unions, and it wouldn't do for me to represent one of the shipowners."

"You mean the union of which this marine machinist is a member?"

"Well, more particularly the longshoremen."

"The International Longshoremen's Association?"

"Yes, sir."

There was silence; the Rutherford brothers exchanged glances.

"U-mmmm," Lloyd hummed.

"That's a departure for you, isn't it, Nate? Union activities?" he asked after another interval.

"I suppose you'd say it was, but I've always been sympathetic."

"Sympathetic with what—and with whom?" J.O.B. asked sharply.

"With the worker, the laborer."

"Against the employer?"

"Not exactly; only when the working conditions are bad and the workers don't get a break."

"Like the longshoremen?"

"Yes, sir, like the longshoremen."

"Good gracious, Mr. Jacobs, if you're familiar with the facts, the shipowners raised their wages ten cents an hour last December; they are receiving eighty-five cents an hour today and a dollar and a quarter for overtime."

"They want a thirty-hour week and a minimum rate of one dollar an hour."

"That's highway robbery! They'll drive the shipping interests to the wall!"

"The men seem to be in an ugly mood."

"Why?"

"Well, because of the conditions prevailing on the waterfront for some years past. I'm sure you know what they are, Mr. Rutherford. The men had to get up before dawn, trudge down to the docks and wait there. If a ship came in, there'd be a mob of forty to fifty longshoremen hanging around the entrance to the pier, waiting for a straw boss to pick and choose. It might be cold; it might be raining. The men who did the hiring just pointed out those they wanted. 'You,' they'd say, and 'you' and 'you.' The fellows who weren't chosen slunk away, drank a beer or two in the back room of some saloon, and slunk home. The only way they could get work was to slip the straw boss money—five or six dollars. When a longshoreman got a job, he might have to work twenty-four to thirty-six hours at a stretch —without a letup. A job might last one day, two days, and then the chap would have to look for another one. There wasn't enough work to go round. Then another thing, the hiring bosses almost universally ran saloons, and a longshoreman who wanted work would have to patronize these joints, treat and be treated, spend his money. There's been graft going on down at the waterfront for the past fifteen years, and the men are sick of it. They want their own hiring halls and they want to run their own affairs——"

"And dictate to us how we shall run ours!" broke in J.O.B. "It won't do, Mr. Jacobs; it won't do. We'll break your unions and run the malcontents out of town. San Francisco must be kept a free port."

Jacobs spread out his hands deprecatingly.

"You asked me, Mr. Rutherford, how and why I happened to become interested in the men's problem."

"Yes, yes. I don't mean to be rude. I'm really interested."

"Take the sailors, for instance," Nate continued; "an ordinary seaman gets thirty-five dollars a month; an A.B. fifty. Some of the companies don't pay even that. J. P. Lobenthal pay their men only twenty a month; their A.B.s, thirty-five. A sailor can't marry on that, make a home for himself, start a family. While he's aboard ship, he and seven other sailors share the same quarters—eight of 'em in one room, piled up in tiers. Each has a small locker about the size of a hatbox to store his clothes. All use the same bucket to bathe in and wash their clothes in; one bucket for eight men; one toilet. In many cases their quarters are below the water line and there is no ventilation——"

"Rubbish," J.O.B. interrupted again; "they have the same system of ventilation as passengers who occupy inside cabins."

"Excuse me—there are not eight passengers in one inside cabin. I have been in those fo'c'sles, and the stench is often overpowering."

"They are a lot of dirty animals at best."

"Some of them are, perhaps, but their living conditions do not make them want to be anything else. Take the matter of duty. There are three watches, eight to twelve, twelve to four, four to eight. It's a tough schedule, but the sailors are not grumbling about that. They do grumble about two-watch ships where the men start to work at

six and work until noon, are on again at six in the evening and work
until midnight. The food is pretty bad. The oatmeal is full of cock-
roaches, the eggs are cold-storage eggs, the meat is poor, and one
thing in particular sailors object to: coffee can only be had at meal-
time; at no other hour can a man get a cup. I think they're entitled
to it."

"You make out quite a case for them. You are endowing these men
with a refinement they don't possess or even aspire to have."

The visitor laughed easily.

"Well, sir, the sailor ashore is pretty much of a laughingstock.
He's the prey of prostitutes, holdup men, and his boarding or lodging
house is a proverbial place of corruption. Men are slugged, drugged,
and shanghaied—and that's been going on for years. Sailors are at
sea most of the time; they are never on shore long enough to organize; it's up to the longshoremen to start the ball rolling. They insist
on running their own hiring halls, they want an increase in wages,
recognition——"

"We've never refused recognition," J.O.B. snapped, "and the San
Francisco Bay longshoremen receive wages equal to the highest paid
anywhere in the country. Moreover," he went on with rising heat,
"the real issue is a closed-shop agreement in which the shipowners
are supposed to recognize only the International Longshoremen's
Association. If we did that, it would be contrary to the law. Section
7a guarantees to each employee the right to organize and bargain
collectively. The National Recovery Administrator has ruled that
closed-shop contracts are equivalent to employer coercion and are
contrary to law. . . . Let 'em go ahead and strike. Believe me, Mr.
Jacobs, we'll keep the ships moving!"

J.O.B.'s face had suddenly congested, the blood beat up into his
temples, and his head shook as he wagged his finger.

Lloyd cleared his throat. "Take it easy, J.O.B. It will all be straightened out. Do you really think the men will strike on the twenty-third,
Nate?"

"They have every intention of doing so, now."

"I don't believe it is the sentiment of their leaders."

"Perhaps not, but it is most certainly the sentiment of the men
led by Rory O'Brien."

"Who's Rory O'Brien?"

"Haven't you heard of Rory? I assure you you will hear a good deal about and from him as time goes on—unless somebody takes a shot at him. So far he's won the workingman's confidence. He's bitter, he can't be bribed, and he intends to fight to a finish!"

"A Communist?"

"Perhaps, but," said Jacobs with an admiring laugh, "he isn't afraid of God, man, or the devil. He's all for the worker, and he's a great leader."

CHAPTER III

THE DIRECTORS' ROOM of the American-Asiatic Steamship Company was filled with men. At the long, polished oak table down its length were seated some twenty representatives of the shipowners, and there was a sprinkling of other businessmen besides. A dozen stood. Percy Grant, president of the Grant Line, presiding at the meeting, was on his feet at the head of the table, making an address.

"And so, gentlemen, we have a strike of major proportions on our hands, and we shall have no such easy time in meeting it as in 1919. Through the intercession of President Roosevelt, the strike was postponed from the middle of last month. Yesterday the longshoremen walked out. Already we are having trouble. Negro longshoremen, of no union affiliation, working on one of our docks were threatened by a mob of menacing stevedores, and bloodshed was averted only by the intervention of the police; police also had to be mobilized yesterday to prevent interference with the arrival of a steamer from Japan; confidential information which your committee has received states that the Teamsters' Union, Local 85, has been approached and urged to stage a sympathetic walkout. We shall have trouble indeed if this should happen. In Portland and in Oakland an embargo has already been placed by teamsters on freight handled by strikebreaking stevedores; in Portland sailors and bargemen have joined the longshoremen and walked off their ships. If the teamsters go out, we face a situation with gravest danger . . ."

After the meeting, J.O.B. and Stan walked to the corner and

boarded a California Street cable car, bound up the hill. As they clung to the supports of the dummy, the former said to his son:

"I wish the shipowners would get together. As Percy Grant says, we're in for trouble. This strike ought to be smashed at once. I think it is up to the Waterfront Association to present a united front. There's too much bickering and too much jealousy going on——"

"And too much rivalry, too," his son contributed.

"Yes, yes. Everybody mistrusts everybody else and they won't play ball with Ahearn, Percy Grant, and myself—the committee."

"Is Percy a good man, Dad?"

"Oh yes—but he's looking out for the best interests of the Grant Line, and he's stubborn as a mule."

"And Jim Ahearn?"

"Oh, Jim wants his own way like all the rest. He's thinking of the stockholders in the American-Asiatic Steamship Company. I tell you, Stan," his father continued, his tone sharpening, "it's a crime we don't pull together better than we do. Lobenthal, I understand, is willing to compromise with the men! God, that would be fatal! Suicide!"

"It's these damn radicals," Stan chimed in. "The *Western Worker* is an out-and-out communist paper published right here in San Francisco, and it's doing everything in its power to poison the men's minds. The same Reds who run it are backing another news organ, a cheap mimeographed affair called the *Waterfront Worker,* and it is distributed daily up and down the Embarcadero."

"Well," J.O.B. observed as he drew a troubled breath, "if the teamsters go out, we'll have a tough fight on our hands, and it'll cost us a lot of money. . . . But let's have it," he interrupted himself to say grimly; "we can't be dictated to by a bunch of Reds!"

When the cable car had reached the top of the hill, the two men descended. Their club, where they were to lunch, was on the corner. They mounted the stone steps; an attendant pulled back the heavy glass door. As they gave their hats and coats to the cloakroom boy, J.O.B. was handed a note. It read:

"Please call your daughter immediately. Urgent."

It was with difficulty that J.O.B. wedged his great bulk into one of the telephone booths, and even when he had partly succeeded it was impossible to close its door, so that Stan, standing hard by, could hear not only what his father said but the words of his excited sister.

"Listen, Dad—listen! I just got a cablegram. It's from a man, Vincent Oliver, assistant engineer on the *Jabberwock*. Listen, Dad— the *Jabberwock's* been wrecked! Six of 'em—I don't know how many —have been drowned! Chris and Lester Armitage and a couple of others have been saved. That's all!"

J.O.B. cleared his throat, wet his lips.

"Let's have that again, my dear, and don't speak quite so fast."

Daisy repeated what she had said, trying with difficulty to control her shaking voice.

"Where's the message from?" her father asked.

"From a place called Cocos. I don't know where that is, do you?"

"Read the cable."

"'JABBERWOCK' WRECKED PORT CULEBRA. BAXTER, ARMITAGE, BALDWIN, DILLON RESCUED. ALL OTHERS DROWNED. PROCEEDING TO SAN JOSÉ. VINCENT OLIVER.'"

There was a faint "Good God!" from Daisy's father, and then on a firmer tone he said, "Stan and I'll be right out."

"You heard?" he asked his son, extricating himself from the booth.

"Yes."

"We'll get home. Hope she's been sensible enough not to let Chris's mother know. Wouldn't do any good. Your grandmother will be bad enough. . . . This is a hell of a note! Five or six of 'em! Did that wire say anything about Williams—Johnny Williams? Can't remember. . . . Port Culebra is off Costa Rica, and San José must be its capital."

They found Daisy and her mother sitting side by side in the drawing room.

The girl rushed to her father and threw her arms about his neck.

"Oh, I'm so glad you're home, Daddy dear! What are we going to do? The *Jabberwock* wrecked and all those men drowned!"

"We ought to find out what really happened before we tell Charmion and Reggie or even Grandmère, don't you think?" Frances quavered nervously. "I thought of telephoning Visalia, and then I thought it would be foolish. Don't you think it would be foolish until we know?"

"Yes, most certainly," her husband told her; "come on, let's see the cable."

He read the message carefully, his teeth sunk into his lower lip, fingers holding fast to his goatee, and then read it again, this time aloud for Stan's benefit.

Stan took it from him and studied it.

"Why didn't Captain Dillon send this or why didn't Chris?" the young man asked.

The others did not meet his inquiring look; they stared at each other, each thinking the same possible explanation.

"Oliver's the assistant engineer, you say?" Stan pursued.

"Yes."

"Why did he send the cable to you? Why didn't he send it to Dad or Uncle Lloyd or Grandmère?"

"I know him; he's a friend of mine. We had a talk the day the *Jabberwock* sailed. He just thought of me, I guess—thought I was the right person to notify. . . . What do you suppose happened, Dad? There were eleven persons on that boat. Chris told me the day he sailed. Six of 'em must have been drowned. What *could* have happened?"

"Let's get an atlas and see exactly where Port Culebra is, and I want to locate San José. I'm almost positive San José's the capital of Costa Rica."

Frances, who had been standing by with anxiously clasped hands, now trod heavily from the room, returning immediately with a red-covered *Atlas of the World*. Anxious fingers fumbled with its pages, and all four heads bent over it as J.O.B.'s thick forefinger sought to locate names.

"Port Culebra. He must mean Culebra Gulf. Here it is just south of Cape Elena. I know the spot. Excellent harbor. They probably put in for fresh water, but, good God, it should be safe enough! Here's a town—Liberia. But where the devil do you suppose Cocos is? . . . I'm right. San José *is* the capital of Costa Rica. Mountainous down there. Must be a good two hundred miles away; the roads are sure to be abominable, and of course no trains. 'Proceeding to San José.' What do you suppose that means? . . . And why?"

"There's nothing any of us can do," Stan observed. "We'll just have to wait until we hear from him again."

"You'd better telephone Charmion and Reggie. They've got to know sooner or later, and Charmion would resent it if we kept her in the dark. You'll just have to convince her there's nothing immediate we can do and that Chris must be all right. And I dare say I'll have to go across the street and break the news to Bessie and Mother. She'll raise a row—Grandmère, I mean—but there's no help for it. I wish to God I didn't have to tell them until we had more definite information."

"Listen, Dad," Stan said, raising his head from the study of a telephone directory he had opened on his lap, "I've got an idea; just been looking up something. Costa Rica has no consulate in San Francisco, but I'll bet anything Costa Rica is represented by Nicaragua or Panama, both of whom have consulates here. Those countries adjoin Costa Rica, and one of them must look after Costa Rica's interests. I'd like to find out just how far Liberia *is* from San José and when we're likely to get more news. I thought too we might get hold of the consul—whichever country represents Costa Rica—and get him to cable his Government and tell them to look out for Chris."

"Excellent! Excellent!" his father approved. "Go ahead; do that. I'm going to telephone Lloyd—probably I'll catch him at the club. Lloyd always knows what to do."

§ 2

It was four days before they had further information. The newspapers had the story before that—and ran it with photographs of the *Jabberwock,* Chris in a yachting cap, another one of Stan and Eleanor taken on Harbor Day, standing arm in arm on the forward deck of the boat, waving American flags.

Vincent Oliver's second cable, this one from San José, read:

ARRIVED HERE BY PLANE. BAXTER IN HOSPITAL. NO DANGER. EXCELLENT CARE. CAPTAIN DILLON CONCUSSION. ARMITAGE OKAY. NEED FUNDS.

OLIVER, HOSPITAL SEÑORA, GUADALUPE.

"Oh, merciful God, he's sick too!" thought Daisy, her hand at her lips as she digested the message and her eye lingered on the signature and the address. Why a hospital?

She read the cable over the telephone to her father and then to his secretary, who took it down in shorthand, typed it, and brought it to J.O.B. He studied it a long time, pulling at his beard; then he flipped up the switch in the interoffice communicating box, said:

"Send Mr. Stanley up here, will you?"

And presently his son, tall, handsome, and dependable, was standing before him, and J.O.B. surveyed him with satisfaction. He handed the message to the young man and waited while he read and reread it.

"Guess you'll have to fly down and take charge. You can get a plane to Mexico City and, since he speaks of flying to San José, my guess is that you can fly there too. I'd feel better if you went, so would your mother, Chris's parents, the whole family. Take plenty of money and cable me daily."

§ 3

There was serious trouble along the San Francisco waterfront, in ports up and down the coast, and the effect of the strike was creeping inland. Lumber mills in the northwest were shutting down, grain shipments were being delayed, a vast number of other industries were forced to suspend operations for lack of essential raw material. At San Pedro a longshoreman was shot by the police in attempting to scale a stockade where strikebreakers were quartered. In Oakland, a mob of strikers broke through the barricade around the piers, boarded the steamship *Oregon Maru,* and mauled and seriously injured six men attempting to load the freighter. Ninety-four vessels were tied up in San Francisco Bay, and some twenty-five hundred freight cars had been sidetracked outside of San Francisco. The teamsters' union, the most powerful in the city, agreed to haul only as far as the gates of the docks but not upon the docks themselves. On May 15 the sailors, marine firemen, and water tenders joined the walkout, and a week later the marine engineers, a thousand strong, and these were followed within a few days by the masters, mates, and pilots.

In spite of a city ordinance prohibiting picketing, all day long a picket line of several hundred men marched up and down the closed portals of the docks along the Embarcadero. No one dared to enforce the ordinance; rioting and bloodshed would have been the result. Efforts of union heads and employers to reach some compromise were fruitless; the rank and file of the unions refused to be led by their officials. The situation had become no longer a struggle between the shipowners and the sailors and longshoremen; it was affecting every business interest in the entire community.

On May 21 the president of the Chamber of Commerce issued the following statement:

The San Francisco waterfront strike is out of hand. It is not a conflict between employers and employees—between capital and labor; it is a conflict which is rapidly spreading between American principles and un-American radicalism. As president of the San Francisco Chamber of Commerce, it is my duty to warn every businessman in this community that the welfare of business and industry and the entire public is at stake in the outcome of this crisis.

The so-called longshoremen's strike has spread since the morning of May 9 to include sympathetic walkouts by unions that have presented no demands. On April 2 the workers and employers were in complete agreement on every point but wages and hours and the President of the United States had set up machinery by which these differences would have been amicably and promptly settled through mediation.

The longshoremen are now represented by spokesmen who are not representative of American labor and who do not desire a settlement of their strike, but who desire complete paralysis of shipping and industry and who are responsible for the violence and bloodshed which is typical of their tribe.

The Assistant Secretary of Labor, sent here from Washington in a last effort to terminate the strike, has indicated that the situation is hopeless and that all negotiations have failed.

There can be no hope for industrial peace until communistic agitators are removed as official spokesmen of labor and American leaders are chosen to settle their differences along American lines.

This was replied to by the executive committee of the striking longshoremen as follows:

The "Red Scare" issued by the San Francisco Chamber of Commerce is a typical propaganda effort.

Any strike in history is a conflict between the pocketbook of the capitalist and the stomach of the employee.

On April 3 the Longshoremen's Association entered into a verbal agreement with the employers of longshore labor from various Pacific Coast ports.

This agreement was openly flaunted by the employers in one or more ports and was nullified in others by the shippers or their agents.

The statement that the International Longshoremen's Association is represented by communistic agitators is false and misleading.

The members of the International Longshoremen's Association are a true cross-section of Americanism. The strike is in effect to procure work enough to support their families as Americans.

On May 28 the picket line on the waterfront swung over to Pier 18, where a ship was unloading, and covered its advance with a shower of bricks and cobblestones. Police on horse and on foot drove the men back and forced them to the other side of the Embarcadero. A free-for-all scrimmage ensued; the Embarcadero was converted into a battlefield; heads were broken; officers were pulled from their horses, four of these badly injured.

A newspaper account reported: "Gas bombs exploded; sawed-off shotguns roared; clubs smashed heads; cobblestones flew."

By this time the strike filled the minds of the whole population. San Francisco was living and breathing strike. Everyone was discussing it. Everybody was trying to understand it. Everybody had something to say about it and something to ask about it. Homes, restaurants, and public places became virtually open forums, with people rapidly taking sides. Bitter disagreements were splitting friendships; at the same time new bonds of sympathy were being forged.

§ 4

"He doesn't look right to me," J.O.B. said. He did not speak until he had closed the door of the hospital room gently behind him and had walked some dozen or more thoughtful paces down the long corridor.

Stan made no comment. The two men passed the turning in the hall that led to the elevators and with measured steps pursued their way to the end of it, where there was a double window which gave upon some adjoining yards. They stood here looking out, seeing nothing, saying nothing, both overcoated, both with fingers linked behind their backs, holding their hats. Finally Stan spoke.

"Chris never was very strong."

"No," J.O.B. agreed; "I've often thought about his narrow shoulders."

"It was that long night clinging to the rocks."

"How long was it before Oliver got him to the hospital in San José?"

Stan drew breath, expelled it with a rush.

"My God, Dad, that young fellow used his head. He not only saved Chris's life with his strength, but he did it again with his brains. I suppose you could say it was all physical, but what I mean is that he not only pulled him out of the water, pushed him up on a rocky ledge, held him there all night, then swam ashore—I guess it must have been nearly a mile—through a rough sea, risked being dashed against the rocks, scrambled up the cliffs, then walked another two or three miles to the customhouse at Cocos Bay and got a boat to go out to the wreck. Then, after he gets the survivors ashore, he walks eight miles to Liberia and persuades them to telephone to San José for a plane!"

"I'm surprised they had a landing field down there."

"It happens that they did, and then Vince had to arrange to transport Chris, Dillon, and the rest by motorcar to Liberia over what they tell me are the worst roads in the world, fly from there by plane to San José, and arrange for doctors and nurses and everything else."

"We'll have to take care of him."

"I should hope so!"

"We'll have to find him a good job on one of our ships."

"Johnny Williams, before he died, told me he was a first-class engineer."

"Did you bury Williams down there?"

"No, I saw his family the day we arrived. They're having the body sent up."

"And Captain Dillon?"

"As far as I can ascertain he had no family. He never regained consciousness, it seems; Vince arranged to have him buried at Cocos Bay."

"He never regained consciousness, you say?"

"Not from the moment he was hit. Vince pulled him out of the water and tied him onto something. As I understand what happened, there was a sudden squall; everybody was below and asleep at the time; the yacht's anchor chain broke, and she drifted onto a half-submerged reef about two miles away; there she hit the rocks and stuck. When she split in two it was the aft and cabin part that sank; the forward part remained. Vince must have gotten hold of a rope or something and tied it under the captain's arms. God Almighty, Dad, that young fellow rescued *four* people! If they didn't all live, that wasn't his fault. He got 'em to shore and he got three of them into the hospital at San José. I'll be damned, I don't know how he did it! He himself must have had the hell knocked out of him. Think of his hiking eight miles to Liberia! It's tremendous!"

"But Armitage, what was he doing?"

Stan smiled sourly. "As far as I can make out, he just let Vince wait on him."

"He wasn't hurt?"

"No! A bruise here and there—and of course scared out of his life. Do you realize, Dad, that they clung to those rocks for over thirty hours! Chris and Armitage are alive today only because of that young fellow Oliver."

"Well, as I say, we'll have to do something for him."

"You bet!"

"But what do you think of Chris?"

"What can you expect? He's had pneumonia, and he was damn sick when I got there. I didn't think he was going to pull through. Vince didn't either. He had it in both lungs, you know. Maybe I moved him too soon."

"Don't believe so."

"The doctors seemed to think it all right. It was a whole two weeks after the wreck; he wanted to get home, and Armitage kept nagging at me. Maybe . . ."

"Oh, you mustn't let yourself worry about that, my boy. Chris is going to get well. Dr. Stewart is one of the best, and he has the finest nurses in San Francisco. If the family would let him alone!"

"We'll have to make 'em."

"It's your grandmother. She's continually fussing—calling the hospital, insisting upon seeing him, asking questions." J.O.B. sighed wearily. "I'm getting to feel like an old man these days," he said. "I've got too much to worry about."

"I wish I could help you."

"Oh, there's no helping. . . . If these longshoremen would get some sense . . ." He exploded on another deep breath of exasperation, thumping the sash of the window before him gently with his fist. "It's this damn Rory O'Brien who's got the men hypnotized. Michael Casey, Joe Ryan—their own International president—a half-dozen of their supposed leaders signed a definite agreement in Mayor Rossi's office to arbitrate everything—and this Communist Rory O'Brien persuades the longshoremen to repudiate the agreement in toto.

"Perhaps you don't know this. You were away. This agreement was all signed, sealed, and delivered in Mayor Rossi's office, and everybody thought the strike was settled once and for all. But the next day O'Brien calls a meeting of longshoremen in Eagles Hall; he sends out runners—a hundred of his own henchmen—to pack the hall; it's jammed to the doors with radicals and Communists, and then and there they repudiate the agreement, shout down everybody who tries to say a word. They booed their own president off the stage; they threatened him with violence, drove him from the hall."

"What is it they want?"

"They demand that the wages and hours and working conditions of every other union that struck in sympathy with them must be adjusted along with theirs. As Ryan said, it's no longer a longshoremen's strike; it's a strike of the entire waterfront. Why, damn it, Stan, the thing smacks of revolution. Some of the idiots are even talking general strike. They're proposing to tie up this whole city just to settle their own selfish demands. I tell you it's communism. The Communists are back of the whole business, and this fellow Rory O'Brien is a rank, out-and-out Red, and it's his purpose to keep on promoting trouble until he takes over the reins of government!"

§5

Bessie and Frances were having tea in Bessie's parlor when Charmion came in. It was very seldom that either Bessie or Frances indulged in tea, but about five o'clock, after the two sisters-in-law had been gossiping for an hour, Bessie had said she "just felt like having a real, good cup of hot tea" and had persuaded Frances without much difficulty to join her. They had had a most satisfactory chat—"so comfortable," Bessie had characterized it; they had talked of Lloyd and J.O.B., of Stan and Eleanor, of Grandmère and the servants of their respective establishments. Wilbur was so conscientious, and Annabel put up with any of Grandmère's whims no matter how unreasonable she was. Well, Martha was competent too; she did all the mending and much of the ironing—Daisy's frocks particularly.

"And only a half-day off each week," Frances had commented with an approving nod.

Ultimately they had reached the topic of Chris, had shaken their heads over his rather alarming condition, and had progressed from this to discussing Daisy's obvious infatuation with the young engineer, Vincent Oliver, who most certainly had covered himself with glory and who was undeniably handsome, but as a son-in-law . . . ? Frances was not so sure.

It was at this point that cumbersome Charmion came in, puffing and blowing to such a degree that it was a moment or two before she could get her breath to answer the two other women's immediate inquiries about Chris. She had just come from the hospital. She sank into a chair, loosened her wraps, and unceremoniously jerked off her hat and dropped it on the floor beside her.

"I'll tell you in a minute," she panted, patting her large bosom. "Those hills——" Presently she swallowed, drew a deep breath, said:

"About the same. Weak and listless. He lies there in bed, and all he wants is cigarettes, and it seems to me they make him cough too much. . . ."

"I'll take him some playing cards tomorrow," Frances announced; "teach him a few games of solitaire. It will keep his hands busy. 'Keep their hands busy,' my old Carrie used to say, 'and they don't fret.' Daisy and I often play. Why shouldn't Chris? Amuse him, don't you think?"

"Is there anything *I* can do?" Bessie asked solicitously.

"No, not a thing," Charmion assured her. "I thought of taking him home with me, but I guess he'd better stay where he is for a while."

"Oh yes, I think so," her companions chorused.

Bessie suggested tea, but Charmion declined.

"We owe an undying debt of gratitude to that young engineer," she said; "Chris tells me he saved all their lives, the survivors, I mean."

Bessie and Frances exchanged looks; the latter shook her head dubiously.

"We were just discussing him," Bessie volunteered. "Most certainly he behaved very well, and Stan thinks the world of him. . . ." She allowed her voice to fade away.

"Why, what seems to be the trouble?" Charmion inquired. "Your tone implies something . . ."

"Oh no, no, no. He behaved magnificently, as I've said. It isn't that. It's Daisy."

"What's the matter with her?"

"She seems to be hopelessly infatuated."

Charmion frowned as she considered this.

"Well, I don't know exactly what's to be held against him. He's handsome enough, and he's an engineer, isn't he?"

"Yes, I know, but after all . . ."

"After all . . . ?"

"Well, he was an employee—engineer or assistant engineer, I don't know what he was—but Chris hired him; he was in Chris's employ. Don't you think that makes a difference?"

"Fiddlesticks! So's Stan an employee of his father."

"That isn't the same thing at all. Don't be foolish, Charmion."

"I think it's *you* who are foolish, Fran. The young man's a ship's officer. There's nothing disgraceful about that."

"Oh yes, I know, but I've just been wondering. . . . I haven't a single thing in the world against the young man. He may come from the finest American stock, for all I know. He's pleasant, and if he drawls a little, that's not his fault. The whole thing is this, Charmion: I was just telling Bess before you came in, I rather thought—I rather hoped Daisy would make more or less of a brilliant match. There's nothing reprehensible in that, is there? Mothers have the right to wish for the moon, don't you think?"

"Well, of course, but I was just thinking . . . Tell me about Eleanor and the beautiful Mr. Armitage."

"Who? You mean this motion-picture actor?"

"Yes."

"She wouldn't look at him!"

"He certainly's looking at *her*."

"Rubbish!"

"Not rubbish at all. I've seen them together, and I tell you he's after her."

"Nonsense. She wouldn't be bothered with him."

"I'm not so sure."

§6

Within a day or two, sartorially resplendent, Lester arrived from Hollywood and became immediately a very decided factor in the Rutherfords' lives, and in particular Eleanor's. Grandmère eyed him critically, treated him distantly; Eleanor condescendingly accepted his attentions; her mother was cordially polite; Lloyd indifferent. It was Stan who actively disliked him.

"Oh, he's so stuck on himself," he complained to his sister on a certain night about a week after Armitage's appearance, when both he and Daisy happened to arrive home at the same hour and lingered to gossip in the drawing room. Stan had been at a meeting of one of the subcommittees of the Shipowners' Association, and Daisy had been to a movie with Vincent Oliver. Stan and Vincent had had a scotch-and-soda together, and then the latter had departed and brother and sister were alone.

"Armitage is one of those body lovers," Stan continued, "and the body he's in love with is his own. Oh, I admit," he diverged to say, "he and Eleanor make a very handsome couple, but each of them is conscious of the fact, and I believe that is what draws them together. But the fellow is a softy. I saw Chris this afternoon, and he was telling me——"

"How is he?" the girl interrupted.

"Not so good. They took some X-rays this morning. I suppose they're looking for t.b."

"Oh, Stan!"

"Well, he's been through a tough experience, exposure and all that, and he never was particularly strong. He told me that at the time of the wreck Armitage didn't show up very well. He bawled and yelled and thought only of his own safety. I suppose that's natural, but that guy . . . I guess he's after Eleanor's money."

"Oh no, Stan; I don't believe it. He doesn't look mercenary. He's not that type."

"He certainly must be aware that she's not a pauper. We don't know anything about him. During the time I was with him in Costa Rica, he never said a word about himself—oh, plenty about his tremendous success in pictures and how the various studios were fighting to get him, but not a word about his home or his people. You know, Sis, it doesn't take much brains to draw conclusions about people when you're thrown in intimate contact with them under the kind of conditions we were in at San José. Armitage did nothing but bellyache about getting back to the States, talked about his agent and the star parts waiting for him. He didn't think anything about them when he accepted Chris's invitation to go on a yachting trip for three months! Whereas Vince—— Say, Sis, how well do you like that chap?"

Daisy's delicate coloring deepened a little, but her shining blue eyes did not falter as she returned her brother's questioning gaze.

"He's wonderful," she said softly.

"You like him?"

"Yes."

"Love him?"

"More than I ever thought it possible for me to love a man."

"Humph, I thought so. Well, he's a fine fellow."

"He's the most magnificent person in the world. Oh, Stan, what can he possibly see in an empty-headed little simpleton like me?"

"Has he asked you to marry him?"

The girl shook her head, but her radiant expression did not alter.

"You're sure, are you?"

She nodded happily, and her brother smiled affectionately and caught her hand.

"But oh, Stan," she hurried on breathlessly, "suppose he should change his mind, suppose he was too afraid? He *is* afraid! He's had such humble beginnings—a widowed mother who's an invalid now—and all that. At least he's awfully humble, and he's so shy and so—so sort of hesitant and unassuming. He doesn't think he amounts to anything. He just thinks of himself as a sort of glorified sailor—an engineer's assistant, if you like—but you and I know he's one of the finest of the fine. But he's afraid; he won't believe how much I care."

"Have you told him?"

"Oh no, but of course he knows. I suppose he thinks of me as Father's daughter—daughter of J. O. B. Rutherford of Wickwire, Rutherford & Company. He won't lift his eyes. You know what I mean! He thinks he would be presuming, he thinks—oh, I don't know!—he thinks he doesn't dare——"

"We'll find a job for him. I know Dad has it in mind; he's spoken to me about it two or three times. As soon as there's a vacancy. He likes Vince, and he'll give him a job on one of our boats and let him work things out. You know how Dad feels about you; he'd buy you a Hottentot with a ring in his nose if you wanted him!"

Daisy laughed, but the laugh quickly died, and again her eyes were troubled.

"Oh, but I'm afraid."

"Afraid of what?"

"That he'll go away and I'll never see him again and perhaps he'll change his mind. He'll be on a ship and he'll be away for weeks at a time."

"It's up to you to see he doesn't change his mind."

"He's *so* handsome. . . . That hair, those eyes, that dark skin and white teeth! Oh, he's a man; he's not a bit like that Hollywood Lester Armitage."

Suddenly she was in her brother's arms and softly crying, clinging to him almost desperately. He patted her, amused and touched by her emotion.

"Don't worry, Sis. Vincent Oliver is a grand guy. He won't let you down."

§7

It was the next afternoon that Stan and his father were told that Chris had tuberculosis and in a very advanced stage.

"His whole system is riddled with it," Dr. Stewart said; "it is just as if his body had been pumped full of buckshot. He must have had the bugs in his system for a number of years and the pneumonia acted like a spark that scattered them. Both lungs are affected; the right has a cavity as big as your fist; the left has several bad spots. I doubt if we could collapse either lung. He's running a degree and a half to two degrees now. When he starts to gain, put on some weight, we'll see what we can do. The only treatment is to get him into some first-rate sanitarium, keep him quiet, build him up, get his temperature down."

The physician's pronouncement was made to father and son as they entered the hospital and were about to pay Chris a visit. They met Dr. Stewart in the corridor.

"Well, where?" J.O.B. asked heavily after a silence. "Arizona?"

"No need to move him so far away. We have some fine sanitariums down the Peninsula; Dr. Willabrandt's California Sanitarium at Belmont is one of the best. You could make your own arrangements with him, and I'd drop down from the city and see the young man a couple of times a week. There's nothing more to be done for him," the physician said as he turned his eyes from one grave face to the other; "he must get some strength back first and we must get that temperature down."

"But what do you think," Stan asked slowly, "what do you think his chances are?"

Stewart shrugged.

"My dear Mr. Rutherford," he answered, "I wish I knew. Nobody can tell. Sometimes these cases—ones as bad as his—recover, and sometimes they don't. It's going to be a long, hard fight at best. Much depends on the boy himself. I should say his chances were fifty-fifty."

CHAPTER IV

ON JULY FIRST, the Industrial Association of San Francisco, demanding police protection, announced its intention of opening the port. At 1:27 in the afternoon of the third, the steel doors of Pier 38 on the Embarcadero rose, and five trucks, loaded with perishable merchandise, rolled out, preceded by eight radio patrol cars.

Since daybreak that morning hundreds of pickets and labor sympathizers had swarmed the waterfront; at eleven the police, on foot, on horseback, and in cars, moved in and proceeded to clear the area in front of the pier. As the trucks came into view, the strikers surged forward and the Embarcadero became a vast tangle of fighting men. Bricks flew and clubs swung. The police fired over the heads of the mob with revolvers and riot guns; clouds of tear gas swept upon the oncoming rioters and sent them to the right-about with streaming eyes. Armed with any sort of missiles, with crowbars and railroad spikes, the men returned to the attack. Officers were dragged from their horses and pulled from their cars. Men went down right and left with cracked heads. At short range the police discharged gas shells from their revolvers. As the crowd fell back, the bluecoats threw hand grenades of gas and shot other grenades from gas guns. Dense crowds lined every rooftop and leaned from every window in the neighborhood. The gas seeped into the buildings, restaurants, and factories, driving those inside to the streets. By midafternoon the Embarcadero had been cleared, and a casualty list recorded twenty-five maimed and wounded—thirteen police, twelve strikers.

It was but a preliminary skirmish to the battle which was to be fought two days later. The Fourth being a holiday, no unloading was attempted. Promptly at eight o'clock on the morning of the fifth, as trucks began to transport more merchandise from Pier 38, a crowd of five thousand strikers surged out to stop them. Eight hundred police officers were on hand and with gas and clubs routed the rioters, and once again the Embarcadero was cleared and once again it was littered with prostrate bodies. The strikers retreated to the slopes of Rincon Hill. Firing their revolvers and swinging their long riot sticks, the police charged up the hill, driving the men up the steep slope. Tear-gas shells ignited the dry grass, and presently the hillside was in flames. The fire department arrived to the scream of sirens and turned high-pressure streams of water on grass and pickets alike. Gas and gunfire at last drove the men into the city, and the police took command of the hill.

From the windows of the president's office in the Wickwire, Rutherford Building, J.O.B., his son Stan, Syd Watterbury, and three other officials of the company stood watching the melee, only part of which was visible, but the roar of battle, the crash of splintering glass, the crackle of gunfire, the angry shouts of men, and the sound of fighting, struggling, and grappling was terrific.

"My God, it's a riot! It's murder and bloodshed!" Stan exclaimed.

"It's revolution," his father said sternly.

At noon there was an interval, but shortly after one o'clock the battle recommenced. A large crowd of strikers had gathered at the Longshoremen's headquarters on Steuart Street and filled the narrow thoroughfare from wall to wall. The police proceeded to disperse this crowd and charged with tear-gas bombs and clubs. Presently there was the angry bark of pistolfire, and a score of men littered the sidewalks, either lying silently where they fell or crawling painfully away on hands and knees. Two were dead.

At five o'clock the same afternoon the National Guard, fifteen hundred strong, helmeted, bayoneted, equipped with automatic rifles and machine guns, moved in and took charge of the Embarcadero.

The governor of the state issued the following statement:

Forbearance with the striking longshoremen in San Francisco has passed the point of common sense and good citizenship. The acknowledged leaders of the strike defied the state government and sought to overthrow the authority of the state government in its operation and maintenance of the state harbor facilities at San Francisco.

The situation cannot be endured. I have ordered the National Guard of California to move into the San Francisco strike area, safeguard life, protect state property, and preserve order.

§ 2

The following day the Joint Marine Strike Committee, of which Rory O'Brien was a member, published and widely distributed among labor circles a bulletin calling for a general strike.

The National Longshoremen's Board appointed by President Roosevelt announced that, in compliance with its request that all issues be submitted to arbitration, replies had been received from employers and the strikers. The longshoremen insisted that the matter of a closed shop and control of the hiring hall be agreed to before arbitration began. They also reiterated their position that the grievances of the seamen be considered before any union on strike would return to work. The employers insisted on the open shop—freedom to hire union or non-union workers at will, and refused to recognize the Strike Committee.

On Sunday, July 8, at a mass meeting of the Teamsters' Union, Local 85, in Dreamland Auditorium, members of that union voted to stop hauling on the following Thursday unless the maritime workers' strike and the longshoremen's strike had at that time been definitely settled. If the teamsters walked out, their action would completely paralyze all movements of freight or merchandise in the community.

Public sentiment in the city was crystallizing rapidly. People in every walk of life were mobilizing at opposition polls of opinion. Lukewarm or undecided attitudes were rare. San Francisco was a city divided into two clear-cut factions—those supporting the strikers and those opposed to them.

§ 3

On Monday following the day in which the two men had been killed, the Longshoremen's Association staged an impressive and dramatic funeral for them. At half past twelve, services were begun at the International Longshoremen's headquarters on Steuart Street, in front of which the men had fallen, and in which their bodies had lain in state since Saturday. The parade was well organized, and in solid ranks, eight to ten abreast, thousands of strike sympathizers, with bared heads, accompanied the trucks bearing the coffins up Market

Street to an undertaking establishment in the Mission two miles distant.

It was a spectacular and stirring sight, as thousands of men and women, to the solemn cadences of Beethoven's dirge, silently followed the dead and the attendant trucks piled high with wreaths and floral tributes. With measured step the vast procession of mourners marched up the main artery of the city. The police, at the request of the longshoremen, were nowhere in sight, and the latter, with blue bands about their arms, directed traffic. Sidewalks were lined with women, children, and sober-faced men of every walk of life. Hours passed and still the column moved onward. A great hush lay over the line of march, broken only by the rhythmic tread of trudging feet. Tramp—tramp—tramp, on the workers plodded, bareheaded, no talking, not even a cigarette. Tramp—tramp—tramp, grave and grim, on they came; there seemed to be no end to the procession. Long after the trucks bearing the coffins and flowers had passed from sight and the strains of the funeral music had been lost in the distance, the phalanxes of the marchers escorting the bodies of their fallen comrades continued. It was a demonstration dramatically conceived, dramatically carried out, and it left Stan Rutherford with a feeling of solemnity and respect, and a feeling of apprehension as well.

He and Syd Watterbury had gone out to lunch together, and as they emerged from the restaurant after their meal the long column of labor sympathizers was solemnly passing in the street. Stan had been aware earlier that morning that there was to be a funeral procession, but he was unprepared for the drama of the spectacle—the endless ranks of sober faces, bared heads, and the slow cadence of marching feet. Tramp—tramp—tramp. No noise except that. The band with its muffled drums and its somber music had long since passed. He recognized that he was looking upon something vastly more significant than a tribute to two longshoremen who had been shot by officers of the law. On the marchers came—hour after hour—ten, twenty, thirty thousand of them. Tramp—tramp—tramp. There was no break in the march; there was no division into corps or companies; there was no halting or hesitation. A solid river of men and women who believed they had a grievance and who were expressing their resentment in this gigantic demonstration.

For half an hour Stan and Syd stood silently, watching the marchers; then Stan on a deeply drawn breath said:

"There's going to be a general strike for sure. These men—they
may be misguided and misled—but they're desperately in earnest.
We're in for trouble."

"I'm afraid you're right," Syd agreed solemnly.

And then it was, or perhaps a little later, that Stan heard two men
talking behind him. At first he did not hear what they had said, but
presently he was aware that their words had some significance for
him. He strained his ears to listen.

"Been some time since I seen you, pal," one said.

"Been busy," answered the other in a harsh, unpleasant voice.
"Some show, isn't it?"

"Oh, you bet. Why ain't you in the parade?"

"Been out to Dugan's and I've got to meet some of the Strike Committee at Eagles Hall. Why aren't you marching?"

"Wife's sick; got to take care of the kid. Guess this show will make
some of those damn shipowners think once or twice before they
start pulling any more of their tricks. My God, it makes a feller feel
proud."

Stan glanced briefly over his shoulder. A weazened little man stood
close to him, his cap clutched in his hand; he looked like a dock
worker. Stan did not glimpse his companion.

There was a silence for a few moments, and then the first speaker
in his harsh twang said:

"One of those men being buried today isn't being buried under his
right name. The papers have him down as Knute Larsen, and that
was what he was known by down at the hall. But his real name is
Frank Rutherford, and he's the son of that old bastard Lloyd Rutherford and the nephew of another son of a bitch, J. O. B. Rutherford,
the president of Wickwire, Rutherford & Company. The police, by
orders from the mayor, who takes his orders from the shipowners,
shot him down, killed him like a dog. I wonder how old Lloyd
Rutherford would like it if he knew his son's funeral was passing in
the streets of the city today."

"You mean one of the dead uns isn't a longshoreman?"

"Sure he was. One of the best. He quit his father's home years ago, ran away to sea, changed his name, struck out for himself and did what he could to help his fellow workers. Now they're burying him."

Stan stood frozen, his nerves taut, his spine ridged. He wheeled, but as he did so the two men who had been standing close to him turned their backs and pushed a passage through the lines of bystanders, pulling on their caps. He started to overtake them, but as he hesitated the crowd intervened, a woman jostled him, and the men were gone. Shaken, not knowing what to do, he began again to watch the passing procession.

Could it be true? Could one of the men whose funeral he was witnessing be Uncle Lloyd's runaway son, Frank, the black sheep of the family? It *might* be so; he *had* taken to the sea. "A waterfront bum," he had been described. Very probably he had changed his name. Sailor or longshoreman, what mattered it? The unions would say he was theirs, proclaim him a martyr, make a hero of him. They would not care what his real name was or his lineage. The last Stan had heard of him—from whom or where he could not remember now— was that he had drifted to Australia—or had it been New Zealand? But if this dead man was in reality his cousin Frank . . . ?

To Syd he said:

"I've got to run along now. Must see my father about something."

§ 4

He found J.O.B. in his office and told his story while the latter stroked his goatee and eyed him under sharply contracted brows.

"How did he know, whoever he was?" Stan finished in a troubled voice. "How could he have known who *I* was? I'm sure I never saw either of the men before. One was a pale-faced, weazened little runt; I didn't see his companion—the one who spoke. It seemed to me that they wanted—*one* of them wanted me to hear what he was saying."

"Let me see. How long's it been since Frank ran away?" his father asked.

"Ten years, I think. You ought to know. Do you think we ought to tell Uncle Lloyd? If it *is* his son . . ."

Stan's voice trailed off to silence, and J.O.B.'s brows knit more deeply and the hand pulling at his goatee paused. He stared hard at his son, and there was a long silence. The clang of cable cars, the honking of motor horns, and a reawakened bourdon from the street below announced that the parade had passed and traffic had been resumed.

"Yes, I suppose so," J.O.B. said at length. "Guess we'll *have* to tell him. Better come with me. I'll break the news to him first—he'll take it pretty hard—and then I'll call you in and you can tell him what you heard and saw."

§5

"Chief Quinn's office? May I speak to the chief? This is Lloyd Rutherford speaking. . . ."

"May I talk to the mayor personally? Lloyd Rutherford speaking. . . ."

"Try Nate Jacobs," J.O.B. suggested; "that smart aleck knows everything, and he's hand and glove with the strike leaders."

". . . Sorry, Mr. Jacobs is not in his office right now. May I take a message?"

"This is Lloyd Rutherford speaking."

"Oh, I'm sorry, Mr. Rutherford. Mr. Jacobs I don't think will be back today. The funeral of the longshoremen, you know . . ."

Lloyd hung up the receiver.

"He's out, too," he announced in a dull, flat voice.

Stan felt a wave of sympathy for the man. His uncle's fine old face was very white; it had become drawn and haggard as if some harsh, unfriendly hand had dragged at his cheeks and with an iron forefinger marked deep the lines about nose and mouth.

Heavy-lidded and pale, Lloyd stared at his brother, his white eyebrows twitching, his knuckled and wrinkled fingers locking and unlocking. In the strained silence unasked questions and unvoiced answers passed between the two.

"I've *got* to know," he said at length.

J.O.B. turned to Stan.

"Where were they taking them—the bodies, I mean?"

"I don't know, but I guess we can find out without much difficulty."

"Wait," said his uncle and pushed a button. Almost immediately his secretary, the capable Miss Hodgins, appeared, made a note of what information was wanted, departed.

While she was gone there was a trying silence. Lloyd's hand shook as he accepted the cigar his brother offered. Stan, trying to think of something to fill the interval, asked:

"What are we going to do if they call a general strike?"

"Break it," his father declared without waiting for Lloyd to speak. "There's never been a general strike in history that's been successful. They broke it in London, and we'll break it here. A parcel of discontented labor unions, inflamed by a lot of incendiary talk by a few soapbox orators, cannot dictate to a community like ours; the public won't stand for it. You can't deny people their inalienable rights."

"I predict they're going to try," Stan pursued. "This fellow Rory O'Brien is a demagogue; he's bent on mischief, and the longshoremen, sailors, and maritime workers swear by him. He heads the radical element, and the radical element is in the saddle."

"I'm told he's an Irishman," Lloyd said.

"His name would imply as much," J.O.B. commented sarcastically. "A Communist?"

"I haven't any doubt of it. He ought to be locked up in jail."

"There's no statute by which he can be imprisoned for being a Communist."

"Suppose he's a citizen?" J.O.B. asked.

"How should I know?"

"Well, if he's an alien, by God, we'll have him deported. He's a damned Red—there's no question about that—and if he's an alien, we'll send him back to where he came from. Maybe in Russia they'll know what to do with him. I fancy he wouldn't get along very well in Ireland!"

"Well," Stan commented, "before we can get round to ridding ourselves of him, I'm afraid we're in for trouble and've got a strike of major proportions on our hands. That parade today has inflamed the mind of every worker who participated in it or saw it."

His father's face became congested, and he raised his fist as he was about to make an explosive statement when Miss Hodgins knocked and entered.

"At Dugan's Undertaking Parlors at Sixteenth and Valencia," she announced.

Lloyd's trembling fingers stroked his chin. Stan's father stared at the floor, and Stan, watching him, knew he was thinking hard.

"Well," said he then, lifting his head, "shall we go?"

Lloyd's answer was to rise with some difficulty and take down his hat from his office closet.

§ 6

"Stop at the corner," J.O.B. directed the driver as the taxi approached their destination. There was no doubt they had reached the right place. A great crowd filled the sidewalk and the street in front of the undertaker's establishment; men stood about in small groups, talking earnestly and in hushed voices. Before the door of the funeral parlors two sentries in veterans' uniforms were on guard.

Leading the way, J.O.B. worked a passage through the throng, but at the steps they were halted.

"Your business?" the sentry demanded curtly.

"It's important," said J.O.B.

"What's it about?"

"If we could see Mr. Dugan or somebody in authority . . ." J.O.B. suggested persuasively.

The guard hesitated and then, evidently impressed with the visitors' clothes and the importance of their bearing, motioned to someone within, said in a loud whisper:

"Parties to see Mr. Dugan."

The corridor and front rooms of the undertaker's establishment were packed to suffocation; solemn and sober-faced, men stood about silently, shifting from one foot to the other, while heads were bowed, eyes searched the floor, and hats and caps were turned in nervous fingers. The heavy scent of flowers was overpowering. A tense silence pervaded the crowded rooms, broken only now and then by a hushed, sibilant whisper.

Stan's father, signaling to him and to Lloyd to wait for him, followed an attendant and disappeared into an inner sanctum. They did not see him again for many minutes. The air in the small, ill-ventilated undertaker's parlors was stifling; the odor of warm humanity, closely packed, mingled sickeningly with the enervating fragrance of strong-scented flowers. As newcomers forced a way through the throng there was a constant squeezing and elbowing. At length Stan saw his father with a large gesture of hand and arm beckoning them over the intervening heads, and it was his and his uncle's turn to work a passage through the press.

Following the older men, Stan suddenly found himself in the chapel where the two coffins reposed on biers. Crosses, wreaths, floral tributes of all sorts were ranged in serried tiers around them. In an opposite corner a group of men in dark clothes watched silently, and at the foot of each of the coffins a soldier in a veteran's uniform stood at attention. Guided by one of the undertaker's assistants, the two elder Rutherfords approached each casket in turn and peered at the lifeless face of its occupant. Stan, from where he waited, could just see the white tufted satin lining and the black hair of the dead inside. Neither his uncle nor his father changed expression as they bent over the coffins. Then silently they bowed their thanks, passed from the room, pushed their way once more through the choked corridor and gained the street.

"No, neither of them. Quite impossible, thank God!" J.O.B. said to his son in whispered tones, careful not to let his brother hear his words.

§ 7

The same day as the funeral, the President's National Longshoremen's Board began its series of open hearings on the issues of the strike. These hearings lasted for three days. On the third and final day, the Waterfront Employers offered to submit all issues between the shipowners and longshoremen to unconditional arbitration. This proposal was rejected by the longshoremen on the grounds that the closed shop and the control of the hiring hall were not debatable; they insisted, too, that they would not sign an agreement unless the demands of the seamen were also met. The Waterfront Employers replied that this was impossible, as they had been unable to discover who the seamen's representatives were or what the seamen wanted.

On Wednesday evening the Teamsters' Union confirmed their Sunday's poll and decided to go on strike at seven o'clock the next morning. Twenty other unions promptly followed their example.

Violence immediately broke out. Picket lines barred all roads leading to the city, trucks were halted, turned back, or capsized, and in many instances their contents, perishable or edible, were ruined by kerosene sealed in electric-light bulbs thrown into their loads.

On Sunday 115 of the 120 unions in the city—each union represented by five delegates—voted for a general strike to begin at eight o'clock the following morning.

Industry promptly came to a standstill. Factories shut down; streetcars ceased to run; taxicabs disappeared from the streets; grocery stores, already stripped of most of their stocks by foresighted housewives, closed their doors and put signs in their windows, "Closed Till the Boys Win" or "Closed for the Duration of the Strike." Highways leading to the city were blocked and picketed. Nothing moved except by "permission of the Strike Committee." Deliveries of gasoline, food, vegetables, milk, coal, wood, and other necessities of life stopped. Movement of all supplies was paralyzed within a distance of one hundred miles north, east, and south of the city. Food on hand was not sufficient to last the inhabitants of the Bay region a week.

Three thousand more troops were ordered to San Francisco, and the area of martial law was extended to include the fruit and vegetable districts adjacent to the waterfront. Streets were barricaded and the approaches manned by machine guns mounted on trucks. The mayor appointed a "Citizens' Committee" of five hundred representative men. Oakland's mayor announced he had sworn in three thousand citizen vigilantes. An additional five hundred were mobilized in Berkeley and five hundred more in Alameda. At the Labor Temple some nine hundred union delegates were in almost continual session. At the same time large orders of gas equipment were immediately placed by the police department, and in addition gas and gas grenades were ordered by the Waterfront Employers, various packers' associations and warehouse distributors, a prominent San Francisco daily, a number of commercial houses, and the Occidental Oil Company of California. Every union man in the Bay district was out except the electrical and typographical workers, who voted to continue at their jobs, thereby assuring the community light, power, communication, and newspapers.

The morning the walkout became effective, the Strike Strategy Committee announced that regular deliveries of all commodities would be made to the families of the strikers, but no provision was made for supplying food to the rest of the city's population. Nineteen restaurants at scattered points in the downtown section were permitted to remain open so that the workers might be fed. All theaters, night clubs, and barrooms were ordered closed, and the sale of intoxicating liquor was prohibited.

§ 8

"Who's running this city?" J.O.B. demanded, shaking his fist in the faces of the family circle grouped around him. "Our mayor and supervisors, or this damned, self-appointed Strike Committee? They permit nineteen restaurants to do business so that they and their hooligans can be fed! The rest of us can starve. Do you call that taking over the reins of government or not?"

"But what's going to happen?" Frances asked anxiously. "My grocer, my butcher tell me: 'Sorry, Mrs. Rutherford, we're cleaned out!' They have some canned goods, but we can't live solely on them— and how long will *they* last? The Government ought to take over, don't you think? Why, we haven't any gasoline for our cars! We can't even get downtown! The streetcars have stopped!"

"You're telling me!" her husband growled. "Don't I have to walk to my office every morning and walk all the way back! It's lucky we have the telephone. What're you going to do when they shut off your light and your water and begin to sack your homes and stick up folk in the streets?"

"Oh, oh, oh," wailed Bessie, "can't we go somewhere? Can't we get out of this terrible city? Surely there's some place that's safe!"

"They're just after my furs and my jewels," Grandmère asserted, sitting bolt upright in her chair and shaking the white curls of her marcelled wig. Her wrinkled hands were crossed in her lap, and every now and then her false teeth clicked audibly. "I'm not going to be run out of my home. I'm going to stay right where I am. Let them come and try to rob me if they dare."

"What will you do if they do?" Lloyd asked amiably.

"I'll have the law on them," Grandmère replied stoutly.

"Well, there isn't any," Lloyd reminded her.

"You men—you men—you men," cried Grandmère, her choler rising, "you've got to *do* something! You can't sit round here like a lot of nincompoops and let that rabble run our town. Where's your manhood? I declare, I'd do something, and do it in a hurry, before I'd let women and children starve."

"To say nothing of the livestock that's cooped up in pens down in Butchertown," Stan tossed in casually. "I only heard today that there are twenty-seven hundred hogs locked up down there that haven't had a single thing to eat for the past five days."

"Oh, don't tell me such things!" cried Grandmère.

"Couldn't we—all of us—go down to Charmion's and Reggie's at Visalia?" Frances queried. "Surely they have plenty to eat down there. Wouldn't that be a good idea? They'd be glad to have us, don't you think?"

"I won't budge an inch," Grandmère asserted.

"But, my dear," Bessie pleaded unhappily, "what are we going to eat? I've got a ham and a few chickens, and that's about all. The cook hasn't a bit of flour or sugar and not even an egg!"

"If you decide to go to Visalia," J.O.B. put in, "how do you propose to get there? Of course you could walk from here to the ferry, take a train, and we'd carry your suitcases for you . . . well, we might even have to do that," he ended soberly.

"I have an idea," he said after a moment when nobody spoke; "I've got an idea of how to break this strike," he continued, "if only I can get co-operation of a sober-minded, clear-thinking element in this town. If I can persuade some of those boys to work with me . . ."

His voice trailed off into silence. The others looked at him expectantly, but J.O.B. only stared at the floor.

Lloyd finally asked: "What you got in mind?"

"Well, if we could run some of these radicals out of town, the communist element and the Reds—this fellow Rory O'Brien, for instance—the conservatives might swing some weight."

"How do you propose to go about it?"

"It would take some strong-arm methods, of course," J.O.B. said thoughtfully. "I can give 'em the information—I can get it from the Industrial Association—but they'll have to furnish the man power; I can promise them all the police protection they want."

He fell silent again, scowling and thinking. Then with sudden determination he turned to Stan.

"Come on," he said, "let's see where we can get with this scheme."

§ 9

"We'll supply you with gasoline for your cars and the cars themselves if you need them," J.O.B. said to the two men seated across the table in his office, "and we'll give you the names of the places— every Red spot and every communistic headquarters in the city; you do your stuff, and I'll guarantee the police won't arrive until you're out of the way. They'll do the mopping up. It's up to you to get 'em first. Understand?"

"How do we know we won't get into trouble?" one of the men asked. "We're entirely in sympathy with you, and I know lots of the boys who would thoroughly enjoy a cleanup like that, but, you know, they'll want more assurance than just your word."

"How would an official okay from headquarters satisfy them— definite assurance from . . ." J.O.B. dropped his voice and whispered a name.

"Can't want anything better than that!" the other man, who was swarthy and beetle-browed, said with a nod. "You give us the dope and we'll clean house."

"How about compensation?" J.O.B. smiled, pursing his lips.

The eyes of the two men fixed his.

"I don't think any's really necessary, Mr. Rutherford. The boys—I know 'em—would have a lot of fun doing what you want."

"But for a good clean, finished job?" J.O.B. said encouragingly.

"Well-l," drawled the dark-skinned man.

J.O.B. took a pencil from his pen tray and wrote down a figure of four digits on the top sheet of a yellow pad and shoved the pad across the table.

"Whew-w-w," breathed the dark-skinned man.

"I don't care what you do with it. Distribute it as you like or keep it between you, for all I care. But I want this job done right. No bungling, and every rat's nest cleaned out. I'll give you a complete list, and five minutes after you've done *your* job the police will show up; not before. I'll have a man go along with you to send in the call. It will be all organized, and not one of you will get into the slightest trouble. If somebody does, we'll take care of him. You do your stuff and then come round to see me, and you'll get that." He pointed to the figure on the pad, then ripped the sheet from it and tore it into small pieces.

"Okay?" he asked.

"Okay," both men agreed.

"When do you want this to happen?" one asked.

"The sooner the better. I'll get the complete list and all the details over to you this afternoon. Phone me when you're ready."

"Maybe tomorrow night."

"Can't happen soon enough to suit me—and my friends," said J.O.B. with a smile.

§ 10

On the evening of July 17 a series of mysterious raids occurred. It was given out by the press the next day that thirty-five vigilante squads, armed with axes and pick handles, had started out in automobiles to clean up the meeting places of the radicals. Who these vigilantes were, nobody was ever able to discover. Their first onslaught occurred in the afternoon and was directed to an open-air meeting of the Workers' Ex-servicemen's League on Howard Street; the vigilantes moved in with fists and pick handles; after they had departed the police arrived, rounded up and placed under arrest a hundred and fifty men they still found there.

During the evening and late into the night the tactics of the raiding party continued. A caravan of automobiles—their crews wearing leather jackets—drew up in front of the headquarters of a known or suspected communist organization; a hail of stones followed, and windows were smashed; then the raiders swarmed into the premises, cracking heads, wrecking furniture, hacking pianos to pieces, throwing typewriters out of the windows, leaving the place a shambles. Then they scurried back to their cars and drove away. A few minutes later the police appeared, arrested any or all persons found in or about the building and marched them off to jail. If some were too badly injured to walk, ambulances were called.

After the quarters occupied by the Workers' Open Forum at 1223 Fillmore Street had been sacked, three men with broken heads were shipped to the Central Emergency Hospital. Nobody wounded or injured was found at the offices of the *Western Worker,* news organ for the Communist party, but fifteen arrests were made; presses were hacked to pieces; the place gutted. A three-storied building at 1212 Haight Street, that had once been a Young Men's Hebrew Association but had recently been turned into a Workers' School where classes in Marxianism and trade-unionism were conducted, was left in ruins. Communist headquarters at 37 Grove Street shared a similar fate, as did also the Mission Workers' Neighborhood House at 741 Valencia. The cavalcade of vengeance moved from building to building, and when the list of communist centers or suspected meeting places was exhausted, the raiders started in on the homes of radicals. By midnight 270 persons accused of being Communists or communistic sympathizers had been landed in the city jail, charged with vagrancy. In Oakland the raids were conducted with equal thoroughness. Every communist hall or gathering place was demolished. Scores of men and women were arrested and locked up.

In San Francisco's papers the next morning appeared the following:

KEEP THE STREETS CLEAN OF LOAFERS AND VAGRANTS!

That order, issued by Police Chief William J. Quinn early today, resulted in the arrest of nearly three hundred men. All are booked at the city prison as vagrants or drunks.

The police are under orders to pick up every man found on the streets who cannot give a good account of himself. The order is effective from sundown to dawn.

Bail for those charged with vagrancy was set at $1,000 each. Police cruising about the city last night arrested every man who was unable to give good reason for being on the streets.

There was considerable speculation in the press as to who had made up the raiding parties. Some declared the "vigilantes" had been members of the Teamsters' Union out of sympathy with their striking fellows, but this was vigorously denied by that union. Police said they did not know who the men were but they believed they were "aroused citizens." There were reports too that the raiding squads had been made up of strikebreakers imported from Los Angeles by the Industrial Association to run scab trucks. Others had it that the gangs were composed of young businessmen, clerks in commercial houses, and adventurous members of the industrialists' white-collar staffs. Nobody knew for sure,—or ever did.

§ 11

Rory O'Brien had been in consultation with the General Strike Committee when the word reached him. It was young Nate Jacobs who unceremoniously burst into the room and, with one arm around Rory's shoulders, whispered the news. Rory's face stiffened, and with a single movement of his body he stood upright, his knuckles whitening as he clutched the edge of the table at which he had been sitting.

"Come on, Steve; come on, Mike—and you too, Rodinsky. Let's see what they've done," he growled.

Thundering down the wooden stairs, they climbed into Nate's car, waiting at the curb.

Twenty minutes later Rory stood amidst the wreckage of his home. There was not a thing in it that had not been hacked to pieces or destroyed. The windows were jagged holes of glass; the few pictures that had hung on the walls had been flung to the floor and ground to pieces beneath the stamp of savage heels; the bed had been demolished, blankets and sheets ripped, the iron framework of the bed itself twisted into a shapeless mass, every stick of furniture —chairs, tables, bureaus, a radio set—had been smashed, telephone cords had been ripped from the wall, rugs and carpets had been slashed, even the fixtures in the bathroom had been cracked and shattered.

Rory gazed at the ruins about him while his friends' faces filled the doorway and peered in at the appalling desolation the one dangling electric light revealed.

They saw him stoop and pick up from the debris about his feet the remnants of a smeared and tattered photograph which once had had a frame about it. For a long minute he looked at the dirtied, tattered bit of cardboard, then tossed it aside, but not before Nate Jacobs recognized a woman's face.

Then Rory raised a clenched fist and looked upward at the ceiling, on through it to the sky and the heavens above him. The hand and the arm shook, but the man's gaze was steadfast.

§ 12

At the breakfast table the next morning, the newspaper before him, J.O.B. pulled at his goatee and nodded with satisfaction. He brushed his mustache from side to side and wet his lips. Then, as Stan entered and took his place, his father handed him the newssheet, indicating a headline with his thumb. He waited until Stan had finished reading.

"Well," he said, meeting his son's eyes with an amused twinkle in his own, "guess your old man's idea wasn't a bad one after all; guess the boys did a tiptop job for us—hey what? Hope they got Rory O'Brien, but that rabble rouser always has himself surrounded by a goon squad of twenty bruisers. However, he may hesitate before sticking out his neck again, and some of his fellow agitators may take the hint. We're going to hear a great deal less from them, and the men are going to listen to the good advice of their conservative leaders. I believe we've got 'em licked and the men will go back to work before the week's out."

§ 13

His words proved more prophetic than he dared hope. The general strike was over within the next two days. Several factors contributed to its collapse.

The Strike Strategy Committee permitted the men operating the municipally owned streetcars to return to work, since, being under a civil-service status, they would lose their jobs and all privileges unless they did. The committee also authorized the opening of thirty-two additional restaurants; while Rory O'Brien still railed and harangued the labor delegates, the group which usually supported him was either absent or had grown strangely inarticulate. It was clearly apparent that the ranks of the radicals had thinned, and there was less incendiary talk. Addresses by conservative leaders were no longer greeted by catcalls and boos, and their advice and admonition could be heard. The partial restoration of streetcar service and the opening of more restaurants gave the impression that the grip of the Strike Committee was loosening. This had a disheartening effect on the unions across the Bay who were just beginning to organize; there did not seem to be much use in promoting general strikes elsewhere if the strangle hold in San Francisco was weakening. Primarily it was public opinion, fanned by the press, and hourly growing more vociferous and exasperated, that ended the general walkout. It was the highhanded ruling of the Strike Committee, permitting certain restaurants to open while others remained closed, which more than anything else aroused people's indignation.

At quarter past one in the morning of July 19, after a turbulent all-day session, a resolution to terminate the general strike was put before the delegates of the various unions. By a standing vote of 191 to 174 it was adopted.

The next day labor poured back into industry in a great sweeping tide. Traffic was resumed, autos honked, trucks rumbled through the streets, chimneys smoked, hammers rang, saws whined, steel clanged, whistles blew, restaurants began serving customers, and thirsty men crowded barrooms.

The longshoremen and seamen, however, refused to capitulate, and the teamsters still boycotted the Embarcadero. The Market Street Railway employees too decided to wait until they were assured their lot would be ameliorated.

A week passed, and finally the longshoremen decided to ballot secretly, with the result that by a majority of four to one the men approved going back to work, provided their differences with the employers were settled by arbitration and the demands of the seamen would be taken care of as well. The Market Street Railway strikers also agreed to arbitrate. The next day the governor of the state ordered the evacuation of the troops from the Embarcadero.

The President's Mediation Board lost no time in arranging for a vote by the seamen to decide who should represent them in collective bargaining. Prior to the strike some seamen belonged to the Marine Workers' Industrial Union, a larger group to the International Seamen's Union, and a still larger group to no union at all. The vote when counted advocated a return to work pending arbitration and named the International Seamen's Union as the official bargaining representative.

Thus the waterfront strike came to an end.

The next morning forty thousand men returned to docks and ships which for so many weeks had been empty and deserted. Once more engine rooms resounded to men's voices; oil cans limbered up long idle machinery; fires flared; boilers grew hot; pistons and turbines under the hot pressure of steam awakened from lethargy; decks were scrubbed; brasswork polished; smoke billowed from stacks; pots and pans rattled in galleys, and longshoremen dug their hooks into the mountains of congested freight. The great endless river of cargo which had given San Francisco its place among the major cities of the world began moving again.

The Mediation Board handed down its award to the longshoremen on October 12. The seamen did not get theirs until April 10 of the following year.

The longshoremen gained practically everything they had asked for: a six-hour day, a thirty-hour week, and time and a half for overtime. Wages were set at ninety-five cents an hour straight time, a dollar and forty cents for overtime. All hiring was to be done through a dispatching hall jointly controlled by employers and the union. The agreement was to hold for a year and was to be renewed on the thirtieth day of each September thereafter.

The seamen did not fare so well. Their award was handed down by a special arbitration board set up by the union and representatives of the employers. In it the arbitrators pointed out that operating a first-class American vessel between American and Asiatic ports cost American owners $60,000 more per year than it cost the owners of a British ship of similar type, and $85,000 more than it cost a Japanese owner to operate a first-class Japanese vessel. Wages therefore were not materially increased, and in some cases—notably the wages of sailors employed on freighters—were set as low as forty-five dollars a month. Overtime was paid for, not in cash, but in "off-time" when, in the employers' judgment, a sailor's services could best be spared. Men could be hired from the pierhead or from the union hall at the discretion of the employer. The sailors, however, obtained considerable improvement in living conditions, especially in the matter of food and quarters, proper bedding, blankets, linen, and in the location and operation of mess halls.

§ 14

J.O.B., after a long study of the longshoremen's award, took off his spectacles, sank his head into his hands, finger tips closing eyes, and shook his head in discouragement. Stan, concerned, waited for him to speak. His father presently raised his head, drew a long breath and, tapping the paper in his hand, said:

"More trouble; lots of it. They've made a botch of things. I hoped this would end our troubles, but it is just a breeding ground for more. Why, look here, Stan—read this Section II: 'The employers shall be free to select their men within those eligible under the policies jointly determined, and the men likewise shall be free to select their jobs'; next, 'The employees must perform all work as ordered by the employers.'

"The words contradict themselves; one paragraph says the men must perform all work ordered by the employers, and another says that the men shall be free to select their jobs.

"When a disagreement arises, what's going to prevent the men on the docks from walking off? We can call for another gang of longshoremen, but they may decide that the work we want them to do is not to their liking; we call again, and the union sends us still another gang, and they too may refuse to work. They are 'free to select their jobs'! Why, damn it, Stan, these stoppages of work are what they call 'job action'; there have been twenty-nine such stoppages between here and San Pedro since the men agreed to submit everything to arbitration. Instead of settling things, only trouble lies ahead. The longshoremen have everything they want now; all their demands have been granted; they ought to play fair, but they won't as long as they listen to that unprincipled scoundrel, Rory O'Brien."

CHAPTER V

IN HER LIMOUSINE Grandmère drove down to see Chris at the Belmont sanitarium three or four times a week. She tried to go every day except Sunday, but the effort tired her physically as well as emotionally, and sometimes she had to stay at home and rest in bed and was, in consequence, irritable and ill-tempered because she felt she was being remiss in her attendance and that her frailness and lack of strength was somebody else's fault.

"I declare," she would complain, "it does seem to me that an old woman my age could do as she pleased! There's no use of pampering me that way, Bessie. . . . Annabel, kindly take that comforter off my knees and open that window; I'm suffocating. . . . I don't know why you are hanging around here all day, Eleanor, sucking your fingers. Why don't you go down and see Chris and cheer him up? I suppose you're waiting for that flibbertigibbet picture actor to phone or come to see you! It does seem to me . . ."

Her voice would trail off disconsolately, but her face would remain pettishly angry.

But on a day when she felt well enough to make the trip, she was affability itself and considerate to everyone.

It was so on a crisp Monday morning early in November. By eleven o'clock she was cloaked, hatted, and gloved and was fussily checking the small gifts she proposed to take with her. These had all been carefully assembled half an hour earlier by the ever efficient Annabel and had now been placed side by side on the table in the hallway, to be counted once more by Grandmère. The old lady trusted details to nobody.

"Those the artichokes?" she said in an inquiring note, touching a carefully wrapped package with her gloved finger tips. "Where's the mayonnaise? . . . Oh, here. I see. Must take the boy some of Hing's mayonnaise. The stuff they concoct and serve the patients down

there, I wouldn't feed to a sick cat! . . . And the fruit? . . . Yes.
And this is the ice cream; in dry ice, you say? . . . And that's the
jigsaw puzzle and the magazines. You had better put the ice cream
in on the seat with me; it might melt up in front or on the floor of
the car."

She was off presently, gliding past pleasant homes and gardens,
then on through more congested neighborhoods of small shops and
markets, bumping gently and easily over car tracks, past factories
and wholesale houses until the car came to the Bayshore Highway
and sped on its way over smooth macadamized roads unhampered
by traffic or intersections.

The day was a warm, golden, autumnal glory such as only California knows. The great arm of the Bay, jutting southward nearly
fifty miles, was cupped and ruffled by a gentle breeze; overhead gulls
wheeled in white circles or else floated on poised pinions; a few
ducks placidly rode the wavelets, and amateur fishermen squatted
on rocks along the shore, poles in hand, while their waiting automobiles leaned haphazardly at an angle on the sloping, grassy ground
beside the thoroughfare. Toward the west, modest little homes,
peaked-roofed and white, dotted the slopes of the bare round-topped
hills. Now and then the wings of an airplane in the blue sky caught
the rays of the sun and sent flashing messages back to earth. Grandmère lay back against the luxurious upholstery of the limousine, her
wrist reposing comfortably on an armrest, and felt at peace with the
world.

But her serenity deserted her once she had reached her grandson's
bedside and stood holding between her gloved hands his thin, bony
one, so like a claw, and gazed at his white, sunken face. His eyes,
though set in deep pools of shadow, still held much of their old
sparkle, and his mouth could still twist itself into the roguish smile
of impertinent gaiety which had always found its way to her heart.
But there was something almost ghastly about it now as it bravely
strove to brighten his ravished countenance.

A boardwalk led to his cottage, and there was a narrow railed
wooden approach to his door. This gave first upon the quarters
occupied by his nurse, and in turn upon his room, which was hardly
a room at all but a screened porch open on three sides to all the

fresh, clean mountain air which stirred by day or night. The back of his bed was next the door, so that Chris had to turn his head at the sound of steps and look well over his shoulder to see who it was who was coming; then, if it were someone other than a nurse or a Filipino boy with a tray or a glass of milk, his rare smile of pleasure would contort his thin features into a most appealing and heartrending grin. It caught at Grandmère's heart like the clutch of a hand; she always wanted to put her frail old arms about his frailer body, hold him to her, and lay her wrinkled cheek against his colorless one. But this was not permitted. Whenever impulsively she would stoop to kiss him, Chris would stop her with a detaining hand.

"No, no, Grandmère, *ma petite*—'tain't allowed, you know. I got the plague, the Yangtze Kiang plague, and you'll break out with the seven years' itch if you waste one of your precious smacks on me. Save 'em for Uncle Lloyd or my other distinguished uncle with the bay window!"

He always made her laugh—that is, in the first days of her visits; but of late she had found him drowsy and dopey from the effect of drugs which she knew were administered hypodermically to save him from violent spells of coughing.

Today he was propped up in bed, the pieces of a jigsaw puzzle spread out upon a flat thin board of triple-ply wood which she had had made for him, his thin fingers gently moving here and there as he tried to fit the pieces into place.

"Oh, hello, Archangel," he said, greeting her with his wan and tragic smile. "What have you got there?" he continued, referring to the numerous packages Greenwood, the chauffeur, was arranging on a near-by table; "the entire contents of Hale's Big Bright Busy Basement?"

His cough stopped him; it racked his whole body as he strained, his face purpling.

Grandmère watched him, stilling the quivering of her own lips as she did so. He seemed weaker.

"What kind of a night?" she asked when, after a few moments, he had recovered.

"Oh, fair. Those damn children in the next cottage started to raise hell at six this morning just as I had fallen into a swell sleep."

Grandmère glanced at Miss Pringle, the nurse, and asked by a look if this nuisance could not be stopped, but Miss Pringle studiously avoided her eyes and carried a tray from the room. She was careful not to return while Mrs. Rutherford was there.

"I'll speak to Dr. Willabrandt," Grandmère said decisively.

"Oh, don't bother," Chris protested weakly, and then, with a quick glance after the departing figure of the nurse, said feverishly:

"Quick, Grandmère. God, I've been waiting for you since daybreak."

"Now, Chris . . ."

She knew perfectly well what he wanted: cigarettes, which were forbidden, and although she always carried a pack in her handbag especially to gratify his craving, it was a regular part of the little scene for her to protest in the beginning.

Chris's face congested with impatience.

"Cut out the hoo-ey," he cried irritably, stretching out a hand, trembling in anticipation. "Don't be a silly. Come on; hand over."

She gave him the pack. He broke it open savagely, quickly extracting a cigarette, lit it, and tucked the package beneath his pillow. Then he leaned back, and his eyes half closed as he inhaled the smoke deep into his lungs.

"They're such damn fools," he said contentedly after a moment. "I know this doesn't hurt me, and you can't take *everything* away from me! I would just as soon die if I can't smoke."

"Don't talk nonsense," Grandmère said, her teeth closing on a sharp click of disapproval. "We'll have you out of here in no time. All you have to do is to rest and build up your strength. I tell you what I'm going to do as soon as you're well enough, and that is to give you any kind of a yacht or boat or flagship you want, and you can sail away to the South Seas or go around the world if you like."

"Swell," Chris said apathetically. "Say, Grandmère, leave me some matches, will you? Old Pringle's a hawk, and she hides the matches on me, too."

It was pleasant sitting in a low wicker armchair in the screened room beside the boy's bed. Grandmère thought how really restful it would be to change places with him and lie there in the comfortable hospital cot, looking out across the green foliage of the garden at the rolling California hills which had already lost some of their summer's dry brownness. There was just a suggestion of green, like a faint film, covering their clean contours. Birds twittered and chirped among the flower beds, a gramophone in some distant room was droning out a languorous waltz, and faintly from the hospital kitchen came the cheerful clicking and clattering of pans.

"Just about the same," the resident physician told her when she stopped at the office on her way home for a report. "He's still running a degree or two. Until that abates, we can do nothing. Just rest, complete rest for the present, is the only treatment we can recommend."

"But you think he *will* get well?" the anxious old woman asked.

The doctor shrugged.

"We can only hope," he told her noncommittally.

§ 2

An hour later, when she entered her own home in the city, she found Eleanor with Lester Armitage at the table in the dining room, finishing luncheon. Eleanor's mother, Grandmère saw, had not been there; no place had been set for her. There was something decidedly intimate in the little scene, the old lady decided, as, with one foot on the first tread of the stairs, she glanced in again at the pair through the folding doors. Eleanor sat where her mother usually did, and her guest was on her right; he was leaning toward the girl, talking animatedly, and it was evident from her expression that she found whatever he was telling her engrossing. The tablecloth was strewn with walnut shells and raisin stems; their coffee cups stood empty; the air was filled with the blue smoke of cigarettes.

As Grandmère started to climb, Eleanor caught a glimpse of her.

"Oh, hello, Grandmère," she called gaily. Immediately she rose and came out into the hall, followed by Armitage.

"How is he?" she inquired, referring to Chris, her face sobering. Hardly waiting for the reply, she asked:

"Had your lunch?"

"Annabel will bring me a tray. Only want tea."

The old lady glanced from Eleanor's face to Armitage's and back again. Eleanor's manner certainly conveyed something. Gay, merry—

Grandmère was almost ready to admit the girl looked radiant. She swiftly took in the tall young man, weighing him as a Rutherford, because whomever the children married, the new husband or wife became a Rutherford in her mind. She was not impressed. Her teeth clicked. Well, if the girl wanted to make a fool of herself . . .

She turned, raised her overlong skirt with both hands, saying as she mounted the stairs:

"Tell your mother I'd like to see her when she comes in."

"I surely will." Pause, then: "Oh, Grandmère——"

"Yes?"

"You using Greenwood this afternoon or tonight?"

"No." Without turning, Grandmère asked: "What do you need him for?"

"Oh, we thought we'd see a picture this afternoon—there's a good one at the Clay—and tonight it's opera."

"That's right. *Tosca.*"

The old lady continued to mount the stairs.

"Your father going?"

"Think not. I hope to get Stan to go. It seems such a shame—Vincent Oliver has no evening clothes, otherwise we'd make him take Daisy. The box holds six comfortably."

"More power to him," the old lady muttered.

"What say? I didn't hear."

Grandmère had reached a landing by now; she paused, one hand on the balustrade, and looked down at the young couple below.

"Fine feathers don't make fine birds," she observed with a brisk nod and disappeared from view.

§ 3

An hour later Bessie found her in bed, her lace cap tied firmly beneath her chin, her puckered old lips drawn together like the mouth of a drawstring bag. Her wig and teeth were nowhere to be seen; her glasses rode the high bridge of her nose, and on a thin board across her lap, similar to the one she had had made for Chris, she was arranging a deck of cards preparatory to some solitaire. Over the rims of her spectacles she fixed her daughter-in-law with a scrutiniz-

ing look, as that lady somewhat out of breath dropped into a chair, removed her hat, and with vigorous fingers began to massage her scalp.

"Eleanor going to marry that popinjay?" she demanded.

Bessie breathed deeply, catching her breath.

"Well," she committed herself at length, "I suppose she is."

"What for?"

"The usual reasons, I suppose."

"What's he after? Her money? I don't propose to leave her a cent."

"Oh, he has plenty of work to do. He's been making a picture this
last month. Think he plays opposite Matilde von Behrens, that German actress. I forget the name of the picture. They only finished it
last Saturday. That's why he flew up. . . . Why, what have you
against him, Grandmère?"

"A whippersnapper."

"Eleanor seems to like him well enough. I can't find any objection
to him."

"What does Lloyd say?"

"I don't think that Lloyd knows."

" 'Ren't you going to tell him?"

"Eleanor will tell him soon's she's ready."

"You going to announce it formally?"

"I dare say. She'll give a girls' luncheon or a tea or something——"

"When?"

"Oh, mercy me, Grandmère dear, I don't know all the answers to
so many questions. I don't suppose Eleanor knows herself yet."

"She'd better make up her mind pretty quick. . . . Give me that
black queen, Bessie; it fell on the floor."

§ 4

Meantime, in one of the back rows of the darkened Clay Street
Theater, Eleanor and Lester sat shoulder to shoulder, his left hand
holding her right one, while the other—stretched across the back of
the seat—stroked the fleshy part of her arm through her dress with
gentle caressing finger tips. It made the girl shiver now and then—
not actually, but she could feel the shiver inside. She closed her eyes
and let the picture go on unheeded. She thought about the touch

of those finger tips. Why should they make her shudder? She tried to analyze it. He was handsome, well groomed, had a fine build, all the manners and aplomb of a gentleman; he was intelligent, well spoken, considerate—and apparently much in love with her. Yet somehow all was not right. She shut her mind to it. If there was something wrong, she would change it. She was proud of this handsome man; she was proud to be seen with him on the streets. She would be proud to tell her girl friends she was going to be Lester Armitage's wife. He had asked her and she was going to marry him.

§ 5

The telephone rang. Daisy flew to it.

"Yes, yes? Hello?"

"Hello, is that you?"

Vincent's drawling voice! She had waited all day to hear it, even since early morning, although he had wired her from San Pedro that the *San Gabriel* probably would not dock until late afternoon. As first assistant engineer of one of Wickwire, Rutherford's newest freighters, he had been gone since September—a long, dreary six weeks—to New Orleans and back. She had had a letter from there, a half-page from Beaumont, postals from Balboa and Panama. There had been only a scribbled word or two on the postals, and the letters had hardly been more satisfactory, giving her starved heart such unimportant items as when the ship had docked, what repairs were needed, the state of the weather, their sailing date, and the next port of call. She had tried so hard to find more in them than that! Had he thought of her—oh, one *tenth* the number of times she had of him? Did he still care? Had he changed? Had he been only half interested? No way of telling—not from these noncommittal words!

He had been overwhelmed by his new job. J.O.B. had had a talk with him and promised him quick promotion but had stressed loyalty to the company and cautioned him against the unions.

"I want to feel, Oliver," he had told him, "that you belong among the men employed by this company whom we can trust—on whom I personally can rely. Now I want no trafficking with this Marine Engineers' Beneficial Association; that's the absurd name the trade unions give their organization of ship engineers; we have our own union—the American Society of Marine Engineers—and if you join any union, I want you to affiliate with that. It used to be a company union; it isn't supposed to be any more because of this damn Wagner Act, but the heads of it are friendly with the shipowners and we get along. The point is this: I'll take care of you, and in the meantime— and always, for that matter—you take care of us."

He concluded the interview with a pleasant nod of understanding and rose to shake hands.

Daisy had known all about this, almost at once. Vincent had told her; her father had confirmed it, adding when he did so:

"I like that young man. He impresses me as a person who knows his business."

This had been said at dinnertime, and Stan, catching his sister's eye across the table, had smiled at her quick rush of color.

Six—almost seven weeks ago! Vincent had sailed away on the *San Gabriel* in his new position as first assistant to the chief, and before he had said good-by he had held her in his strong young arms and kissed her many times as she clung to him and laid her head against his breast and cried a little, but he had told her nothing—not even that he loved her—only:

"Gee, you're a cute kid."

Now he was back, would be in port a week while his ship was being unloaded and reloaded, and then he would sail away again, this time to Seattle and Puget Sound.

A sailor's wife, she had thought a little tremulously and a little scared. He'd be away from her half his days—at sea! But nothing would matter once she was his wife and she was certain of his love.

Her heart was pumping so violently now as she held the telephone receiver to her ear and heard his voice that she could not speak, and he had to ask:

"Dais? . . . Are you there? . . . I'd like to speak to Miss Rutherford, please."

"Oh, this is me," she said, swallowing hard. "Where are you? What are you going to do?"

"Well, I'm off duty now. Could come and see you right away, if that would be okay."

"I'll be waiting."

It was an hour before she heard his ring at the front door. She rushed to open it. There he stood, bronzed, black of hair, showing his white teeth, his eyes, agate brown, alight with flecks of gold like glistening mica in deep pools. He came in awkwardly, fingering his hat. She closed the door and met his warm, embarrassed glance with a serious, searching one; then without another moment's hesitation she went into his arms with a little cry like the cheep of a bird, and he laid his dark cheek against her bright crown. So they stood for a moment, and presently she raised her lips and he met them with his own in a long kiss.

She drew him into the living room with its curtains of brocade and overstuffed chairs, and they sat down on one of the wide couches whose cushions were embroidered richly with gold thread.

"Well," he said haltingly then, "I've been afraid you'd forgotten."

"How could I?"

She leaned towards him and he took her in his arms, and their lips met and met again.

"Darling," she kept repeating between kisses.

"Golly, you're sweet."

There followed murmurs of endearment, words of inconsequence, long, happy minutes when neither spoke.

He stayed for dinner, respectfully listening to J.O.B.'s observations, watched Stan out of the corner of his eye to see in just what order he made use of fork, knife, spoon, was politely attentive to Daisy's mother, and sometimes, meeting the girl's glance, smiled, his brown eyes turning browner and warmer. On her part she was in a flutter of excitement, swallowing nervously every now and then, playing with her food, watching him anxiously and with admiration. Her complete infatuation was apparent to all.

They too went to a movie that evening and held hands in the darkness, and then Vincent piloted her to a fish grotto and they ate unconcernedly of shrimps in their shells and cracked crab, and he had beer and she coffee. All the while they talked, he of shipmates and ship experiences at sea and in port, and she of everything she thought might interest him. Towards one o'clock he took her home in

a taxi and kissed her a dozen times in the shadowy recess of her door
—and so left her, promising to call early in the morning.

They spent the next day together and the next, and the one following. There was something almost frightening in Daisy's ecstasy. Stan
noticed it and was concerned, for he foresaw the problem his sister
and the young engineer must face. He knew his emotional and tender-
hearted Daisy; he had learned to respect the integrity and character
of the man; he doubted if Vincent would accept an heiress as a wife.

He spoke to his father.

"Money shouldn't stand in their way," said J.O.B. "Go see the
young fellow; talk to him. After all, Daisy's been brought up like a
flower, surrounded by luxury; your mother and I have given her
anything and everything she wants. She'll have an income no matter
whom she marries. He shouldn't expect her to live on an engineer's
salary. It wouldn't be fair to her—and really not fair to him."

"I'm afraid he won't ask her to marry him unless he can support
her and she's willing to live on his salary," Stan said dubiously.

"Nonsense. The girl's pin money amounts to two hundred dollars
a month. Explain that to him. He's got a future—here in the company. Maybe he'd like to come ashore and take a position in the office
and we could groom him for an executive's job. Sound him out."

As Stan suspected, Vincent had no intention of marrying a girl
with money.

"You see how it is," he said, marking the cloth on the luncheon
table between them with a blunt thumbnail. "You—you . . . I guess
you know how I feel about Dais; she's tops with me, but I can't see
her marrying a man with an income like mine, and I can't accept
anything from her. Sorry, Stan, I was just brought up that way—it's
part of me—it's just the way I am; I can't do it."

"Do you think it's fair to her?"

"I'll have to wait, I guess, until I make enough. My mother has
arthritis; she lives down in Redwood City, and I have to pay a nurse
to take care of her. Lord, Stan, I'm in no position to marry——"

He stopped with a savage frown, knitting his brows.

"You wouldn't consider giving up your job as an engineer and taking one in the office? There'd be more salary after a while. Dad spoke
to me about it."

Vincent shook his head.

"'Coming in over the transom'? That's what they call it, don't they, when somebody gets a slick job because he has a pull with the boss?"

"Like me," Stan said good-humoredly.

"No," Vincent countered with decision, "you're different. You're the old man's son and you're going to fill his boots someday. Besides you've been trained, you've been to Harvard's Business School and you know things, while I've had only an ordinary college education and the kind you get playing football! I'd hate to give up the sea, Stan," he went on earnestly. "Besides, get this: If I came ashore and got a job in the office and married Daisy, it would be—everybody would say it was because I had married the boss's daughter—I'd be Mr. Rutherford's son-in-law! I can't do it!"

"What do you propose?"

"Well, damned if I know. I just got to wait and ask her to wait— well, until I can save something."

§ 6

Vincent talked earnestly to Daisy that same evening.

"You see," he said in his drawling way, "I don't think it's right for you to tie yourself up with a guy like me——"

"But I want to," she took him up as he hesitated; "I don't want anybody else but you."

He smiled and shook his head.

"But you see, Dais, I'm not going to hold down an engineer's job on board a ship—even if it is the position of first assistant—and have you living here in San Francisco in some swell apartment, lavishly furnished. Your father has been awfully good to me. He's stepped me up a couple of grades already. Why, it might have taken me ten years to get as far as I am now if it hadn't been for him. I can't accept any more favors from him. I've got to prove myself first and prove to him his confidence hasn't been misplaced."

"I suppose so," she said apathetically.

"It isn't as if I didn't think a whole lot of you."

She longed for a stronger phrase, but she knew him well enough by now to know he did not use stronger phrases.

She sat silently beside him, a limp hand in his, and her heart sank within her.

"Then we'll just have to wait," she said.

"What else?"

"I could learn to cook, to wash dishes, to make beds——" she began.

"Of course you could, but there's my little old mother so crippled she can't move a finger——"

"I know," she said heavily. And then on a great breath of rebellion she went on:

"But it does seem a shame when there's so much money all around us, so much to spend and to waste and actually to squander, that we can't even make your mother more comfortable, and—and do what we want——"

She stopped, her heart quailing as it so often did with the dismaying thought that perhaps he did not want her as she wanted him. Maybe all these reasons were but excuses . . .

She blinked hard to keep back the tears, but they had to come, and miserably she leaned against him and cried silently into her handkerchief, while his encircling arm held her close and he kissed and kissed her hair. It was good to feel herself so firmly held, to feel herself against his heart, his strong arm about her waist—but she wanted more than that: she wanted him to crush her, to wrench at her wrists, drag her to an embrace, tell her with fierce words that he loved her with all his soul!

She pulled away and through swimming eyes tried to read what more there was behind those brown ones of his, now full of sympathy and tenderness. She wanted so desperately to be sure.

"Vincent," she said, steadying her voice, "you *do* love me?"

She asked the question with all the seriousness she could command.

"You know I do."

"You'd tell me if you didn't—you'd really tell me?"

"Why, Dais——"

"No, no, I mean it. If you weren't sure, if you weren't *positive* how you felt, you'd tell me?"

"You bet."

"And are you?"

"What do you mean?"

"Are you sure you—you love me?"

"Why, of course."

"Say it, then. Tell me so as if you meant it. . . . Oh," she cried with sudden vehemence, "lie to me, *lie* to me! *Don't* tell me the truth! Say you love me even if it's a lie! I couldn't stand your saying you didn't."

"Now look here, Dais"—his voice was grave—"this is crazy talk. You know how I feel about you. You're tops with me. Just because I don't plunge into marriage without enough money to support you in the right way doesn't mean I don't think a whole lot of you. You mustn't get a bunch of silly notions in your head."

"But you do love me?"

"Yes, sure."

"You what?"

He stared at her, troubled and perplexed.

"You 'what' about me?" she prompted.

"I don't get you."

"Oh, you do *love* me?"

"I've told you so."

"Then say it, say it, say it out loud so I can hear it."

She beat upon his chest with her small fists.

He laughed and caught her in his arms.

"Why, sure I love you, baby—love you big."

Her arms tightened about his neck, and she strained him to her with all her strength, tighter, tighter, until the veins swelled in her neck and temples.

Then she wilted and sank down upon him, eyes closed, panting a little as she lay spent in his arms. At last on a deep sigh she whispered:

"I could die for you—give my life for you."

§ 7

On Saturday he went away. The *San Gabriel* sailed from the Encinal Terminals in Alameda, across the Bay, leaving her moorings at six in the morning to catch the outgoing tide. Daisy was there to wave good-by. Greenwood had driven her over in the limousine, and the car waited while she watched the sturdy freighter, her funnels striped with the colors of the Mission Fleet, slowly growing smaller and smaller as she dipped and gracefully moved toward the great bastions of concrete on which stood the giant towers of the new bridge, now being built. Vincent had gone below with a final wave of his visored cap as the hoarse whistle of the *San Gabriel* sounded her raucous signal of departure, but Daisy stood on, her small hands clasped against her heart while the tears drenched her cheeks. At last when the ship was only a far distant smudge in the morning mist, she turned and, hardly seeing where she stepped, made her way back to the car.

Home then, through Oakland's still deserted streets, crossing the Bay by ferryboat, crowded now with commuters, up over the steep hills of San Francisco to find when she reached her house that neither her father nor her brother had as yet come down to breakfast, and her mother was still asleep. Grateful to escape to her room, and dressed as she was, she threw herself on her bed and, seizing in both hands the silver framed photograph of Vincent—so handsome in his engineer's uniform!—she studied his face through swimming eyes which she wiped and wiped again.

Life took up its customary course after that, and days were filled with their small round of important and unimportant happenings, but all were equally lacking in interest for her.

Thus, with the New Year, Stan was promoted to traffic manager of Wickwire, Rutherford & Company; her mother came down with a bad case of shingles; her father and Uncle Lloyd went to Washington— the former to interview Senator Wagner, chairman of the National Labor Relations Board, the latter to argue a case before the United States Supreme Court; Uncle Reggie and Aunt Charmion, up from Visalia for the holidays, prolonged their stay to see more of Chris and talk to his doctors; Aunt Bessie and Grandmère had a furious quarrel, refused to speak to each other for days, and unexpectedly and surprisingly Eleanor announced her engagement to Lester Armitage.

This last event somewhat roused Daisy out of her lethargy, for she was present at the luncheon Eleanor gave when the news was told, and immediately must attend a series of social affairs arranged for Eleanor and Eleanor's fiancé, but her heart as well as her life stayed empty. The *San Gabriel* was far up the Columbia River, and it would be weeks before the freighter would return.

Twice Daisy went to see Vincent's arthritic old mother in Redwood City—a pathetic, withered little creature, snow-white of hair and skin, who smiled at her out of a shriveled face and stroked her hand, while a matronly woman in a starched apron came in and out of the small room, closing doors noisily and eyeing the visitor suspiciously, her curiosity aflame to account for the limousine before the door.

The wedding of Eleanor and Lester was set for June, and Daisy was to be one of the bridesmaids. . . . Would Vincent be in town? . . . The young couple were to be married in Grace Cathedral, and the reception would follow at the home of the bride's parents. The newspapers had much to say. Lester Armitage, popular screen idol, was to be ushered by Carey Douglas, Sherwood Powers, and other motion-picture actors. All Hollywood, it was reported, planned to be present when this Metro-Goldwyn-Mayer's star was united in marriage to San Francisco's beauty and heiress—Eleanor Farthingale Rutherford, only daughter of the eminent jurist Lloyd Rutherford, and niece of the distinguished shipping tycoon, J. O. B. Rutherford. An event—so said the evening *Call-Bulletin*—which would make social history in California.

§ 8

Vincent Oliver was in San Francisco in late February, was gone in March, this time on the long voyage to the Gulf. Daisy's father, back from Washington, discovered her one afternoon sobbing on a couch in the ornate living room—the same couch with its heavily gold-embroidered cushions where she and Vincent had talked so often and where he had kissed her and held her in his arms.

"Well, honeybunch, what's all this, what's all this?" J.O.B. said. He had come home earlier than usual that day, and Daisy, not hearing his step or his keys as he opened the front door, had no time to recover herself. He drew up a chair and, squatting precariously on its seat, patted her knee sympathetically as she straightened herself and attempted to dry her eyes.

She could not answer immediately. She blinked into the light, mopping her wet lashes, striving to still her quivering breath.

"It's as bad as all that, hey? Well," he went on when she did not speak, "I respect him. He's a fine young fellow—worth waiting for."

And, as she still offered nothing, he continued:

"You won't have to wait long, I fancy. The boy's going to make good; he's loyal; you can depend on him. I had an excellent account of him the other day. His chief—that's the chief engineer on his ship—sent in a report I happened to see. We've been having some trouble with the unions, you know, the Marine Firemen's Union. I don't know what the beef was about, but they sent a ship's delegate out to the *San Gabriel* to make some complaint. The chief was not on board at the time, but your young friend, Oliver, was. There was an altercation, I understand, and the ship's delegate became abusive. Oliver knocked him off the side of the boat with his fist, and the man damn near drowned. That's the kind of officers we want in our employ, and I'd step him up even if my little girl didn't think the world and all of him. You leave the matter to me, and I'll see you get your man."

Then with some difficulty her father bent his ponderous body over the girl, kissed her forehead, and mounted heavily to his room.

Vincent was not due in port until June 4; the wedding was scheduled for the eighteenth. Daisy asked Stan if it could not be arranged for the *San Gabriel* to be held in port until after the ceremony, or if Vincent could not be detached and allowed a vacation.

"I think he deserves a vacation, my dear," Stan said, nodding his head judicially. "Let me see, how long has he been with us? September? Well, that's almost a year. Suppose I speak to Syd Watterbury and see if he can spare him for the last two weeks in June. Of course he may have to change ships—we can't hold the *San Gabriel* in port while one of its engineers takes a fortnight off!—but perhaps he'd *like* another boat——"

"You darling," Daisy cried, flinging her arms about his neck and reaching to kiss his cheek; "you're just wonderful, Stan. It's going to make such a difference to me to have Vincent here when Eleanor's married."

June arrived and wedding plans proceeded at an accelerated pace, excitement among the Rutherfords mounting steadily. Eleanor's wedding gown was being made of a heavy, gleaming white satin, fitted tightly to her superb figure, and with a long, wide-spreading train, and her veil was to be an exquisite piece of rose point. She must visit her dressmaker every day or two, and Daisy and the other bridesmaids must see to their own costumes—pale, salmon-tinted silks under gauzy salmon-tinted tulle, with salmon ruffles and bows, and adorable salmon-hued hats with salmon ribbons to be tied beneath the chin, high up on one side just under an ear. The church had been reserved, the bishop interviewed, the decorators had been consulted, the orchestra and caterer engaged, invitations were in the mail, and presents were arriving daily by express, by mail, and by delivery—when suddenly all this came to a dead stop. Word came that Chris was dying.

Daisy learned the news from her father. He came home one morning unexpectedly before noon. One look at his sober face and she knew something had gone wrong. *Another strike!* her swift thoughts ran. *Those ruffians again!*

"Come upstairs, my dear; I have some bad news for you and your mother," he said, putting a large arm around her.

In his wife's room he told them; it was only a question of hours, he said.

"Charmion and Reggie are at the sanitarium now; they came up from the country early this morning; the doctor telephoned them about seven o'clock. I didn't know Chris had taken a turn for the worse, but presumably they were aware of it at the hospital last night. Reggie—he called me about an hour ago—says that Chris is unconscious, doesn't know a thing, has a good deal of difficulty breathing, and can't last much longer. They have him, he said, heavily drugged, so he does not suffer."

He heaved a long sigh.

"This will go hard with Grandmère. Lloyd's over there now, breaking the news to her. We came up together in a taxi."

There was a long silence. Daisy felt her chin quiver and her eyes fill as she looked at her mother's grave and set face. Frances' gaze was upon her husband.

"We'll have to—we'll have to postpone Eleanor's wedding, don't you think?" she asked slowly.

"Oh yes; decidedly," J.O.B. said. "We just couldn't go through with it. It would be unseemly even if we had any heart for it. No; I talked it over with Lloyd as we were coming here. We thought it would be best to put it off."

CHAPTER VI

SOME WEEKS AFTER Chris's funeral the two Rutherford brothers were having luncheon together at their club. They had chosen a small table at one side of the spacious golden dining room where they could talk confidentially and where they would not be interrupted.

"What's the lowdown on this Modesto affair?" Lloyd asked, buttering a biscuit. "At court this morning I ran into that little busybody, Nate Jacobs, and he claims the whole thing is a frame-up and that those men are being railroaded to the penitentiary."

J.O.B. shrugged, and his big mouth twisted into an expression of incredulity and contempt.

"Well-l," he said, "there's more to it than perhaps meets the eye. Percy Grant, Jim Ahearn, two or three others, and myself among the shipowners have been attempting to do a little—well, underground work to break up this damn Maritime Federation which that rascal Rory O'Brien has been trying to organize. You know, Lloyd," J.O.B. diverged to ask, bitterness and strong feeling coloring his tone, "you know how many stoppages of work we've had down on the water-front since the longshoremen's award was handed down a year ago and the seamen's last April? I'm telling you the God's honest truth. Over five hundred and fifty! And they're happening every day. The men call 'em 'quickies,' and they're the damnedest nuisance! If either the sailors or the longshoremen don't like the superintendent or the officer in charge, or they don't like what they are asked to do, they just quit, and the work stops until some adjustment is made. These union leaders don't know what honor means, or what giving their word or signing an agreement amounts to! It's come to a point where we can't go on, and Grant and I and the others determined we had to do something about it.

"This tankers' strike which ended in the Modesto trouble was at its very outset an abortive thing. The row was between seamen on the oil tankers and the oil companies. The oil companies are run by pretty competent executives, and they're loyal to each other, play each other's game—which is a damn sight more than I can say for the shipowners! At any rate, they were hiring a good many non-union men and getting away with it. Swenson called a strike of all tanker seamen, which was all right with the oil companies because they felt pretty sure they could break it.

"What interests you, I know, is the case of these fellows who were arrested transporting dynamite into Modesto. It was the result of a pretty slick deal engineered by the Occidental Oil Company. One of the men, a chap named Hal Mosher, was employed by the oil company; the other, Scanlon, was a private detective. Both pretended to be labor sympathizers. The union got wise to the fact—or they suspected it—that the Occidental Oil was housing strikebreakers in a hotel near Modesto. They decided to send some of their own men down there to see what was going on. I don't know whether they meant mischief or not—probably they did, because those chaps don't handle scabs with kid gloves. Somehow Mosher and Scanlon got themselves included in the party, but before they left, Mosher tipped off the oil company that both cars were loaded with dynamite. On the outskirts of Modesto the cars were stopped by private guards in the employ of the Occidental Oil, and they put the whole gang under arrest."

"Nate Jacobs asserts that the dynamite was planted in the cars and the men knew nothing about it," Lloyd interposed.

"What if it was and they were as innocent as lambs?" J.O.B. demanded. "It would be no more of a trick than some of the things the unions have been doing to us. Of course, a frame-up is the natural hue and cry of the Communists and their damn Red news organs like the *Western Worker*. Personally I believe it was all over and aboveboard, and that those chaps had every intention of blowing up Occidental Oil property or blowing up everybody in the hotel. If we could send a few more of such gentlemen to the penitentiary, it would be an excellent thing for the country at large and San Francisco in particular."

"What do you think of that case up in Sacramento where those eight young people were convicted under that criminal-syndicalism law and sent to the penitentiary?"

"What do *you?*" J.O.B. countered.

"Well, it's a pretty moribund law in the first place; it was enacted during the days of hysteria following the war, and its terms are so vague that under it almost any person could be imprisoned for anything. The D.A. told me personally that it is so manifestly undiscriminating that he refuses to make use of it, and I think he's right. You want to remember one thing, J.O.B., and that is there is nothing criminal about being a Communist or being sent to jail for belonging to that party——"

"When it advocates the overthrow of the United States Government by force or violence?" The brother's tone was indignant.

"Oh, I don't know as all Communists want to do that. But let it pass——"

"I won't let it pass!" J.O.B. cried angrily; "not when we know for certain that the Reds of Russia helped organize the general strike here last fall!"

"You're not sure."

"I *am* sure! They sent men out here with the set purpose of getting it started. Their own paper, the *Communist,* in the October issue of last year says frankly that it took long and careful preparation. They say—right out in cold print—that they sent 'militants' first to small unions and then tackled the big ones. Why, damn it, if that isn't flagrant rebellion and subversion, I don't know what it is! The Communist party in New York—that's the headquarters of their organization in this country—sent their special representatives out here to promote that strike, and they get their orders straight from the Comintern in Moscow!"

"Well, well, perhaps you're right. But I don't believe that many of those young people—eight of them, weren't they?—advocated the overthrow of our Government by force and violence. They were more interested in raising the price paid per hour to cotton pickers, and they *did* raise it from sixty to seventy-five cents——"

"And how, in the name of God, do you expect our farmers to make their farms pay? You should hear Reggie on the subject. He and the other big farmers round Visalia depend on these migratory workers. They keep moving from one end of the state to the other as crop follows crop. They're mostly Mexicans and riffraff of the lowest order.

"Damn it, Lloyd," J.O.B. broke off to say with rising indignation, "sometimes you talk like a Red yourself! I never heard such nonsense. You don't know what courageous work that organization, the Associated Farmers—composed of big banks, big oil companies, big fruit packers—is doing for the agriculturists of this state. Our orchards and farms would be overrun with these damn Red lice if it weren't for their help and campaigning."

Lloyd waved his brother's tone of challenge aside, said with a shake of his head:

"I can't believe this young chap, Pat Curtis, who's only in his early twenties, and who organized these same shiftless migratory workers into some sort of a body of protest, ever had any thought of overthrowing the Government by force or violence, and yet he's a convict over here at San Quentin right now, and he'll be there for years to come. I think they gave him fourteen years.

"That trial was a good deal of a farce," Lloyd continued, eyeing the tip of his cigar reflectively; "in the first place it was one of the longest in California court history, lasting four and a half months. I read Mr. McAllister's impassioned address to the jury, and I must say it was rather hysterical. The whole business won more sympathizers for those on trial than it did for the state. I'm surprised he got a conviction, and I think the judge was unnecessarily severe. Whatever Pat Curtis did, I don't believe he merited fourteen years in the penitentiary."

J.O.B. rose in impatience, dusting off the crumbs from his vest and ample lap.

"You try my patience, Lloyd. You'll be telling me next you believe in unionism and a union-owned town. San Francisco is being throttled by organized labor, and until we throw off labor's yoke we'll be a city of stagnation. As long as Roosevelt remains in office, what are you going to expect? He fosters industrial strife, urges the worker to organize and impede the wheels of progress by unreasonable demands.

I tell you, we need a new leader in the White House, and the quicker we get one, the better off we'll be. What do you think of Landon?"

"A sound conservative, I should say. He's done a fine job for his state. I agree with you, we should have a change in Washington. The unemployed situation is just as bad as it was four years ago for all the money Mr. Roosevelt has thrown away. Personally I should like to see Hoover run again.

"Which leads me—I don't know exactly why," Lloyd continued on a new note, "to speak of Eleanor's wedding. Bessie thinks it would be all right to have it in September."

"How's Mother?"

"All right. She has an indomitable spirit, you know—Mother has. Chris's death was a terrible blow to her of course. She idolized him—I think more than any of the rest of us. Perhaps it was just as well the young scapegrace went as he did. He would never have settled down, never have taken a responsible view of life, never been of any material help to either Charmion or Reggie. I think Mother came to see that herself toward the end, although she naturally doesn't admit it. Family pride, of course. She never forgets she is a Breckenridge of Savannah and a lineal descendant of Lord Oglethorpe."

J.O.B. acknowledged this with a smile, and the two men left the dining room together.

"You think then we can hold the wedding next month. You don't think it is too soon, hey?"

"Oh no. It will be three months since—since . . ." J.O.B. did not finish, but presently asked:

"Eleanor. Does she seem very eager for the event?"

"I fancy so; the young man has been hanging around so long now that I think Bessie fears that unless she gets them married pretty soon, the affair might not come off at all! I hope Charmion and Reggie will feel like coming up for it."

§ 2

Not until Lloyd's daughter went to the City Hall with Lester to get their license did she learn that his right name was Emil Gittelsohn. It was a great shock to her, and she could not conceal the fact. He was amused by her agitation.

"My dear," he said, laughing at her expression, "what do you expect? Would you have me appear in pictures and with my name headlined as 'Emil Gittelsohn'? My fans wouldn't know how to pronounce it!"

"But—but you've never told me anything about your people, your . . . your family," Eleanor reproached him.

"There isn't anything to tell. My father has a small business in Trenton, New Jersey. Manufactures shoes. I haven't heard of or from him in years."

"And is your mother living?"

"Oh, I think so—but, as I tell you, I've lost all contact with my parents."

Not very satisfactory, but she had to accept it. Legally, to the end of her days, she thought, she would always be "Mrs. Emil Gittelsohn" —a secret never to be shared with anyone. She would beg Bishop Boggs to call him "Lester" during the ceremony. Anyway, she consoled herself, her promised husband was distinguished-looking, a popular screen idol. He might not always be a screen idol, of course, and then what would the future hold for them? But he'd always be handsome—and there'd always be money!

After the wedding, they planned to motor leisurely southward, stay for some weeks at the Ambassador in Los Angeles and look around for a house to buy or rent in Beverly Hills. It should be exciting to know the movie colony and the big stars whose names came so readily to Lester's tongue and of whom he spoke so familiarly. Eleanor knew she was beautiful, and Hollywood was a place where beauty was appreciated and courted. There would be men—and women, too— who would be interesting and fascinating; she was determined to play her cards carefully and come to know only the nicest people.

But that awful name—Gittelsohn! She shuddered whenever she thought of it.

Preparations for the wedding, now less than a fortnight away, for a second time got under way, and she was caught in the excitement of arrangements and engagements.

The society columns of the newspapers were full of squibs, paragraphs, and half-columns about the approaching nuptials and gave full space to the dinners, receptions, and cocktail parties which were arranged to honor the young couple. There was Mrs. Bradly Ottinger's dinner, for instance, of forty-two covers in the old Ottinger home on Nob Hill, and the supper dance at the St. Francis given by Mr. and Mrs. Jacques Toussaint, and the informal soiree at the Burlingame Club, at which the popular bachelor, Mr. Tobias Anthony Fitzgerald, was host. There were many other luncheons, receptions, and dinners, where the appointments were carefully described and the guests meticulously enumerated.

The wedding, announced the press—postponed from last June because of a death in the family—would take place in Grace Cathedral, and the appointed hour was to be nine o'clock in the evening, after which the city's social elite would assemble for the brilliant reception to be held at the stately mansion of the bride's parents, Mr. and Mrs. Lloyd Gordon Rutherford.

But at this time, to everyone's embarrassment, the more gossipy journals began to make much of an impulsive remark Eleanor made which presumably had been overheard by a listening reporter.

"I'm sure I don't want a lot of flat silverware and junk," she had said thoughtlessly at a luncheon Mrs. Percy Grant was giving for her at the Fairmont. "I'm bound to inherit all of Grandmère's old flat silver—you know, the Breckenridge armorplate!" Eleanor had garrulously continued—"and there'll be plenty of checks from the family, and when we are settled in Beverly Hills, I can pick out my own furniture and the things I like without having to try to fit a monstrosity some well-meaning friend has given me into a house that isn't suitable for it at all. I'll have all the clothes I want—Mother and Father have just been too lavish!—so what is there? People have asked me, and I've told them—frankly—jewelry; I don't care if it's no more than a pair of ten-dollar clips from Magnin's. You can always use jewelry—at least I can!—and you can wear it now, tomorrow, or any day till kingdom comes! Then there's another thing about jewelry: if it's too horrible or loathsome, you can always give it away, or exchange it. They can't *mark* jewelry!"

In a lighthearted tone, half serious, half humorous, Eleanor had expressed herself in this fashion to an admiring group of her intimates, but quoted—when it appeared in the paper and touched up with an added word or two by a none too sympathetic reporter—it sounded neither gracious nor becoming.

"Oo-ooo," Daisy gasped as she read the article and clutched the sheet to her breast with an inward stab of pain.

Other papers promptly reprinted Eleanor's remarks. They made good copy, choice reading. Thus one evening newspaper headlined: "'Send Me Only Jewelry,' Says Bride-to-Be."

There was far too much talk about it, thought the Rutherfords, but they did not discuss the matter. Perhaps Bessie and Lloyd in the seclusion of their bedroom shook their heads over it regretfully; perhaps Frances and J.O.B. exchanged tut-tutting noises and frowned. Stan *did* say in confidence to Daisy when they were alone one day:

"Why're all the papers boobing Eleanor? I think it was kind of a silly remark for her to make, but why all this hullabaloo? You'd think she'd slapped Mrs. Vanderbilt's face! Maybe we aren't popular in this town. I thought we were."

Many of Eleanor's friends and some of the family—in particular Grandmère—had taken Eleanor's wishes literally, and, before the unpleasant publicity broke, from Shreve's and other leading jewelers expensive and unique pieces of jewelry had been ordered by these well-wishers. An enterprising but scurrilous reporter in some underhanded way found out what a few of these actually were to be—most of them had been ordered specially—and a list promptly appeared in a morning paper:

Cuff bracelet with gargantuan pink tourmaline, 127 carats, set in two-tone gold—modern leaf design.

Flexible necklace of gold—supporting a superb topaz of warm, golden brown, 102 carats.

Amethyst ring of princely purple, 28 carats, gold mounting set with diamonds.

Gold ear-clips—in whimsey leaf design—set with ruby heads, topaz and diamonds.

More regrettable still—through an untraceable source—one paper learned that Grandmère's wedding gift had been ordered from Tiffany's, and a description appeared in bold type:

A brooch like a comet with a center diamond of colossal size and sprays of diamonds and rubies making the tail.

"It's none of their vulgar business," Grandmère snorted when Eleanor's unhappy mother showed her the item. She snapped her teeth together in audible indignation. "I declare, it seems to me there're a lot of busybodies round this town! It's my privilege to give my granddaughter what I like without these envious reporters with their disgusting noseyness commenting upon it. . . .

"Why, what is there to it?" she went on with mounting exasperation. "I asked Lloyd to tell my broker to sell some United States Steel Preferred I own—there were only two hundred shares—and to deposit the money to my account in the bank. I intended to give the child half of it in the form of a check, and I thought it would be a pretty gesture to pin the brooch to the paper. Goodness sakes alive, what business is it of theirs anyway! I should think I could do as I like with my own!"

§ 3

Daisy determined she would *not* tremble when she walked up the aisle; bridesmaids always did, and on this occasion she, for one, wouldn't. She decided to think of Vincent and imagine that her small hand was safely and securely tucked in the crook of his elbow and that he and she were taking a stroll someplace—oh, it might be along a street or on a beach, or—or down the aisle of a motion-picture theater. . . .

As she stood waiting to enter the church, she let her thoughts carry her to him, keeping in mind only that she must listen for the first strains of the wedding march which would be the signal for the great leather doors to be pulled back and for the first pair of ushers to commence their measured march to the altar. Vincent was due in New Orleans about the first of the month, and he had promised faithfully to air-mail her a letter from there. Her heart was full as she dreamed of him. Wickwire, Rutherford would be launching a new boat—the *San Marco*—next month at the Morse Dry Dock Company's yards in Alameda, and she was going to christen her—the third of the Mission Fleet whose names she had conferred upon them—and she knew, although Vincent did not, that he was to be made the chief engineer of this new boat as soon as she was commissioned. Then maybe in the spring of next year, or at the latest in June, they would be married, and the next time she walked up the aisle of a church for a wedding it would be for her own and he'd be waiting for her at the altar—and Stan, of course, beside him as best man. . . .

Boom—boom—de-dum . . .

There it was! She came out of her dream with a start. Turning to look, she saw Eleanor standing motionless in her glamorous satin and rose point. A woman, on her knees, was straightening and arranging the wide-spreading train, another the soft, exquisite lace that covered her hair. Somebody else handed her her bouquet, and Daisy saw Uncle Lloyd, looking distinguished and magnificent in his brand-new evening clothes, white tie, white vest, white gloves, white boutonniere and all. Now the ushers, arranged two by two, were beginning to step forth: Larry and George, Dave and Barney; then Syd Watterbury, who was paired with Stan, and finally Peter Evans and Willie Pratt. Eight smartly turned-out, handsome young gentlemen. But no motion-picture stars among them. She was glad of that. It appeared that none of Lester's movie friends could leave Hollywood—all busy making pictures—but he had succeeded in persuading Gordon Morgan to act as best man.

Now it was the bridesmaids' turn. She watched the two girls ahead of her take their initial steps; she counted twenty, exchanged glances with Laura Nickel and set forth, right foot first. Steadfastly she clutched her bouquet, held it firmly against her so that by no possible chance could the delicate buds of the sheaf of salmon-pink roses shake and betray her nervousness.

The great nave of the cathedral was a huge bower of fragrance and loveliness. The decorators certainly had outdone themselves, and never, it seemed to her, had she seen so many people crowded into one church. Now they all turned around, beaming and staring, while from all sides rose the sibilant whispers of admiring women.

It was happening all too quickly! Hard to believe that Eleanor could be married in so short a time. Standing before the chancel rail, steadily gazing at the row of flickering candles ranged tier on tier upon the altar, and at the lovely cascade of evergreen arches that balanced one another on either side, hiding the severe stone walls of the church, Daisy did not glance at the bride. She heard the familiar words of the service intoned by the venerable bishop in his fine cultured voice; they seemed to come from a great distance. She heard them, but her mind was occupied with other things: the vast assembly behind her, the lovely decorations which softened the awesome cathedral with its lofty pillars, the hushed throbbing of the organ, which she could hardly hear but which she was sure she could distinctly feel, herself, her costume, her posture, the bouquet—and Laura's roses, which were pitifully trembling. That morning while dressing she had told her mother she was certain to cry during the ceremony, but somehow it had all slipped by her—the emotional part which she had anticipated with secret dread.

Suddenly it was over—oh, much too soon! There was a great rustling and bustling behind her, a burst of sighs, exclamations, even a sniffling sob or two, and then the organ boomed out, and Eleanor and Lester turned to march up the aisle, smiling and bowing right and left, and there was Gordon Morgan taking out the maid of honor, and Syd Watterbury offering Daisy his arm to escort her in their wake.

Eleanor was Lester Armitage's wife now. Nothing could change that. He might die or they might be divorced, but whether she married again or not, in this day and year of our Lord, 1935, she had become his wife!

Such a lot of fuss for so short a few minutes!

§ 4

Crowds and lights and a long queue of cars—moving, stopping moving again, inching toward the curb, headlights sending forth long, gleaming antennae of light as they approached, while camera bulbs popped and flashed, blinding the bridal couple and attendants indiscriminately. Laura Nickel and Stan, Syd Watterbury and Daisy found themselves huddled into one limousine, where, because of the frailness and crushableness of the girls' gowns, the bridesmaids preempted the back seat, the men finding uncomfortable perches on the less roomy jump seats, holding their silk hats in their white-gloved hands, complaining because they could not smoke. Crosstown traffic impeded their progress now and then, while unconcerned pedestrians sauntered leisurely along the sidewalks, unaware of the momentous social event that had taken place in the city that night. Presently the limousine was slowing down to take its place in the line of other limousines converging toward the awninged entrance of the Rutherford residence. The house gushed light from every window, and gay music came invitingly from within, and here were gathered more photographers with flashing, flaring bulbs, a fresh crop of gaping spectators, and a squad of blue-coated policemen hovering about to open car doors, direct traffic, and keep back the crowd.

Blue and silver, blue and silver—the house had been metamorphosed into a glittering pavilion of loveliness and enchantment with azure-tinted hydrangeas and spiky delphiniums alternating with clusters of white peonies and snowy plumes of feathery phlox. The ugly electric fixtures hung with hundreds of dangling prisms had been removed, and now concealed flares shone upward from the floor through tinted screens and cast a soft radiance on walls and ceilings draped and canopied with folds of lusterless blue silk. The carpeted floors all had been canvased, and in the dining room stood a sumptuous buffet table garlanded with ropes of silver and blue, surmounted at either end by towering silver candelabra. On the threshold of the half-opened pantry door, a swarm of caterer's men was poised, awaiting the signal to sally forth with trays of foaming goblets of champagne, and from a leafy arbor beneath the stairs the orchestra played a sprightly waltz.

Denuded of furniture, the rooms looked empty, but Daisy knew that in less than a quarter of an hour they would be swarming with a brilliant crowd of friends.

§ 5

By eleven o'clock the reception was at its height. Most of the company had completed felicitating the bride, congratulating the groom, politely shaking hands with some of the bridesmaids, embracing others whom they happened to know more intimately. Now the steady line of well-wishers had thinned, and presently the bridal party of lovely girls in their salmon-pink costumes, the gorgeous bride, the handsome groom, the well-tailored young ushers had gathered about the bridal table and could be observed by admiring guests, who whispered their praise and nodded their heads in approval.

The bride's parents had been part of the receiving line for only a short time. Bessie had said she had "things" to look after; Lloyd declared his presence only spoiled the picture and had been anxious to circulate among his guests.

Stan suspected that Grandmère had been somewhat disgruntled by their departure, as she had felt obliged to follow their example. The old lady was magnificently arrayed in black and silver and wore all the diamonds she could crowd upon her person. A new wig, made for the occasion, glistened and shone upon her head—a mass of tortuous silky curls—and if she wore any artificial gems, they were the deep blue amethysts arranged effectively in her luxuriant crown. She looked the grand duchess, played the part, and would have been happy to have remained in the receiving line, between her glamorous granddaughter and distinguished-looking son, greeting San Francisco's elite with all the royal mannerisms at her command. She still carried herself regally as she moved about, affecting a slight condescension in greeting casual acquaintances, bestowing on closer friends a gracious wrinkled smile, pleased when some courtly gentleman raised her gloved hand to his lips.

"Your grandmother seems to be having the time of her life," Syd Watterbury said to Stan across Daisy, who was seated between them at the bridal table.

"She's the grand dame de luxe," Stan agreed with an affectionate smile. "A great old girl born too late; she belongs to the court of Louis XIV or to the Vienna of Franz Josef."

"Well, neither of those gentlemen ever saw any more magnificent scene than this," Syd commented.

It was indeed a brilliant spectacle, Stan thought. If it could be said that San Francisco boasted a nobility, all of it had assembled this night at his uncle's house. Everyone of any social prominence was present, the women bedecked and bejeweled, the men in faultless evening attire—white ties and tails. Milling among themselves, acquaintances greeted one another, gathering momentarily in knots, dissolving to form fresh groups, moving against a soft harmony of blue and silver tones, presenting a pageant which might well have graced a royal court.

J.O.B. and a group of his business cronies were gathered beside the buffet table, glasses in hand, discussing the latest "beef" along the waterfront; Bessie in lacy lavender circulated among the company, drawing friends together, greeting old and new acquaintances; Frances piloted the curious upstairs to view the array of wedding gifts; Lloyd held forth to a circle of his own beyond the folding doors leading to the hallway. Stan from where he sat at the bridal table could hear his pontifical pronouncements above the general hubbub.

"The court vacated the injunction, restraining the police from interfering with the pickets," he was saying.

Suddenly amid the gabble of voices and general laughter, the clicking of crockery and the clink of glasses, Stan heard a sharp noise which did not belong to the scene. First came a splintering of glass—not of a dish or wineglass—then three pistol shots, sharp staccato stabs in the night, and the whine of bullets. In the abrupt silence that followed, an object, black, pear-shaped and smoking, rolled almost to his feet. He stared at it, horror filling heart and brain as he recognized what it was; then it exploded with a great billow of smoke. Instantly he was seized with a spasm of coughing, gagging, his eyes smarting as if red-hot rods had been plunged into their sockets. The smoke obliterated everything, the room, the house, those close at hand, while all about him rose cries of anguish. Someone shouted:

"Tear bomb! Everybody out!"

Others took up the cry.

"Get out of doors! Get to the street!"

The blue-and-silver rooms became a shambles of struggling, gasping men and women fighting blindly to make way for themselves and reach fresh air. Stan fell over a woman on her hands and knees sobbing miserably. With streaming eyes, unable to breathe or see, he managed to seize the unhappy lady about her waist and drag her in the direction of the pantry door. Though the tear gas had already penetrated here, it was less dense and there was more space, for servants, cooks, and waiters had fled. His outstretched hand found a familiar door, and through this he carried his now unconscious burden. Finally there was the garden and the street and he could draw breath with some relief, though smarting eyes and nose streamed water and his head was aflame.

Willing hands met him. Someone relieved him of the woman, and a policeman guided him to a seat on the running board of a car, while about him a crowd gathered.

"In there—in there," he pointed in anguish to the house.

"They're all out by now, Mr. Rutherford," someone said. A man squatting in front of him mopped his face with a wet towel.

"My mother—Daisy, Eleanor!" Stan gasped.

"All safe. The cops and chauffeurs rushed in and dragged 'em out. Maybe one or two's fainted, but all the windows are open and they are beating out the gas."

"Some stinker threw a bomb through one of the windows. There were two or three fellas with him," another said.

"Yeah," contributed a bystander, "I seen 'em. One of 'em had a red beard and a bum eye."

"Waterfront bums," the first speaker stated.

"We took a couple of shots at them," the policeman said, "and one of our patrol cars took after 'em, but the gang had everything planned for a quick getaway."

"Can you imagine the kind of a guy who would do a thing like that?" asked a man.

Suddenly a wild shriek like the wail of a banshee screamed into the night.

Stan struggled to his feet.

"Easy, Mr. Rutherford," the officer said, placing a restraining hand on his shoulder. "It's nothing. Somebody's turned in a fire alarm, or maybe it's the riot squad."

CHAPTER VII

"She's remarkable," Daisy said.

"Your grandmother?"

"Grandmère, yes. She had no ill effects; apparently the whole terrible experience didn't bother her in the least. Aunt Bessie fractured her hip. She was dazed and I guess couldn't see. She got to the front steps, then stumbled and fell to the sidewalk, and they had to call an ambulance and take her to the hospital. She's in a cast now and is terribly uncomfortable. But Grandmère . . . she's indestructible. It was a frightful humiliation for her, of course, a hurt to her pride; she couldn't understand how she, a Breckenridge and a Rutherford, could be subjected to such indignity. Imagine, her own granddaughter's wedding, she, the hostess, presiding at the reception, and then to have the affair spoiled by such bru——brutality, so unprovoked, unwarranted, and later to have all the unpleasant notoriety. But after a few days in bed, she rose undaunted and is her old self again."

"Nobody knows who did it?"

"No one, but certainly it was someone connected with those villainous labor unions—someone with a grudge. Of course there was all that silly talk about Eleanor's wedding presents in the papers; unquestionably that enraged some disgruntled person."

"But how is it possible for a vicious thing like that to happen in a decent, civilized city like San Francisco and the offender go scotfree?" Vincent asked indignantly. "By the Lord, I'd drum every lousy union stiff off the waterfront if I had my way. I'd jail 'em, hang 'em, run 'em out of town. They're a lawless bunch, Dais. They think nothing of beating up some poor guy who doesn't want to join their organization, and if he tries to make a living in his own way, they call him a 'scab' or a 'fink,' and one fine day his body's found floating in the Bay with his skull laid open—drowned and dead!"

"Oh, goodness me!" moaned Daisy, drawing a troubled breath. She knew that what Vincent told her was no exaggeration; too often she had heard similar tales from her father and brother. "Oh, I wish," she continued unhappily, "I wish you weren't—I wish you had nothing to do with stevedores and sailors and horrible men like that."

He laughed in his slow way, his agate-brown eyes alight with amusement. "I like it," he said; "I like dealing with such men, and I wouldn't swap my job for any other in the world. That kind of hoodlum can't scare me; I'm not afraid of any of 'em. I'd plug the first roustabout who sassed me and knock him cold; I've done it a couple of times already. I'll stand for no lip from their delegates or from their leaders. They can't dictate to me. I run my life and my engine room the way I please. I'm only responsible to the company, and I shall be eternally grateful to your father for the hand-up he's given me. Imagine! Me, a chief engineer at twenty-eight!"

When the *San Marco* had been launched in October, Stan—gladly following his father's suggestion—had told Vincent he had better leave the *San Gabriel,* come ashore, and begin studying for the Government's marine examinations, for if he passed them he was to be chief engineer of the new freighter. So Vincent had happily gone to live with his invalid mother in Redwood City and spent days and nights poring over books on navigation and engineering to prepare himself for his promotion.

During this interval Daisy had seen him twice a week on the evenings when he came to town for coaching by a retired engineer who knew all there was to know about navigation and a ship's engines. After these hours of instruction, Vincent would come out to her house, tell her of his progress, hold her in his arms, and kiss her ever-ready, eager lips. He did not leave her until it was time to catch the twelve-fifteen train home, but she lived for these glimpses of him and wrote him almost every day.

In January he successfully passed the Federal examinations—a three-days' trial—and on this Saturday in March he had come to say good-by, as the *San Marco* was to sail with the tide from the Alameda Estuary at noon the following day. He was to stay for dinner, and later they planned to slip away, perhaps to a movie, their favorite diversion. But they were not to be parted long this time; the *San*

Marco had only to make Seattle, and after that, one more trip—a long one through the Canal to New Orleans, but home again in June— and in June—Daisy could hardly contain herself whenever she thought what June held for her. They were to be married then, and although she had offered to live with his arthritic old mother in Redwood City, Vincent would have none of it. They would find a little flat or a house, he told her, somewhere in Oakland or Berkeley or Alameda—the Rutherford freighters always docked at the Encinal Terminals—and then, while he was at sea, she would be near her friends and family.

"Only," Vincent had stipulated, "it must be on what I can afford."

"Oh, I agree, I agree," Daisy had assured him. "Of course. I'll budget beautifully, save money, and go to see your mother every week."

Her eagerness to be his troubled him. He loved her—as much as his nature was capable of love—but he saw difficulties ahead, his life and interests divided between his home and the sea.

"There'll be children," he told himself; "at least I hope so, and they'll fill her days, keep her happy."

They had had a long, satisfactory talk this afternoon, and Vincent had felt more hopeful of the success of their marriage. No matter how he reasoned, no matter if indeed he was a chief engineer at twenty-eight, he thought of himself as unworthy to be the husband of this exquisite girl, daughter of such doting, wealthy parents. Vincent Oliver, he reminded himself, was a nobody. While his father, old Pat Oliver, had worked in the Redwood City Garage for many weary years, he, the son, had been a roughneck, hashing his way through college, playing football, and later coming to know the waterfronts of various ports with all their shoddiness and corruption. Who was he to marry his boss's lovely daughter, so gently reared, so pampered and shielded, so surfeited with luxury?

But today he felt more confident. Surely no girl so obviously eager to link her fortunes with his could be unhappy as his wife, and it would be wonderful to think, as the bows of the *San Marco* turned toward San Francisco, he was headed for his home and wife.

Thinking of this, he took her in his arms and pressed her closely to him, kissing her ardently, thrilling to her softness and surrender.

"That's it, that's it," she cried breathlessly, shoving him from her as he released her, her small fists against his breast. "That's what I want! That's what I long for. I want you to crush me—crush the breath out of me! I want you to love me like that—always and always."

There was a rattle of keys in the front door. It opened heavily, slammed shut, and a moment later J.O.B. entered the drawing room in which the lovers sat.

"Ah, Vincent," he said cordially; "don't get up, don't get up. No, no. Let me take this chair and sit down awhile—if I'm not intruding! Need to catch my breath. It's been a hard day."

He sank into one of the big armchairs and reached in his inside pocket for his cigar case.

"How's your mother?" he asked his daughter.

"All right, I guess. She's been down sitting with Aunt Bessie most of the day."

Her father frowned as he bit off the end of his cigar.

"You know," he said to Vincent, "my sister-in-law broke her hip last September—and quite badly."

"Daisy was telling me. How's she getting along?"

"I wish I could say 'fine,' but the bones didn't knit satisfactorily the first time; they had to take the cast off and drive an actual nail through the joint and put her back in a cast again. God, what that woman has gone through!"

"But she *is* on the mend?"

"Can't tell until the cast comes off, but it will be a long time before she can walk—and then with a crutch or be pushed about in a wheelchair. I was talking to my brother about her at lunch today. She's been at the Dante Sanitarium since—well, let me see—it's six months now. A long pull. They hope she can come home in a few weeks; she's sick of the hospital—and, Lord knows, I can't blame her. I don't know when they'll remove the cast, but they won't let her go until they take it off and see if the fracture's properly mended. It will be some weeks yet. She's been remarkable through it all. You'd think my mother would have been the one to suffer, but she's as hale and vigorous as ever. Apparently the experience did her no harm."

"You've never been able to find out who did the job?"

"Not so far. The police are so damned incompetent. Of course it was perpetrated by some union sympathizer, one or a gang of those scoundrels. Who else would know about a tear bomb, or have one? And why should anyone else in this town have a grievance—fancied or otherwise—against us as a family? I was talking to Lloyd today, and I'm thinking of hiring a detective agency and having that rascal Rory O'Brien shadowed day and night. He knows something about it, I'll bet my hat; anyway he's responsible for most of the trouble-making in this town. He's got a grudge or something."

"Well, the city certainly is in a mess."

"Yes, and it's got to be cleaned up. The award handed down by the board Roosevelt appointed is ridiculous. In the first place it stipulated that the shipowners and the unions were to establish a hiring hall, the expenses of which were to be divided between us. Well, the unions are doing all the hiring—we haven't a word to say—but we still pay our share of the cost and maintenance. Of course you know all about it. It's outrageous! The agreement comes up to be signed again this fall, and it's not going to be renewed, that's all. We're determined to stay in business and operate our ships at a decent profit, and we're not going to let these Reds tell us we can't!"

"What can you do to shut them up?" Vincent asked.

"Starve 'em! Did you ever hear of a lockout, my boy? Just close our doors and let 'em whistle. I'm meeting Ahearn on Monday to discuss the matter. If we can get enough shipowners in this town to co-operate, we'll just quit—close up shop and wait until these damn unions and their leaders come to their senses. Two can play at the quitting game, and this time it will be the employers who do the striking. There's no placating these Communists. If it's to be war, let's have it."

"Lord, I hope you can swing it!"

"I don't think we'll have any difficulty. By the way," he diverged to ask, "you having any trouble on the *San Marco?*"

"Not more than usual. I had a visit from one of the officers of the Firemen's Union today; he came to see me along with the ship's delegate about some overtime pay for one of the oilers. A small matter, and we adjusted it amicably, but I'm sure we are in for more and more 'beefs.'"

"Was that that man Dempsey who came to see you?"

"Yes, same fellow. He's a patrolman for the union."

"He's dangerous; just wants to make trouble. Why, Vincent, if you gave those confounded hooligans everything they ask for, they wouldn't be satisfied! Fomenting strife is the breath of life to them; give 'em peace and they wouldn't know what to do. What's the use? As soon as we get organized we'll have a lockout; then see what happens. How do you like your ship?"

"She's a humdinger." Vincent's slow smile showed his white teeth. "She behaves like a darling, steers like a baby carriage, and those engines . . ." He paused, unable to go on. "They turn over as smoothly and as rhythmically as . . ." He stopped again, an adequate simile failing him. "We can make fourteen knots in the foulest weather. I've never handled a finer boat."

"Than what?" asked a pleasant voice, and Stan came into the room. He took Vincent's outstretched hand and shook it warmly.

"Oh," Vincent answered, with smiling embarrassment, "I was getting a little rhapso . . . a little rhapso-something or other; can't think of the word! . . . I was just raving to your father about the *San Marco;* she's the finest boat I've ever set foot on. I'd sail her to kingdom come and back again if I had to."

"Good, and your skipper?"

"Captain O'Day? They don't make 'em any better. We get along swell, and he knows his onions, too."

"Nice to hear things like that," J.O.B. commented; "nice to hear that somebody's happy and likes his job in these dark times of grumbling and discontent."

§2

The following day, Sunday, the family gathered at J.O.B.'s house for one-o'clock luncheon—midday dinner, rather—for Frances always served pork and beans and a salad at suppertime on this day of the week, as it was the cook's night out. Eleanor came with her father and grandmother; she had only arrived from the southland that morning, and Daisy thought she looked sober and stern. The younger girl—from what source she could not have said—had gleaned the fact that her cousin's marriage had not turned out entirely satisfactorily. Grandmère had telephoned her mother earlier in the day to say that Eleanor was coming up from Los Angeles and would be there for the luncheon. Daisy had heard her mother, the receiver at her ear, ask in a constrained voice: "Is there anything wrong?" and there had followed a long cackling and buzzing reply from her grandmother, no word of which the girl had been able to understand, but she had seen her mother's face cloud and noticed the swift look she had cast in her own direction. Then, after an interval, her mother had said: "Very well, Grandmère; I understand. We'll expect you all a little before one."

No explanation, but Daisy had long suspected that something was amiss. She was not surprised, therefore, when Eleanor appeared, to note the girl's repressed manner as she greeted the rest of the family.

Ever since the wedding in September, and even before that, during prenuptial days when the bride-to-be and her fiancé had been going to cocktail parties and to dinners, Daisy had had her misgivings. Eleanor had not seemed happy, not wholly happy the way *she* was about Vincent, and certainly her cousin had never conveyed the impression that Lester filled her heart the way the man she loved filled hers. She had had letters from Eleanor after she had moved to Beverly Hills—hardly more than notes they had been—describing the charming bungalow she had found, with a patio, Spanish tiles, and a garden, but containing only the briefest mention of Lester; he was in a new picture, had a fine part, was playing opposite a glamorous star of the moment, was on location, was away on a fishing trip to Catalina with Gordon Morgan and Rupert Tate, a stag party—Bruce Steinart's yacht. They were not the letters of a radiantly happy wife.

Daisy's thoughts carried her to Vincent. He had telephoned her that morning again to say good-by; he had just arrived in town, had spent the night with his mother in Redwood City, was off now to his ship, due to sail with the noon tide.

"I'll be seeing you in less than five weeks, honey," he had told her; "don't forget to write. Expect me next month; I'll have only one more trip to make, and then . . . oh well, you know what!"

Hardly conscious of what she did, she now pressed to her lips the unpretentious ring he had brought her the night before. It had been his mother's—a small square garnet, set on each of its four sides with a tiny diamond. Its setting was old-fashioned and it was too small for the proper finger, but she prized it more than if it had been the Koh-i-noor. Tomorrow she intended to take it downtown to Shreve's and have it made larger.

But Eleanor?

She studied her cousin's cold, beautiful face. No lightness there— no gaiety or happiness. . . . She remembered——

A ring at the front door scattered her thoughts. Martha was at the moment clearing away the soup plates.

"I'll go," Daisy said, halfway to her feet.

"Nothing of the kind," her grandmother cackled. "Let the maid answer it. Whoever it is, let him wait."

"Let me," Stan volunteered, but his sister was already in the hallway.

A pleasant-looking young man faced her as she opened the door— black-haired, black-browed—who instantly whipped off his hat as he inquired:

"Mr. Rutherford in?"

"Well . . ." Daisy hesitated.

"I'd like to ask him a question or two. Do you mind? I'm from the *Chronicle*."

"Oh," the girl said, uneasily. "I'll see. Won't you step in?"

The young man did so, and Daisy returned to the dining room.

"There's a reporter from the *Chronicle* to see you, Dad," she announced.

"What's he want?" J.O.B.'s face clouded.

"He didn't say."

"Well, you'll have to excuse me," he grumbled, large hands on either arm of his chair as he pushed it back and raised his big bulk. "You'd think," he growled, "that on a Sunday, in the bosom of one's family, they'd leave a man——" With the sentence unfinished, he left the room.

Daisy caught the murmur of the men's voices and then heard them cross the hall and go into the drawing room.

The hearty midday luncheon proceeded, Grandmère picking at the bony fish in front of her, clicking her teeth, complaining she was sure Bessie wasn't getting the proper treatment.

"I declare, Lloyd," she said tartly, "I'd get another doctor. There's no sense in letting her go on day after day in such misery."

"Stewart's one of the best," Lloyd observed mildly. "After all, it's been a most difficult case. You must remember, Bessie isn't a young woman any more. However, as soon as they take the cast off, I propose to bring her home. We'll see what the X-rays show, but I'm sure she'll be more comfortable."

"She seemed quite cheerful when I saw her this morning," Eleanor remarked. "I thought she looked quite pretty—much better than I expected."

"She's a saint," Frances said; "complains hardly at all. The nights are hard; she tells me she sleeps badly. They ought to give her some pills, don't you think?"

"I thought I'd go down to see her again this afternoon," Eleanor observed, "but on Sundays so many people drop in, and I want to talk to her alone."

So—thought Daisy—Eleanor did have something to talk over *alone* with her mother!

J.O.B., just behind her, spoke suddenly, startling her.

"Lloyd, Stan," he said, "will you both come here a minute?"

There was an unusual gravity in his tone which made Daisy turn to look at him. Her mother asked anxiously:

"What is it, John?" She rarely called him by his first name, and Daisy had a feeling of alarm. Silence held the women as the men left the room, and the girl strained her ears to hear what was being said. Only their low tones reached her, but suddenly she heard a startled "Oh, my God!" from Stan.

Then all four gathered in the hall, and her father came back to the dining room, kissed his wife, said:

"We've got to go, my dear. Something rather serious has happened, and we all must see about it."

"But what is it?" cried Frances. "Tell us what it is!"

"We'll be back soon's we can," her husband told her.

"You going, too, Lloyd?" shrilled Grandmère.

"I think I'd better."

Stan came to where Daisy was sitting, put his arm around her and kissed her hair, filling her with a fresh feeling of apprehension. Then the men departed, and the heavy glass-paneled door closed behind them with a reverberating bang.

§ 3

"It was never a marriage—never, never, never! Not from the day that bomb broke up the reception! I should have known then—I should have recognized it as a sign! The whole thing was destined for failure!"

Eleanor's face was hard; she clasped her hands tightly, fingers interwoven, and now and then she tilted her head ceilingward to wink back her tears. She would not cry. She would not give in.

It was soon after the disrupted luncheon that the two girls found themselves alone in Daisy's bedroom. In contrast to Eleanor's determined self-control, her cousin's cheeks were wet in sympathy.

"But I don't understand," she faltered.

"You wouldn't, you wouldn't," Eleanor rushed on; "he wasn't in love with me—never was! He was in love with himself, with his looks. With his fan mail!" she added contemptuously. "He insisted on reading such slush to me and telling me about some woman in Kalamazoo who had written to say she thought he had a classical face, and about another—a sculptress, I think she was—who wanted to model his head! He lived for such flattery. He couldn't pass a mirror in the house without stopping to look at his reflection, turning his face first to one side and then to the other, asking me if the color of his tie was right and if I approved the collar he had on! . . . It made me sick!

"We went to some parties at first, and I met a lot of movie stars; I liked that, but most of the people were just the same. I couldn't abide the women. Fluffy-haired idiots without a thought in their heads, who talked only of themselves and regaled one another with studio gossip. 'Fritz is going to cast so-and-so for the lead' and 'Arabella sprained her ankle on the lot yesterday' and 'I saw the rushes of so-and-so's latest yesterday and they're simply wonderful!' I grew so *tired* of their gibberish! But I believe I could have come to endure it; I didn't have to go to their stupid parties after all. It was Lester I couldn't stand. He was no more of a husband than a sleek, silky dachshund. He made me creep every time he came near me. I repeat he didn't love me; he loved only himself—his body, his clothes, and his looks. I tried—I really did. I arranged some nice little dinners for him and his friends; I shopped, and I had a good cook. I tried to make things gay, turned on the radio, proposed we dance. No good. He and his pals just wanted to sit round and talk about themselves and what was going on in the studios and how good or how bad each one's agent was. I thought—God help me!—I was marrying a man—not a sexless Narcissus. He used to paw me at night! I thought I'd go out of my senses. He wouldn't give me any peace or rest, worrying me and teasing me until . . ."

The angry tears came now—tears that only a proud and humiliated woman could shed.

Daisy sank to her knees and tried to put her arms around her while tears flooded her own cheeks, but Eleanor would not unbend. The hurt that had been done to her had gone deep. She did not want comfort or sympathy. It was her home-coming that was hard to face, confessing to her own people that she had been shamed by the man in whom she had believed. She must tell them one by one her tale of ignominy and humiliation.

She rose now, almost rudely pushing Daisy aside, and went to stand at the window, looking out with unseeing eyes at the leafy, overgrown garden which lay beneath the gabled old house and the street. She stood there for a time, composing her twitching face, stilling her trembling lips, but no sound escaped her. Daisy, on the floor, cried into her sodden bit of handkerchief. She felt so sorry for Eleanor; she knew better than anyone else what this failure of her marriage meant to her. It would take courage—a great deal of it—to resume her place in San Francisco society, "Mrs. Armitage—divorced wife of . . ."

Was there *going* to be a divorce?

"What do you intend to do?" she asked at length.

A long minute, before Eleanor answered.

"Divorce him, of course," she said grimly; "I can stand anything, face anybody, as long as I never have to see him or hear from him again."

Another interval, and presently she continued:

"I talked to Father when I got in this morning. I had telephoned him the day before I left, told him I was coming home and not returning, so he knew what was in the wind. He'll arrange everything —pay Lester off if he wants money!—and I'll apply, so Dad tells me, for an interlocutory decree. It will take a year, but I don't care about that. I want to be back with my own family and be rid of that toad once and forever."

All the fuss, thought Daisy—all that unpleasant publicity about the presents, all the discussion about arrangements and decorations and the endless arguments as to who should be invited to the reception and who should not! For what? The futility of it! . . . It wasn't going to be that way with Vincent and herself. She wouldn't have a soul at her wedding but just the family, and then, as soon as they were ready, after the ceremony, they would borrow Stan's car and drive down to Redwood City to see his mother. Oh, there would be no such nonsense when they were married! She didn't blame Eleanor, but her own marriage was going to be different. After all, Vincent was no motion-picture actor!

Thoughts like these were perhaps unkind and ungenerous to her unhappy cousin just now. Resolutely she wiped her eyes, got to her feet, and went to her mirror to powder her nose and redden her lips, determining she would give Eleanor all she would want in companionship, and she would do all she could to make life bearable for her. She kissed her shoulder as she passed her, slipping an arm about her waist. As she did so she heard steps in the hall, and a knock came at her door. Opening it, she was surprised to see her parents. Her mother had been crying, and her father's face was set and dark.

"Daisy," her mother asked, "may we come in? I'm sorry," she said to Eleanor, "I'm sorry to interrupt you, but Daisy's father and I must see Daisy alone just now."

The older girl flashed uncle and aunt a startled, questioning look, straightened, and left the room. J.O.B. gently closed the door behind her.

Frances sank upon the bed, and at once her tears began to flow again. She held out her arms to her daughter.

"My baby, my poor baby!" she sobbed.

J.O.B., in a chair by the window, said admonishingly:

"Now Frances—now Frances."

Daisy looked from one to the other, terror filling heart and soul. She flung herself on her knees beside her mother, and Frances gathered her into an embrace, weeping uncontrollably.

"What is it—what *is* it?" the girl demanded.

Neither would answer her. Frances continued to cry; her father sat staring at the window, his florid, jowled face scowling darkly.

Daisy crawled across the floor to him.

"Daddy, Daddy, tell me! What is it? What has happened? . . . Is it Vincent?"

She knew it was Vincent!

J.O.B. nodded, his averted eyes fixed upon the window beside him.

"Tell me!" the girl insisted. "Tell me!" She shook him fiercely.

"He's had an accident," her father began slowly. Then he turned to her and put his hands about her two arms, gripping them tightly.

"You've got to brace yourself, honey. You have to remember the rest of us who love you. . . . Vincent is gone."

Daisy stared at him, horror dilating her pupils.

"He must have gotten into some sort of argument with someone. We don't know the details. He was a fine young fellow, and whatever he did was right."

"Go on," Daisy breathed, her voice now a whisper.

"There must have been a fight, or——"

"Or *what?*" The last came in a scream.

"Or foul play."

"He's dead?"

"Yes; they—they killed him."

The room swam about her in black circles. She clutched at her father with taloned fingers.

"I want to know," she said, a steely steadiness in her voice.

"In his cabin. They found him—one of the crew found him. It must have happened soon after he came aboard at about eleven this morning. He'd gone to his cabin to change his uniform, and they must have been waiting for him. . . ."

"Yes?"

"He didn't have any enemies we know of. I talked to the captain;

he says the crew all liked him. He was loyal to us, of course. Unquestionably it was someone—or a gang—connected with these waterfront rowdies, stevedores, or this Marine Firemen's outfit with whom
we're having trouble just now. Vincent had an altercation yesterday
—I think it was—with a man named Dempsey who came aboard the
San Marco to settle some differences with him. We'll find out. The
labor unions knew he wouldn't traffic with them, and they were out
to get him. But we'll find the murderer or murderers, my dear; we'll
track down every last one of them, and they'll pay the full penalty of
the law. . . ."

Daisy sank back, gazing steadfastly into her father's eyes, flaming
now with hate and vengeance.

"It was that *Chronicle* reporter who came while we were at luncheon," blubbered Frances. "It was he—he brought the news; the first
we heard . . . Oh, my baby, my poor baby! You loved him so!"

"Yes," repeated Daisy dully, "I loved him so."

She continued to stare at her father.

"Did he suffer? Was there much of a struggle?" she asked evenly.
"I'd like to know."

"No, I think not; evidently there wasn't any time. They were lying
in wait for him."

"He didn't have a chance?"

"No, they killed him, struck him down brutally."

"How?"

J.O.B. swallowed, a hand at his throat.

"Knife wounds, my dear; they stabbed him to death."

She swayed crazily then, and fainted.

§ 4

Stan came down to the dining room early the next morning to
read the newspaper account before his father appeared. He sat at the
breakfast table, the *Chronicle* before him, and had just finished the
half-column when his father's heavy step sounded on the stairs and
J.O.B. entered.

"Morning, sir," Stan said. "There it is."

He handed his father the newssheet, his thumb marking the head-line.

SHIP'S OFFICER MURDERED ON VESSEL IN BAY
Engineer's Body Found in Cabin with Knife Wounds in Back

J.O.B., settling himself in his chair, adjusted his glasses, scowled as he scanned the heading.

Stan made no comment while his father read the article.

Struck down by a mysterious assailant in the cabin of his ship, the *San Marco,* at the Encinal Terminal on the Alameda Estuary shortly before noon yesterday, Chief Engineer Vincent Oliver was found murdered a few moments before the ship was due to sail.

Five wounds, apparently made by a stiletto, were found in his back, while a heavier wound, which apparently had caused death, was directly under his heart.

The body was found by Captain Simeon O'Day, summoned by a member of the crew when Oliver failed to appear in his engine room.

A quarrel between Oliver and his first assistant engineer, B. C. Smith, preceded the actual death, but both Captain O'Day and the police said Smith could not have been in the vicinity of Oliver's cabin.

The *San Marco,* a Wickwire, Rutherford freighter, was due to sail for the north at twelve o'clock noon. She was held, however, until the killing had been investigated.

Captain O'Day places the time of the murder at between 11:05 and 11:20 A.M. Oliver and himself reached the ship at eleven o'clock, Oliver go-ing immediately to the engine room.

There, according to Smith's story, he berated Smith because two of the engine-room crew, who he said were "Smith's pets," had not reported back from shore leave.

Smith went to the captain at 11:05, according to O'Day, and declared he would not sail with Oliver. O'Day quieted him, and Smith returned to the engine room.

Oliver had in the meantime gone to his cabin to change his clothes. When he did not return to the engine room one of the other seamen went to Oliver's cabin to investigate and found him lying helpless beside his bunk.

Going to the cabin, Captain O'Day found Oliver had been murdered.

"Terse," J.O.B. snorted, contemptuously throwing the paper onto the table. Stan knew it was not the write-up which incensed his father.

What he wanted—indeed expected—was to have the news of the murder headlined in bold type clear across the front sheet.

"A man can be knifed to death in broad daylight on board his own ship by a gang of union thugs and they'll give it no more space than that! Well, by God . . ."

He did not finish, but pushed his chair nearer to the table, his heavy-jowled face flushed with anger. He gulped off his glass of fruit juice and rang sharply for his coffee and toast.

"I have Percy Grant and Jim Ahearn meeting me at ten tomorrow morning in Ahearn's office," he said. "You'd better be there, and Syd too. I've asked Lloyd to come. We've got to get together on this thing. A man like Vincent Oliver can't be murdered in cold blood and the murderer—or murderers—get away with it. I'm going to track 'em down and hang 'em if it takes the rest of my life."

§ 5

Excerpts from the morning *Chronicle* the following day read:

Investigation into the brutal knife murder of Vincent Oliver, chief engineer of the ship *San Marco,* Sunday, just before the vessel sailed, proceeded with mounting interest yesterday.

Norwood Tharp, inspector for District Attorney Dan Sheridan of Alameda County, spent the day searching for witnesses and interrogating those who might possibly throw light on the mystery. At the Encinal Terminals the death ship was marooned by law and its crew of thirty-six were held incommunicado.

B. C. Smith, Oliver's assistant, who admittedly had quarreled with the victim shortly before his death, was questioned but not taken into custody or removed from the ship.

Convinced the murder was an outgrowth of marine labor difficulties, the Industrial Association of San Francisco posted a reward of $1,000 for the arrest and conviction of the guilty person or persons.

At the same time a like sum was posted in connection with the murder of Otto Blaczinsky, a dock engineer on the steamer *Minnesotan,* whose throat-slashed body was dragged from the Bay near Pier 28 on October 22, 1935.

Mr. Sydney Watterbury, general manager for Wickwire, Rutherford & Co., owners of the *San Marco,* later in the day posted $2,000 reward for the apprehension and conviction of the murderers.

Clifford Kelly, Deputy District Attorney, said he had the names of four witnesses who saw two unidentified men leave the ship between the time when Oliver was killed and when his mutilated body was found in his cabin. Both were white, of ruddy complexion like men who work out of doors, and were about thirty-five years old. One wore a light gray checkered cap and a mackinaw; the other had on blue jeans, a dark suit coat, and a dark cap.

Oliver's body will be shipped this morning to Redwood City. Interment will probably take place tomorrow.

§ 6

On Tuesday, shortly after ten o'clock, a number of men were grouped about the long mahogany table in the directors' room of the American-Asiatic Steamship Company. Jim Ahearn, genial, pleasant-faced, and gray-haired, presided; Percy Grant was on his left; J.O.B., his brother Lloyd, Stan, and Syd Watterbury sat opposite; others included Jesse Lobenthal of Lobenthal & Company, Felix Hobard of the Hawaiian Fruit Company, Horatio Nickel of the Nickel Line, Clifford Kelly, deputy district attorney, Norwood Tharp, an inspector, and Joe Halliday of the Industrial Association.

J.O.B. had held his peace during the earlier part of the discussion, but now, flourishing a folded newspaper in his hand, he struck the table a slap with it and cried:

"Well, *somebody* killed him! *Somebody* drove that knife into him! He just didn't do it himself!"

"Just a moment, Mr. Rutherford," Norwood Tharp cautioned. "Of course somebody did it. We'll have to find out who did. Smith has been questioned and put through the mill. It is true he did have an altercation with Oliver just before the murder, but he had nothing to do with it. He was in the engine room, had on his dungarees at the time; one of the oilers who was with him can vouch for it. Somebody came up the gangplank after Oliver came aboard, or was waiting for him after he went into his cabin——"

"Damn it," shouted J.O.B., "we know that! But who was he? What's his name? Who sent him there?"

Lloyd put his hand on his brother's sleeve.

"No use in getting so excited, J.O.B.," he said. "We'll find out who he was, and he—or the gang with him—will be brought to justice. It looks to me as if it were carefully planned."

"Oh yes, I think that's evident," Norwood Tharp agreed; "the getaway was too perfect. No doubt some one of these labor leaders is responsible. Oliver was definitely at odds with one and all of them. They had had trouble with him, were out to teach him a lesson. It was carefully worked out."

"By whom?"

"That's what we must discover!"

"What about Rory O'Brien? D'you suppose he was mixed in it?"

"I very much doubt it," Clifford Kelly put in; "he's too shrewd, and besides, I don't think he's that kind of a guy. . . . But we'll find out."

"The shipowners' contract with the longshoremen comes up for renewal next month," J.O.B. observed grimly. "We'll take care of Mr. O'Brien and his wharf rats then."

"It would be to our advantage, I think," said Jim Ahearn, "if we could establish the fact that this murder was planned by some of those left-wing leaders and executed by their henchmen. It would help us with the public."

"Well, there is no question, is there," asked Horatio Nickel, "that somebody connected with the union did the job? You say," he went on, "he didn't have any enemies."

"None that we know of," Stan offered.

"Let's see. Oliver had most of his dealings with the firemen, oilers, and water tenders—the Marine Association. Who's head of that union now?"

"Man by the name of Detrich—Emil F. Detrich."

"What do you know about him?"

"Hard-boiled; helped organize the Maritime Federation and recently has been made head of the Marine Firemen's Union."

"We've had a lot of trouble with him," Percy Grant said.

"And Dempsey—the man who called on Oliver the day before he was killed?"

"A patrolman for the firemen; lately has been organizing a Fish Reduction Workers' Union here."

"And that's the fellow who came aboard the *San Marco* with the ship's delegate last Saturday?"

"Yes."

"It's a natural," J.O.B. said with satisfaction.

"But there wasn't any trouble at the time," Stan offered. "You told me yourself that Vincent told you that they merely discussed a matter of overtime pay, and there wasn't any row or anything unpleasant."

"So *he's* innocent, and *Detrich* is innocent, and Oliver just killed himself!" J.O.B. barked. "Our dead friend was a fine man; he didn't have an enemy in the world except these damn dirty waterfront bums! He was loyal to me and to my company. He wouldn't have anything to do with that kind of scum. I know for a fact—I happened to see a report made by his former boss, the chief on board the *San Gabriel*—that Oliver once had an argument with the ship's delegate, and when the man became abusive Oliver knocked the fellow off his ship and he nearly drowned. They were out to get him, I tell you —and I'm going to track the killer or killers down and see that they all swing for it. The company I represent will set aside a fund of $200,000 to convict his murderers, and I'll see that they're hanged at San Quentin!"

He rose angrily and jerked his head toward the door.

"Come on," he said to Lloyd, Stan, and Syd Watterbury; "we're just wasting time here. When you've got anything to report," he added, addressing Clifford Kelly, "give me a ring. Maybe I'll have something to report first." He nodded and left the room.

Fifteen minutes later he was closeted in his own office with his brother, his son, and Syd. J.O.B. was still fulminating, raging and cursing.

Stan, thinking that he himself had more reasons to be concerned over Vince's death than his father, was disturbed by the latter's fury.

Lloyd leaned forward in his chair and rested his forearms on the edge of his brother's desk, fingers clasped.

"Listen," he said in his calm, well-modulated voice. "There's no need of your getting so wrought up about this. We're all in sympathy with you, and we're going to find out who killed young Oliver and see that the perpetrators of the crime are brought to justice——"

"I don't want any poor dope to swing for it," J.O.B. countered; "I want to get the principals who planned it—this man Detrich, and Dempsey——"

"Yes, yes; we understand all that. It will take time; you've got to expect that and be patient. After all, it's the district attorney's job to find the murderer or murderers; that's what he's elected for."

"You mean Dan Sheridan?"

"Yes."

"What d'you know about him?"

"Good man."

"What's he want? . . . 'S he political?"

"Probably. When they get to be the D.A. of a small county, they all expect political preferment."

"Let's find out." He turned to Stan. "Go over and see him this afternoon. Sound him out. He'd like to be governor, I presume; maybe senator sometime! Well, we'll make him governor if that's what he wants. Tell him so in so many words. We'll back him—every last one of us. But he's got to understand that he must pin this crime on some of those damned radical labor leaders. I want to see a few of them hanged by the neck and a lot more of 'em sent to jail. Get that over to him. If he's a sensible man, he'll see the light. Takes a potful of money to make a man governor or senator, but we've got the jack and can get the votes. Make him understand that we want some of these union labor leaders *hanged!*"

CHAPTER VIII

"She won't eat—won't take a thing," Frances Rutherford complained tearfully, "or see anybody. Just lies there in her room and doesn't seem to care whether she lives or dies. The nurses tell me she isn't in any particular pain, doesn't complain; it isn't grief she suffers from; it's shock—shock to her whole nervous system, and she doesn't get any worse or any better."

"What's the doctor's opinion?" asked Stan.

He was seated on the edge of his mother's bed, had breakfasted, and had come up from the dining room to give her a morning kiss before going off to his office. His father was away, had flown to

Washington the week before to discuss with Madame Perkins the threatening labor trouble that would loom on the Pacific Coast by the end of September when the contract between the unions and ship-owners came up for renewal. Stan had found his mother propped up in bed, supported by a mound of soft pillows and wearing a pretty silk negligee with a frilled and fluted lace cap upon her as yet undressed hair; her finished breakfast tray lay beside her on the bed. They had been discussing Daisy, whose condition had been a subject frequently upon their lips during the past four months. Now, to his question, Frances answered:

"Well, Stewart talks about psychosis—whatever that means. He called a specialist yesterday. They were very vague, used awful words that frightened me. The nurses are still feeding her intravenously, and they won't let me see her! They say she doesn't want to see me, doesn't want to see anybody! They say I might upset her! . . . Oh, Stan, Stan, I don't know what to do! It seems a terrible thing to me that a mother isn't allowed to see her own daughter! . . . I'm afraid, I'm terribly afraid that the shock of that poor boy's death has unhinged her mind!"

Stan patted her round bare arm reassuredly, but his own face was set and unsmiling.

Unaccountable, he was thinking, that his lovely little sister with her china-blue eyes and fly-away gold hair should remain helpless so long. In the beginning—for some weeks—there had been nights of horror when she had awakened screaming, roused from her lethargy when apparently the full consciousness of what had happened came upon her. She seemed to see the tragedy of that Sunday morning on board the *San Marco* in all its terrible details—the knives, the bloody hands, the stab after stab that had sent her sweetheart to his death. Nurses hurried to soothe her, opiates were administered, the hypodermic needle resorted to. Since then, on many a night, Stan had wakened suddenly, imagining he could hear those wild cries of terror ringing through the house. Mercifully that time had passed. Now Daisy lay in a stupor, growing weaker and thinner day by day, indicating fear or alarm only when something happened to distress her or hallucinations troubled her. In March she had been stricken; now it was September.

Her brother shook his head.

"I wish Dad were here," he said, drawing a deep breath. "I wish he hadn't gone away."

"Oh, so do I! I feel so lost without him. When do you expect him back?"

"Next week or the week after. You know how slowly things move in Washington. He may be there until the end of the month. . . . If it weren't Saturday," he continued, again upon a sigh, "I'd try to see Dr. Stewart this afternoon, but I don't suppose he'd be in his office."

"What could he tell you?"

"I don't know, but he might be more frank with me than with you. I'd like to have his opinion."

"I doubt if he has any."

A silence then, and presently Stan asked about Aunt Bessie.

His mother's troubled face grew graver still, a frown gathering between her eyes.

"Oh, that's another worry," she moaned. "Poor Bessie's very sick; they talk about pneumonia now. Good gracious! She's had a year of misery, and she might well want to leave it all behind her. But I don't believe a word about this pneumonia. I saw her only yesterday, and she was just about the same."

"Who told you?"

"Grandmère. She telephoned last night; was so upset. She says that Eleanor is of no help, and Lloyd shows no concern at all——"

"Nonsense. Perhaps he doesn't believe she's threatened with pneumonia either. We Rutherfords," he added grimly, "all seem to be under a curse. First Chris——"

He did not go on, but kissed his mother's soft, cool cheek, and left with the promise that he would try to see Dr. Stewart sometime during the day, but although he had not finished his sentence that began "First Chris——" the thought he had had at the time recurred to him as he walked downtown to his office.

It was a fine summer morning, with no hint of fog—unusual for early September—and though it would take him until ten o'clock to reach Wickwire, Rutherford & Company, he preferred to stretch his legs rather than ride a streetcar or drive there in his automobile.

"First Chris," he reflected as he strode along, "and secondly Eleanor, who acts like a lost soul; then Aunt Bessie, and next Vince, who surely was like a member of the family and would have been if . . . And now poor Daisy!

"I wonder what's happened to Uncle Reggie and Aunt Charmion? I haven't heard anyone speak of them in a long time except Dad, who said Reggie had written him he was having a lot of trouble with 'stoop' labor. Neither of them came up for Eleanor's wedding, nor for Grandmère's last Christmas breakfast. I suppose Chris's death must have hit them both pretty hard. This family seems to be a target for somebody's ill will!"

§ 2

It was a few minutes after ten when he reached his office. Miss Chambers, his secretary, brought him a basketful of mail; there was a message from Uncle Lloyd—he was, please, to call his office—another from Syd who wanted to speak to him as soon as he came in, still another from the district attorney of Alameda County, and a long night letter from his father in Washington. On good authority, J.O.B. wired, he understood the President planned to name a Maritime Commission which, when appointed, would be charged with settling all labor disputes. His father wished Stan to pass this information on to Percy Grant, Jim Ahearn, and Joe Halliday and tell them to sit tight and wait for the existing contracts to expire.

It was easier to dispose of Syd first, so Stan picked up the interoffice telephone.

"I'll be down to see you in five minutes," Syd told him.

"What's the matter with my coming up to see you?" Stan suggested.

"No, it's better for me to come down; we can talk better in your office—and don't answer any outside calls until I see you."

"The D.A.'s office in Alameda left word for me to ring them."

"Don't do it. Wait until I talk to you."

"My uncle wants me to call him. That all right?"

"Sure, I guess so, but don't say anything—you know—important. Your wire may be tapped."

"*What?*"

"Yes; we're in for a lot of trouble, and you might as well get set · for it."

"Okay."

"I'll be down in a few minutes."

Stan called Lloyd's office; got Miss Hodgins.

Mr. Rutherford had left for Sacramento that morning, she told him.

"He wants you to sign that affidavit you made about hearing somebody, the night of the wedding reception, say that one of the men running away was a person with a 'red beard and a bum eye.' Remember?"

"Yes, very well; I dictated it to you in your office."

"I've been holding it, waiting for you to drop in. Will you sign it if I send it over, and have it notarized?"

"Certainly."

"I'll send it over by messenger, and can you get it back to me this morning—or drop it in the mail so I can have it Monday?"

"Of course. What's Uncle got? A clue or something?"

"He didn't say. He just asked me if you'd signed it, and I was ashamed to tell him I had neglected to ask you to. May I send it over now?"

As he was talking, Syd came in and sat down on the other side of the desk and watched him with a fixed look until he hung up the receiver.

"Well, what's up?" Stan asked.

"They think they've got the men who killed Vincent. They've arrested Detrich, Dempsey, and a man named Kerrigan, all of whom had something to do with the Firemen's Union at the time of the murder. One of 'em is head of the outfit, I think Kelly said. At any rate, the D.A. has picked up a chap named Walters; arrested him in Brownsville, Texas; he was a wiper and also a member of the Firemen's Union. He'll testify, so Kelly says, that Detrich asked him to 'go on a job' which meant Detrich wanted him to kill or beat up somebody. Then Kerrigan—the ship's delegate who came to see Vincent with Dempsey the day before the murder—was arrested in Seattle. Evidently the police put the bee on him and got a confession. He's in custody now over in Oakland. All four of them, and a man named Muscowitz who's skipped the country, will be indicted for murder by the grand jury tomorrow. Well, now, where we must watch our step is that there's going to be a hell of a yell from the unions and they're going to claim a frame-up. That damn little squirt, Nate Jacobs, is back of it. A mass meeting is to be called next week at the Scottish Rite Auditorium, and Jacobs asserts there'll be seventeen thousand workers of the Bay region present. The hall can't possibly hold more than fifteen hundred! But there's going to be a lot of mud thrown. Here's a copy of the stuff he's putting out."

He handed Stanley a typewritten sheet of paper. It read:

What are the people of the United States going to do about these infamies? Scores of labor union members are railroaded to prison every year; some of them come out in a few years, but a great many of them are doomed to stay the rest of their lives unless a mighty effort is made to release them.

Appeals to the courts can be made, but justice is hard to get in cases like this one, especially in California, since millionaires can put District Attorney Dan Sheridan and his hand-picked judges into office. Mooney and Billings, proved innocent years ago, are still in prison; California courts refuse to turn them loose. The nine Modesto boys proved to be victims of a frame-up, but five of them are still prisoners and the other four are only out on parole.

Only when the people of California and the United States put *their own men* into office will these frame-ups stop. Labor and progressive people can and must put men into Dan Sheridan's place who will take orders from the people, not from shipowners and their brother millionaires.

Frame-ups and police violence will continue just as long as political parties controlled by millionaires run our courts, our city councils, our legislatures, our Congress, and our law-enforcement agencies. The beginnings of a People's Party already exist in labor's Non-Partisan League, the American Labor Party of New York State, the Farmer-Labor Party in Minnesota, the Commonwealth Federation in the state of Washington, and the People's Legislative Lobby in California. When these organizations take government out of the hands of the millionaires and put it into the hands of the people, then the frame-up victims will go free and frame-ups will end.

Stan studied the script, rubbing his chin.

"Did Jacobs write this?" he asked.

Syd shrugged. "Somebody did."

"Why don't they come right out and say 'Communist Party' instead of 'People's Party'? It's just flagrant propaganda! . . . Where did you get this?"

"Does it matter? It is being set up in print right now and will be distributed in pamphlet form by the thousands, one of which will be handed to every person attending that mass meeting at Scottish Rite Auditorium."

"It rather puts the finger on us, doesn't it?" Stan smiled ruefully. "I wonder who heard my father raving. Of course I don't believe a word of what they are trying to imply. Dan Sheridan is an honorable man with an impeccable record. We've helped him all we could —naturally—to track down the murder, but he made no requests of us except to ask us to carry the officers of the *San Marco* on our pay rolls for a while so's to keep them on hand in case he wished to call them as witnesses. They did not care as long as they got their monthly checks, and neither did we. . . . I think Dan Sheridan's done a swell job and doesn't deserve any such vilifying."

"There'll be a lot more mudslinging before this affair is ended," Syd observed. "Like you, I believe in Sheridan, but you can rest assured he wouldn't indict these men unless he was certain he can convict them.

"And one thing that will interest you! Ten minutes after I got through talking over the phone with Kelly, a representative of a detective agency we employ—I'd prefer you didn't know anything about this, its name, or who they are or anything about them—came round to see me, and just gave me this tip-off—not to say anything over the telephone which might be wrongly construed or that might give desirable information to the radicals——"

"Why," Stan exclaimed, cutting in sharply, "he must have been listening in when *you* were talking!"

"I don't know whether he was or wasn't, but I *do* know that this agency is looking after our interests and is protecting us. I just thought you'd like to be wise to the fact that when you're talking over the wire, somebody may be listening in. I'm going over our own personnel with a fine-tooth comb."

"I'd better have a talk with Kelly or Sheridan this afternoon," Stan observed after a moment's thought, "only I promised my mother . . ." With a frown he added: "Well, that can wait."

"Kelly, of course, asked for you when he phoned. Our operator inquired if I'd do, and he said okay."

"I think I ought to go over and see him just the same," Stan persisted. "I ought to find out what he knows——"

The door opened, and Miss Chambers came in and laid on his desk a long, legal-sized envelope bearing in its upper right-hand corner the name of "Poltney, Campbell, Rutherford & Hart."

"Oh yes," Stan acknowledged before she could speak. "I know what this is." He glanced at the clock on his desk top. It was after twelve.

"God Almighty, Syd," he cried, "we've been gassing a long time! I've got a pile of work to do—haven't even looked at my mail yet. . . . Miss Chambers! . . . Ask her to come in when you go out, will you, Syd? I'll see you Monday morning, or if there's anything important turns up, I'll phone you."

"Be careful," Syd warned, departing, as Miss Chambers came in.

"Is there a notary in the building?" he asked her. "I've got to sign this paper before I leave."

"I'm afraid . . ." the girl said doubtfully. "It's after twelve and a Saturday, and I think . . . However, I'll see and let you know."

Stan turned to his mail, sorting it with an impatient hand.

Those damn Reds, he was thinking, *trying to smear my father, his friends, and blackening the reputation of an honest man like Sheridan!*

He made an impatient spitting noise with his tongue and shuffled his letters, scowling at them angrily.

"That can wait—that can wait—and so can that, and that, and that——"

Mary Chambers came in.

"Our own notaries have all gone, and the one on the third floor didn't show up today. I telephoned Miss Hodgins, but their office is closed, too. However, there's a Miss Welch in the Pitcairn Building on Sutter Street who says she'll be there until one o'clock."

"Thanks; I'll go over at once."

He picked up the long envelope and stuffed it into an inside pocket.

"Hold that mail until Monday morning, will you, Miss Chambers? None of it is important. I'll get down early. And I wish you'd telephone the district attorney's office in Alameda and tell them that I . . . No; guess you'd better not. I'll phone myself after I'm through with Miss Welch and have a bite of lunch.

"Let's get rid of this damn affidavit first," he said to himself irritably, as he crowded into the already crowded elevator cage and dropped swiftly to the lobby floor.

§ 3

The corridor on the ground floor of the Pitcairn Building was lined with small business offices. The opaque glass door of one of these bore the legend: "Catherine Welch. Life Insurance. Loans. Notary Public."

Stan went in. A woman with short curly dark hair clustering about her head under a small hat sat at a desk, busily typing.

"Miss Welch?"

She raised her eyes, took him in with a swift glance, said with a pleased smile:

"Mr. Stanley Rutherford!"

An odd inflection in her voice made him look at her closely.

"You know me, hey?"

She smiled again, broader this time.

"Everybody knows who Mr. Stanley Rutherford is," she said.

A rather heavy-faced woman, he thought her, with a big nose, eyes set far apart, and a large mouth. Likable. Her smile was ingratiating.

"You've been expecting me?"

"No, someone—a girl telephoned. I presumed she was a clerk; she said her boss—well, she didn't say her boss exactly, but I thought that's what she meant; at any rate she said a man was coming in to sign something and wanted a notary. I told her I'd be in until one, and then, before I could ask anything further, she hung up. But I didn't expect *you*, Mr. Rutherford; I'm glad to meet you."

She half rose, extended her hand.

Stan took it and was aware of its warm clasp and friendliness. He returned her smile.

"It's a pleasure to know you, Miss Welch."

"Sit down," she invited. "What is it you wanted me to acknowledge? Will you need a witness?"

"I think not. It's just an affidavit, already drawn up."

He drew the envelope out of his pocket, broke its seal, and picked out the paper. He ran his eye over the typed statement before he handed it to her. He was aware she was watching him as he did so, and she met his eye with a broad smile as she accepted the document. They both smiled—Stan a little uncomfortably. He felt embarrassed.

"May I read it?" she asked, almost roguishly.

"Certainly."

She spread out the sheet on her desk and glanced through it with a slight puckering of her brows.

It was his turn to study her.

She was attractive—youthful in spite of her years—with a fine figure, curved slightly across the shoulders, large, beautifully shaped hands, and round firm breasts. A woman who had known many ups and downs, he decided, who depended on her own wit and charm and had lived among men—perhaps with them. She intrigued him.

He put his hat on a near-by chair and reached for his cigarette case while she concentrated on the brief document before her. He was mildly surprised that it should interest her. Usually a notary—the few with whom he had had dealings—perfunctorily witnessed his signature, scribbled down his or her name, affixed the date, stamped the paper with a seal, and collected fifty cents. But Miss Welch plainly was engrossed with what she read.

When she looked up, it was to smile once more—again with coquetry.

"May I smoke?" he asked, tapping a cigarette on the cover of his case.

"Assuredly."

"And will you have one?"

"Don't mind if I do."

He held his lighter to the tip of the cigarette between her rouged lips. She puffed on the blaze, inhaled and blew out the smoke in a long upward spiral, controlling amusement with visible effort.

"So you want to sign this?" she asked with an arch look.

"Yes, why not? My uncle asked me to, and to have it back in his office today. I don't know what he wants it for, but I *did* hear somebody say that he thought the man who threw the bomb had a red beard and a bum eye."

"You don't know exactly who said it?"

"No, of course not."

He frowned. Why was she quizzing him?

She reached out and touched his arm lightly and gave him the full benefit of her smile—a big smile with two deep parallel parentheses on either side her wide mouth.

"You mustn't think me impertinent," she said, "but do you know Rory O'Brien?"

"Rory O'Brien! No, I've never seen the man!"

"That describes him."

"What does?"

" 'A man with a red beard and a bum eye.' "

He met her look with a level one.

"Do you suppose *he* threw that bomb?" he asked.

"How should I know?"

"If he had a red beard and a bum eye, it must have been him."

"There aren't many men with a red beard and a bum eye," she admitted. She was very easy and friendly, almost flirtatious.

"You know him?"

"Very well."

"Why should he have done a thing like that? What prompted him? Did he know the misery he was going to cause? My aunt, Mrs. Rutherford, broke her hip that night and has been very ill ever since. I suppose he thinks he has a grudge against us, or a grievance?"

"I didn't say I thought he did it. I just wondered whether or not you knew him and were trying to identify him as the man who threw the bomb."

"You mean—make a false affidavit?"

"Not necessarily. Many things are laid at Mr. O'Brien's door for which he is in no way responsible."

"What kind of a man is he?"

"One of the best. Don't judge him by his looks; he was badly burned once—at sea. He's a great humanitarian."

"He couldn't be—if he threw that bomb."

"You're jumping at conclusions, aren't you, Mr. Rutherford? Presumably your uncle would like to connect him with what occurred."

"He hasn't told me so. He hasn't mentioned Rory O'Brien's name in connection with the matter. My uncle's ways are dark and mysterious."

"Like the 'heathen Chinee'?"

"Well, I don't know what use he wishes to make of that affidavit, but I certainly can swear to the statement."

"Okay. Sign here."

He bent over to write his name and was aware of her femininity. There was no fragrance about her exactly, no perfume, but she exhaled something that caught at his senses. She added her own name and date, then stamped the paper.

"There you are," she said laughingly.

"Fifty cents?"

"Make it that, or five dollars."

"I'd rather take you out to lunch," he said, putting the silver coin on the corner of the desk.

"Oh, that would be amusing," she caroled; "Mr. Stanley Rutherford taking Caddie Welch out to lunch!" She laughed again, enjoying her mirth.

"I don't understand," Stan said, puzzled. "What would be so funny about it?"

"Well . . . You know I'd like to accept," she told him, firming her mouth, "only I have a date."

"Presumably I must eat alone," he said regretfully, reaching for his hat. "Anyway I have to take a taxi and keep an early appointment across the Bay."

"With Mr. Dan Sheridan of Alameda?" she asked with jeering good humor.

The pleasant look left his face; he stared at her, brows thickening.

"Oh, I know all about you, Mr. Rutherford," she went on as he did not speak; "and I know just why you want to see Mr. Sheridan or his assistant, Cliff Kelly. It's about those unfortunate boys they are trying to railroad to the gallows."

Stan held his peace, fearing to say something injudicious.

"Oh, now listen," Caddie Welch continued, "don't get huffy with me. There's two sides of a question—and I don't believe that any of those boys had anything to do with that murder. If I tell you I know for a fact that Kerrigan, whom the police picked up in Seattle, was given the third degree, padlocked to a chair, and quizzed by the cops for two days and nights running, without allowing him a wink of sleep or letting him see an attorney, until he finally broke down and signed a 'confession,' you wouldn't believe me, would you?"

"Certainly not!"

"It's a fact, just the same; he's over in a hospital in Oakland right this minute, a physical wreck, running a temperature, and frightened out of his wits—but not so frightened as not to repudiate promptly the confession he signed. A lawyer finally was permitted to see him, and the first thing poor Kerrigan did, when he knew a friend was standing by him, was to deny everything——

"But look who's here!" she interrupted herself to say; "here's the man who's befriending him; he can tell you more about it than I can."

The door had opened, and as Stan looked up he saw Nate Jacobs.

"Oh," he muttered, rising at once.

"Nate," said Caddie Welch, "you know Stanley Rutherford."

"I think we met a couple of years ago," the young attorney said, putting out his hand. Stan accepted it, but he felt now that the quicker he was free of the company of these two the better.

"I think I'll run along," he said stiffly.

"No, no," Caddie Welch protested. She turned to Nate. "Mr. Rutherford has just asked me to go to lunch with him; I told him I had a date, but we can include him, can't we?"

"Why not? Come along," Nate concurred cordially.

"Sorry, it's impossible." Stan smiled perfunctorily.

"He's going over to see Sheridan in Alameda this afternoon," Caddie said, "and I thought it might do him a lot of good if he knew some of the facts about this frame-up and got it from some of us who know what's going on."

A quick glance passed between the two men, Stan's cold and inimical, Nate's easy and good-natured.

"Come on," he urged.

"I think not."

"Suit yourself," Nate told him; "but you're like all the rest of your class; you only hear one side of a case; you refuse to hear the other; you shut your ears and decline to listen to people who don't agree with you. That's what makes beefs along the waterfront; that's what makes strikes—and that's what's going to tie up the waterfront next month."

His words caught Stan's interest. Tie up the waterfront! This was news. He had thought that that was what the shipowners secretly planned to do; two or three times his father had spoken of it. Perhaps the unions . . . ? He might learn something—and without having to tap wires! He hesitated.

"Oh, come along, Mr. Rutherford. Don't be so standoffish. We'll go down to a little restaurant at the foot of California Street; they have booths there, and we can talk things over—a lot of things. Let your friend, Dan Sheridan, wait. I assure you, you can find out a lot more from us than from him."

"You won't incriminate yourself?" Stan asked, weakening. "I might use it against you!"

"We'll take a chance. Come on."

§ 4

"I'm not going to waste time discussing this ship murder case," the young lawyer began when they had established themselves in one of the booths of the restaurant and were waiting for drinks and their food. "I'm not going to waste time discussing it," he repeated. "They will try those boys sometime this fall, and Sheridan will do his damnedest to get them hanged, but, believe me, they're innocent. I don't know who murdered Oliver, but I'm as certain as I'm sitting here that Detrich, Dempsey, and Kerrigan had nothing to do with it. Let's skip it. You follow the trial; go over to the courthouse and watch Sheridan's tactics. Just why does he want to pin the crime on these particular men? Because they belong to the Firemen's Union, part of the Maritime Federation of the Pacific, and the contract between the shipowners and the unions comes up for renewal the end of this month. The case won't be settled then, and it won't be settled for some time. If Sheridan can implicate these union men, he'll arouse public sympathy and make it tough for the unions to get their just demands. It's as clear as day! A frame-up—a rotten, damnable frame-up—just as sending those boys accused of carrying dynamite to San Quentin and Folsom was a frame-up."

"Why, I thought that was a clear-cut finished case!" Stan exclaimed. "It was proved, wasn't it, that they were illegally in possession of dynamite and were on their way to blow up a rooming house in which some strikebreakers were lodged?"

"That's what *you* think—and what most people believe. But I'll give you some brand-new information that will surprise you.

"A man by the name of Hal Mosher was a stool pigeon in the employ of the Occidental Oil Company. He became the prosecution's star witness and testified that he was one of a party who went to Modesto with the definite intention of blowing up Occidental Oil property. Well, the prosecution got a conviction all right and the men went to prison, some of them with a sentence of five years.

"It was on the basis of Mosher's testimony that the oil-tanker strike of last year was broken, but all he got for his trouble was a five-dollar-a-day job in a gasoline station in Culver City, while another guy who participated in the frame-up—a dick by the name of Scanlon—was handsomely rewarded. Mosher got sore. He complained of his treatment to friends of the men who had been jailed. They encouraged him to talk and finally asked him to a card party at one of their homes, where they persuaded him again to recite his grievances. There were five persons in the room at the time, and three more were clinging to the rafters of the attic just above; these three were equipped with dictaphone paraphernalia; everything Mosher said was recorded and later transcribed onto records—eighteen of them! Mosher stated he had been hired by the Occidental Oil, that he had been supplied with the sticks of dynamite and had placed them in the two automobiles the boys were going to use, and that nobody but himself and Scanlon knew that they were there. Then he urged them all to go to Modesto, where they were arrested. He admitted he had perjured himself at the insistence of the district attorney, and that's just what's going to happen to Walters and Kerrigan—again at the 'insistence of the district attorney.'"

"I don't believe it!" Stan said with heat. He stopped, reminding himself he must keep his temper if he was to learn just what the strike leaders intended to do about the contract with the shipowners.

"I remember my father and my uncle discussing that case," he went on in a calmer tone; "they both said that the district attorney branded the charges as 'wholly and completely false.' All evidence presented at the trial, he said, was corroborated; the same charges of perjury were made at the time and were not substantiated."

"Well, let's not get excited about that affair," Caddie Welch interjected; "we'll see what happens across the Bay, but I'll bet you you'll find out, Mr. Rutherford, that a lot of pressure will be put on those witnesses Dan Sheridan has turned up. We'll fight all we can. Nate, here, has offered to defend them."

Stan shrugged indifferently.

"When this contract comes up for renewal," he said, "I don't see how the longshoremen have a leg to stand on, since the shipowners have agreed to submit everything to arbitration."

"The unions," Jacobs replied, "won't agree to arbitrate, because there are some questions which are not arbitrable."

"The employers have signified their willingness to confer with your committee," Stan countered, "and notified the longshoremen to that effect as long ago as last July. They've not replied. Sixty days before the contract expired both sides were to get together and discuss terms which would be mutually agreeable."

"The committee believes that fair negotiations and conciliation might obviate the necessity for arbitration," Jacobs stated.

"I have failed to observe," Stan said, "any indication on the part of labor or the committee representing the unions to negotiate fairly or be conciliated. They resort by preference to highhanded murder as the easiest way to achieve their ends!"

"Oh, come, come," Caddie Welch interposed, "that sort of talk won't get us anywhere!"

"Of course you won't agree that there are fundamental principles not open to arbitration," Nate Jacobs said.

"Certainly I won't agree," Stan answered; "the employers are paying the longshoremen the highest hourly wage anywhere in the world, and have given them a six-hour day——"

"Only because they were forced to!" Nate interposed.

"It was agreed," Stan continued, ignoring the interruption, "that all differences between the employers and longshoremen should be referred to a Labor Relations Committee in each port; if this failed, then the differences were to be submitted to an arbitrator, and his decision was to be final. Rory O'Brien himself signed that agreement in Judge Shotwell's office last April. All provisions of the National Longshoremen's Board's award, renewed by mutual agreement a year ago, were okayed.

"Please let me finish," he said, lifting a hand as Nate started to speak. "Judge Shotwell was appointed arbitrator by the Secretary of Labor. When the question of hot cargo came before him, what happened? He decided that the unions had no right to refuse to work or stop work merely because they did not care to handle cargo they declared 'hot.' The unions have ignored his ruling. Since Rory O'Brien, representing the longshoremen, signed that agreement, there have literally been hundreds of unlawful stoppages of work in this port alone, 'quickies' you call them, or job action, tying up ships from a few days to weeks and months. These job actions have been openly approved by your own Maritime Federation in a published bulletin in which it is asserted that 'quickies' are justifiable as a means of gaining concessions not specified in the agreements.

"May I continue?" Stan asked as his companions, now silent, watched him with condescending amusement. "I'd like to get this off my chest while I'm thinking clearly.

"A year ago," he proceeded, "the Waterfront Employers appeared before the arbitrator and asked that mutual penalties be established for all parties concerned. The longshoremen refused to agree to this. The employers also petitioned to have disputes with the sailors referred to the Labor Relations Board. The sailors likewise refused. The shipowners have appealed to the Federal Government; they have been told the Government is powerless. Very well, the time for the renewal of the agreement signed last September comes up the end of this month. We can't go on as things are now. Schedules of vessels have been seriously interrupted, and traffic and cargo diverted to their destinations by rail and truck. Where do you fellows come off if all merchandise is shipped by rail and truck?

"Let me state the position of the employers, and then I'm through," Stan begged as he paused for breath. "The shipowners claim first the right to select their own employees; second, the right to expect a continuance of work free from strikes and stoppages; lastly, the right to expect a fair day's work for which they are willing to pay top wages. They want no more slow-downs, or pilfering and stealing, which are ten times worse than ever before. Do these demands seem reasonable?"

Nate Jacobs smiled and tapped off the ash from his cigarette.

"You put up a good talk, Mr. Rutherford—I'll say that for you—but you don't speak for all the shipowners; I'm not convinced they are as sincere as, I am sure, you are. They are a crooked bunch, if you'll excuse my frankness. It is true, last July the shipowners *did* serve notice on the unions that the contract now up for renewal required readjustment. Why? Because they considered wages too high and planned to reduce them in defiance of those established by the President's appointed board——"

"That's a damn lie!" Stan cried. "The shipowners have no such intention. I'm sure of it. If there is a question of wages, let it be submitted to arbitration."

Jacobs shrugged, dismissing the point with a careless gesture.

"Perhaps wages can be adjusted that way," he said, "but there are certain things which cannot. Take the matter of hot cargo. I don't care what agreement Rory signed. You employers are trying to prevent our unions from assisting fellow workers in labor trouble. Look," he said. He drew from an inner pocket a folded newspaper. Stan saw it was a copy of the *Pacific Coast Longshoreman*. "See," Nate invited; "glance your eye over that editorial. I wrote it."

He handed the paper across the table. It read:

Arbitration has its values and its uses, but there are matters which strictly are not arbitratable. In our estimation, support for sister locals in the association in a labor trouble is one of them.

Stan met Jacobs' eye.

"You say 'in the association,' " he said; "what about the longshore-men in British Columbia who do not belong to your association, and though they do not, you refuse to handle any cargo carried in American vessels going to or coming from Vancouver? One ship was tied up here for two months last year because the longshoremen would not unload her."

"Perhaps," Nate answered with his easy smile; "but we espoused the cause of the striking Canadian longshoremen because they're workers."

"The shipowners have no authority to deal either with the employers or the longshoremen in British Columbia," Stan returned.

"Too bad," Nate said mildly. "The workers' strength lies not only in union in the United States, but in union the world over."

"In other words, you want the world run by the workers. That's communism, isn't it?"

Again Nate smiled.

"Read on," he urged, indicating the paper.

The Shotwell award on handling "hot cargo" is loaded with dynamite for our organization.

It is not difficult to conceive that cases may arise where our own union may be compelled, by obeying such a mandate, to act as strikebreakers against a sister local. There are some things more important than arbitrators and awards.

"In other words," Stan challenged, "the 'some things' are more important to your unions than their solemn pledge to the Government of the United States and to their employers? Yet you expect us to be bound by agreements which you yourselves disregard at will!

"I assure you," he continued, his voice rising, "the shipowners have no quarrel with responsible union labor. We have recognized and accepted unionization of our employees and have unanimously offered to continue our agreements—or make a fresh adjustment of terms through an arbitrator—for another year. But for you fellows deliberately to violate your contracts with us in an attempt to use us to force the unionization of other industries and ports on other seaboards is beyond the bounds of reason—and we will not do it!

When you say that the employers are trying to use the longshoremen and the seamen as 'strikebreakers,' it is just damn outright misrepresentation."

"Oh, let's have a drink," broke in Caddie; "I'm dry."

"Just a minute," Stan began; then, catching her eye, he grinned, said, "Sure, go ahead. I'll have scotch. But I'd like to find out one or two things from Mr. Jacobs before we stop. Mind if I ask a couple of questions?"

"Shoot."

"What do your unions want? Are you able to speak for them?"

"Well, I'm pretty close to Rory, and he knows what he's after. The men believe in him and will stand back of him."

"Okay. Then what does Mr. O'Brien want before he'll sign an agreement?"

"Increased wages, decreased hours, control of hiring."

Stan drew a deep breath, held it a moment in exasperation before he continued:

"We've been paying both the licensed and unlicensed personnel on our ships the highest wage anywhere in the world. We've been paying the longshoremen tops as well. The question of wages and hours can be adjusted by arbitration, as I have said, but we must have a new understanding regarding the matter of hiring. The unions have complete control of it now, and they have put into operation a so-called rotation system of assigning men to jobs, the idea being—obviously—that all longshoremen and sailors will get a piece of the cake. That takes away from the shipowners the right to select the men they believe most competent or to employ those best fitted for the job. They also want the right of keeping good men, not having them rotated merely to comply with a mechanical system which classifies all men—the fit and the unfit—as the same. And most certainly the shipowners cannot be dictated to in the selection of their masters, mates, and engineers.

"Why," Stan rushed on, excitement gathering, "the officers are the shipowners' executives on the high seas. We are responsible under Federal laws for the safety of the lives and property on board our ships, and we cannot countenance any interference with the men we choose."

"Oh," said Caddie, "let's have another drink."

Nate Jacobs glanced at his wrist watch.

"Sorry, I can't join you," he said; "I've a date at three. I'll pay the check."

"Oh no, no," Stan protested; "I asked Miss Welch to lunch with me and you were included."

"Well," said Nate, collecting his briefcase and reaching for his hat, "you pay the next time. Keep Caddie company. I really must run, and I'll settle at the desk."

"We'll have luncheon together soon again," Stan told him. "I've enjoyed exchanging differences of opinion."

"Good business, as long as you don't get sore. Fun to argue. So long," he said, and then in the aisle he paused, waved his hat, smiled, added:

"Don't forget to give my regards to Dan Sheridan!"

"Clever," Caddie observed, sipping her drink after he had gone; "and you certainly gave him back as much as you got. I didn't know you were that good!"

She smiled archly at him, and he warmed to her company. She was amusing herself with him, but he did not care.

"Oh well," he said, settling back comfortably, "I'm afraid I get too excited when I argue. You should hear my uncle Lloyd addressing a jury or a judge. He's as calm as a summer's day; nothing ruffles him. He presents his case with such deadly composure that, listening to him, you get frightened. You feel as if he has a knife up his sleeve and is suddenly going to stab you."

"Like what happened to Vincent Oliver, hey? Whoever killed him, those men Sheridan's trying to send to the gallows had nothing to do with it."

A shadow darkened Stan's face.

"I don't know whether or not you know it, but Vincent Oliver was engaged to my sister. They were to have been married last June."

"Oh, I *didn't* know!" There was instant sympathy in Caddie's voice.

"I didn't, didn't know," she repeated. She reached out and touched his sleeve. "I'm very sorry."

"Maybe you'll understand now," he said, "why we're so keen to find out who murdered him. He was one of us. We all liked him; I think I could use a stronger word. He saved my cousin's life in Culebra Bay—that's down off the coast of Mexico—and he saved three others' lives very much at the risk of his own."

"Tell me," Caddie urged, sobered.

"Well . . ."

It was some time before he completed the story, and drinks came, had been finished, and fresh rounds had taken their place. He had not been conscious of how or when they had arrived or when they had been drunk, or of the passing minutes as the hour hand of the clock above the bar slipped to three and then to four and on to five.

It was very pleasant sitting there talking to this attractive companion. They returned to the mounting struggle between employers and workers in the city, and Caddie's even-tempered observations did not irritate him the way Nate Jacobs' assertive pronouncements had. Although he differed with her about almost everything, she was disarming in expressing her opinions.

"The laboring man has had a tough time of it from the beginning of things," she said; "he's always been exploited and taken advantage of by the employers. If you'll notice, every labor board and every arbitrator who has sat in judgment in this city to settle a dispute has invariably given the worker more than the employer would have voluntarily conceded. It wasn't so many years ago that the Union Iron Works paid Chinamen ten cents a day for hammering off old paint from the sides of vessels under repair. Huntington built his transcontinental railroads by coolie labor, and in early days New England textile mills had whipping posts for the kids they employed, and heaven knows what iniquities have been perpetrated in garment sweatshops. Seligmann, who was boss of the Tex-Mex pecan shellers, once complained that 'they eat too many pecans' when he was paying them a nickel an hour. Labor has always had to fight for its rights and fight for a living wage——"

"By what methods?" Stan interrupted.

"Oh, frequently by lawlessness and violence. I'm not contending that labor has won recognition with clean hands, but it's the worker who creates wealth, not the employer."

"Why, Caddie," Stan protested, "you can't say that! What would the worker be unless there was someone to employ him? If labor continues demanding more and more, employers will be driven to the wall and there won't be any more."

"Then the workers will take over."

"And be paid by whom?"

"The State."

"That's rank communism!"

"Perhaps; I believe in it."

"You can't!"

"Isn't there a respectable divergency of opinion there? Haven't I a right to believe in a State owned and operated by the workers?"

"Yes, yes, of course," Stan admitted, staggered by such a question from so likable and intelligent a person. "Then you're a Communist?"

"I'm not saying," she replied, "but if you ask me to have one more drink, I'll not refuse!"

Her words brought him to a sharp realization of the passing time. He was amazed to see that it was half past five!

"Surely; let's have another. Waiter!"

Where had the afternoon flown to? What had happened to his plans for Alameda, and to his call on Dr. Stewart?

Now he was uncomfortably aware of the liquor he had drunk, and passed his hand over his face, wiping his mouth.

But the hours had not been wasted. This woman . . . He had never met anyone more pleasant, more enjoyable!

"It's awfully late," he said.

"It's been fun, hasn't it?"

"Oh sure; lots of fun. It's been great getting to know you."

"And getting to know *you*."

"I've learned a lot."

"I told you you would."

"But I'm not convinced. I think you and your friend Jacobs are all haywire. You just want to make trouble."

"I've heard that before."

"So have I, and I can see now how true it is."

"Let's finish this and go," she suggested.

Outside in the air Stan was again conscious of the alcohol he had consumed, but he was very happy.

He slipped his hand beneath Caddie's arm and squeezed its round hard firmness. She was delightful to him. An essence about her tugged at his senses; he had noticed it before—when he had bent over her in her office. They walked along slowly, not talking now, but comfortably in step, aware of each other's nearness.

I'm being a fool, Stan said to himself.

He shook the thought from him. It was too pleasant being with this woman. He did not care whether she was a Communist or not; he liked her.

"I suppose this is very reprehensible," he said after a while.

"What is?"

"Being with you, and—and a little drunk!" He laughed carelessly.

"I don't think it's reprehensible to be with me, and I don't think you're drunk."

He hugged her arm. Presently she remarked:

"You're a great discovery."

"Discovery?"

"Yes—finding you to be as nice as you are."

"Think I'm nice?"

"Very."

"I think you are, too."

This was silly talk. He was just plain drunk. He'd say good-by at the next corner and board a streetcar. Yet he did not want to. He walked another block with her.

"Where do you live?" he asked.

"On Pine Street. It's only a little way. Why don't you find out where I am, so you'll know where to go when you come to see me?"

"Am I going to see you?"

"Don't you want to?"

"Sure, of course."

This was wrong—all wrong. He didn't care whether what she had said was meant to be an invitation for more intimate relations or not. He had no intention of going to see her or of ever meeting her again.

She lived in an unpretentious apartment house with brass-covered letter boxes on one side of the shallow tiled entrance and a row of bells for the tenants' names on the other. She slid her key into the lock and opened the glass-paneled door curtained inside by a shirred strip of faded silk. Within was a small foyer made ugly by some garish red hangings and a shabby bronze elevator cage.

"I think I'd better leave you here," he said.

"Won't you come up and have one more drink?"

"I think I'd better not."

"Oh, come on."

Obediently he entered the lift as Caddie held back its sliding door for him. They got out on the fifth floor, and she unlocked another door—"5-A."

Inside it was almost stifling. The small apartment was unaired and smelled of something he could not place at first. Then he recognized what it was: Caddie! It was neither scent nor fragrance, but a curious emanation which exhaled from her which he found oddly pleasing and exciting.

"Oh, it's suffocating in here," she cried.

She pushed past him in the narrow hallway and half raised a window in the room beyond.

"Throw your hat anywhere," she called to him; "I'll get the drinks."

The sitting room he entered was crowded with furniture and furnishings. There were long, tasseled drapes at the windows, with lace curtains inside, some large overstuffed chairs, and a stiff-backed sofa with curving arms, plush pillows at either end; there was a mantel over a false fireplace, and this and a number of tables, taborets, and wall cabinets were cluttered with knickknacks, ornaments, and souvenirs—souvenirs by the score!—while on the wall hung gaudy colored chromos in gilt frames and behind the sofa a tawdry piece of tapestry; on stands in the corners stood artificial ferns, and at the base of the mantel squatted a stone bulldog almost life-sized.

He went to the window, pushed it up as far as it would go, and breathed deep of the fresh air outside. His head was buzzing. Night fog was coming in; torn scarves of it were trailing over the roof-tops.

This is all wrong, he thought again and once more stilled his conscience.

What was he doing here? An impossible room and an impossible hostess!

He fumbled for a cigarette and was looking for a match when

Caddie came in with a tray of glasses, a siphon bottle and one of whisky.

"Over there in that china pig," she said, indicating where the matches were. "I'm sorry," she continued, "I haven't any ice." She placed the tray upon the seat of one of the chairs, cleared a small table, set the tray upon it.

"Doesn't matter," he said thickly. "I'll just have a swallow and be on my way. It's late."

"Say when." She poured the whisky. It was a stiff portion, and he watched her dully as she squirted water into the tumbler.

He was revolted. He didn't want another drink; he didn't like the woman who was pouring it; he didn't like the room or the situation in which he found himself!

She had removed her hat and slipped off her jacket. He noticed her snug silk waist and how trimly it was tucked inside the band of her skirt. She shook her curls and held out her glass.

"Well, here's looking at you, Stan," she said with her big smile, "and here's to better acquaintance."

He touched his glass to hers and drained some of the drink. It was warm and frightfully strong.

"God, that's p-powerful!" he gagged and set down the glass.

"No more?"

"No, no—heavens, no! I've got to go. It's awfully late."

"One more swallow," she urged.

"I couldn't."

She raised her own glass to her lips and half emptied it.

"That was your share," she told him and smiled her big smile again.

Then she sobered, caught him by the lapel of his coat, stood close, looking up into his face.

"I like you," she said.

"I like *you*," he repeated.

They remained so a moment; then, with a quick movement, she caught him about the neck with a forearm and pulled his lips down to hers.

"Well," he managed, disengaging himself and unconsciously wiping the lipstick from his mouth, "I'll be seeing you."

"Call me up sometime soon, will you, Stan? We'll have lunch together. My name's in the book, you know."

"Sure, I'll do that."

"Soon?"

"Yes, soon."

"We can talk some more."

"That'll be fine."

He picked up his hat. She went to the door with him, opened it.

"I like you," she told him again.

"Good," he said; "I like you, too."

§ 5

Although there was a vacant seat on the dummy of the cable car,
he stood on the step, clinging to a stanchion so that the night wind,
laden with fog, would blow in his face. He was aware of a great
dissatisfaction with himself, but he would not think about the afternoon. He was concerned about his mother now, conscious she would
have been expecting him for some time, and he did not want her to
suspect he had been drinking.

When he reached home he let himself in noiselessly with his latchkey and mounted quietly to his bedroom, deciding he would shower,
soak thoroughly, then dress even if dinner was kept waiting. But the
roaring noise of the water brought his mother to his door.

"Stan! Stan!"

"Hey, wait a minute."

He turned off the faucet, stuck out his head from behind the
shower curtain. The bathroom door had remained open.

"What is it?"

"Oh, Stan, Stan!" she cried. "Aunt Bessie is awfully sick. They
don't expect her to live!"

"Well," he said, shocked, "I'll be with you in a jiffy."

§ 6

Mrs. Lloyd Rutherford died at four o'clock the next morning.

CHAPTER IX

REGGIE AND CHARMION BAXTER came up from the country for the funeral. J.O.B. was held in Washington, unable to secure plane reservations, but the rest of the family was present. Not Daisy, of course; she had begun to mutter and moan alarmingly now, but otherwise showed no change. Her nurses continued to hover over her night and day. Bessie's sudden death and her daughter's unhappy state had all but crushed Frances.

The Rutherfords arrived at the church in deep mourning, Lloyd looking tragic with a colorless face beneath his snowy tight-crimped hair. He seemed, Stan thought, to have aged many years in the last two days. Grandmère carried herself with cold dignity and reserve; her white wig, carefully dressed, was surmounted by a black bonnet trimmed with jet, and from this dangled a black veil bordered by a deep black band. Eleanor, tall, regal, strikingly beautiful in her somber, well-fitting tailored suit, reflected something of her grandmother's bearing and steely composure. Stan's mother and Charmion, both swathed in sable, clung together, the former sniveling unhappily during the service, the latter holding her black-gloved hand between her own, patting it in sympathy.

The great church was crowded with friends; flowers were lavish, their heavy scent stifling; Bishop Boggs intoned the ritual in well-modulated tones; the music was beautiful.

It had been arranged that, in following the hearse to the cemetery, the women should ride in one limousine, the men in another. Up until the last minute they had hoped J.O.B. would be with them, but the wire explaining his delay had reached his brother only that morning.

Sitting on one of the jump seats of the car half facing his uncle, Stan was struck afresh with the man's pallor. The dignified attorney so widely known and respected was, after all, so his nephew reflected, getting on in years. Reggie too had aged—grown paunchy, balder, more careworn. The atmosphere within the car was strained and depressing, Lloyd looking out of one window and Reggie out of the other, no one speaking.

To relieve the silence, Stan asked:

"How are things down your way, Uncle Reg? Having any trouble with the Okies? Many of 'em drift up to Visalia?"

Reggie adjusted his weight against the cushions at his back, widened his eyes in a stare before answering.

"Do they? Oh, you bet your life. We're having a devil of a time. I'm sure I don't know what we California farmers are going to do."

"How do you mean?"

"Every labor union in the state is after the farmer. Each one wants recognition. First it's the teamsters; then it's another local belonging to the A. F. of L.; now it's a damned communistic outfit. They tell us that everything we own on wheels must be unionized; we must have only union labor in our dairies, only union men can harvest our hay, our sheep can be sheared only by union shearers and our wool packed only in union bags; otherwise our produce is declared hot, and the longshoremen, the drayers, and the retailers won't handle it."

"It's a holdup, isn't it?" Stan prompted.

"Holdup is right," Reggie went on; "but it's the Okies who are causing us the most trouble; they're just driving us off our farms and driving us out of the state. Thousands of these homeless vagabonds and their families pour into the state. They come from Oklahoma, Missouri, Texas—from the dust bowl, and they all want jobs. There's too many of 'em. We can hire some at full time and pay 'em at a rate of two dollars a day, or if they prefer to divide the work, we'll divide the pay. They fight among themselves. Along come the Communists. They organize those who can't get jobs, declare a strike, and prevent those who have them from working. We send a sheriff after them, and of course there's trouble. An agent of the American Civil Liberties Union comes to investigate; we don't like the agent, so we take him for a ride into the desert and leave him there."

"Be a good thing for the country if we could take all the Communists into the desert and leave them there," Stan said.

"But think what we're up against!" Reggie continued, warming to a recital of his grievances. "These migratory workers and their ragged, half-starved families are welcomed at the border by agencies of the Federal Government, who give them money, groceries, comfortable living quarters. They are not entitled to state or county relief; they have to remain in California a year before they get that. The Government builds camps for them, dozens of 'em, with running water, hot and cold shower baths, recreation halls; they have music, dancing, and movies. Our County Fair Grounds have been turned into an Okie playground, and naturally the Okies think it's pretty soft. Listen. This year I ran short of cotton pickers, tried my damnedest to get some; there were none to be had. Why? Because they are being supported by the Government and didn't want work. By the end of one year they are allowed to vote in this state, and of course they vote for a governor and a legislature who will keep 'em on relief."

"You're quite right," Lloyd agreed with a nod of confirmation.

Stan was pleased his interest had been aroused, and he was about to prod Reggie further, but the latter needed no urging. He was too full of bitterness, and it was moving and pathetic as well to see how, in his cumbersome, awkward way, he gave vent to it.

"I tell you, Lloyd, we don't want these people," he proceeded, edging himself farther forward in his seat to give more emphasis to his words; "they ought to be sent back to where they came from. They aren't our business! What we need in this state is a peon class. We've always had one—until these damn Okies came pouring in on us. We've had Chinese, Mexicans, Filipinos, Japs, and we sowed and plowed and cultivated our orchards and acres believing we were always going to have them. Such people never kicked. They were glad to work and were satisfied with what we paid them. It's only since this white trash came here that there's been trouble. Why, there's a thousand families parked in Tulare County right now, two thousand in Kings County, fifteen hundred in Kern County, and so on. Two hundred and fifty thousand of 'em all together!

"There's no sense in the way we're trying to run things," he went on, a certain fluency coming to him as he grew more earnest. "I have a thousand acres in oranges farther south; part of the crop I sell to the Government at a certain fixed price on condition I let another part rot on the ground, while a third part I send to market—if the unions let me!—and then I'm expected to make expenses! It drives you crazy!"

"What can you do?" Stan asked.

"Well, we're trying to get together—all the farmers in the state; we're trying to form an organization called the Associated Farmers. We hope to put an end to labor racketeering, stop the Communists, maintain the open shop, and see that the law's enforced and there's no more disorder. We've spent three million dollars in the past two years putting up tent platforms and shacks for the migratory pickers and cannery workers. It's this damn rascal Rory O'Brien who's causing us most of our grief."

"Our old friend Rory again," Stan said.

"Seems he's at the bottom of every labor trouble," Lloyd observed.

"Well, he *is!*" Reggie declared. "There's no doubt he's a Communist; he's surrounded by Communists, and he uses communistic methods. He doesn't want to settle anything. He's out to knife the wage system. He doesn't *want* it to work. His business is to see it works badly. He likes to get folks fighting. The contented worker is his despair. 'Boring from within,' they call it. By gravy, I'd like to bore *him* from within!"

Stan laughed.

"I don't know what you can do about him," Lloyd said. "He's protected by law unless it can be proved he believes in the overthrow of this Government by force and violence. If he doesn't believe it, you can't shut him up or jail him just because he's a Communist."

"He *is* a Communist, isn't he?" Reggie demanded.

"I don't know; he acts like one."

"Anyway, he's an alien—and ought to be deported."

"He may be an alien; he may not. My guess is that he has as much right to be in this country as a lot of the rest of us. Many of our forbears were aliens, and all of us were emigrants once. . . . Did you ever stop to think, Reggie," he diverged to say, "of some of the inconsistencies of our law? For instance—though it is unlawful for an employer to black-list a worker because he's union, it is perfectly lawful for workers to boycott an employer because he is anti-union."

"You're too deep for me, Lloyd. I know what I'm up against, and

I don't see any way out. Some old malcontent down there in Visalia was making a radical talk one evening in the high school; he said we farmers ought to give a few acres away to each dust-bowler. How ridiculous! It takes money to operate a farm—even ten acres. Takes more money in California than elsewhere. We have to do all our own irrigating and cultivating; takes machinery and costs plenty. What does this bozo expect me to do? Give every Okie who comes my way part of my acres and then endow him with enough money to operate them? Why, average taxes come to about eighteen dollars and fifty cents an acre, water costs the same; a grower must earn an overhead charge of thirty-seven dollars an acre before he can have a chance of profit. The fellow's crazy!"

"Guess we all are, or getting that way," Lloyd commented.

The procession had found its way to the gates of the cemetery, and there was a brief pause at the entrance before it moved on again. The short wait brought silence once more to the three men in the limousine.

§ 2

Stan was talking to Syd Watterbury on the interoffice telephone. Miss Chambers came in and stood waiting until he had finished. When he flicked up the switch cutting off the connection, she said:

"There's a Miss Welch on the line who wants to speak to you. She says it's important. I think she's the notary public you went to see a few days ago."

Stan looked at his secretary for a long moment while his thoughts raced.

"Okay," he said; "put her on."

Miss Chambers went out, and when his buzzer sounded he picked up the receiver.

"That you, Stan? This is Caddie."

"Yes, I know. How are you, Caddie?"

"Fine. I've been trying to get you all week."

"I got your messages, but I've been terribly busy. My father arrived home a few days ago from Washington. He's been running me ragged."

"I wanted to tell you how sorry I was to hear about your aunt."

"Thanks."

"It was quite sudden, wasn't it?"

"She'd been sick a long time. You know—ever since she was hurt at that wedding reception."

"I'm awfully sorry. What was it? The newspaper said pneumonia."

"That's right; very sudden. She caught a bad cold after she came home from the hospital. She was pretty run-down."

"I'm awfully sorry, Stan."

"Well, thanks."

"When am I going to see you? You promised to ring me."

"I've been busy. My father——"

"Can't we have lunch together today?"

"Oh, I—I don't think that's possible."

"What's the matter?"

"Engaged."

"How about tomorrow?"

"Can't promise."

"How's Saturday?"

"You don't understand, Caddie; I'm up to my neck."

"Don't you want to see me, Stan?"

"Of course."

"Then why can't you make it today or tomorrow?"

"I tell you, Caddie, I'm awfully busy."

"Listen, Stan, can't you come up and have a drink with me late this afternoon?"

"No, no, no! I can't talk over the wire very well, Caddie."

"What's the matter?"

"Someone might be listening. Can't tell. Mr. Watterbury, our general manager, had his private files rifled yesterday."

"His what?"

"His confidential office files."

"I don't believe it!"

"It's true just the same."

"But Stan——"

"Really, Caddie——"

"Stan, I've got to see you. I've some very important news to tell you. Something that will interest you a great, great deal."

He paused, frowning.

At the request of the Maritime Commission the settlement of the dispute between the shipowners and unions had been postponed until there could be a hearing. The shipowners had agreed to a fifteen-day truce. Caddie, of course, might be able to tell him something of real importance.

"Well," he said uncertainly, "I couldn't make it today or tomorrow."

"Saturday? At El Jardine's? At one. Nobody's there on Saturdays and we can have a talk. . . . I'm crazy to see you."

"All right," he agreed. "Saturday, but I may be a little late."

"I'll wait."

§ 3

Sitting opposite to her in a booth at the restaurant on Saturday, he decided she was more attractive than he remembered. Her face seemed smoother, and her hair curled becomingly up around the brim of her small, close-fitting hat. He had forgotten her big smile with the double parentheses on either side of her wide mouth, and he had forgotten, too, the friendly, understanding look in her quick-moving eyes. She wore a tight-fitting brown jersey—the top of it encircled her white throat—with sleeves stopping at the elbow, showing her clean strong forearms. The sweater defined her breasts and nicely fitted her rounded, well-shaped shoulders. There were her hands also—finely modeled and expressive. She used them effectively. There was that peculiar essence about her, too, of which he was immediately conscious. He was glad to see her, glad he had come.

"Let's have a drink," she said after greeting him. He had taken her hand, and she put her free one over her right as she clasped his and drew him down toward her.

"Sure, let's have a drink," he agreed, "but I've got to go easy this afternoon. None of the carousing we did the last time."

"Was that carousing?" She widened her eyes. "I didn't think so. We had such a nice time, and I felt I had acquired a new friend. . . . I'm *so* glad to see you again."

"I'm glad to see you."

"Are you?"

"Very."

"Let's have that drink."

"Waiter! . . . Scotch?" he inquired.

"Yes, with soda."

This was pleasant, he thought. There was some strange quality about this woman! It was something of a thrill to be sitting here looking at her in anticipation of the good talk ahead of them.

"Well, what is that you've got to tell me?"

"That can wait, can't it? What are you shipowners planning to do? Stage a lockout?"

" 'Re you trying to pump me?" he laughed. "I thought you were going to tell me something important."

"What does that commission Roosevelt's appointed think they're going to accomplish out here? They haven't any authority. It's just an investigating committee to report."

"We've offered to arbitrate."

"To them? They're no arbitration board."

"Well, to somebody—Paul Sinsheimer, Harry Rathbun, Dean Morse—anybody acceptable."

"The unions won't arbitrate."

"Why?"

"Because Rory knows that you'll try to persuade any arbitrator to amend the 1934 awards. You want to change our hiring halls, reduce wages, lengthen hours. These fundamental principles the maritime unions have won, and they won't relinquish them."

"We'll see. You and I are not going to fight."

"We never do, do we?"

"No, I can't say we do. You're a very stimulating person. Here's our drink. Let's have it and order another with our lunch."

§ 4

An hour later, as he stirred his small coffee, he leaned his elbows on the table and blew a plume of smoke from his pursed lips.

"There's one thing, Caddie, I wanted to ask you about. I've been thinking about asking you some questions for—oh, for a long time. I don't know the answers myself, but my guess is you do. What about this Associated Farmers organization? My Uncle Reggie was telling me about the mess he's in. Between the unions and the Government's surplus restrictions, he doesn't know which way to turn. He's a prosperous farmer—or was! He says he can't turn round without some union trying to hamstring him."

He gave Caddie a summary of Reggie's grievances.

"First of all, he says that the shiftless Okies who are pouring into the state ought to be stopped. Just as soon as they cross the border some union gets hold of 'em and tries to sign them up. He says that the Government has had to build a dozen or so camps to take care of them."

Caddie laughed. She sucked on her cigarette.

"Who's this uncle of yours? I didn't know you had another one. Tell me about him."

"He's the father of that cousin of mine, Chris, whom Vincent Oliver rescued when his yacht was wrecked."

"Oh yes, I remember. . . . Did he tell you there were *dozens* of government camps in California taking care of these poor refugees?"

At Stan's nod, she said:

"He's loony."

"He said he thought he was!"

"As a matter of fact there are only two—one at Arvin, another at Marysville. They accommodate about two hundred families each. But why should the Government take charge of these migratory workers at all? Why shouldn't the rich farmers do it?"

"My uncle says the farmers are being hijacked by the unions. That's why they, the farmers, have had to organize."

Caddie laughed again.

"I don't know anything about your esteemed uncle, but do you know the kind of farmers who make up the bulk of the 'Associated Farmers'? They aren't farmers; they are great land companies, banks who hold thousands and thousands of acres in the San Joaquin Valley; they are corporations with stockholders and boards of directors, only interested in returns from their investments. They appoint superintendents to run their farms, and these gentlemen naturally are anxious to hold their jobs, so they hire the cheapest labor they can get.

"Let's go back a bit," she said, "and review the history of farming in this state. First came the Chinese—thousands of them who, after they had built the railroads, went to work in the fields and were paid something less than a dollar a day. Then came the Japanese, next the Filipinos, and after them the Mexicans. All contract labor. Folks in California resented them. Immigration laws were passed, quotas established, and eventually these undesirables were deported. When there were no more of them, labor contractors distributed handbills and put advertisements in local papers to attract what you describe as 'Okies.' Okies come from the drought country, where their small farms have either been blown away or have dried up because of lack of water. The handbills and the ads promised good wages for pickers in California. The poor devils responded by the thousands. Thirty thousand came in since January of this year; more are on their way."

"Why does the Government allow them to come?"

"You can't prevent them very well."

"Then it's up to the Federal authorities to take care of them."

"I don't think that's the solution. These poor people who've been encouraged to come here ought to be provided for by those corporations and banks who advertised for them. That's the answer.

"Anyway, Federal camps can't solve the problem," she went on; "fruit when it ripens cannot be harvested by local help. A large peach orchard which requires the work of twenty men the year round will need two thousand for the brief period of picking and packing. There are the vegetable crops of the Imperial Valley, where lettuce, cauliflower, tomatoes, cabbage must be picked and packed; in Kern County and in the San Joaquin Valley there are grapes, cotton, pears, melons, beans, and peaches; Salinas grows lettuce, and in the Sacramento Valley there are more vegetables and fruit. The pickers must jump from harvest to harvest. A short time before the actual picking begins there is a scurrying on the highways, families in open cars hurrying to the ready crops and hurrying to be there first. The growers always welcome twice as much labor as is necessary so wages may be kept low.

"The pickers establish themselves in squatters' camps, usually located on the banks of rivers under trestles or near an irrigating ditch. You should see these camps—litters of rags and scrap iron, houses built of flattened cans, paper, while inside there are perhaps three old quilts and a soggy, lumpy mattress. The money necessary for food cannot be spent for soap or clothes.

"Pickers are needed, and they are hated. They are hated because they are ignorant and dirty, because they are carriers and breeders of disease, because they require more policing, and if they try to organize, they can—simply by refusing to work—wipe out an entire season's crops. Your reverend uncle wants a peon class, does he? My God, if he is right, then California has no place in a democracy!

"These Okies, as you call them, are white folk, Stan. You only have to look at some of their strong, purposeful faces, often filled with pain, marked by hunger, and more often—when they see the idle lands held by the banks and the corporations—filled with anger. When you study their faces, you know that these people are here to stay and they must be taken care of. Old methods of repression, of starvation wages, of jailing, beating, and intimidation will not work with them.

"Suppose there is an epidemic in one of these squatters' camps, say typhoid or scarlet fever; the county doctor will come to the camp and promptly hurry the infected cases to the pesthouse. But malnutrition is not infectious, nor is dysentery, which is a common rule among the children."

"That's just sob stuff—and isn't so!" Stan cried indignantly. "I know for a fact that many of the large ranches maintain pleasant, comfortable houses which they rent cheaply to their pickers and cutters."

"So?" Caddie said with her big smile, her brows elevated. "As a matter of fact, they are one-room shacks, without a rug or water, not even a bed. Water is supplied from a spigot at one end of the street, and at the other is a double toilet with a septic tank, serving one hundred to one hundred and fifty people. Near by are armed guards —deputies with guns and clubs—and always there is a company store run by the management where merchandise may be purchased on credit—at *company* prices!

"Workers are herded like animals. Every possible method is used to frighten and intimidate them. At the slightest suspicion of organizing, the organizers are run off the ranch at the point of a gun. At the gates there are more guards, and the roads are patrolled.

"Can you blame these miserable people for wanting to organize? They've got to live. They have a right to live. They deserve decent wages."

"Well, a lot of different unions are trying to help them, and rowing and killing each other's organizers in the process!"

"True enough. Unions—several of whom differ in their ideas and have no love for each other—are all interested in giving a hand-up to these ragamuffins because their need is great."

"Boloney!" Stan exploded. "The unions are interested in organizing them because they want to shake them down for their dues! What about this 'march inland'?"

"Call it what you will. It is the hope of responsible and intelligent labor leaders to get this unfortunate flock together and assist them."

"It smacks of communism to me," Stan said.

"So what? You keep coming back to that again and again, as though there were some awful stigma attached to communism."

"Isn't there? If there isn't, there should be."

"You talk like a schoolboy, my dear—but I love you just the same. We have jurisdictional rows, I admit—lots of them right here in San Francisco, and many all over the country; but these are labor pains—I don't mean to pun!—giving birth to a great labor movement which will unite the workers into one great powerful army, and then what labor says will become the law of the land."

"If that isn't rank communism, I'll eat my hat!" Stan cried.

"Certainly that's communism—and it's coming, my dear friend, just as sure as we're sitting here."

He fell silent, distressed, unhappy. He felt Caddie was confusing him, befuddling him with words. She talked very convincingly, but he felt somehow that her arguments were unsound.

"Well," he hazarded at length on a troubled sigh, "what do you propose to do about these poor, unfortunate Okies who have been driven off their homelands in the Middle West—by billows of dust and greedy land-grabbing barons who have discovered the modern tractor will do the work of hundreds of men? How are you going to take care of these shiftless ragamuffins who have been enticed out here by false promises of high wages made by unscrupulous, crafty, money-grubbing farmers?"

Caddie threw back her head with a rich laugh.

"Well," she said, sobering after a moment, "it *is* a problem. A lot of 'em are going to starve before we can do anything for them; they *are* ignorant and shiftless. This might be a solution for the time being: Establish a migratory labor board with branches in every agricultural center where seasonal labor is required. Before the picking begins, the board should canvass the district, discover and publish the amount of labor needed and the wages to be paid. Such information should then be placed in the hands of the unions and a specified number of workers be dispatched to that district."

"A hiring hall, huh?"

"Exactly."

"And what unions would you endorse to accomplish this altruistic work?"

"Does that matter? It will work itself out. The need for unionization is there, and agricultural workers should be encouraged and helped to organize. They must be protected even from themselves. They must receive a decent wage; they must be taught to save for the lean months of the year. About the fifteenth of January the dead time sets in. There is no work. First the gasoline gives out; then the food. And with the coming of the rains, the hungry children begin to develop colds because the ground in the tents is wet, and the colds turn into pneumonia. Next year the hunger will come again, and the year after that. If you buy a farm horse, Stan, and only feed him when you work him, the horse will die. No one complains about the necessity of feeding the horse when he is not working, but farmers complain about feeding the men and women who work their lands when they are idle!"

"That's all very fine," Stan said after a pause; "boost the poor pickers' and cannery workers' wages, raise 'em until they've got all they want; in the meantime tax the farmer on his lands and his crops, make him deal only with union labor, pay the exorbitant rates it demands, hold him up until he goes bankrupt or blows out his brains, and then what have you got? No farms, no vineyards, no orchards, no cotton, no fruit, no nothing! Where will your picker and cannery worker be then? Your teamster and the rest of your union racketeers? Just out of luck, that's all. They haven't the brains to run a farm, grow grapes, or raise cotton—any more than your longshoreman and your sailor know how to run a ship!"

"Some of them know more about running ships than their owners," a near-by voice said easily. Two men approached the booth. "Howdy, Caddie? Good afternoon, Mr. Rutherford."

The backs of the newcomers were against the light, their faces in shadow. Stan recognized neither at first; then he saw that the speaker was Nate Jacobs. He had a premonition that something disagreeable was about to happen.

"Oh, hello," said Caddie. "Hello, Nate. Hello——"

She stopped. There was a moment's awkward pause.

Stan looked at the second man, and a spasm closed his throat. He seemed to have seen that face before—a malevolent face with a red, uneven beard, one sunken blind eye, covered by a half-closed lid and a drooping eyebrow, the other glittering flame, while the jaw was misshapen and crooked—the result of a burn or an injury. A death's head—grotesque and horrible.

"Hello, Rory," Caddie went on hastily; "I don't think you ever met Mr. Stanley Rutherford—J. O. B. Rutherford's son. Stan, this is Rory O'Brien."

Wedged between his seat and the table, Stanley could only partly get to his feet. He felt antagonism. The man's baleful eye fixed him coldly.

"Won't you join us?" Caddie suggested nervously. "Let's all have a drink."

"Thank you, no," Nate declined. "We're going to stand at the bar for a quick one."

Stan and Rory continued to regard each other, the former unsmiling under slightly contracted brows, the latter gimleting him with his one good eye.

Stan acknowledged the introduction with a nod, but words failed him. In a rasping bass, Rory said:

"How d'do."

No cordiality; the tone was hostile, the look one of arrogant contempt. He turned to Caddie, asked pleasantly:

"What are you doing here, my dear? Taking an afternoon off?"

"Making a convert of Mr. Rutherford—I hope."

"I see." He measured Stan with another quick look.

"Mr. Rutherford is a champion of Dan Sheridan," Nate observed cheerily.

"So I've heard," said Rory.

Stan felt the blood burn hotly in his cheeks. Awkwardly he half stood, supporting himself with one hand against the wall behind him, the other clinging to the edge of the table. Caddie laughed. He felt mortified, ashamed. He hated this man with sudden hate. Coarse epithets and phrases raced through his mind. He sensed Rory's sneer as he moved with Nate to the bar.

" 'Lo, Mr. O'Brien," the bartender cried genially, greeting him. "What will it be? Same as usual?"

Evidently it was a privilege to wait upon the labor leader!

Stan sank down into his seat. He wanted to cover his face with his hands until composure returned. Instead he bit his lips hard and clasped his hands fiercely beneath the table. Caddie was solicitous, but he did not hear what she was saying. Every instinct within him cried out for self-control. He did not know what it was that affected him so deeply; he felt chagrined, shocked, affronted.

To his companion's persistent queries, he could only shake his head.

What troubled him? It had nothing to do with the mere meeting of this man. It went deeper than that! He knew all about Rory O'Brien, what he stood for, who he was. . . . No, there was something more.

"What *is* it, Stan?"

He bowed his head.

"Didn't you ever see Rory before?"

"No."

"Well, he isn't a very pleasant-looking object, I'll admit."

He said nothing.

"But I don't see . . . I can't understand . . . You went bright red, and now you're as pale as a ghost."

He wiped his face with a napkin, reached for the remnant of drink in his glass, drained it.

"Just a minute, Caddie," he pleaded.

Presently, as the men at the bar prepared to depart, he felt normalcy returning.

"So long, Caddie," Nate Jacobs called. Rory made a gesture with his hand. They went out.

"Well, that's that," Stan breathed with relief.

"My dear," Caddie said with concern, "I'm sorry you're upset. Rory may be an odd-looking person—but he's magnificent. He's got one of the greatest minds I've ever known—a tremendous thinker and a born leader, and he's devoting his life to help his fellow man. He's a saint —I don't care how ugly he looks. He wasn't born that way. When I first knew him, he was one of the handsomest . . ."

She did not finish.

"Yeh?" Stan said apathetically.

A silence. He was aware of a sudden desire to get out of this place, rid himself of his company, be alone. He moved restlessly.

"Shall we have another drink?" Caddie asked.

"No; I have to be getting home."

"One more, huh?"

"No, thanks. I don't want any more. I've got to go."

He would not meet her eyes, although he knew she was looking at him.

"I've got to go," he repeated.

"Very well." She was hurt; he gave no heed.

Beckoning the waiter, he paid the check, slid toward the end of his seat.

"Really going, huh?"

"Yes, I must."

"When will I be seeing you again?"

"Soon."

"Don't leave me this way, Stan!"

Impatience gripped him.

"Sorry," he said, "I must go."

"Call me up?"

"Sure thing."

He waited for her while she slipped on her jacket over the brown sweater and collected her bag and gloves. Then he pulled back the entrance door of the restaurant, held it for her to pass through. In the street he lifted his hat.

" 'By," he said. He did not touch her hand; he left her standing where she was, turned sharply and walked rapidly away.

CHAPTER X

"WHAT WAS THAT WORD?" Frances asked, her lips trembling.

"Catatonic. It's a term we use to describe such a condition," the physician said.

Dr. Lorenzo Beardsley was the specialist whom Dr. Stewart had called in to examine Daisy.

The family—J.O.B., Frances, Stan—had gathered in the octagonally shaped drawing room of the Rutherford mansion to hear his verdict. Eleanor had slipped in; Dr. Stewart also was there.

For some time it had been noticeable that Daisy was steadily getting worse. The start of her decline had begun with mutterings, protesting and complaining, and then one afternoon the screams had recommenced. At any time of the day or night one of the paroxysms might occur. Frequently she fancied she was seeing the actual murder, Vincent entering his cabin, the assassin creeping upon him with his raised knife. In agony she tried to warn him, screaming to him of his danger, imploring him with shrieks and strangling sobs to guard himself. These hallucinations lasted for several minutes while one of her nurses tried to soothe her and another hurried to prepare the hypodermic needle.

There were times, too, when Daisy was both tractable and quiet, although her jumbled thoughts were always of her beloved. On one of these occasions, at his mother's suggestion and with Stewart's approval, Stan went in to see her. Although he had been forewarned that she looked badly, he was unprepared for the shocking change in her. Her skin was drawn tight across her cheekbones, and her lips were stretched across her teeth, baring them and giving her the look of a ferocious little animal—frightened, cowering, and ready to snarl.

Quietly he approached the bed, and after a time she became aware of his presence; she was puzzled at first, and then with a fluttering pitiful cry she held up her sticks of arms to draw him to her. She covered his face then with little bites of kisses, hugging him, crying and whispering meaningless endearments between her feeble and rapturous embraces. She thought he was Vincent come back to her!

"I can't promise you anything, I'm sorry, Mrs. Rutherford," Dr. Beardsley now said, his finger tips joined as he sat in a big chair, elbows on either arm. He was a distinguished-looking man, Stan thought, and his tone carried conviction. He liked him.

"Certainly," he continued, "no good can be accomplished by keeping her here——"

"Oh, oh, oh . . ." sobbed Frances.

"You want your daughter to get well, don't you?" Beardsley asked.

"Of course, of course."

"She won't in your home. In the first place, the only way to control her in one of her mental disturbances has been by injections of morphine. The dose to be effective has had to be steadily increased. It's not good for her and might eventually prove fatal. Her system is impoverished; she needs treatment——"

"But I can't let you take my baby from me!" wailed Frances.

"My dear," J.O.B. remonstrated, "try to control yourself; be patient; listen."

"Dr. Stewart has done all he possibly can for her," continued the specialist. "It must be obvious to you that the poor girl's vitality is on the wane. She's a very sick child. We don't fully understand the disorders of the human mind, Mrs. Rutherford. Your daughter has had a terrible shock——"

"And I did it! I did it!" moaned her mother.

"Nonsense," said J.O.B.

"Oh, it was I who told her——"

"Please, please," Dr. Beardsley interposed. "The girl eventually would have had to know. Nothing could have prevented that. It was as well she heard the tragic news from her parents."

A whimper escaped from Eleanor here. She fumbled hastily for her handkerchief and covered her eyes with it.

It was all very terrible, thought Stan—far more terrible for his mother and father, Eleanor and himself, who loved his little golden-haired sister so much, than it was for the girl herself with her un-balanced mind, reposing at the moment peacefully upstairs in bed.

Dr. Stewart spoke.

"I think what Dr. Beardsley says is entirely right. There was no way in which the news of the shocking event could have been im-parted to her without consequences. Evidently her mind was a nicely balanced one——"

"That's true, that's true," agreed Frances on a quivering breath, interpreting the physician's words as a tribute to her daughter.

"Well, we'll have to try to get that balance back," Beardsley said, kindly. "Now there is a psychiatric hospital here in the city—a very nice, comfortable place, not far from here. It's run by a good man—a Dr. Gustav Müller. He's a foreigner, comes from Carlsbad in Ger-many, knows his subject. He has a soothing treatment for his patients when they become violent——"

"Oh, don't say such things!" wailed Frances.

"Well, when they become hysterical or their distorted minds play them tricks. The point I'm trying to make is that Dr. Müller will not administer any more morphine; instead he will use his treatments; they are very efficacious but cannot be administered here. And then there will be therapy—electro shock therapy—and while I'm not familiar with his methods, I *do* know he gets results. Then of course there will be massage and diet——"

"But Daisy won't eat a thing!" cried Frances.

"Dr. Müller's business is to see that she does. Appetite will be stimulated by massage and exercise. As I say, I am not familiar with his methods, but he specializes in just such cases as your daughter's—mental derangements—and I've known him to effect some remarkable cures.

"You want your daughter to live, don't you?" he said, directing his question pointedly at Frances. "You want her to be well and strong once more—in full possession of her wits?"

"Oh yes, yes," she agreed passionately.

"I assure you she won't be if she remains here. You might try Dr. Müller for a time, see if there is any improvement; then, if you are not satisfied, try something or somebody else. The Mayos, Johns

Hopkins, any of the great medical centers, I promise you, are not the places to take your daughter; this is a psychiatrist's job. Give Dr. Müller a trial and see what he can do."

§ 2

Joe Halliday of the Industrial Association was addressing a large luncheon gathering at the Palace Hotel; almost all the members of the association were present, most of the shipowners and a large number of businessmen. Stan, sitting with his father, his uncle Lloyd, and Syd Watterbury, noticed, scattered among the tables, the vice-president of the Occidental Oil, the president of the Sierra Nevada Mining Corporation, the general manager of Hesperian Steel, Hotch-kiss of Sunset Gas & Electric, Judge Shotwell and his partner, Judge Ainsworth, Zachariah Nugent of Nugent & Peabody, old man Sylvester of the Sylvester National Bank—a fine turnout of prominent San Franciscans.

Halliday read from a script carefully prepared. He said:

"We must have industrial freedom in San Francisco; no group can be permitted to capture control of our business enterprise for its own selfish ends.

"Today we are faced with the challenge of a closed-shop labor monopoly. It is fifteen years since this city was a union-bossed town. In that day a man couldn't get a job, build a home, open a store, or start a factory unless he received the permission of a union labor boss.

"Up to the year of 1921, the strangling grip of the closed shop was so tight on the city that the vast web of union rules and regulations, mercilessly enforced by dictatorial union chiefs, was referred to and known in union circles as 'The Law.' Some of these laws were:

"A bricklayer could not lay more than eight hundred and fifty bricks a day.

"Electricians could not install more than eleven outlets per day.

"A painter could not use a brush more than four inches wide.

"A plumber could not bend a pipe or use a bent pipe.

"Only the sons of union plumbers could be hired as apprentices.

"No employer could supervise his own job more than two hours a
day.

"The union could put as many men on a job as it saw fit, regardless
of the wishes of the employer or the needs of the job.

"All labor-saving machines were barred.

"Those were just a few of the laws. Why did the union chiefs have
such power? Because they had insisted upon and secured the closed
shop, and their power rested upon an absolute control and monopoly
of the labor supply. We broke that strangle hold in 1921 by resolute
measures.

"The closed shop does not mean simply high wages. If that were
all, some compromise would be effected. But it really means ineffi-
ciency, extortion, graft, and the poisoning of the very lifeblood of
industry and business.

"Every union in San Francisco wants the closed shop. Some unions
already have it, and others are demanding it. It is part of every set
of demands. Only one thing can stop it. Rock-ribbed resistance!

"Let us proceed to a consideration of the situation which confronts
us on our waterfront today. The ordinary citizen wonders what all
this turmoil is about. He asks, 'Is it true that the shipowners and the
men have a signed agreement dealing specifically with wages, hours,
and working conditions?' When he is answered in the affirmative,
he naturally thinks: 'There must be something wrong somewhere'—
and he's right!

"He's right because the men in command of the San Francisco
Local of the International Longshoremen's Union do not want the
agreement to work for the purposes for which it was written, namely
—peaceful, continuous profitable operation of ships and docks under
conditions fair to both employer and worker. This is hard to believe,
yet it is a fact.

"There is no assured peace on the waterfront from day to day,
week to week, or month to month for the simple reason that the men
in the longshoremen's unions are not satisfied with the limits imposed
by that agreement. These limits are the essence of that agreement:
fair wages, fair working conditions, and fair treatment of stevedores.

"The radical leaders pretend they like the agreement, but what they really want is a complete control over the conduct and operation of the marine transportation industry and over shore industries dependent upon movement of commodities by water.

"Why do these men want such control? Because such control would be an effective instrument in the ultimate revolutionary objective of an international conspiracy to seize all private property in the United States and other countries.

"There will be no permanent peace on the San Francisco waterfront until the leaders of the San Francisco marine unions give up their revolutionary objectives. These leaders are intent on overturning our economic setup for their communist dream of a classless, profitless, propertyless class.

"The awards of the President's National Longshoremen's Board were designed to operate under the American system of private enterprise. They will not work under any other system or for any other purposes than that for which they were intended.

"The hope of peace in the immediate future rests upon the fact that the name of Mr. Rory O'Brien is at the bottom of an agreement signed in Judge Shotwell's office in April of this year. His name is at the bottom of this contract reaffirming the award and its provisions for the elimination of job action and hot cargo strikes because the Waterfront Employers' Association had the courage to threaten to sever relations with the unions unless he signed it. At that time—April 21 to be exact—Mr. O'Brien agreed to observe the agreement and decisions of the arbitrator which he had violated and defied in the past.

"However, Mr. O'Brien's signature to this agreement is a pretty shaky foundation on which to pin our hopes for an abiding peace. Mr. O'Brien is working hand in hand with the radical leaders of other maritime unions on the Pacific, Gulf, and Atlantic coasts. Their combined objective is the organization of a powerful maritime federation embodying *all* marine transport workers on *all* American docks and ships of registry. If this is accomplished, they will command the most powerful union in the United States. It would consist of several hundred thousand men, embodying all dock workers and the personnel of all ships from the captains down to the cabin boys. The plan is to keep it, if possible, within the American Federation of Labor and take control of that organization.

"Mr. O'Brien is afraid that if he goes too far the local charter of the International Longshoremen's Association will be lifted and he and his friends will be thrown out of the American Federation of Labor. The Sailors' Union of the Pacific has already lost its charter and is now making frantic efforts in and out of State and Federal courts to regain its status within the International Seamen's Union which gives it an affiliation with the American Federation of Labor.

"It is not easy to prove that Mr. O'Brien or his clique are actually members of the Communist party, but neither can it be denied that they have successfully used the Communist technique in instituting labor unrest and strike.

"The hope of peace in San Francisco lies today in peace along the waterfront. We are committed to collective bargaining, and we are content to deal with the legitimate representatives of our employees chosen by them. But if that means a closed shop, the Industrial Association of San Francisco is opposed to it and will fight it with all its strength. If it means that no man can work in this city without joining a union, we will fight any coercion to make him do so. Employees have the right to join or not to join any union as they prefer. We believe that this right adheres to each individual and that the individual should be protected in its exercise."

§ 3

"Listen, you fellows!" J.O.B. caught Jim Ahearn by the arm and blocked Percy Grant's path as they emerged with the crowd from the luncheon.

"Listen! Come here a minute!" J.O.B. was excited; his florid face, so easily flushed, was copper-hued. "Let's go somewheres where we can talk. Find Nick; we'll need him. Your office is handy, Jim. Get your hats and we'll all meet there. Huh? . . . All set? Come along."

Twenty minutes later the four men, representing the four biggest shipping lines on the Pacific Coast, were gathered in the office of the president of the American-Asiatic Steamship Company.

"Tell 'em you're out, will you, Jim?" J.O.B. requested. "Won't take me but twenty minutes to spill my idea.

"That was a great speech of Joe's, wasn't it?" he continued, when assured of privacy. "Don't you think so, Percy?"

"Sure; he talked sound sense."

"I didn't think Joe could make as good a talk as that."

"Old Sylvester seemed impressed. I saw him chewing the end of his cigar; he forgot to light it!"

"What do you think, Nick?"

The president of the Nickel Line rubbed his expansive stomach with both hands, pursed his lips.

"Good," he said.

"It all comes down to the question of who's running this town, doesn't it?" J.O.B. proceeded. "It's the Reds or us—and to break their grip on our industry, we've got to break the union——"

"You'll just get in trouble with the NLRB," Jim Ahearn interrupted.

"Well, if we can't break the unions, we can get rid of their radical leaders."

"That's just what Joe said," put in Percy Grant.

"For God's sake, tell me how you're going to do it," Horatio Nickel demanded.

"Have the rank and file throw 'em out—make them disgusted with them. . . . Listen here. I'm pretty well fed up with this Rory O'Brien and his gang. He's cost me a lot of grief, one way or another. That boy, Vincent Oliver, was going to be my son-in-law. Did any of you know that? Well, he was. What did they do to him? Murdered him! Stabbed him in the back in his own cabin on board his own ship! Oh hell, you fellows know all about that! No use my getting so disturbed about it! But my daughter who was engaged to him and who was going to be married to him last June is in an institution now, a mental case, as a result. And there's Lloyd's wife—my sister-in-law. When they threw that tear-gas bomb into her home, somebody killed her— just as sure as I'm sitting here. She slipped that night, fell and broke her hip. Last month she died. If I'm bitter, you'll understand why. . . ."

With an effort he curbed his mounting emotion.

"Now . . ." He paused, swallowing, and gripped his goatee. "I learn from my son, Stan—he's been talking to some of their people—that the unions refuse to arbitrate any differences they have with us. All right, if they won't arbitrate, let's just sit tight and let 'em starve. There's no justice in their refusal to arbitrate. We've told 'em we will. I don't see how we can do much else. Certainly I won't compromise with them—not if I fight 'em single-handed and my company has to close its doors! I won't compromise, and we can't bring in a lot of strikebreakers——"

"Nothing doing!" interrupted Percy Grant.

"I'm not even suggesting it!" J.O.B. shouted. "But I *am* saying that we've got no other course open to us but just to shut up shop. We've been talking about it—and talking about it—and talking about it! Nothing happens. What I want to know here and now is, are you men with me? Do we sink or swim together? No one of us can get anywhere alone, but if we all *stick* . . ."

Silence followed as he left his words in the air. Jim Ahearn reached in his vest pocket for a cigar, thoughtfully clipped its end; Percy Grant scowled, drummed the arms of his chair with his finger tips; Horatio Nickel rubbed his stomach, pursed his lips.

"We'll offer to arbitrate," J.O.B. resumed; "if they won't arbitrate, there's to be no further dealings with them. Understood? I want it agreed amongst us that there'll be no private negotiating on the side. We arbitrate—or we quit. Tie up the ships, close the docks! We can jockey things around so we won't lose much. If the men won't arbitrate, to hell with them! Let 'em strike—and stay struck! There won't be any more jobs for any of 'em until they're ready to talk turkey. All we got to do is a little forward thinking. I want to be sure that the four of us will stick together, that's all. What d'you say? Are you with me, Jim?"

"You know me, J.O.B."

"How 'bout you, Percy?"

"Okay."

"And you, Nick?"

"It will cost a lot of money!"

"Course it will—but you've made a lot. You just can't throw us down, Nick."

"All right; count me in."

"We'll pool our losses, work it out later. Anything suits me—just so we don't advertise it. We've got to keep this agreement among ourselves; if the press ever got wind of it, there would be a lot of blatherskites blowing their heads off and talking about conspiracy, a lockout, and some other goddamn nonsense. You know how it is. Let's shake on it. The unions will arbitrate, or we quit! Agreed?"

"All right, J.O.B.; we're with you. It's going to take a load of worrying off my mind."

The four men shook hands solemnly.

§ 4

The seven unions comprising the Maritime Federation of the Pacific struck on the twenty-ninth of October. The port of San Francisco and all other ports from San Diego to Alaska, with the exception of Canadian ports, closed; shipping was completely tied up; 229 ships in various harbors were deserted by their crews, their holds either choked with cargo or standing empty. The Warehousemen's Union, affiliated with the Longshoremen's Union, seized the opportunity also to declare a strike. Seventeen commercial warehouses, four feed and milling warehouses, three cold-storage warehouses in the city shut their doors. Fifty million dollars' worth of supplies were strike-bound, and in addition hundreds of cars were stalled in railroad yards. Mayor Rossi of San Francisco declared a state of emergency existed.

In November of that year the Spanish rebels began their drive on Madrid; President Roosevelt was re-elected for a second term with the greatest presidential victory in the history of the United States; Hitler at Nuremberg declared: "All states have experienced the destructive effects of democracy. The spiritual presupposition for the inauguration of anarchy—yes, the spiritual basis of every anarchy—is democracy; the rock foundation of the state is an authoritarian will! Bolshevism seeks to destroy culture, as we see in Spain, where eighty per cent of the leading personalities are Jews. Just as in Russia, ninety-eight per cent of the entire present-day leadership of the Soviet republics lies in the hands of Jews—who never were either workers or peasants but simply overcultured parasitical intellectuals in search of another feeding ground—so do we see, in recent weeks, with Marxism raging in Spain, the same process of slaughter of racially Spanish state leadership through the Jewish element!" Mussolini again warned the world that Italy was prepared to defend her conquest of Ethiopia. "I am sure," he declared to his countrymen, "that in any eventuality you will be ready to change your workers' jackets and put on soldiers' uniforms." The world was wondering whether King Edward VIII would announce his engagement to Mrs. Wallis Simpson and relinquish the throne. In Tampa, Florida, at the annual convention of the American Federation of Labor, it was overwhelmingly voted to suspend the ten unions comprising the Committee of Industrial Organization, tantamount to expulsion, and on the twelfth, thirteenth, and fourteenth of the same month, the San Francisco-Oakland Bay Bridge celebrated its opening.

§5

Leaving the Wickwire, Rutherford Building a little before four o'clock on the afternoon of Christmas Eve, Stan ran face to face into Caddie, accompanied by a man. He tried to pass her with only a polite lifting of his hat, but she caught him by the sleeve.

"Oh, I'm so glad to see you! Merry Christmas!"

"Merry Christmas to you!"

"I haven't seen you in ages! Where you been?"

"Around." He smiled a trifle uncomfortably. "These are troubled days, you know."

"Course I do. I've been frightfully busy myself. Stan, do you know Mat Swenson? Mat, this is Stanley Rutherford—J. O. B. Rutherford's son."

Stan looked with interest at the man she introduced. Mat Swenson was the leader of the Sailors' Union of the Pacific, one of the militant leaders of the striking unions. He was a big man with wavy blond hair and frank blue eyes under well-marked blond eyebrows; he wore no hat, and his tieless dark blue flannel shirt, open at the throat, revealed a bull neck which rose in a round bronze column from between his powerful shoulders.

"Glad to know you, Mr. Rutterford."

He spoke with a pronounced Swedish accent, and the hand which grasped Stan's was strong.

"Well, I'm glad to know you, sir."

The two men took each other's measure, and Stan was aware of liking the big sailor. There was something singularly straightforward and honest about him. He could readily understand how the men he led had confidence in him.

"You are de shipowner's son, heh?"

"Yes, I am."

"You are a tough bunch of bastards."

It was said easily, amiably.

"Well," Stan smiled, "as I was saying to Miss Welch, these are tough times, and I guess we have to be tough bastards."

"Yah, dat goes for everybody," Swenson agreed.

Stan was pleased with this encounter and warmed to the blond giant. "Say," he proposed, "I have to get a couple of Christmas presents before I go home, but couldn't we have time for just one drink? That Jardine place is only a block or two from here, isn't it?"

Mat Swenson shook his head, his blond hair waving like a lion's mane.

"No," he said shortly; "no."

"Oh, come on, Mat," Caddie pleaded.

"No," he said again; "it's my schtomack; Ay cannot do it."

"Ulcers," Caddie explained. "He won't drink a thing except coffee, and drinks twenty to thirty cups a day."

"He could have that while we were having something stronger," Stan suggested.

"No," Mat reiterated with impatience. "No time now. Ve got to go; come on, Caddie. So long, now. Vish you a Merry Christmas."

He gestured with one of his large hands and turned away, pulling Caddie with him.

"Call me soon, will you, Stan?" she cried, departing. "Please—an' . . . and a Merry Christmas to you."

She laughed gaily as Swenson carried her off, waving her bag at Stan as she and her blond companion disappeared in the throng of Christmas shoppers that choked the sidewalk.

Stan was aware of an odd feeling as he stood looking after them.

He felt abandoned and, in some curious way, hurt. Caddie—and this man, this big Swede with the bull neck! What in the name of God did she find . . . ? He wished . . . Oh, he didn't know what he wished! He was conscious of a pang somewhere—in his head, or in his heart.

Christmas Eve! He'd get those presents now—something for Grandmère, and something his mother could take to Daisy when she went to see her at the sanitarium in the morning. Just what? Well, something for a sick girl, a girl who had been ill a long time; something that might amuse her, or make her think of him—and a brother's love. . . . If Caddie had come along, she could have advised.

He moved away, walking slowly, head bent. The interest he had had earlier in the afternoon in selecting his presents had vanished.

§ 6

Only six gathered at Grandmère's Christmas breakfast table the following morning. Three years ago the group had numbered eleven. Now Chris was gone, and Aunt Bessie, too; Daisy was in the sanitarium. Her mother was much encouraged by her improvement and spent all her days visiting her, bearing small gifts, specially cooked dishes, regaling her with gossip of the family and the town, reading to her for hours. The other two who were missing were Reggie Baxter and his wife; there had been no word from them since the funeral in September. Grandmère had written, urging them to come to her for the holidays—plenty of room now; no need of their going to a hotel!—but there had only been an unsatisfactory Christmas card by way of reply with an inky scrawl in Charmion's hand along one side of it, regretting they could not come this year.

A sober company seated itself about the large oval table; everyone was conscious of the smaller circle and of the missing faces, but all put on a brave air. Grandmère, Stan thought, as he surveyed the group, had changed the least in the intervening years. She was still an indomitable figure with her wrinkled, animated face—creamed and powdered and rouged—her white wig with its carefully curled ringlets, her wide dog collar of sparkling rhinestones about her lean neck, her gnarled fingers thickly ringed, her black satin dress. Stan's mother too was in mourning still, a dark worsted, expensive and ill-fitting, her cheeks a little more tremulous than of yore. It made little difference, Stan reflected, what his mother wore. Her hips were wide, her abdomen prominent; no garment could hide her bulging figure, but she looked kind and motherly, despite her clumsy shape and the thick-lensed spectacles she wore. She was more composed this Christmas morning than he had seen her in some time. Daisy was definitely better.

Eleanor, robed in steely gray, was—as always—beautiful. She was past thirty and was no longer the imperious, haughty girl of a few years ago. She had changed; she was a woman now, as reserved perhaps as ever, but a becoming dignity had come to her. Her unfortunate marriage undoubtedly was responsible for this, but it was responsible for a good deal more, for she was gentler, kinder, less self-centered. As the butler, the austere Wilbur, passed the waffles and Grandmère urged another helping, Stan wondered what fate awaited this stately cousin of his. She deserved something better than to be for the rest of her life Lloyd Rutherford's daughter and the divorced wife of Lester Armitage. Eleanor had possibilities; she was not merely decorative; she had a mind and a personality.

Her father definitely had aged. There was only one phrase, Stan decided, which described him now: he sagged. Some iron quality that had characterized him all his days, and had found expression in his suave and courtly manner, was gone. Lloyd was over sixty—not broken exactly but unquestionably failing. His hands trembled slightly as he reached for his water glass; his spoon rattled as he put it in the saucer beside his coffee cup.

There was less noticeable change in his brother. J.O.B. was still vigorous, still healthy, vituperative and choleric, but the last three years had taken their toll of him as well; he was heavier, slower of motion, an easier prey to his emotions.

And lastly there was Stan himself, but he could hardly form an opinion there, except that he knew that recent years had brought unwelcome responsibilities, unquestionably robbing him of youth. He felt the burden of the family; he felt the weight of the business, the everlasting quarrel with the unions. He was living other people's lives; he wondered if there would ever come a time when he could call his days his own.

"Well, children—what say? Presents, now?"

The old familiar words which ended the sumptuous breakfast; the moment for gift-giving had arrived. How Stan had thrilled to them once, watching his grandmother's face for anxious minutes, waiting impatiently for her to say them! Now it was time—as it had been in all the previous years—for the family to push back its chairs and adjourn to the parlor. Here—where it had always stood—was the resplendent tree, aglitter with colored balls and tinsel, effectively ensconced in the embrasure of the front bay window, while stacked about its base, as in the past, was an impressive heap of gaily wrapped packages and parcels. Grandmère, guided by Lloyd, arranged herself in her customary gilt upholstered chair; the Rutherford brothers sat beside one another, exchanging brands of cigars; Stan placed himself next his mother on the sofa, and it devolved upon Eleanor to distribute the gifts.

This she did gracefully and becomingly—not with the girlish excitement of Daisy, but with charm and gentleness. There followed the usual snipping of string and ribbon, the usual rustle of tissue paper, the usual exclamations of surprise and pleasure, the usual thanks. All were conscious of the effort everybody was making to recapture some of the lightheartedness of bygone days.

"Come, Lloyd, it's time for the servants."

The long-established ritual!

Stan summoned them.

In they filed, Wilbur first, then Annabel, next a new lady's-maid, followed by Greenwood, the chauffeur, Hing, the grinning Chinese cook and little Kay, his helper.

Grandmère rapped with her ringed fingers.

"All right, Lloyd," she commanded.

Holding the pages of the Scripture a little closer to his eyes than in former years, the leaves of the book trembling slightly in his hands, Lloyd began:

"And there were in the same country shepherds abiding in the field, keeping watch over their flocks by night. . . ."

§ 7

Later that morning, as the two brothers gossiped over freshly lit cigars, Lloyd said to J.O.B.:

"Have you met Byron Mackey—you know, the man Madame Perkins sent out here?"

"No; I've only heard about him, that's all—and read some of his wisecracks in the newspapers. He's no friend of ours."

"Meaning?"

"He was sent to us as a conciliator, and as far as I can see he conciliates the unions and not us."

"He's quite a person."

"Where'd you meet him?"

"At the club. Zachariah Nugent had him up there for luncheon the other day. I tell you, he's unusual—a most interesting individual."

"What's his background?"

"Oh, I'm not sure. New York, I guess. I think he was a state senator when Roosevelt was governor. College of the City of New York, LL.B.—that sort of thing. He's young—nearly forty, I should say. He's a labor sympathizer, I suppose, but he's stimulating."

"Why did you ask about him?"

"Thought I might have him out here to dinner some night during the holidays; it wouldn't do you—or him!—any harm to meet."

"Oh, my Lord, Lloyd, I don't want to have any dealings with one of Perkins' stooges."

"Yes, you do. You fellows—you and Jim Ahearn and Percy Grant, the whole lot of you—are far too inclined to stay on your mountaintop and leave it to Joe Halliday to talk for you."

"Mackey's just an emissary to do what he's told and report what's expected."

"No, that isn't so. The man's got a fine, analytical mind; he thinks. He's sincerely interested in trying to end this fracas; I know he's doing his best, because he told me he was staying on in California over Christmas and New Year's instead of returning to Washington, hoping his presence might solve our local problem. The man is baffled, confused, and I believe it would do him good to listen to you—

and you wouldn't lose by it. I've often found in law, J.O.B., that more flies can be caught by honey than by vinegar, and that if parties in litigation can be brought together for an exchange of views, it's usually effective. . . . Oh, I don't want you to try to convince him of anything, nor do I expect him to make you a convert to his liberal ideas, but he's worth listening to."

"Oh, well," said J.O.B. indifferently; "go ahead; ask him whenever you want to. Sometime next week, if you like. There'll be no progress made in settling the strike until after the New Year."

"Then you'll come?"

"Sure; certainly. . . . Is he married?"

"No, he's a bachelor, I believe."

"Well, thank God I won't have to talk to his wife!"

CHAPTER XI

THE FIRST FRIDAY of 1937 was New Year's Day. Stan did not go to the office until the following Monday. He drove downtown with little interest in the day, and with little interest in the days to come. On the twenty-ninth of December any possibility of peace with the unions seemed to have ended once and for all. He read in the papers that the masters, mates, pilots, and engineers insisted upon preferential employment—which meant that the shipowners would no longer be able to select their own captains, mates, or engineers; the owners' coast committee had rejected the proposition, and negotiations had broken off. It was another brand added to the bonfire that was rapidly becoming a conflagration.

The newspapers were full of the strike, now going into its third month; their editorials reflected the public's mounting indignation. The speeches Jim Ahearn had made—a notable one at a public meeting in the Civic Auditorium—the full-page advertisements presenting the views of both sides, the radio addresses, the literature in pamphlet form which had been widely distributed by the employers and the strikers, all seemed to have accomplished nothing; on the contrary they appeared only to have fanned the flames of discord. Resentment against the shipowners was growing; the general attitude of the people was that they could afford to give in. Stan was sick of it all. He wanted to get to work, once more begin to route the Mission Fleet to Honolulu, New Orleans, and Seattle.

The one bright spot in the New Year's gloom had been his visit with his mother to Dr. Müller's sanitarium on Sunday. It had been his first glimpse of Daisy since she had been in Dr. Müller's care. He had found her—in some unaccountable way—smaller. She was thinner, more quiet and subdued, pathetically docile, but she had smiled bravely at him when she saw him and had even cried a little when her two frail little arms had encircled his neck and she had drawn him to her and rested her small cheek against his shoulder. But he could see she was better; the wild, frightened look had disappeared wholly from her eyes.

He had been at his desk less than half an hour that Monday morning when his uncle's secretary called him. Did he know where his father was? asked Miss Hodgins; Mr. Rutherford was anxious to speak to him. No, Stan had no idea. Had she tried J.O.B.'s office? Yes; he wasn't in.

"Just a minute, please; Mr. Rutherford would like to talk to *you*."

"Stan? Uncle Lloyd speaking."

"Yes, I know, sir."

"I got that man, Byron Mackey; he's coming to dinner tonight. I want your father to meet him. Will you get in touch with him? Tell him I expect him at seven-thirty. And we'd like you and your mother. . . . Black tie."

"Very good, sir; I know he's anxious to come, and thank you for including me. We'll all be there."

§ 2

Byron Mackey had not put in an appearance by the time J.O.B., Frances, and Stan arrived, but he came in a few minutes later. Lloyd went into the hall to welcome him as the butler relieved him of his hat and overcoat; they exchanged greetings, and then Lloyd piloted him into the parlor where the Rutherford clan was waiting.

The moment Stan's eyes fell upon him, he recalled having seen him before—once in Joe Halliday's office and another time talking to Nate Jacobs in the lobby of the Palace Hotel. He had not known who he was then, but he had been struck by his looks. He was stocky, with a big head and wide shoulders which stood out at right angles from his neck. His black hair was sleek and swept back like a raven's wing over his head; his eyebrows also were black, bristling black, and he had deeply set black eyes; his jaw was square, as was his face, a thin line marking his close-set lips. He walked with an exaggerated step, taking long strides as though to lessen the effect of his squat stature.

With the exception of Grandmère and Frances, all rose as he entered. They must present a rather formidable group to a stranger, Stan reflected. Grandmère gave him the benefit of a slight nod and her finger tips, J.O.B. scowled as he took his hand, but Stan stepped forward and shook it cordially, and Eleanor vouchsafed him one of her best smiles. She was beautiful tonight, Stan noted—tall, gracious, wearing a long, black dinner dress of lusterless silk, cut modestly low in front and cleft almost to her waistline in back; it was severely plain, relieved by her string of diamonds and by two glittering pendants at her ears. It was obvious that Mackey was impressed. After he was seated his eyes traveled more than once in Eleanor's direction, Stan noted.

Talk began with polite stiltedness, Lloyd carrying the brunt of it.

How long had he been in San Francisco? With the exception of two brief flights back to Washington, practically two months. Did he like it here? Delightful, fascinating. They were going to have a wonderful Fair year after next. Yes, he had visited the site a couple of weeks ago—a most amazing engineering feat. Someone had told him the number of cubic feet of fertile soil which were to be dredged up from the bottom of the Sacramento River and brought down on barges to cover the sandy earth of the Island, so that trees and flowers could grow there. Staggering figures!

The butler came in and passed canapés and cocktails. Presently Grandmère rose, indicating it was time for dinner.

Not until the lifeless meal was over and the company had returned to the parlor did the conversation become interesting. As soon as the men began to discuss labor problems, Grandmère and Frances excused themselves and went upstairs, but Eleanor remained, following the talk closely. She offered nothing, but her eyes traveled from face to face as the men spoke, her expression one of rapt absorption.

"I'm sorry, Mr. Rutherford," Byron Mackey said, answering one of J.O.B.'s salty observations, "I cannot agree with you."

He enunciated evenly, without emphasis, and Stan thought he had never heard a man speak with such assurance. He was not more than forty, yet he carried the aplomb of a person half again that age.

"Let me remind you," he proceeded, "that the Maritime Commission the President appointed has no authority to settle the present dispute. It has jurisdiction only over those operators who receive a Government subsidy for carrying mail. The unions quite rightly refuse to recognize the commission as a board of arbitration. Mr. Jacobs, on behalf of the unions, declined to accept the commission's authority to dictate the conditions under which they should work. He decided to withdraw, and I think Admiral Hamlet made an error when he permitted your Mr. Halliday to attack the unions when they were not represented."

"I don't believe you fully understand the conditions," J.O.B. began, but Byron Mackey stopped him.

"Oh, I think I do," he said amiably. "I have been here two months now, and I think I am familiar with every phase of the disagreement."

"From the beginning we were willing to leave everything to arbitration," J.O.B. persisted.

"I fully understand that, but if a board of arbitrators should favor you, the men might be deprived of their most precious gains, gains secured by the 1934 award."

"I don't see how!" J.O.B. said testily.

Lloyd raised a fine, blue-veined hand.

"Let's not go over old ground," he said. "Mr. Mackey has come to tell us something, and I have invited him here so we can listen."

"Well, I don't know what you have in mind."

"I recall some of the remarks you made at the club the other day which I thought extremely interesting."

"If I remember correctly, I was holding forth about our industrial relations in general, the relations between capital and labor, without any reference to the local controversy."

"Exactly," Lloyd confirmed.

"I think I was saying that it is demonstrably true that industry in this country has for a long time closed its eyes to the toll that it has been taking from the workers. Many of our industrialists have remained blind to conditions and have consistently resisted the enactment and enforcement of factory legislation and laws bettering working conditions. Mr. Roosevelt——"

"Don't quote that pirate to me!" interjected J.O.B.

"Please!" remonstrated Lloyd.

Byron Mackey's thin lips smiled.

"I have always thought that neither employers nor employees, nor both together, have a right to settle their relations either by contest or agreement in disregard of the public interest, and I have consistently held that some plan should be adopted by which labor controversies shall be regarded as involving the three interests of the employer, employee, and consumer.

"Mr. Gompers was a genuine patriot and a great man, and he knew perfectly well that he could remain president of the American Federation of Labor only so long as he did not give the radical and violent elements in his organization an opportunity to unseat him. As a consequence he was often driven to approve publicly things which he privately deplored. 'I want no laws regulating labor,' he used to say, 'and I want no court to have any power in labor disputes.'"

"Bravo!" cried J.O.B. "That's exactly what old Michael Casey of the Teamsters' Union used to say. He wanted no interference from Sacramento or the supervisors. He didn't believe in strikes if they could be avoided. He was a wise counselor of labor in '34."

"The privilege of striking is labor's natural weapon now," Mackey continued; "Washington is backing just such legislation——"

"And sending the country to the dogs!"

"Excuse me," Lloyd said, ignoring his brother's interruption. "There is just one observation I'd like to make. It is undoubtedly true that the present administration is labor's ally, but don't you think, Mr. Mackey, that the present Wagner Labor Relations Bill and the National Industrial Recovery Act—presuming both are constitutional, which I very much doubt—are bad legislation? I regard their philosophy as profoundly erroneous. You know as well as I do that they both proceed upon the assumption that there is an inevitable class struggle between men who work with their hands and the people who work with their heads to find work for people to do with their hands. I don't believe there is any such inescapable opposition of interest, and I don't think it's fair to charge all industrialists with a desire to oppress labor or all labor with a desire to rob capital; that's why I don't trust Federal legislation which recognizes any such conflict as either necessary or proper."

"Excuse me, Father," spoke up Eleanor. "Would you think me impertinent if I, too, asked Mr. Mackey a question?"

All turned to her, pleased at her interest and charmed with her beauty.

"Certainly not, my dear," Lloyd encouraged her. "I'm sure Mr. Mackey won't mind. We're all pumping him."

"Of course, Miss Rutherford."

"I'd like to ask what you think the future holds for us? What's going to happen to us? What's going to happen to Europe? To Asia? To the whole world? By what code are men to live? What form of government will survive—democracy, fascism, or communism? And if they all fail, how will men govern themselves—or how will they allow themselves to be governed?"

The visitor smiled broadly and held out his hands in a helpless gesture.

"Ah, Miss Rutherford, you shouldn't ask me things like that. I have my own opinions, but they are strictly my own, and I don't expect others to share them. I'm afraid your father and uncle and your good-looking cousin over there wouldn't agree with me."

There was an encouraging murmur for him to proceed.

"Perhaps what I have to say might prove to be more acceptable if I began by asking a question myself."

He paused; there was attentive silence.

"Do you believe," he asked, "that capitalism—the present economic system by which we live today—is going to continue?"

No one answered.

"Personally I don't see how it can," he said, smiling pleasantly with his thin lips. "It cannot go on many years longer because of certain obvious reasons. First and foremost there is the matter of unemployment—mass unemployment—which is steadily on the increase; just now we have some eight million persons out of work, and their number is constantly growing; second, we continually have periods of boom followed by periods of depression—when hunger, poverty, and want stalk our streets; third, the volume of public debt is steadily increasing and will sooner or later reach a point where it will topple us into ruin; fourth, our present economic life depends upon a free money exchange between this and other countries. That hoard of gold buried at Fort Knox is of no value to us because it has no value to other people in other parts of the world. Under capitalism production is carried on for profit and for no other reason, and it is the demand for profit which in the final analysis, provokes war. Next there is our agriculture, sunk now in debt and poverty which even state subsidies can hardly keep alive. Mr. Roosevelt has tried various kinds of 'pump-priming,' including the expedience of plowing under a fourth of our cotton crop, reducing our wheat acreage by twenty per cent, destroying five million pigs. A wanton waste. Lastly there is our failure to find uses for the funds stored in our banks. During the past ten years new capital investment has come almost entirely from the State, not from private sources. There are a number of other good reasons which point to the collapse of our present economy, but with these I do not need to bore you. Personally I think the end of capitalism will come in the next ten or twenty years."

"What's to succeed it?" Lloyd asked, as he paused.

"Well," Byron Mackey answered, giving each of the listening group about him another thin, disarming smile, "there is the mounting strength of labor. I see it everywhere—in strikes, in demonstrations—labor growing into a dominant, aggressive army—labor demanding its right, its privileges, its recognition—and whether you sympathize with these demands or not, labor is going to get them. And so I envisage a labor party—a workers' party——"

"Like Russia's!" J.O.B. growled.

"No, not like Russia's. I'll come to the difference between them in a few minutes. The present split in labor's ranks is, in my opinion, one of the most regrettable tragedies that has happened to its cause in all the years of its history. I do not care who is right—William Green or John L. Lewis; both of them will be dead before long, and labor will reunite and go on its triumphant way, but for the time being, they have decimated labor's power just when a united front of all workers is essential to labor's march. Their differences will be healed eventually, their present leaders will disappear from the picture, and in a few years you will see a solid labor coalition again.

"Just now," he continued with slow impressiveness, "we have in this country forty million workers, our biggest sector of society with a common interest—and we will have half again as many in a short while. They *must* have a voice in the Government. Eventually they will take over the reins of government, and I can see no reason why they shouldn't *become* the Government. If we are to exist at all as a nation, our hope lies in labor.

"When that happens, there will be a new setup in our economic system—a new New Deal. I foresee the abolishment of all private property, everything—utilities, transportation, factories, mines, all the processes of production and manufacture—becoming the property of the State——"

"And the State will make a pretty mess of them!" snarled J.O.B.

"Not necessarily. Today our Government operates to everybody's satisfaction the postal system, the building of highways, pipe lines, the successful management of the TVA and the WPA. Think of the many municipally owned utilities and power plants throughout the country. For instance, the able administration of the Port of New York Authority which has charge of the George Washington Bridge and the Hudson and Lincoln tunnels, and your own state commission which manages, on behalf of the people, your San Francisco-Oakland Bridge and the Golden Gate Bridge! Yes, I can see successful government management of all enterprises now privately owned."

"You believe, then, it is right to eliminate the incentive for individual effort?" Lloyd inquired.

"Everybody would be working for the Government—for themselves, just as the employees do in a department store or factory which the owner has turned over to them. They take a keen interest in the business they own and see to it that it is properly managed."

"And all private property, all enterprises and the inventions which man's ingenuity has created—all these rights of ownership will be confiscated?" J.O.B. demanded in a rasping voice.

"Some scheme, I should say, will be worked out by which private owners will be compensated. It would take a number of years, of course, before they could be paid in full——"

"It's revolution!" cried J.O.B.

"Yes, revolution, but not necessarily a sanguinary one. You fail to see that a revolution is already taking place, and it will come much faster when labor is united and elects its own congressmen, senators, and its own President.

"I see no other future for our country, Miss Rutherford," Byron Mackey said, turning pleasantly to Eleanor; "our only hope to exist lies in labor's strength. There won't be any more Republicans or Democrats in a few years; there is very little difference between them even now. The struggle, as I see it, is the forces of capital versus the forces of labor, and the rising tide of labor is certain to triumph."

"So you advocate communism—Russian bolshevism!"

Mackey laughed mildly.

"We're a different people from the Russians. Most of them are illiterate peasants; we have no peasant class, and most of our workers both read and write; moreover they think, and think for themselves; they don't have to be told, as the Russian peasants do, that they are being exploited.

"But the USSR is still in the throes of evolution, and in order to achieve the goal Lenin had in mind, it is ruled today with the iron hand of dictators. There are nearly two hundred million citizens in the Soviet Union, and these two hundred million are ruled by four and a half million members of the Communist party. There is no secret about this. As the only legal party, the Communists enjoy a complete monopoly in the political field. Automatically the decisions of the Party become the Soviet law of the land. Members of the Party are commissars in the cabinet, are heads of the trusts and universities, staff the high commands of the Red Army, hold key positions in the labor unions, co-operatives, and the press. Upon its members the Party depends for carrying out its policies. If they do not, it straightway discredits, demotes, or deposes them. Within the last year or so thousands have been stricken from its rolls; nearly half a million have been expelled. Not only have they been ejected from the Party, but many have been arrested by the secret police, the NKVD. Eight generals of the Red Army and thirty-seven leading

Bolsheviks accused of being antagonistic to the existing regime have been shot, while tens of thousands of their followers have been jailed, exiled, or put in concentration camps. Russia speaks in the name of freedom and sets up a totalitarian dictatorship. No subversive attacks upon, or even criticism of, government policy is permitted in the press. Stalin says 'No,' and there is an end of it. It will be different here."

"You bet it will!" J.O.B. chimed in.

"I fully expect the capitalistic elements in the United States will attempt to thwart the will of the workers, and they may go as far as to resist by force. In that case the party in power must be prepared to crush the aggressive capitalists with swiftness and severity in order to keep scattered violence from developing into full-fledged and nation-wide revolt. If the die-hards start trouble, it will be their own fault if they get hurt. But I don't believe it will come to that. We are a democracy, and I think we will remain a democracy, and if the majority of the people elect representatives to Congress to carry out their wishes, the rest of us will fall in line.

"How many capitalists are there today in this country who approve of Mr. Roosevelt's policies? Not many, I should say, and yet they obey the laws he recommends to Congress, and we bow our heads to the NLRB and the WPA and pay the taxes that are imposed. No, I do not believe there will be any violence. Lots of grumbling, of course; but no forceful resistance."

"There will have to be some necessary enforcement of the law, won't there, if you are going to confiscate people's property and take away from them what they rightfully believe belongs to them?" Lloyd inquired.

"Very probably. A military arm will be essential."

"Despotism backed by force!" J.O.B. growled.

"Call it what you will——"

"What about the Bill of Rights?" Lloyd interposed.

"They will have to be modified."

"You mean abrogate the civil liberties guaranteed our people by the first ten amendments to the Constitution?" Lloyd was aghast.

Mackey smiled.

"Well," he said, "consider how civil liberty is denied many of us today. Let me remind you of the persecutions under unconstitutional state syndicalism and sedition laws, the use of injunctions against the rights of labor, the forbidding or breaking up of meetings and demonstrations, the practice of police brutality, the censorship of newspapers and books, the theater, the motion picture, and particularly of the radio. Air censorship is rigidly controlled by Washington today. That's restriction of free speech, isn't it? Consider too the arrests for the dissemination of birth-control information, the persecution for religious principles—such as refusal to salute the flag—the legal discrimination in many states against atheists and persons disbelieving in religion; I have only to remind you of the trial of John T. Scopes, who was convicted and fined for disobeying the Tennessee state law against the teaching of the theory of evolution in tax-supported schools. If today we ignore and wink at observing freedoms guaranteed our citizens, I can see no logical reason why a labor-controlled Government in Washington should observe such guarantees to the letter."

"And the Judiciary—the Supreme Court?" Lloyd asked.

"Abolished by constitutional amendment.

"Look here," he broke off to say abruptly with another easy smile for each one of his listeners, "I don't think this is quite fair. You've persuaded me into describing certain advanced ideas I entertain. I had no wish to express myself so freely. Miss Rutherford asked me about the future, and I tried to give her a picture of what I think may happen. I have been studying tendencies throughout the country; I have traveled into every state and sat in on hundreds of disputes between employers and employees. Everywhere it is strike, strike, strike, often accompanied by lawlessness and strong-armed methods. While such strikes must be curbed—we cannot countenance bloodshed and murder—these strikes indicate, I think, a steadily growing strength on the part of the workers, a strength which one day must assert itself into a unified objective. I'm sorry I have let myself run on this way; I have no wish to offend you."

Lloyd reassured him.

"That's quite all right, Mr. Mackey; we're deeply indebted to you for giving us the benefit of your ideas; they will set us all to thinking——"

But J.O.B. was roused. He heaved his big bulk up from his chair, his red face redder than usual, his large head trembling a little, and, shaking a finger at Mackey, cried:

"Look here! Do you mean to tell me that after all the years of hard work I have put in, after all the years of thought and conscientious management I have given to making my business one of the great shipping companies on the Pacific Coast, such hoodlums and rough-necks as Rory O'Brien and Mat Swenson are going to come along and take it away from me? I'll fight them with every drop of blood I have, with every ounce of strength! And what's more, my dear sir, I refuse to belong to a nation which robs its citizens of the fruits of their labor! I refuse to belong to a nation where there is no reward for thrift, perseverance, and brains! I refuse——"

"Now, come, come, J.O.B.," Lloyd urged, soothingly; "Mr. Mackey obliged us by telling us what he thought the future promised. Mr. Mackey is not making the law, is not prescribing the conditions under which you and I are going to live. He's telling you what he *thinks* may happen, and what he *thinks* a government controlled by labor will expect of you and me and everyone."

"Dictatorship!" barked J.O.B.

"I'm afraid so," Mackey admitted amiably; "I'm not going to like it any better than you."

"Preposterous! If a mongrel like Rory O'Brien and his wharf rats are going to hijack us, browbeat and murder us, are going to take charge of our lives and our country——"

"No, no, no," Mackey hastily interposed. "I said no such thing, nor do I believe they ever will. O'Brien and many of his followers un-doubtedly are radicals and advocate reforms which they promise will ameliorate the lot of their fellow workers, but I am not certain just what motives actuate Mr. O'Brien and his friends. No doubt he is prompted to some extent by a desire to help his unions, but unques-tionably ambition plays a part. His strength lies in making trouble, and he knows it. It contributes to his personal power. To obtain it, he does not hesitate to sow the seeds of discontent——"

"He ought to be jailed!"

"Perhaps, and I am not defending him or his methods. I say only that the power of labor is on the increase, and a united labor front is an element which we must weigh and consider in predicting the future."

Lloyd had placed a hand on his brother's arm and now put himself between the two men and backed J.O.B. out of the group, murmuring an admonition.

Stan, striving to digest some of Mackey's unpalatable statements, had his thoughts diverted by the sight of his cousin. Eleanor's face was glowing, her red lips were parted, her eyes sparkled. He had never seen the girl appear so animated, so beautiful. She approached Mackey now and held out her hand, taking the one he gave between her own.

"Thank you," she said fervently; "*thank* you."

The man's expression changed from one of polite acceptance of a tribute to sober contemplation, unsmiling and intent.

"May I also express my appreciation?" said Stan, stepping forward. "You have a good deal of courage, sir—if I may say so—to beard the lions in their den."

"Daniel got away with it," Mackey replied easily.

J.O.B. came back to where they were standing.

"My brother has been giving me a good call-down, just the way he used to when we were small boys. He's the older and has always been the wiser, fairer one. He tells me I have been discourteous. My apologies, Mr. Mackey."

"Oh, please! Not at all necessary! I understand your prejudices and sympathize with them. I really shouldn't be so free and easy with my ideas; they always get me in trouble. It was your daughter— is she . . . ?"

"No, no, Eleanor is Lloyd's child."

"Your niece, then. She caught me off guard; she seemed to challenge me. I was just thinking out loud."

"Well, I hope that for my sake and the sake of my friends your dream of the future doesn't materialize until after we're all dead!"

"I doubt if you have any cause of worry on that score; it probably won't happen for many years."

"Tell me, Mr. Mackey—I hope I'm not speaking out of turn—but what do you think is going to be the outcome—what *should* be the outcome of this local fracas? What do you believe we shipowners ought to do?"

Mackey shrugged.

"Negotiate, I suppose. Make a deal that's acceptable to each union, approach them separately. I think that's all you *can* do—that is, if you wish to resume relations. I honestly believe all of you want this strike over. If it is not ended soon, the revolution of which I have been speaking may come sooner than I predict."

"Maybe you're right," J.O.B. said, thoughtfully.

"Meet the strikers halfway," Mackey pursued; "I'm convinced they are in a chastened mood and are willing to compromise, perhaps modify their demands."

J.O.B. stood frowning, pulling at his goatee.

"I'll have to consult some of my fellow shipowners," he said.

"Why don't you? You mean Mr. Ahearn, Mr. Nickel, and Mr. Grant?"

J.O.B.'s eyebrows impulsively twitched.

"I'll think it over," he said, "and maybe take your advice. Certainly we're all sick of the quarrel."

CHAPTER XII

IT WAS MIDNIGHT when Stan and his father left; Byron Mackey remained talking to Lloyd and Eleanor; Frances had long ago slipped across the street and gone home.

"What do you think of him?" J.O.B. asked.

"He seems to know his own mind," Stan answered evasively. He had been impressed with Mackey although agreeing with very little of what he had said, but he was in no mood at this late hour to start a discussion with his father.

"He's one of those theorists who likes to hear himself talk," J.O.B. commented caustically; "he's just plain fascist. We may have to have a totalitarian government, but it won't be controlled by labor; it may well be a military one so as to keep rioting off the streets and workers where they belong."

Stan was too tired to reply, and without further words his father fitted his latchkey into the door lock and they entered the house.

On the hatrack, conspicuously displayed, was a small folded piece of paper addressed in the maid's handwriting: "Mr. Stanley." Unfolding it, Stan read:

"Miss Welch called you. She said for you to phone her when you came in. Important, she said."

As his father heavily climbed the stairs on his way to bed, Stan hesitated, then looked up Caddie's number in the telephone book and dialed her. She answered immediately.

"Oh, Stan! Forgive me, please, but I just *had* to talk to you tonight; tomorrow'd be too late. I've been over at the courthouse in Oakland all day today and all day last Saturday listening to the murder trial and hearing the lawyers scrap—Nate, Dan Sheridan, and the others— and oh, my goodness, how they fight!—and tomorrow the judge is going to instruct the jury. It's thrilling! And listen: I've got a pass for two. I stood Nate Jacobs up after court adjourned this afternoon, and I told him I simply *had* to have one, so he got it for me—and, well, can you go over there with me tomorrow?"

"Lord, Caddie—this is pretty short notice. Today's the first day I've been to the office."

"I know, but—oh, come on, Stan. You'll get the kick of your life out of the fireworks. Why, the attorneys do everything except call each other names, and the judge is constantly admonishing them. I'm certain he's going to instruct the jury in the morning, and there may be a verdict tomorrow afternoon or tomorrow night. Oh, *please* say you'll come. We'll have to take the eight-twenty boat because they start at nine-thirty——"

"What's the matter with driving over the bridge?"

"Oh, you'll *come?*"

"I think I'd like to."

"Stan, I could *kiss* you! I haven't been over the bridge yet, haven't been anywhere near it. Oh, that will be simply *wonderful!* Doing it with you! Oh, Stan, Stan, will you really drive me over there? I can't believe it! I'm simply drooling! This case is positively the most interesting you've ever listened to! I wish I could write it! I wish I could tell everybody—the world—about it! It's *terrific!*"

He was smiling into the telephone's mouthpiece. Her excitement and enthusiasm were those of a little girl.

"Where shall we meet?"

"Oh, anywhere you say. Can't you pick me up in front of where I live? I'll be out on the sidewalk waiting for you at eight o'clock."

"Well, say," he said, "you'd better find out where the courthouse is. I don't know my way round Oakland, and I don't think I've ever driven over there—certainly not by the bridge."

"Don't give it a thought! I'll find out just how to get there—every turn. Oh, Stan—you're just a darling!"

§ 2

At the appointed hour he met her. She wore her tight-fitting jersey suit, firmly belted; about her neck was a fur scarf, and as always her wavy hair curled up and around the brim of her small hat. She was radiant and, he thought, beautiful as, laughing gaily, she climbed in beside him.

"Oh, this is fun!" she cried. "And what a morning!"

There were heavy clouds to the south filled with the promise of rain, but the sun shone brave and glittering over the crest of Mount Diablo and tipped each hurrying wavelet of the dun-colored Bay with gold.

Bubbling with eagerness, she began to tell him about the trial.

"Those lawyers! They're continually at each other's throats. You see, there are four defendants; Walters, who confessed, and who is trying to implicate the three others, and each one of the accused has his own attorney, and then there are the district attorney and his assistants. They row all the time—oh, and they mean the things they say to one another! The judge gets furious.

"You understand, don't you, Stan? Sheridan got a complete confession from Walters, who frankly admits he was one of the men who stabbed Oliver; he says another man helped him, a fellow named Muscowitz, but he escaped, went to Russia they say; anyway they haven't caught him, and on the strength of Walters' say-so, the D.A. is doing his best to convict the others—all members of the Firemen's Union—of conspiracy. It's ridiculous, of course."

There was no checking her; her rush of words confused him.

"Walters has contradicted himself a hundred times," she rattled on; "the poor dope can't either read or write, and Nate has just made hash of his testimony. And the defense—that's Jacobs and the other attorneys representing the accused—put on a surprise witness last week —Jack Crosby, the second assistant engineer on board the *San Marco,* and he swore he saw Walters with his hand on the doorknob of Oliver's cabin within a minute or two of the time the murder was committed, and that there was positively no one else in sight."

She spoke breathlessly, repeating herself, reciting unrelated details of the proceedings without regard to their sequence. He could not follow her, but he liked the sound of her eager voice and the passionate emphasis with which she spoke. He was more concerned with the problem of finding the proper approach to the bridge, but presently he made a left turn and the broad six-lane highway of the great structure stretched out magnificently before them.

Caddie uttered cries of exultation. Wasn't it terrific! Wasn't it simply stupendous! What stately towers—so tall and graceful! And, oh, you could see all the strike-bound ships riding at anchor at their moorings or tied up at the docks—hundreds of them without a single man on board, except perhaps a single watchman! Now came a glimpse of the site where the fair was to be. You could see the roofs of some of the temporary structures over the top of the bridge rail. It was going to be the finest ever—and wasn't it a shame that New York had decided to hold a fair of its own exactly at the same time!

"Are you going to listen to Mayor Rossi on the air tonight?" Stan asked, carefully watching the tracks of a car he was following.

"Oh yes, but he won't say anything."

"I don't know why not! It's time somebody said *something.* We're in a fine mess; the unions are just killing San Francisco as a city— making a ghost town of it!"

He fished into an upper vest pocket and pulled out a folded newspaper clipping. "Read that," he told her; "I tore it out of the *Chronicle* this morning and brought it along just to edify you."

Caddie opened it. In a box, headed "Today's Strike Headlights," were listed the various strikes in progress at the moment within the Bay area, and beside them the number of days each one had lasted. It read:

Maritime Strike .... 68th day	40,000	men idle
Warehousemen's Strike .... 67th day	350	men idle
Bay Industry Strike .... 53rd day	550	men idle
Shipyard Strike .... 58th day	2,500	men idle
Machinists' Strike .... 21st day	133	men idle
Cigar Makers' Strike .... 97th day	46	men idle
Upholsterers' Strike .... 76th day	100	men idle
Battery Workers' Strike .... 98th day	110	men idle

"That's a fine summation," he said, watching her as her eyes took it in. She crumpled the clipping in her hand and tossed it away.

"Old stuff," she said with a disdainful shrug. "The inference implied by the worthy *Chronicle* and by the rest of San Francisco's newspapers—all privately owned, and all of whose revenues come from their advertisers—is that the unions are all to blame. It's always the poor unions."

"I don't see how!"

She made no rejoinder, but after a moment said brightly, "Well, I can tell you this much: the warehousemen's strike will be settled this afternoon."

"Really?"

"Yes; they've agreed to compromise."

"Who've agreed to compromise?"

"The owners of the warehouses, of course; they'll settle for an increase in pay—as they should."

"How do you know?"

"Oh, I know all right. They'll not give the men as much as they asked, but it will be a raise. Five cents an hour more. They'll pay a minimum scale of seventy-five cents an hour in public warehouses, and seventy cents to men who work in grain, feed, and milling warehouses."

"I suppose an increase of five cents an hour justifies three hundred and fifty men remaining out of work for sixty-seven days."

"You're so prejudiced! You see everything through those green-tinted glasses of yours."

At the barricade he stopped the car and paid their toll.

"It's a tremendous success," he said, referring to the bridge, when again they were on their way; "twice as many cars cross it than was expected. They're talking of reducing the charge to two bits."

"So I read. . . . I think you turn here."

He swung the car to the right and headed for Oakland's business district.

"I hope we're in time," Caddie said.

"It's only twenty minutes to nine!"

"The courthouse is jammed; there's an awful crowd; you'll have a hard time finding a place to park."

"What happened in court yesterday?" he asked, now willing to give her closer attention. "I saw in the paper that Jacobs accused Sheridan of suppressing evidence favorable to the defense."

"Oh, he did! It was perfectly outrageous! Jack Crosby's evidence. He wouldn't call him. Crosby went to the district attorney's office a couple of weeks ago and stated he knew something about what happened on board the *San Marco*. He told one of Sheridan's assistants about it and made a statement which identified Walters as one of the murderers and cleared Detrich and the others entirely; what he had to say was never presented to the jury, but Jacobs put Crosby on the stand and got his statement into the record, and he accused Sheridan of withholding this witness' evidence intentionally. It's just another one of those outrageous frame-ups whereby innocent union men are railroaded into prison——"

"Hold on a minute, Caddie," Stan interrupted. "You've claimed all along that those Modesto boys were framed for carrying dynamite illegally. Their conviction has been upheld by the District Court of Appeals and by the California Supreme Court, and every contention of the defense was analyzed and all evidence reviewed, and finally the Supreme Court of the United States refused to reopen the case. I guess that proves conclusively the men are guilty. . . . Guilty as hell, I'd say!"

"Oh, here we are!" cried Caddie. "Look at that mob! You'd better turn here."

The street in front of the gray-walled, dingy courthouse was filled with a milling, yelling crowd, blocking all passage. Stan drew into a side street and drove two more blocks before he could find a vacant place for his car. The angry rumble of the mob reached them even here, a menacing bourdon beneath the other noises of the city streets. When they again came upon the scene, Stan saw that a demonstration was in progress. A dozen banners—one, the American flag—were being carried through the press, and in addition square-sided lettered signs spelling such legends as "Free Detrich, Dempsey, and Kerrigan," "No More Frame-ups," "Stand by Union Labor's Fight!" "Remember Tom Mooney and Warren Billings!"

"Lord," Stan exclaimed more to himself than to his companion, "that's a fine kettle of fish!"

"What is?"

"This kind of thing—attempting to intimidate a judge and influence a jury!"

"It's the Defense Committee."

"What Defense Committee?"

"The Defense Committee to free Detrich, Dempsey and Kerrigan. Labor won't stand for their being framed. . . . Come on. You'll have to push."

A policeman barred their way.

"We have a pass!" cried Caddie. She fumbled in her bag, produced it.

Shoving and elbowing, they squirmed a passage through the crowd and eventually reached the courthouse doors and found themselves inside the dreary, odorous building. Caddie was panting, but she stilled her breath long enough to address a court attendant she knew.

"Tony, help me, will you? Show us where we are."

"This way, Miss Welch. The old barn's never seen the like of this before."

The man indicated where their seats were located, and inching and stumbling past a long line of knees with many an "Excuse me, please" and "I beg your pardon," they ultimately reached the chairs reserved for them.

The high-vaulted room was crowded, filled with nearly a hundred persons; the air was fetid with the smell of warm bodies, woolen garments, and rubber raincoats. On the wall back of the witness stand hung a large diagram, obviously the deck plan of the *San Marco*. Inside the rail before the judge's dais two long tables were arranged, at one of which sat the defendants and their counsels, at the other the district attorney and his assistants. Stan studied the faces of the accused men. He was familiar with the photographs that had been published in the newspapers: Emil Detrich, stocky, big-shouldered; Joe Dempsey, red-headed and square-jawed; Pat Kerrigan, iron gray, a deep dimple marking his chin; near by, with high cheekbones, eyes wide apart, and a vacant, hangdog expression, sat the confessed murderer, Gus Walters. Each man wore four union buttons in a vertical row on the left lapel of his coat. Of the defense lawyers, Stan readily recognized Nate Jacobs, and he knew the public defender, Otis Keeble, representing Walters, by sight. At the other table sat Clifford Kelly and Norwood Tharp, both assistants to the district attorney, and between them Dan Sheridan. Stan had met Sheridan on several occasions. He was a good-looking man with curling light hair and shrewd eyes that shot rapid, nervous glances right and left through horn-rimmed spectacles. Beyond this table and in a double tier against the wall sat the jury—six men and six women, and as Stan looked—in his line of vision—he suddenly saw Eleanor, very straight and very beautiful, in a seat in the fourth row across the intervening aisle, and next to her was—Byron Mackey!

He was about to exclaim and call Caddie's attention to his cousin's presence, when the bailiff rapped for order and the judge entered. Everybody rose, and as they reseated themselves he whispered to Caddie:

"Who's the judge?" He had a stern face, a bald head and wore glasses.

"Olzendam."

"I thought Duffey was going to try this case."

"He withdrew; said he didn't know enough about murder trials."

The bailiff rapped again for order. There followed the rustling sound of people adjusting themselves to comfortable positions, and the crisp shuffling of paper from the corner where the representatives of the press were congregated. Outside rose the rumble and murmur of the mob. At a sign from the judge the bailiff began to close windows.

"Let the record show that the jurors are all present."

Dan Sheridan rose to his feet.

"If your honor please, may I interrupt just a moment?"

He wanted to apologize, he said, for certain remarks he had made during his closing argument the previous day. There was a low exchange between the two; then Sheridan resumed his seat and the judge cleared his throat.

"May it be stipulated," he said, addressing the attorneys for the defense and the prosecution, "that the Court may instruct the jury orally, the reporter to take down the instructions in shorthand and later transcribe them?"

"This is *it!*" Caddie whispered, pinching Stan's arm.

"Ladies and gentlemen, before instructing you in the law applicable in this case . . ."

Caddie inched herself to the edge of her seat and leaned forward in close attention. Olzendam droned a little; he mumbled his words, addressing himself exclusively to the jury, making no effort to have his voice reach the rest of the courtroom. Only now and then could Stan hear what he was saying.

"First," he asked, "was Vincent Oliver killed on or about the twenty-second day of March 1936 in this county and state, and if so, did the person or persons who perpetrated the act of killing commit the crime of murder, and in what degree in so doing; second, are these defendants or any of them criminally responsible for the crime of murder?"

The crowded courtroom was tense with hushed expectancy. Occasional smothered coughs accentuated the stillness. The rumble of the mob outside rolled on in muffled waves.

The judge reviewed the evidence and proceeded to describe the wounds from which Vincent had died.

Stan glanced at Eleanor, wondering how it happened that she was there with Mackey. Only last evening they had met, and while it had been obvious to him—and presumably to the rest of the family—that she had been attracted to their guest and he to her, still it was odd that they were here today. After he and his father had left the house, had Mackey suggested this expedition? Evidently. His thoughts were interrupted by the judge dispassionately describing Vincent's injuries —a T-shaped wound in the back of the head, a stab wound in the right shoulder, a stab wound in the spine, a stab wound in the liver, penetrating the pancreas, and a wound in the back of the left thigh, cutting both the large artery and the vein in the leg. Stan wondered how Eleanor was taking all these unpalatable details. Apparently she seemed unperturbed, sitting tall and straight in her seat, closely listening, her classic profile set, expressionless.

Olzendam droned on. Often he made use of the phrase, "to my mind." It was "to my mind" this, and "to my mind" that. Frequently he referred to the diagram on the wall.

"The defendant Walters testified he was standing at the point marked 'W-1' . . . which is inconsistent with the testimony of the witness Smith who asserted he saw Walters and another man at the point marked 'J-1' . . .

"The testimony of these two witnesses, Griffiths and Crosby, if believed, would be strong evidence tending to identify the defendant Walters as the, or one of the, actual killers. . . . However, their testimony is not convincing to my mind."

Caddie snatched from her bag a pad and pencil and hastily scribbled:

"Rot! Walters and Muscowitz killed him and *nobody else!*"

Presently another scrawl:

"Walters lied to save his own neck—promised to incriminate the others so he wouldn't hang!"

Olzendam began now to recount in detail the story Walters had told on the witness stand—how Detrich had asked him in the Union Hall to "go on a job"; how in Dempsey's office he had heard it said, "that God damn fink, he belongs to some company union; he needs a lesson"; how he had accompanied Dempsey, Muscowitz, and another sailor, whom he didn't know, to the dock where the *San Marco* was moored.

Stan lost the thread of what he was saying. The courtroom, after the first hush of silence, was vibrant with small noises—sounds of twitching and fidgeting, half-stifled coughs, sibilant whispers, rustling and snuffling. With the windows closed, the room grew suffocatingly warm, and he became more and more conscious of the unpleasant odor of perspiring humans closely packed together. Caddie strained to hear what the judge was saying, blinking her eyes, faint wrinkles puckering her forehead.

". . . would, in my opinion, justify your belief as to the existence of an unlawful conspiracy. . . . His testimony is, however, to my mind, inconsistent with the physical facts."

"Oh!" gasped Caddie. She drew the outline of a large exclamation point and blacked it in with fierce scratchings of her pencil.

"This testimony"—Stan gathered the judge was discussing the reported confession of Kerrigan, who had been arrested in Seattle and grilled—"required over four days of the trial, and I therefore see no reason of again stating it."

"Oh!" scribbled Caddie, underlining the word three times.

The judge expressed his doubt that the confession had been wrung from Kerrigan by extortion.

"Blackguard!" wrote Caddie.

"As to the participation of the defendants Detrich and Dempsey," continued his honor, "the testimony of Walters finds corroboration in that of the witness Magee."

Caddie turned to Stan fiercely; her face was flushed; her eyes blazed; her nostrils quivered.

"Why, he's plainly telling the jury just what verdict he expects them to bring in!" she whispered. "Those are *instructions* all right!" she sneered.

A murmur, accompanying her whisper, swept through the courtroom like wind ruffling leaves. The bailiff rapped for silence.

"Whether the defendant Detrich is to be believed," continued the judge, "must therefore depend upon the credibility which you place upon the opposing testimony of Magee and Walters. . . .

"The defendant Dempsey has not denied the accusation against him by the witnesses . . ."

Caddie fisted her hands and pounded them together.

"He's sending them to the gallows himself! I've never heard——"

The sound of her voice reached the bailiff's ears; he frowned and shook an admonishing finger.

"To my mind," went on the judge, "these considerations of an impeaching character do not persuade me that the witness Magee has been deliberately false in his testimony. . . ."

"God!" wrote Caddie. "What good's a jury? Send them home!"

"I again caution you, ladies and gentlemen, that you are the exclusive judges of all questions of fact and the credibility of the witnesses and that you are not to consider yourselves bound, nor influenced against your own judgment, by my comments just given to you."

"Oh no," scoffed Caddie, "of course not! They won't be influenced one little bit! They'll do just as they think best!"

§ 3

Olzendam now began to explain the law and its applicability to the case. At eleven o'clock he ordered the officers who were to take charge of the jurors sworn, and the six men and six women retired to the jury room.

The moment the judge left the courtroom a hubbub broke loose. On their feet, excited men and women began to talk at once, gathering up coats, wraps, hats, preparing to depart. Caddie was too agitated to say more than, "Let's get out of here—quick!"

But Stan wanted first to speak to Eleanor. He called her name, waved his hand.

"Who's that?" Caddie demanded.

"My cousin."

He caught Eleanor's eye, and recognition brought from her a bright smile. Stan fought his way to her side.

"Hello," he said, when near enough to be heard; "what brought you here?"

"Mr. Mackey."

"Howdy," he said, addressing her companion. "Interesting, wasn't it? . . . Eleanor, may I present my friend, Miss Welch? And Mr. Mackey."

An artificial smile for Eleanor was the best that Caddie could manage, but to Byron she said cordially:

"I've met Mr. Mackey before; in Mr. Jacobs' office."

"Ah, yes indeed; I remember," he nodded.

"What did you think of this exhibition?" Caddie asked him.

"I'd've liked to have heard more of the testimony. The judge didn't give the men and women of the jury much leeway about making up their own minds, did he?"

"I should say he didn't!" snapped Caddie.

"It's just a question," Mackey observed, "how much faith they have in the witnesses."

"A frame-up," declared Caddie.

"Don't know about that," Mackey countered. "I doubt if Walters did the job single-handed."

"Muscowitz," said Caddie.

"The fugitive? Perhaps, but there seems to have been some conniving, some concerted plot——"

"Not by those others. They're just being framed!"

"Well, it's up to the jury to decide."

"Going home?" asked Eleanor.

"I have my car," Stan answered; "we drove over the bridge this morning."

He turned to Caddie.

"Not much use in waiting, is there? How long do you think it will take them?"

"About ten minutes," she said scornfully.

"We'll drive back to the city. May take them hours; you never can tell about a jury.

"I'm glad you got over," he said to Eleanor. "Wish your father had been here. His opinion would be interesting."

"He wanted to come, but—you know—couldn't very well afford to be seen here."

"I'll be glad to hear what he thinks, just the same. Well, so long. How're you getting back?"

"Greenwood."

So she had driven Byron Mackey over in Grandmère's limousine!

"I'd like to discuss this case with you," Caddie said to Mackey; "certain things were never brought out in the testimony."

"So?" he observed noncommittally.

"Perhaps you and Nate—Mr. Jacobs, you know—and I could get together for luncheon someday soon."

"Good; call me at the Palace."

"Let's go," she said to Stan.

He waved to Eleanor, nodded to Mackey, caught Caddie by the arm, piloted her through the fast dispersing crowd, and they made their way to his car without further words. When she was seated beside him and they were moving, she said:

"I need a drink—a big, long, tall one."

"Where'd you like to go?"

She thought.

"There's a nice place here on San Pablo Avenue; it's quiet and they have good liquor."

"Show me."

CHAPTER XIII

SITTING OPPOSITE TO HER in one of the curtained booths at "Trader Horn's," Stan noticed with concern her stricken face, usually so animated and given to ready smiles and coquetry. She would not meet his look and sat staring into space, her lips shut tightly, her eyes smoldering. When the tall glass containing her drink was set before her, she let it stand where the waiter had placed it.

"Drink up," Stan urged; "see how it goes."

She had suggested a concoction known as a "Zombie," a blending, she explained, of three kinds of rum with a brandy float. It sounded formidable, but Stan was eager to please her. He found the drink palatable and potent.

Now, at his word, she emptied a third of her glass, gulping and drawing breath as she set it down.

"That's better," she said, and presently began to give vent to her pent-up feelings.

"Take it easy," he cautioned her; "we've got all day."

With an effort she stilled her quivering breath.

"I'm sorry I'm so upset," she told him with a shaky smile. She sipped her drink. "If you only knew what *I* know; if you had followed the case from the beginning! Let me tell you.

"In the first place, Kerrigan was tortured until he was willing to sign anything that was put before him. I don't care what the judge told the jury; they handcuffed him to a chair and gave him the third degree. I got it straight from Nate. He repudiated his statement the minute Nate contacted him. Then Magee—another Sheridan witness!

—testified he gave Dempsey thirty dollars the day before the murder, expense money for a trip across the Bay, its object to beat up Oliver. There is no such entry in the union's books! Next what did they do? They wired Magee's hotel room for sound, and they got him to entice Detrich there in the hope he'd say something incriminating. He said nothing! Then, on a fake charge, they arrested Magee and threw him into a cell with Dempsey, and the cell was also wired for sound! Again their plot failed. Just think! Detrich never saw Oliver in his life, and Dempsey visited the ship the day *before* the tragedy to settle some claim of overtime, and he and Oliver sat down and talked things over amicably."

"That's right," said Stan; "he told my father so—that everything was friendly."

"I wish I'd known that!" cried Caddie. "Nate would have put you on the stand."

"Hearsay evidence," Stan commented.

"Well, it's too late now. But there is something I want to ask you: What about that little matter of Wickwire and Rutherford keeping the captain and the other officers of the *San Marco* on their pay roll ever since last March—ten months?"

"Oh, come, come, come," Stan said with some impatience; "that doesn't make sense, Caddie. The unions are on strike; all ships are tied up. Captain O'Day and the others are important witnesses in this case. What do you expect Wickwire and Rutherford to do? Let 'em get away, find other jobs, perhaps lose track of them? We sent them their monthly checks at the D.A.'s request just so he would be sure to have them on hand when he wanted them."

"Well, let's skip that. Both mates swore that Kerrigan did not come ashore when Walters said he did, and further, Crosby, the assistant engineer, testified he saw Walters—at the moment the man claimed he was more than thirty feet away—with his hand on the doorknob of Oliver's cabin.

"And consider this," she continued, "the Defense Committee offered five thousand dollars to Walters to get himself a good attorney; he refused; chose instead the public defender, Keeble. Why? Because he wanted to save his own wretched neck. He testified just as was told him to do, and was caught in lie after lie.

"Of course," she continued, "the biggest scandal in this farcical affair is the judge. He told the jury, in so many words, he believed Walters was telling the truth and that Kerrigan's confession had been freely made when he knew for a fact it was wrung from him by extortion. Kerrigan was arrested in Seattle, denied legal counsel, flown to Oakland and quizzed for sixty hours without sleep; then, when he was a wreck and he had signed what they put in front of him, with great compassion they took him to a hospital, where the doctors found he had a temperature of a hundred and one and that he was in a highly nervous condition. The jury was never informed of *those* facts! Oh no! They were given the impression that Sheridan has done a fine job of sleuthing and they ought to bring in a verdict of guilty. I haven't a doubt in the world but that those six moribund old men and six crotch-bound old women will hand out a death penalty for all."

She stopped and drained her glass to its dregs.

"Hit me again, will you, Stan?"

He rang for the waiter, ordered a single "Zombie," but Caddie would not have it so.

"You've got to have one, too! You can't throw me down, Stan; not today. I'm not going to drink alone."

"Okay," he said, "but remember I have to drive across the bridge."

"You'll make it."

"You see everything through those green-tinted glasses you accused me of wearing," he told her; "you're so damn prejudiced, you believe only what you *want* to believe."

"That isn't so," she returned. "I know more than they let the jury know, and it's all an outrageous miscarriage of justice."

The second round of "Zombies" came, and they talked on, reviewing the trial, Caddie repeating her criticisms, but with less agitation now. Her smiles returned, and she was agreeable and good company.

Feeling the effects of the drinks he had had, Stan drove carefully as they recrossed the bridge. Caddie had suggested they lunch at "Julius' Castle," a restaurant high on the bluff of Telegraph Hill from which there was a fine view of the Bay. Following her directions, he successfully maneuvered the steep inclines and arrived at the place without mishap.

A table for two next to the window on the glassed-in porch was vacant, and they seized it joyfully. Caddie loosened the fur scarf about her neck, placed purse and gloves on the floor and, with a sly grin, asked:

"A martini, hey, Stan—or have we had enough?"

"Oh no; a martini by all means." He was in fine fettle, and a cocktail seemed right.

The sky had become overcast; rain was imminent. The prospect from their vantage point was fascinating. The city tumbled headlong from beneath their feet to the water's edge in a tangle of gabled roofs, punctuated now and then by tall structures of steel and stone; beyond lay the gray expanse of the Bay reaching out toward Berkeley and Oakland with myriads of foam-tipped hands. Gulls, their pinions poised, floated effortlessly in the gusty air or swooped from sight in precipitous flights. The muffled sounds of motor horns, streetcar bells, and the hum of traffic reached them faintly. The towers of the Bay Bridge stood tall and blackly silhouetted against the gray sky. Tiny trucks and microscopic figures of men could be seen crawling over the sandy wastes of Treasure Island, soon to be transformed into a tropical paradise.

"Oh, isn't this fun?" cried Caddie. "It's so heavenly being here with you. You've been so kind to me today. You soothe me, quiet me. If I were a cat, I'd purr. May I have another cocktail, please?"

"You're a perfect tank, Caddie! You don't want to get drunk, do you?"

"Why not? I don't care. Do you?"

"No. Come on."

The luncheon arrived in due time. First, a mess of raw shrimps in their curving shells, then a delicious minestrone, followed by lobster *à l'américaine,* a savory salad with a faint flavoring of garlic, pastry, cheese, crackers, fruit, and coffee. Stan was considering a bottle of Haut Sauterne, but, warmed by the food and the felicitous hour, he decided upon champagne.

"Oh, we will get tight!" Caddie exclaimed joyfully.

"Look," she said, her face suddenly serious. She put down her knife and fork and linked her long, graceful fingers beneath her chin, her expression sobering him.

"Look," she repeated; "I'm awfully fond of you! I'll tell you something you'd like to know, but you must give me your word never to betray me. Promise . . . All right, I'll believe you.

"You know Mat Swenson and Rory O'Brien have no love for each other. Either would stick a knife in the other's back without a moment's hesitation. Now this strike could be settled in a jiffy if those two men could get together, and it can be settled within the next week if you'll do what I say and tell no one I gave you the tip-off. I have your solemn word on that.

"The Maritime Federation is Rory's darling. It comprises, as you know, the seven unions connected with the shipping business—sailors, longshoremen, firemen, stewards, and so on. Their slogan is—you're familiar with it!—'An injury to one is an injury to all.' In the solidarity of their organization lies their strength. Mat is sick of the strike; his men want to get back to work; their treasury is low. He feels—we all do—that the sailors have had a rough deal; they haven't got as much as the men belonging to the other unions of the Federation have. They didn't get the break that the longshoremen did in the '34 award. He wants a raise for the sailors, and that's the crux of the whole beef. Other unions have tacked on demands of their own, but if the shipowners were to go to Mat privately and offer to boost the sailors ten dollars a month, he'd accept it like a shot and force Rory to call off the strike under threat that if he didn't he would bust the Federation wide open. Rory would never stand for that."

"You're *sure?*"

"I'm not sure, of course. You mustn't modify the gains the stevedores have already won——"

"What about penalties for stoppages of work?"

"Rory'd concede something within reason, or leave disputes to a Port Authority."

"And the licensed personnel? The shipowners will never consent to the unions selecting their captains, mates, and engineers for them. I tell you, Caddie, there's no use trying to settle this strike unless that's understood."

"Make that a condition," she advised. "If the shipowners can get together with Mat and he's willing to sign up to get a ten-dollar-a-month raise for his men, he can force the rest of the Federation to

fall in line. That's just a tip, Stan, but you must promise me—you
have promised me!—never to give me away. I don't think my life
would be worth a plugged nickel if it was found out. I'm telling you
because—because, well, because I like you so much and I think this
stalemate has lasted long enough."

"You really think we can end the strike?" he asked, excitedly.

"I do. Tell your father—or Joe Halliday if you think better—to get
hold of Mat and put the proposition before him. He won't commit
himself right off, but he'll think about it and talk to some of his pals
in the S.U.P. He'll want to make peace, if for no other reason than
to cross Rory."

"I hope you're right, my dear. Here's a drink to you and a drink
to the end of our waterfront troubles, now and forever."

He filled the glasses, and when the foam subsided they touched
their rims and emptied them. As they set the goblets down, their eyes
met and there was tenderness and softness in Caddie's look which
made Stan's blood stir and feel warm in his neck. He met her smile,
and they gazed long and steadily at each other until his vision fogged
and he grew dizzy.

"Whew," he breathed, passing a hand over his eyes.

"What?" she whispered.

"You—you . . ." he floundered; "you get my goat," he finished
clumsily.

"Do I?"

"Yes."

"You've had mine for some time." She paused, continued: "You're
so young and so handsome; you're so . . . oh, I don't know what!
Fine and—and unspoiled!"

He laughed in embarrassment and felt the blood spread to his
cheeks and to his temples.

"I've never met anyone like you," she went on. "I've had an up-
and-down sort of life, and I've known lots of men, always got along
swell with them, but I don't think I ever really loved any of them.
There usually has been something calloused and soiled about the
men I've known—coarse and tough. They've been fighters and rough-
necks. I've never known a gentleman—someone who's fine and good
and . . . and . . . I guess what I'm trying to say is *refined!*"

"Aw, come off!" he expostulated; "let's drink up."

"Have you got a girl, Stan?"

He shook his head.

"Did you ever have one? Been in love?"

"Don't think so. There was a manicurist in Cambridge I liked; we used to go out nights, and she was a good kid. She married some years ago and has a little boy and a girl now."

"I know. While you were in college."

"I took the business course after I graduated."

"But here in Frisco, hasn't there been someone?"

"No—nobody."

She reached across the table and covered his hand with hers.

"I'm glad," she said softly.

His fingers interlaced with hers. She seemed wholly desirable to him at the moment. He formed a kiss with his lips and tossed it to her with a motion of his head. She answered it and squeezed his fingers hard.

Wheels turned within wheels and turned again. Caddie's smiling face swam in a golden light, her brown curls forming a shining halo about it, her eyes grew soft and luminous, her smiling lips, cupped on either side by the double lines that creased her cheeks, were red and inviting.

"Oh," he gulped, trying to tell her with a look what he could not find the words to say.

"Come," she said, disengaging her hand. "Pay your check and let's go. We'll drive to my place and I'll call Nate's office and see if those twelve solid citizens of the commonwealth have reached a verdict."

He signaled the waiter, dropped a bill of large denomination on the check, waved away the change. He rose a trifle unsteadily and thought of his driving. Hell! He could drive Caddie anywhere! Certainly he wasn't going to admit he couldn't! He could drive with his eyes shut!

Any doubts as to whether or not he was able to quickly evaporated as, with Caddie beside him, he released the brakes, touched the starter, and eased the gear shift into low. The fine mist that had begun to fall and the gusty breezes that accompanied it steadied him; he filled his lungs again and again with the cold air.

"Ah," he exulted, "I feel like driving you to the Beach and back! I feel like driving you to Reno!"

"Why Reno?"

"Oh, a place to go; nearly three hundred miles. I could get you there in six hours."

"We'll do it someday, you and me, huh? Just now I want to hear the verdict."

"They looked like a pretty good bunch of eggs," he said, referring to the jury's personnel.

"Not to me, they didn't," she rejoined; "just twelve goons without an intelligent thought among the lot of them!"

He threw back his head in laughter.

"What's a goon?" He reached for her knee and squeezed it.

"Look out!" she cried. "You'll have us in the gutter in a minute. Careful, Stan! For God's sake!"

He gave her a superior smile, but when a red light at a crossing, which he had not seen, suddenly confronted him, he had to jam on the brakes and bring the car to an abrupt stop, throwing Caddie forward so that she narrowly escaped bumping the windshield. He apologized, but she made no comment. He drove slowly now, and it was with a feeling of relief that he drew up in front of the apartment house where she lived and switched off the ignition.

They got out, and he followed her as she unlocked the entrance door and then held back the gate of the tarnished gilt elevator cage for him to enter. As they rose, he was aware of a mounting excitement, and aware too of the peculiar smell she exhaled that was neither scent nor perfume. It had a heady sweetness, and he breathed deep of it.

She opened her door and they went in. It had hardly closed before they reached for each other in the narrow, dim hallway, arms and hands groping, lips finding lips. They clung together for some moments; then she pushed him from her, scanning his face in the half-darkness. With a smothered cry she caught him to her again and kissed him hungrily; then, with his hand clasped in hers, she led him into her unaired, cluttered little sitting room and, tossing aside her hat, drew him beside her on the hard sofa and seized him in her arms, her lips again seeking his.

All thought of time or place, facts or circumstances deserted Stan. His senses were plunged into a vortex of confusion and raised to a plane of ecstasy as he drank deep and ever deeper of her responsive lips. Exhaustion followed, and they lay limp in each other's arms. Time passed.

A clock whirred a hoarse, discordant note, announcing the hour, and Caddie roused herself.

"I believe you're going to sleep," she accused him.

"No, no," he murmured; "just resting."

She kissed him.

"You darling!"

"You, too."

"Do you love me?"

"Course I do."

"Honestly?"

"Better than anyone I've ever known."

"Is that true?"

"Gee, Caddie," he cried boyishly, "I never dreamed there could be a woman like you. I think I've been purposely starved all my life, so I could give you everything I have."

"I adore you," she whispered. "I've loved you and wanted you from the very first minute we met. I'd seen you on the street before that and in different places, and I always thought you were a fine-looking fellow—handsome and big-shouldered and slim-waisted—but from the day you walked into my office, I've been a goner. . . . Oh, no fooling! I've dreamed about you. Oh yes, I have—many a night. It's hard to believe I've got you at last."

"Body and soul," he assured her.

"I don't know," he continued as she ruffled his hair; "I guess I've been robbed of something I ought to have had years ago. I was a pretty serious-minded kid when I was in college, and since then I've been sort of living other people's lives—not my own. I've never had a girl—not in the real sense—and I know now I've never been in love."

She kissed him and looked into his eyes for a searching moment before releasing him. Then she rose, straightened herself, lifting her breasts as she pushed down her girdle, ran her fingers through her curls and drew breath.

"Now, let's see," she said; "I want to ring Nate's office first, and then . . ."

She did not complete her sentence but went into the bedroom, and he heard her dialing, after a minute asking for someone.

"I see," came her voice. "Nothing yet. They're still out. What time is it? Four! My goodness, I had no idea. Well, when you get any news, phone me, will you? . . . Thanks."

She came back to the sitting room. He rose to meet her, gathered her in his arms and kissed her. She pushed him away.

"Now be good," she admonished him. "I'm going out to get some ice, whisky, and a couple of bottles of fizz water. You wait here, and if the phone rings take the message."

He offered to accompany her, but she would not let him.

"No, no," she said; "you stay here. I'll only be a couple of minutes. I'm dying for a drink."

She went into the bedroom again and came out wearing a cape. The early afternoon drizzle had turned to rain.

"Don't run away," she laughed and went out, slamming the door behind her with a smart clap.

He sank back upon the sofa and rested his forehead in his hands, his fingers thrust into his tumbled hair. He tried to think, but his thoughts would not co-ordinate. Something inside him was trying to warn him, but he would not listen. His mouth was dry, and his lips were lacquered with Caddie's lip-red. He was glad she had gone for whisky and soda; he wanted a drink badly.

Rising none too steadily, he took a cigarette from his case, but found no matches.

"Damn," he said softly and looked about the room for the little china pig he remembered. As he reached for it, he stumbled and again swore softly. "Guess I'm drunk all right. What do I care? She's a wonderful woman, and I adore her."

The telephone rang in the adjoining room. Swaying and holding to chair backs, he went to answer it.

"Caddie?" said a man's voice. "That you, Caddie?"

"No," said Stan, articulating carefully. "Miss Welch has stepped out for a minute."

"Who are you?" demanded the voice. Its tone was peremptory. Stan considered a brusque answer.

"Who's speaking?" continued the voice. "Is this Miss Welch's apartment?"

"Yes, it is."

"Well, who's talking?"

A sharp reply such as "What's it to you?" or "It's none of your business" crossed Stan's mind. Instead he answered evenly:

"Stanley Rutherford."

"Oh!"

Silence. Stan steadied himself with one hand on the bureau beside him and pressed the receiver to his ear. When nothing followed, he repeated his name, this time challengingly. No reply. Then the voice said, detached and cold:

"Please tell Miss Welch the jury has just brought in a verdict for all the defendants of murder in the second degree."

§2

He told Caddie when she came in. She dropped her packages into a chair and sank down upon the sofa, covering her face with both hands.

"Oh," she choked, "they couldn't! They couldn't!

"Framed," she continued passionately, lifting her head. "The fools did just what they were told to do. Murder in the second degree! Twenty years in San Quentin! He ordered the verdict! Demanded it! . . . I could have told you!"

In another moment she was angrily pacing the floor.

"Take it easy," Stan urged.

"Take it easy?" she repeated defiantly. "It's the power of money! The power of the privileged class! You shipowners can buy the kind of justice you want, bribe judges and juries, suborn witnesses!"

"Careful, Caddie," he remonstrated.

"Careful? I won't be careful! You and your rich friends think you can run this country the way you please. You can smear the unions with murder because it suits you. You can brand them with crime so you can make a case for yourselves! You'll sentence those unfortunate men to life imprisonment because you want the public to believe they are murderers and assassins. You, the high-minded, honorable, irreproachable citizens——"

"Quit it, Caddie," he said, his temper rising.

"I won't!" she went on hysterically. Back and forth she paced, her arms swinging, hands fisted.

He was perplexed and offended.

"Guess I'd better be going," he said evenly and began to look for his hat.

She stopped her march instantly and ran to him, catching him about the neck.

"No, no, Stan," she all but sobbed. "I'm sorry. Truly I am. You can't help the way you feel; neither can I." She drew him to her and leaned her head against his shoulder. "Forgive me," she hurried on. "I'm wrong. I didn't know what I was saying. I've been so close to this trial—going over there almost every day—that I've come to care too much. I'll take back everything I said. Don't be angry with me, darling. I've just found you; I can't lose you so soon. You said you loved me, and you've made me the happiest woman in all this world. Say you forgive me."

She drew back and scanned his face.

"Kiss me," she commanded, "and forget what I said."

Their lips met, his arms went round her, and all his resentment ebbed away. Fiercely he grappled her to him, his mouth on hers, feasting of its pulsing fervor.

Now there were real tears on her cheeks. He felt them on his face.

"I'm such a fool," she said penitently. "I'm always kicking away any happiness that comes my way. What do I care if those men go to prison? What do I care who sent them there, or whether they're guilty or not? *You're* all I care about and want. Let's never quarrel, my darling. Love me always and I'll always love you. I've known many rough and ugly years, and I've never known such happiness as you have brought me. Kiss me again—and again—and again——"

He did so, and the circles began to wheel again, and colors flared behind his closed lids—mauve and purple and indigo, shot through with darts of yellow and bright orange.

Once more they sank upon the sofa, and she lay in his arms for a long time, her face buried in the hollow of his neck, both wrapped in sensuous contentment.

He had no desire to move; he was tired, and his head had begun to ache, but Caddie insisted on rousing him.

"Let's have a drink," she proposed. "I got a bottle of good scotch. I know you don't like bourbon. I'll mix the drinks."

She disengaged herself, picked up the packages from the chair seat, and disappeared into the kitchen. He remained where he was, eyes closed, aware of a mounting misery.

Caddie brought him a tumbler filled with ice, whisky, and soda. He indicated his distaste by turning away his head.

"Come on," she urged, "don't be silly. It will make you feel better, darling; buck you up. . . . That's a good boy. . . . More! A sip won't do you any good. We have to listen to the mayor's radio speech this evening, remember."

He shook his head, but he managed to empty half the glass. The drink did freshen him and helped clear his mind. He took another swallow.

"That's fine," she commended. "We certainly let ourselves in for a lot of punishment today, that lunch and all that mixture. . . ."

She finished her drink and begged for a cigarette. She drew on it, sucking in the smoke deeply, expelling it in a gush.

"Who do you suppose that was who telephoned?" she asked, making herself comfortable beside him.

"He didn't say. A man spoke, you know."

"Yes, you told me. Perhaps it was Nate, or somebody in his office. Mullens maybe. He's Nate's right-hand man. My guess is that Nate's still over at the courthouse."

"He didn't sound very gracious," Stan said thickly.

"Funny," mused Caddie.

Presently she said: "I suppose those poor fellows won't have a very happy time tonight, knowing they're bound for San Quentin. Olzendam will give them the limit. Nate will appeal, of course."

"Let's not go back to all that," Stan grumbled. He felt himself getting drowsy again. His head bobbed.

"Here," she said, "you're going to sleep. You can't do that. You got to keep awake so you can hear the mayor. I'll get you another drink, and by and by I'll scramble you some eggs. We'll have supper out in the kitchen—just you and me!—and I'll make toast and some good strong coffee."

He had no energy to protest. He ought to go home. His mother would be expecting him for dinner, but it was raining now, and driving in the wet wouldn't be easy. Anyway, he guessed he was too drunk to go home. He toppled over on his side and rested his head on the hard arm of the sofa, his empty glass in his hand. It fell to the floor after a moment, but did not break, nor did he hear its thump. He was fast asleep.

§ 3

He stirred some time later and eased his cramped position. His neck pained him, and the inside of his mouth tasted foully. Lights blazed down from the electrolier overhead, and a loud voice filled the room.

". . . Hundreds of ships and docks up and down the entire Pacific Coast lie idle. Forty thousand workers engaged in shipping walk the streets. Tens of thousands of other wage earners are forced into idleness or else are working part time only."

He recognized Rossi's voice. Its tones beat mercilessly upon his ears.

"A national emergency now confronts us. . . . I call upon the public of San Francisco, in fact of the entire Pacific Coast, to take a hand in this present impossible situation. . . . I urge that they write or wire the President of the United States, asking him to intervene."

Intervene—intervene—intervene! That was a funny word. It didn't mean anything—or did it? He wished Caddie would shut off the radio and turn out those lights. Presently he became aware that his feet now rested in a chair and he was covered with a blanket or an overcoat. By wiggling his toes he could tell his shoes had been removed, and putting his hand to his neck, he found his collar and tie gone. He sighed wearily. His head was aching fiercely; he had no desire to move; he wanted just to be let alone and have that damn radio stopped and the lights turned off. He groaned, shifted his position, and fell asleep again.

§ 4

Hours later he awoke. It was dark. Slowly he realized he was in bed and that Caddie lay beside him. His arm was beneath and about her; her head with its tangle of curls rested on his shoulder; one of her arms was across his chest. Her hair smelled pleasantly, and he felt comfortable and warm. As the consciousness of their proximity came to him, his pulse quickened. He could not remember how he had gotten to bed or how he had undressed, but he was there now, without clothes, and Caddie, breathing easily and regularly, lay next to him. Gently moving his finger tips, he could feel the soft plumpness of her flesh beneath her armpit. He thought of her and thought of himself. There must be no regret and no remorse. He was happy. That counted. He loved Caddie and she loved him. Neither of them could be harmed by such intimacy. He put his lips to her fragrant hair and kissed it softly.

She stirred; her hand found his neck.

"Ah, Stan," she murmured sleepily and happily. "This is wonderful, isn't it?"

"Yes."

"Still like me?"

"Yes."

"You're so young, Stan—so young and strong and clean. I've never known anybody as clean as you are. You're just like a marble statue, like a Greek god——"

"Ah-h-h, baloney!"

She raised herself upon an elbow, leaning over him, and with a forefinger commenced to stroke his eyebrows and with its tip follow the line of his jaw.

"You're pretty nice yourself," he told her.

"I used to be," she said, "but I've gotten fat lately; I've let myself go."

"I like you the way you are—plump and soft, and I like that funny smell about you."

"Good gracious! Do I smell?"

"No, no; it's a fragrance you have. I've noticed it always. It's not a smell exactly; it's something far more subtle—like the perfume of jasmine or heliotrope. I like to breathe it; it's a drug, makes me feel dizzy."

"There's a smell about you, too—a good, strong, clean smell. Not toilet water nor soap nor talcum. You smell of *you*—clean and good."

He laughed.

"Guess we fancy each other."

"I certainly 'fancy' you." She kissed him.

"You love me, Stan?"

"You *bet!*"

"We'll always be friends, won't we? It's so wonderful that way. I don't demand anything of you, nor you of me. I want only to be sure that you're thinking of me occasionally and that I can see you once in a while, and we can have lunch or dinner and an evening together. I hope that's what you want. We'll be good friends and always understand each other.

"You know," she went on, "it's really remarkable—our friendship. You and I think differently about almost everything, but we don't quarrel. We mustn't fight—ever. I may make you a little cross sometimes, but I'm always sorry, and you must forgive me. But you—you never make me cross. I'm never angry with you. You can tell me that every labor leader in this country ought to be hanged and every member of a union sent to jail, but that will never make me mad. You've been raised differently than I've been, and I suppose I naturally take that into account, but it's more than that. You just don't annoy me with the things you say or with your beliefs. I guess it's the way you express yourself. I don't know—but I do know you never anger me."

She rambled on, interrupting herself to kiss him lightly, and now and then he drew her to him for a longer embrace.

Time passed. The alarm clock on the bureau stood close to seven, and Caddie said she must get started for the day.

"What did Rossi say last night?" he asked.

"Oh, a lot of rubbish. Something about Rory holding out here on the Pacific Coast until the Atlantic strike was settled, and a lot of nonsense about his getting a salary of seventy-five dollars a week from the International, plus a salary he receives here as head of the Federation. Rossi's talking through his hat. When Rory *did* receive that seventy-five a week, he turned over every cent of it to the strike funds, and he doesn't get a nickel from the union."

"How does he live?"

"His friends contribute, and of course his expenses are taken care of."

"I'll bet he has big expenses and a lot of loving friends."

"He doesn't fatten his expense account, if that's what you mean. And he *has* a lot of loving friends. I'm one of 'em!"

"Do you contribute to his support?"

"That's being nasty, Stan—and we weren't to quarrel! You promised."

"Okay," he said.

"We'll make a pact and seal it with a kiss. Is that a go?"

"Okay," he said again.

She smoothed back his hair and kissed him tenderly.

"Now, go and shower," she directed, "and I'll dress and get breakfast."

"Holy God," he said ruefully, rubbing his chin. "I need a shave."

"Get it on the way to your office."

After he had bathed and returned to dress, he could hear Caddie moving about in the kitchen. His clothes were in a heap, tumbled into a chair. They looked rumpled and dirty. He eyed them with distaste, considering what to do. A hotel; get a room there, send for a barber, and while he was being shaved in the room, the valet could press his suit. The situation was sordid, and like his clothes, he felt bedraggled. As he adjusted his tie, a framed picture on Caddie's bureau caught his eye. It was a cabinet-sized photograph of Rory O'Brien. He picked it up and examined it. There was something malevolent about the man's face, and a strong feeling of dislike rose within him. As he set it back in its place, a foul word, said with venom and with hatred, escaped him, and he spat at the likeness.

CHAPTER XIV

ON FEBRUARY FIFTH, the hundred-day strike of the unions composing the Maritime Federation of the Pacific, costing an estimated $686,-000,000, dissolved into a rush back to work by the forty thousand strikers of 229 ships. Approximately five thousand men congregated in the hiring halls; eighty-seven gangs of longshoremen were dispatched to handle cargo; shippers estimated fifty million dollars' worth of cargo awaited movement on or off seventy-eight strike-bound vessels in San Francisco harbor, and eighty-four ships in the Los Angeles port of San Pedro where 234,000 tons of merchandise had accumulated. Similar figures came from Portland and Seattle, where thousands of feet of lumber were awaiting shipment.

All unions, excepting the longshoremen, obtained wage increases in the settlement. The longshoremen earned the right of gangs to work at straight time for six hours and receive overtime payment thereafter. The rest of the maritime unions won the establishment of a working day of eight hours or less, and all retained full control of the hiring halls. Employers reserved the right to select their own ship officers and engineers, and agreed to give the sailors a raise of ten dollars a month and cash for overtime.

§ 2

"The other day you mentioned to me something about the shipowners offering the sailors ten dollars more a month and you said you thought that might end the strike. It proved to be a good tip although I think Halliday already had agreed to it. But I've been wondering where you got the idea; was it from that wench you've been running around with?"

Stan was sitting in his father's office; J.O.B. had asked him to come up for a talk. He made no reply to the question, only twisted his lips wryly.

His father eyed him over the tops of his spectacles.

"If you're going around with that kind of a trollop, I'm sorry," he said. "I've been hearing things. Eleanor saw you with her at the trial last month. She's no good, my boy. She's thick as thieves with all the radicals. The quicker you drop her, the better."

Stan's color rose, but he managed to hold his peace. His father continued to study him, and his embarrassment mounted. He felt compelled to say something.

"Looks as if we're going to have peace for a while," he hazarded. "I think the unions have learned a lesson; and I think, too, that other unions, with no connection with shipping interests, will think twice before they go on strike."

"Oh yeh!" jibed his father. "We're going to have peace, are we? No more labor troubles, is that it? Take a look at this, my boy."

He shuffled among some papers in his basket and drew out a sheet of typewriting.

"I got this yesterday from Halliday. It's going into this week's issue of that pamphlet, *Labor Relations,* the Industrial Association publishes. The statistics have been compiled from information given out by Washington, and they answer your question. Take a glance at it, and then tell me whether or not this country is in for a lot of grief."

Stan took the paper and read:

Fist fights, rock hurling, and shooting among strike pickets and workers are more or less the order of the day on the far-flung labor battle-front. The United States Department of Labor states the cost of current strikes to labor and industry exceeds $10,000,000 a day.

A few of the highlights:

Machines and assembly lines in glass and auto-parts factories—28,000 men on strike.
Pittsburgh Glass Company—20,000 on strike since October.
Libbey-Owen-Ford Glass Company's four plants closed—7,000 men idle.
Kelsey-Hayes Wheel Company, Detroit—5,000 men out in two plants.
Berkshire Knitting Mills, Reading, Pa.—14 strikers injured by rioting and hundreds routed by tear-gas bombs.
Aluminum Company of America, Detroit—600 men out.
Sun Shipbuilding & Dry Dock Company, Chester, Pa.—3,000 of the 4,500

strikers voting to return to work; two killed in riots and hundreds injured by bricks, clubs, and tear gas.

Utah mines closed down—1,200 miners idle. Several bloody battles staged between strikers and miners.

Aladdin Industries, Inc., Alexander, Ind.—500 men out.

J. I. Case Company plants, Racine, Wis., closed for seven weeks—1,700 machinists on strike.

Fisher Body Company, Atlanta—1,400 men idle. Fisher Body division of the Chevrolet Motor Company, Kansas City, closed with 2,400 workers in a sitdown strike.

John Morrell & Company packing plants closed at Sioux City, S.D.

Hercules Motor Company, Canton, Ohio, shut down—1,600 men on strike.

Transportation facilities tied up in Flint, Mich.—106 bus drivers on strike.

Philadelphia, Pa.—400 truck drivers and helpers on strike. In excess of $1,000,000 worth of vegetables and meat spoiling along the waterfront markets while truckmen refuse to work.

"A fine summary!" ejaculated J.O.B., as Stan finished. "That's what's going on all over the country. The Labor Bureau in Washington states there have been 7,367 strikes in the United States in the last four years.

"What are you going to do about it? If Byron Mackey is right and labor is going to run this country, I guess it is on its way, but I'm not going to sit still on my fanny and see them get away with it.

"Listen to what that fine friend of Lloyd's has to say; he was addressing a mass meeting last Monday night in Los Angeles. He predicts that every industry in the United States will be unionized within four years. 'Economic revolution is now taking place'—I'm quoting—'the administration is set in the right direction. The biggest factor in the labor movement today are the transportation industries. Maritime workers and teamsters are working into a position where they will be strong enough to refuse to handle goods not union-made. When that day comes *the battle will end*.' Now what do you make of that? This man is supposed to represent the Government; he's appointed as a conciliator by the Secretary of Labor. What right has he to go sounding off like that?"

Stan frowned. He was in agreement with his father, but felt he had nothing to contribute.

J.O.B. whirled about in his big chair, rose, and began angrily to pace the room.

"Where does Eleanor get off running round with this fellow? My mother tells me she sees him constantly. They even *write* each other! Good God, what's this family coming to! You hobnobbing with a tart, and Eleanor consorting with a Communist!"

Stan remained silent. When his father worked himself up this way, there was no quieting him. But unexpectedly this morning he abruptly checked his anger and with a visible effort forced himself to a calmer mood, went back to his desk and sat down. His face worked spasmodically for a moment, but when he spoke it was in tranquil tones.

"Why I sent for you this morning was to discuss a family matter."

He paused, took off his spectacles, and tapping their frame gently on his desk while he stroked his goatee, said:

"It's about Daisy. She's nearly well. I had a talk with your mother yesterday morning, and I saw Dr. Müller last night. He's done a magnificent job. The child's practically herself once more. Of course she's frail, and it will be some time before she's able to go about as she used to."

"Does she know anything about that trial last month?" Stan interrupted. "Does she have any inkling who killed Vincent?"

"Oh no, no. Newspapers have been carefully kept from her. She hasn't heard a word; nothing's been mentioned. She never speaks of Vincent, so your mother says. Just as well. It's a closed chapter.

"Now to come back to what I wanted to say. She's about ready to leave the sanitarium. Müller says he's done everything he can for her, and now it's just a question of time until she gets her bearings. He thinks it would be a mistake for her to return just yet to her home, and I agree with him. There's always the possibility of an unfortunate association.

"A trip might do her good. Jim Ahearn will have his passenger steamers running in no time now, and I was thinking of sending Daisy with your mother to Honolulu and letting 'em stay there for a couple of months, or as long as they want to. Watterbury ought to go too; I want a check on our warehouses and office there. God knows what's happened during the past three months. He'd accompany your mother and sister, look after 'em, manage tickets, accommodations, baggage, and so on. He'd stay a few weeks, but I want the women to remain for some months. What do you think?"

Before Stan could answer, his father continued:

"The *Mauna Kea*—one of Jim's best passenger boats—is due to sail the end of this month. I just called him up; he says she's almost certain to go then. I thought I'd reserve one of those *lanai* suites for your mother and Dais, and send Syd along. . . . Well, I want your opinion."

Stan said he thought it was an excellent idea, but after he had returned to his own office he sat at his desk for some minutes, wondering why the plan brought him no pleasure. Perhaps it was the thought of living alone with his father. He was fond of the old man, but J.O.B. was getting so assertive and opinionated there was little satisfaction in his company. If he wasn't haranguing and shouting, he buried himself in a newspaper, even then scowling and muttering. However, the scheme was fine for Daisy, and God knew, his mother needed a rest.

§3

Miss Chambers came in and said Miss Welch was on the wire. Stan frowned. Caddie shouldn't ring him at his office. There was always the possibility of the company's wires being tapped and a conversation being overheard. He must remember to caution her.

"Okay," he said; "put her on."

"Hello, Stan."

"Hello, how are you?"

"Fine. Why haven't you called me?"

"Millions of reasons. Haven't had the time, for one thing."

"Fiddlesticks! You could have found the time if you wanted to."

Even now, he caught something of her warm personality. Her voice made his scalp tingle and quickened his pulse. He could see her brown eyes, her big mouth with its ever-ready smile, and the twin creases marking either cheek.

"What's doing?"

"Oh, lots. I'm crazy to see you."

Not the kind of thing to say over an office telephone!

"Good."

"When's it to be?"

"Soon."

He *did* want to see her, but not immediately. They had lunched together recently, but he knew what Caddie desired.

"How about coming up for a drink this afternoon?"

"Can't today; driving Father home."

It sounded convincing even if it wasn't true.

"How about dining with me tomorrow night? I'll cook you a *bijou* meal."

"A what?"

"Oh, that's a word a friend of mine used to use. You'll like it, and I'll get a bottle of wine."

No! Things like that shouldn't be said over an office wire!

"I'll call you about twelve o'clock," he told her.

He'd use one of the public booths in the lobby downstairs.

"Okay; I'll be waiting for you, but *do* make it tomorrow night! I'm *so* lonely, Stan. I can't stand not seeing you much longer."

Lord, she mustn't say things like that!

"All right, twelve o'clock," he agreed and hung up.

§4

Then the wrestling resumed—familiar by now. He wanted to see her; he wanted her in his arms; he wanted her kisses; he wanted *her*. Yet some cold inner power of reason told him he shouldn't—he mustn't!

There was a picture in some primer of schoolboy days he remembered. It represented a little boy, with finger in mouth, eyeing a gingerbread cake set on a window ledge to cool. The little boy's expression clearly indicated his thoughts, and above the picture, in bold type, appeared the word: "TEMPTATION," and beneath it the legend: "He would, and he wouldn't! He would, and he wouldn't!"

Stan "would" and he "wouldn't." When he thought of Caddie

there was a tug at his heart that seemed to tear it from his breast. He loved her; she was the only woman he had ever loved; what she offered he could not live without. If this was so, he reasoned, then it was right for him to accept her blandishments and affection. Yet it was playing with fire, and he knew he risked being burned. When he put her out of his mind a thousand things came to remind him of her. He had but to close his eyes, to hear the joyous peal of her laughter, see the swiftly changing expressions in her face, the lovely gestures of her long, deft hands, and, in imagination, feel the warm clasp of her arms and the pressure of her lips.

Thoughts of her relentlessly pursued him for the rest of the afternoon, followed him home, haunting him during his lonely and solitary dinner. His father was at a directors' meeting at the club, and his mother was supping with Daisy at the sanitarium. He tried to concentrate on the evening news, his paper propped before him on a metal rack, but he could not control his thoughts, and suddenly and to his amazement he snatched the sheet from its stand, crumpled it roughly in his hands, and threw it to the floor.

He sat staring into space then, wondering why he had done it. What kind of a reflex action was that? Reflex of what? Should he call her now and see if she was at home? He went into the hall and scowled at the telephone. Wheeling away, he went back to the table, smoothed out the newssheet, set it where it belonged, forcing himself to think of what he read by pronouncing the words aloud.

At eight o'clock he rang his grandmother, asking if she would like to have him come over to play backgammon with her.

"Why, that will be delightful!" Grandmère assured him. "Lloyd's not here; I'm all alone. Wilbur will light the fire and we'll have a nice, cozy little time."

While he shook the dice and moved the ivory counters from one long diagonal to another, he drank several scotch-and-sodas which the butler brought him whenever he rang. He did not count how many he had, but he was aware of their effect as he stumbled home.

In bed, it was a long time before he could get to sleep; then, as he drifted off, he was dimly conscious of a word that kept repeating itself. It was:

"Wrong—wrong—wrong—wrong—wrong . . ."

Shaving the next morning, he remembered it. With razor paused, for some minutes he stood arrested, gazing at his reflection. Another word had taken its place. Now it was "right."

§ 5

He had awakened early that morning and decided to walk downtown.

It was one of California's halcyon February days with a warm bright sun and an intoxicating hint of coming spring. But in spite of the gracious weather he was depressed. His indecision rode him hard, and although he could not make up his mind whether or not to keep his engagement with Caddie that evening, his thoughts were full of her, phrasing words of an excuse in case he should not go, alternating this with imagining the joy of being with her again.

As he strode along, almost everything he saw reminded him of his struggle: a stalled motorcar with a coughing engine striving to make headway, a dog straining at the leash held in the hand of a pretty girl, a heavy truck groaning and laboring up a steep incline, a crowded streetcar being cumbersomely dragged by its cable toward the summit of a hill, two newsboys wrestling at a corner, a bird fluttering at an upstairs window of a house, vainly trying to enter. Conflicts all!

It was a relief when he reached his office. Miss Chambers had just arrived, and a pile of welcome work awaited him. Dictation and routine matters were disposed of first, and these were behind him before his telephone began to ring. Interruptions followed all morning, and noon was upon him before he found time to tackle the job he liked best: drafting a new schedule of sailings from Hawaiian, Gulf, and Pacific ports, an intricate and complicated task, involving the figuring of so many days at sea, so many days in harbor, dates of departure and arrival for the twenty-six freighters composing the Mission Fleet.

At two o'clock Captain Willard of the *San Fernando* dropped in. He had found all the offices empty and was glad to shake Mr. Rutherford's hand and pass the time of day. They talked of the strike, and the captain said he was glad to be at work again; idleness didn't suit him; he liked the sea, particularly when there was a bit of a blow.

Half an hour later he was gone, and Stan toiled on alone and uninterrupted until four o'clock when, with a grateful sigh, he laid down his sharp pencil, pushed away the sheet covered with small figures, and reached for a cigarette. He was pleased. He had worked out a tight schedule. Only one bad spot: the trip the *San Geronimo* would have to make in late March—Puget Sound and back in ten days. If good weather prevailed, she could do it.

Not until then did he realize he had missed lunch—and had forgotten to call Caddie.

He rose stiffly, stretched, and, cigarette in hand, went to look out of the window. The day was still beautiful; not a trace of the usual afternoon fog.

Well, should he go to Caddie's, or shouldn't he?

Still uncertain, he locked the drawer of his desk, put on his hat, slammed the office door, caught an elevator and dropped without stop to the lobby floor.

Market Street was half empty; office buildings were closed. Quarter past four. Too early to go anywhere now. He hailed a taxi and trundled off to his club.

At the bar stood Steve Gallagher and Tom Brophy, rolling dice. He joined them and stood for a round of drinks.

"You certainly told those waterfront bums where to get off," Steve said to him, raising his glass.

"Fine work," Tom agreed, draining his. "Y'ought to have that guy Rory O'Brien deported. Let fellows like him get the bit in their teeth and, like a horse, they're liable to throw you."

"Guess we'll have peace for a little while in this goddamn union-ridden town," said Steve.

Five o'clock. Stan decided to get a shave in the club's barbershop. It was relaxing, used up time, and Tony, the barber, was a nice guy.

"Well," said Tony, rubbing the lather on his chin, "they're after us now."

"Who?" asked Stan.

"Oh, the unions. They're trying to sign up the boys who work in the private clubs. They're going after the big hotels, too. I hear sixteen of the hotels will have to close their doors next month."

Stan opened his eyes to speak, then closed them. He was tired of strike talk. Nothing would be gained by discussing the situation.

At five-thirty, turned loose with a "There you are, Mr. Rutherford," Stan felt refreshed. He recombed his hair and strolled into the bar once more. Steve and Tom were gone, but Zachariah Nugent was there with old man Sylvester.

"Have a drink, Stanley?"

Yes, he thought he would. A martini, please. The two older men continued to chat, their subject of no interest to him; he sipped his cocktail, finished it, waved good-by, got his hat from the check boy at the door, and lightheartedly hurried off in the direction of Caddie's apartment. Now that he was on his way to meet her, elation filled him and his spirits soared. It was easier to trot down the steep hill than to walk.

She gave a little cry of joy as she opened the door to him, and immediately they were in each other's arms. He laughed happily between kisses. He was so glad to be with her again. She wore a negligee, of which he was aware at once, as there was no girdle beneath it; it was soft, lacy, and becoming. He thought her beautiful, and there was the scent of real perfume about her now. He made a face as he sniffed it.

"You said I smelled," she said defensively, "so I dabbed on a little cologne."

"No cologne would make you smell any sweeter than you do naturally," he assured her.

They sought the sofa, and intervals of lovemaking were interrupted by laughter and eager talk.

He held her hand in both of his and devoured her face with his eyes.

It was good to be with her again, and good to be able to tell her without a qualm:

"I adore you! I've been living for this moment!"

"You promised to phone me; why didn't you?"

"Got caught with a lot of work; didn't even have any lunch."

She made drinks and brought him a slice of toasted and buttered

French bread; they listened to the music of a fox trot from the radio, even tried a step or two in the small area the room afforded, Caddie protesting she had never learned to dance. Mostly they talked, holding each other's hands, smiling into each other's faces.

About eight o'clock, she declared she must start dinner.

"Oh, it's all prepared," she told him. "All I have to do is throw it in a pan. The salad's mixed, and I have a divine Camembert, and I borrowed a bottle of champagne from a friend of mine."

"From whom?" he demanded.

"Oh, a friend," she replied archly.

He insisted upon knowing.

"Don't be such an old sill!" she protested. "I bought it, but I thought it might embarrass you to know I did. If you think I got it from a 'gentleman friend,' I assure you I didn't, and it cost four dollars and eighty-five cents at the corner drugstore! So you see, smarty!"

She laughed at his dubious expression, poked the tip of his nose with a forefinger, kissed him.

The little dinner was excellent. The main dish was cut-up chicken stewed in a savory sauce; there was hot French bread, hearts of artichokes, green peas cooked with tiny cubes of ham; there was a salad flavored with garlic, champagne, finally coffee and the cheese, whose aroma filled the room and whose flavor justified its smell.

Later, when she had piled the dishes and refused to let him help her wash them, they went back to the crowded little sitting room, and it amused him to ask where she had picked some of her souvenirs.

"This, for instance?" He held up a small pink china doll dressed as a Turkish houri.

"Oh!" She threw back her head in a gale of mirth. "That's from Santa Cruz. A bunch of us went down there for a week; we rented a beach house, and I never had more fun in my life."

"Who were 'we'?"

"Oh, just a bunch of us. It was years ago. . . . I suppose you saw where they sent Detrich, Dempsey, and Kerrigan to San Quentin?"

The question wiped the brightness from his face.

"Yes," he said frowning slightly; "and Walters, too."

"Walters should have been sent to the gallows! He lied to save his neck."

"Goodness, Caddie," he cried with some irritation, "do we have to go over all that again?"

"Nate's preparing an appeal," she went on, ignoring his protest; "he thinks there's a good chance Olzendam will be reversed. Did you know that the unions have raised over twenty-five thousand dollars to defend those boys?"

He shook his head. The trial and convictions belonged to yesterday. He was concerned that Caddie should still feel so deeply. Green-tinted glasses!

"Look here," he said, "I've got a juicy morsel for you; been saving it ever since I saw it in the paper."

He took a clipping out of his pocketbook.

"Do you remember the day you and Nate Jacobs harangued me about the terrible injustice handed out to those seven thugs who started for Modesto with the intention of blowing up Occidental Oil property? Jacobs claimed they were framed by a stool pigeon in the company's employ, and told a long cock-and-bull story about his talking too much during a card game while detectives, armed with dictaphones, were concealed in the attic above the room and made eighteen records of what he said. Remember?"

Caddie nodded.

"Listen to this: 'Harold Mosher, the chief prosecution's witness in the Modesto Occidental Oil case, told a State Assembly Investigating Committee at Los Angeles last week that he "lied" when he confessed his trial testimony was perjured——'

"Wait a moment," he silenced her as she moved to interrupt. "Let me finish. 'Mosher insisted he testified truthfully at the trial in 1935, saying that his so-called "confession," recorded on dictaphone records, was made to mislead questioners. He told the Investigating Committee that he was "suspicious" of the friends who had invited him to play cards and "lied to lead them on." He admitted receiving six hundred dollars from the Occidental Oil Company after the trial, plus a five-dollar-a-day job——'!"

"You see! There you are!" cried Caddie. "He was paid—*paid* by the oil company to spy on those men and tip off the police!"

"Why shouldn't the Occidental Oil hire someone to protect its property? Don't you hire police to safeguard your home and belongings?"

"But he was a *spy,* and he was *spying* on fellows who believed him a pal!"

She was angry and aroused, and at once he was sorry he had brought the subject up.

"Forget it," he begged; "we'll just get scrapping, and we promised we wouldn't."

"But they *did* pay him six hundred dollars," she persisted; "he admits it shamefacedly—and they gave him a five-dollar-a-day job to boot for doing a neat job of spying!"

Something about this woman in her frilly negligee suddenly struck him as repellent. At the moment he seemed to see her in a new light—a dissolute, tarnished wanton, opinionated and quarrelsome, believing all upright men corrupt and all employers dishonest. Her flushed face, her angry tones were not pleasant.

Perhaps this was his opportunity, his chance to end this unsavory relationship. The way of escape lay open; he need but pretend more anger than actually he felt. Not that what she had said disgusted him so much as did her manner and the way of saying it. She had assured him she would not quarrel; now she had flagrantly begun one. There was no health, rhyme or reason in continuing this intimacy, and there flashed across his mind the memory of his father's words. He closed his lips and began to look about for his hat. Yes, this was the way; she had broken her word; their parting had been provoked by her, and she would remember it had been her doing. He would go now, and the chapter would be closed.

But Caddie, guessing rightly what was passing in his mind, flew to him, clasping him about the neck, mumbling repentance, tears choking her.

He stood straight and unbending while she wrestled with him and tried to reach his averted lips with hers.

He mustn't be angry with her! She was sorry—oh, *terribly* sorry! He must forgive her. Please, Stanley darling—please!

It revolted him, but as her importunities battered at his senses, pity rose to soften him. She loved him, after all—and he had never known love before. Tenderness took pity's place. His troubled eyes met hers, and as she saw him weakening, she redoubled her passionate entreaties.

His arm went round her, and she dragged his head down to hers, her wet kisses interrupted by quivering breaths. Her hand stole to the hat he held; she loosened his fingers, tossed it to a near-by chair, then slowly and persuasively drew him into the bedroom.

§6

Days later J.O.B., his wife, and his son were having dinner at home. It had been almost a week since they had sat down together, for Frances usually had a supper tray beside Daisy's bed at the sanitarium, and J.O.B. had been dining at the club. They were all at home this evening, and plans were being eagerly discussed about the approaching trip to Hawaii. Frances now said she thought it might be wise to bring one of the nurses along just in case . . .

"After all," she argued, "the child's only been on her feet the past three weeks, and it would be safer, don't you think?"

"She's better off without one. It's only four days to the islands, and once you get there you can get all the nursing help you want—that is, if it's needed, which I very much doubt."

J.O.B. spoke slowly, his napkin tucked beneath his chin, emphasizing certain words with vigorous slices of his knife across the thick slab of roast beef on his plate.

"We'll have to get a couple of wardrobe trunks, too," continued Frances; "the child hasn't a thing to wear. She's lost weight, but I can get her clothes in Honolulu; we'll need trunk space to bring them home in."

J.O.B. nodded.

"Where's Lloyd tonight?" his wife asked.

"With my mother probably. I don't think he had any plans for this evening. Eleanor's away——"

"She *is?*"

"So he tells me. She flew up to Portland."

"To *Portland!*"

"Yesterday. It's certainly a funny place for her to go. She told her

father she wanted to visit a friend she used to know at Mills College.
I don't know whether she told the truth or not."

"Why?"

"I may have a suspicious mind, my dear; I hope not—and hope it
wasn't to keep an engagement with that wise guy, Byron Mackey.
He's up there, trying to settle some teamsters' dispute. That I happen
to know."

The telephone rang. Stan's immediate apprehensive thought was
that it might be Caddie. He had not seen her since the previous
Saturday night and had thought it wise to tell Miss Chambers to
say he was out should she call.

Martha, the maid, came in.

"It's for you, sir," she said to his father.

Involuntarily Stan asked:

"Sure it isn't for me?"

"I don't know, sir. The party asked for 'Mr. Rutherford'; didn't
say which one."

J.O.B. ponderously rose, left the room, and after a brief exchange
over the wire, returned. One glance at his face and Stan knew that
it *was* Caddie!

"For you," he said curtly, tucking his napkin back into place and
hunching his chair nearer the table.

Knowing he could be overheard, Stan answered Caddie's eager
questions, briefly.

"Yes? . . . Yes. . . . Yes, you're right. . . . No, I can't. . . . No,
I'm not. . . . Sorry. . . . No. . . . Impossible. . . . Busy—*very* busy.
. . . I'll call you. . . . Sure thing. . . . About noon. . . . Yes. . . .
Good-by."

He hung up.

Silence pervaded the dining room as he slid back into his chair.
His father munched solemnly, a faint frown marking his brows. His
mother, sensing something was amiss, cast apprehensive eyes first at
her husband and then at her son. Now and then J.O.B. cleared his
throat with a rasp.

§7

The next day Stan waited for his father to come downstairs for breakfast. They exchanged greetings, and when J.O.B. was seated he said:

"I'd like to see you in your office this morning if that would be convenient."

His father rustled the paper, threw him a quick glance over the top of his spectacles.

"Any time," he said.

"Nine-thirty?"

"Fine."

At the appointed hour Stan found himself facing his father across his broad, flat-topped desk.

"What's on your mind?"

The young man floundered.

"Shoot," encouraged J.O.B.; "you don't have to be afraid of me."

Something kindly and understanding in the older man's gruff voice brought an embarrassing prick of emotion to Stan's eyes.

"I've been thinking," he began awkwardly. "I've been thinking . . . Well, it's like this," he resumed; "I took a long walk last night—walked 'way out to the Presidio and had a look at the Golden Gate Bridge. They'll be finishing that soon."

"So they tell me. . . . What did you walk out there for?"

"To try to work out something in my mind. . . . Dad, what would you think—instead of sending Syd Watterbury to Honolulu with Mother and Daisy—of letting me take them over to London to see the coronation? . . . It's farther."

There was a subtle implication in the last word. J.O.B. sat staring at his son for a long minute, and Stan saw he understood.

"I see," he said.

"I think I'd like to get away," continued Stan.

"I see," repeated his father.

"I haven't had a vacation for a couple of years, and I think Mother and Dais would get a big kick out of the coronation. It's in May—

the twelfth, I think—but I'd like to start immediately, if that's all right with you and you can spare me."

"I see," J.O.B. said for the third time, jerking at his goatee.

"I'd like to be away a long time; perhaps five or six months," went on the young man. "I thought maybe, if you approved, I'd take Mother and Dais to the Continent after the coronation, show 'em Paris, and perhaps arrange a motor trip through Italy."

J.O.B. continued to pull his goatee, his free hand drumming the while with his finger nails on the desk. A long silence ensued.

"You think that's the best way out?" he said at length.

"Well," Stan smiled, his heart big with gratitude for his father's understanding. "It's *one* way. I don't want to follow Frank's example."

J.O.B. frowned sharply, the reference escaping him. Then, as he caught Stan's meaning:

"Oh, you mean Lloyd's boy?"

Stan nodded.

"I wouldn't want to do that even if you and Mother weren't in the picture and I had no one to consider but myself."

"I'm glad," J.O.B. said.

"We've never heard what became of my wayward cousin, have we?" Stan asked.

His father waved one of his large, fat hands.

"Dead. . . . When do you want to go?"

"As soon as we can. I'll put the heat on Mother; don't worry about that. Daisy's all set."

"Passports?"

"I'll get them."

"I suppose Syd can cut his visit to the islands short. He can go over and come back in a fortnight."

"You'll be short-handed."

"We can manage."

He paused, sat studying his son.

"Well," he said at length, "I guess you're not the damn fool I was beginning to think you were. . . . Okay, Stan; make your own plans and go when you're ready."

"Perhaps tomorrow, or the day after?"

His father's eyebrows elevated.

"What about those wardrobe trunks?"

"New York," said Stan.

"Very well, my boy. I have to congratulate you."

It was as near an approach to an expression of affection as Stan had ever had from his father.

"Thanks, sir," he said and held out his hand. "You've been *very* kind."

CHAPTER XV

OFF TO NEW YORK, London, and the coronation!

On the day of good-by, Grandmère had the departing travelers to a farewell luncheon; Lloyd, J.O.B., Eleanor were present; Syd Watterbury too was invited. Daisy dressed at the sanitarium, and Greenwood called for her and her mother there and drove them directly to her grandmother's house.

It was a festive occasion, the guests of honor in the excited state of all voyagers bound for a long pleasure trip. Lloyd and J.O.B. beamed benevolently; Grandmère radiated good cheer and hospitality, with small gifts for each of the wayfarers; Eleanor smiled cryptically and benignly; Syd grinned with pleasure.

Daisy was the center of attention. Except that she seemed smaller and was quieter, she looked well and happy, her china-blue eyes as clear and translucent as they had ever been, her fly-away gold hair as lovely as before, her face bright with health and excitement. During the last few days at the sanitarium she had been fitted to a trimly cut tailored suit by a downtown dress shop, and had a saucy blue hat with a blue feather to go with it, the shade just matching the color of her eyes. It made Stan's heart grow soft as he looked at her; she had been so near to a life sentence of imprisonment and had been snatched back at the very threshold of a grave far worse than death's!

"You lucky stiff," Syd said to him with an assumed air of grievance; "*I* was supposed to be the one who was to take charge of your mother and sister and see them safely to Honolulu, and now you go butting in!"

"Well," Stan returned, an affectionate hand on the other's arm, "Dad can spare me a lot easier than he can you. He couldn't let you go for six months, and Mother and Dais are just crazy to take a look at the coronation!"

The limousine was to take them to the Mole, where they would board the elegant Overland train. Suitcases, handbags, and hatboxes were stowed in the trunk space at the back of the car. When it came time to go, there was a chorus of farewells, Grandmère dabbing her wet eyes with a tiny lace handkerchief, J.O.B. planting a firm kiss on his wife's cheek, an arm about her waist, everyone taking turns at embracing Daisy, all advising her to take care of herself and have a good time.

Stan gripped his father's hand, said:

"Can't thank you enough, sir. You've helped me out of a bad mess."

The older man scowled to hide any trace of feeling.

"Don't get into any more," he said brusquely; "watch your step and look after Daisy."

Eleanor, to Stan's mild surprise, seemed entirely reconciled to being left at home. The coronation, he knew, was a spectacle she would have enjoyed tremendously, but she showed no feeling of envy whatsoever as she waved good-by and watched them descend the steps and take their places in the waiting car. Syd begged to accompany them to the train, and Stan was glad to have him along.

"I'm sailing the twentieth," he told them when they were rolling down the hill. "The *Mauna Kea* docks on the twenty-fourth, and I'll come back on her next trip. . . . How did you hypnotize the old man into letting you go for so long?" he asked Stan.

Stan made no answer. The car was approaching the Bay Bridge, and he remembered all too poignantly the last time he had crossed it. Thoughts of Caddie brought uneasiness. She was going to be hurt; she would know he was running away!

Daisy was in rhapsodies over the Bridge, and Syd was telling her all sorts of details regarding it—the amount of steel that had been used, the length of the cables and the way the strands were laid, the hoisting of the roadway sections from barges, the masses of concrete in the anchor blocks and the central anchor tower, the early stages of catwalks and the safety devices. Where did he get such information? Stan wondered. Syd could be very interesting when he knew what he was talking about; Stan's mother, too, was entertained.

Two freighters belonging to the Mission Fleet were loading at the Encinal Terminals; Stan could barely make out the striped colors on their smokestacks. They were the *San Juan* and the *San Salvador,* he knew, due to sail the next day. Directly beneath the Bridge one of the Nickel steamers was heading out to sea, bound probably for Australia and New Zealand. Such sights would have no interest for him for months to come; the affairs of Wickwire, Rutherford & Company would not concern him for half a year. . . . Would Caddie have forgotten him in that time?

The long train with its washed and polished Pullmans, its observation car attached to its tail end, brass rails gleaming and a red drum spelling "Overland Limited" hanging over its rear platform, lay waiting for them like an enormous worm. Blue-uniformed porters, silver buttons shining, stood before the steps of each sleeper, rubber-covered stools beside them; tractors dragged bumping lines of baggage trucks through the milling crowd; carts piled high with luggage were being pushed along the station platforms by perspiring redcaps; near by two gray-haired conductors stood, schedules in hand, surveying the gathering passengers, their attitudes inviting questions. The Overland was about to depart!

"Here we are! Isn't this comfy and delightful?"

Daisy stood in the doorway of the drawing room which she and her mother were to share. Its carefully brushed seats, its glistening woodwork, its orderliness looked inviting indeed, promising relaxation and peaceful nights. Stan's compartment adjoined.

"B and C in Car N-74," he told them as they arranged themselves in the drawing room and the redcap stowed away the bags.

"Goodness," cooed Daisy breathlessly, "I think this is the most exciting thing I've ever done in my life! . . . And with the coronation thrown in!"

They laughed at her childishness, and her brother thought he was going to enjoy his sister's unspoiled enthusiasm a great deal on the trip that lay ahead of them.

They interrupted one another constantly now as each gave Syd last-minute commissions: he was to be sure to tell Mr. Rutherford that all the household bills were on a spike on Frances' desk, and she wished he'd remember to tell him, too, she hoped he'd send something "really handsome" to Dr. Müller; Stan asked him to arrange a vacation for Miss Chambers, and Daisy wanted him to thank Grandmère for the lovely orchids delivered on the train. All promised to write, and Syd must remember to tell them all about his trip and forward any gossip that came his way. Their chatter was interrupted by the porter, who put his head in at the door to announce that they would be starting shortly. Stan grasped Syd's hand, and they exchanged a look of confidence and affection, and then Syd turned to his mother, kissed her as laughingly she protested, and kissed Daisy, too. He was gone. They had a final glimpse of him waving his hat as, with an almost imperceptible shudder, the train began to move.

§ 2

If Stan thought that, once aboard the train, his mind was to be at peace, he was grievously mistaken. Thoughts of Caddie haunted him as he gazed at the empty, rolling prairies spotted with frozen snow, as alone in his compartment he sat staring at his folded hands, as he lay in his berth at night and the prolonged whistles of the locomotive wailed into the darkness. He saw her face and heard her laugh, smelled the faint aroma—neither perfume nor scent—that always clung to her, felt the loving clasp of her arms and the tremble of her kisses. What harried him was the thought of the hurt he had given her. He had run away—that was it!—run away without the decency of a phone call, without a word of farewell! If he had only written a note or even wired, saying he was being sent away hurriedly on company business! . . . But Caddie would not have been fooled; she would recognize and properly appreciate any deception. In the papers she would read that he had gone with his mother and sister to the coronation. All that his father had said about her might be true, yet Stan was convinced she loved him . . . and he had treated her shabbily!

If also he had imagined that for a time he was to be spared disturbing news of strikes and labor troubles, once again he was wrong. Newspapers at Salt Lake City, Ogden, Omaha, and in Chicago headlined the latest industrial wrangles. The General Motors strike had finally been settled through the intercession of Michigan's governor, and forty thousand strikers had returned to work in Detroit, thirty thousand in Flint, and thirty thousand in other plants, but at Anderson, Indiana, martial law had been declared and a thousand National Guardsmen patrolled the county line to stop organizers from promoting trouble; at the Fansteel Metallurgical Corporation's plant in North Chicago, sit-down strikers had hurled acid and missiles through a tear-gas barrage, attacking a hundred policemen and deputy sheriffs in a two-hour battle; at Santa Monica, in his own home state, 340 "sit-downers" in the Douglas Aircraft plant, cowed at last by the menace of machine guns and surrounded by a cordon of law-enforcement officers, submitted to arrest and were locked up in jail.

Strike, strike, strike! Everywhere were strikes, turmoil, battle, and hatred! If Byron Mackey was right, were these signs of revolution, labor clamoring for power and domination?

Frances and Daisy played solitaire most of the day and night as the train racketed across the plains. They sat opposite each other in their drawing room, their cards arranged on a sheet-covered table between them, bemoaning their luck whenever a particular game turned against them, chortling if good fortune came their way.

"I'm tired of Canfield," Frances would complain pettishly; "let's try . . ."

"Spiders or Turkish Rug," Daisy would suggest.

Her mother would pout, shuffling her cards.

"How about Life Sentence? That's an amusing game, don't you think?"

"I hate Life Sentence," Daisy would object; "let's try Elba."

"Elba it shall be!"

Stan would watch them as they busily dealt their cards, playing red ones on black, black ones on red, trying to match suits or establish sequences. He could make neither head nor tail of their pastime, but was amused by their seriousness. His mother would draw a quivering sigh of disappointment if she encountered an unsolvable combination of cards; she would scoop them up impatiently and begin to stack them with such a woebegone expression that Stan was tempted to laugh.

"My dear," his mother would say to him then in a tone of despair,

"you might ring for that man and tell him to bring us two ginger
ales. I simply must have something to buck me up."

He would summon the porter as she asked, perhaps giving the order
verbally to him as, leaving the drawing room, he encountered him in
the passageway, and would wander forward to the club car, where
he would find a seat and resume his uninterested contemplation of
the lone shacks and cattle pens which fled past, accentuating by their
infrequency the vastness of the wind-swept barren lands. Sitting there
moodily wondering about Caddie, his eye might catch a glimpse of
headlines in discarded newspapers or held in the hands of fellow
passengers: "Strikers Close Waukegan Plant," "Martial Law Declared
in Cleveland," "75,000 Idle in Chrysler Corporation Pending Strike
Negotiations."

§ 3

They reached New York in a driving snowstorm. Stan had not been
there since Cambridge days, six years ago; his mother's and sister's
last visit had been two years before that, when they had come east
to spend Christmas holidays with him.

Both Lloyd and Jim Ahearn had recommended the Chatham Hotel.
They had stayed there on various occasions, they said, and praised the
management, food, and rooms. The Rutherfords found an enormous
suite ready for them, its spacious rooms filled with flowers—from
J.O.B., Lloyd, Jim Ahearn, Grandmère, and a great sheaf of roses
from Syd.

"Awfully kind of them," Frances said, sniffing a half-open bud of
one of Syd's red beauties. "Flowers take the curse off of hotel rooms;
they always look so cold and bare and inhospitable when you first
come in."

Air-mail letters were waiting, and running through them hastily,
Stan found one from Caddie. Unobtrusively he stowed it away in an
inside pocket.

His mother had immediate plans for the theater. They must go to
see something gay and lively—and, oh, Stan, how about the luggage?
Had he the baggage checks? Would he call the porter and then see
about getting tickets for a show? What was good? Maurice Evans in
Richard II? No, no, much too heavy. She was in no mood for Shake-

speare, and besides Daisy would prefer something light. Well, what about *The White Horse Inn?* Yes, that would be perfect. Would he see about three seats for that evening?

An hour passed before his suitcase was unpacked, his creased clothes given to the valet, his toilet articles arranged in the medicine cabinet of his bathroom. Then he eased himself into a chair by the window, took out Caddie's letter, and slit open the envelope with a penknife.

Four closely typed pages, corrected, interlined, smudged with ink, and with many sentences scratched out. It was what he had expected, full of reproaches and self-blame, pathetic repetitions and vigorous underscored words.

"I wanted nothing of you," she wrote, "I asked nothing. I told you so again and again. I only wanted your companionship, your friendship and—if I earned it—your love. What did I do? What turned you against me? Did I deserve this from you? Wasn't I entitled to *one word? One minute* to say good-by?"

No; he hadn't treated her fairly! At least he might have written a note, mailed it the day he left. Poor Caddie! And after a long time, in his thoughts, he added, "Poor me!"

§ 4

New York caught them immediately in a mad whirl. First came theaters and then the shops. Daisy still had her luxurious mink coat to wear, but she had practically nothing else and needed sports clothes for deck attire, street clothes for town, evening gowns for dinners, two or three "formals" for dress occasions. Her mother must have a tweed suit, a few frocks; both required hats, shoes, gloves, all the necessary accessories. One pleasant morning Stan accompanied them to a luggage shop, where they picked out three enormous wardrobe trunks and, at his mother's insistence, ordered them striped in red, white, and blue.

"I'm not going to splurge on clothes in New York," she declared several times in her children's hearing; she repeated this, her son suspected, more to stay her own improvident instincts than to still any extravagant ideas on their part. "No, I'm not going to splurge here; we'll get what we have to for the steamer and for London, but I'm going to wait for Paris to outfit Daisy, and there we'll find something chic and up-to-the-last-minute at Worth's or at a salon of one of those fashionable couturiers."

Stan was glad her days and his sister's were so well filled, for he had much to do himself. After lengthy discussions, they had decided to cross on the *Manhattan,* a United States Steamship liner, and he must see to their tickets. The general manager, whom he interviewed, told him that while reservations had been spoken for, long in advance, owing to the rush of Americans to witness the coronation, he would see to it that the Rutherfords had satisfactory cabin space. Stan must arrange, too, for seats for the pageant itself, and must get passports, a letter of credit, travelers' checks, and he must have some clothes— a new dress suit, a new tuxedo, and a warm, camel's-hair overcoat. Other obligations entailed a call on Mortimer Weeks, Wickwire and Rutherford's agent in New York, offices at 90 Church Street, who promptly had him to lunch and made him set a date when he, his mother, and sister could dine with Mrs. Weeks and himself in their Park Avenue apartment and afterwards go to a show of their own choosing. There was also the agent of the Grant Lines who had received word from the president of the company, Mr. Percy Grant, to get in touch with them at the Chatham and do everything possible to make their stay in New York pleasant. Lastly there was Mr. Douglas MacConaughey, local manager of the American-Asiatic Steamship Company, who insisted upon arranging a luncheon for Stan at the University Club, to which he bade some members of his office staff, Monsieur Jules Quartremain, an official of the French Line, and a standoffish, good-looking young Englishman named Rodney Castaigne of the British consulate.

Californians telephoned the hotel, wanting the Rutherfords for lunch, cocktails, dinner, the theater, and constantly there occurred the odd circumstance of encountering friends in the street who exclaimed, "What on earth brings you to New York? Where are you staying? When can we get together?" But to these importunate people the Rutherfords could reply with just a touch of airiness, "Oh, we're leaving next week; off to the coronation, you know."

§5

The S.S. *Manhattan* sailed upon a windy April afternoon at four o'clock. The bugle sounded the last warning for going ashore, steel cables were loosened from the bitts along the dock, splashed into the water, rose dripping as they were hauled on board, the last gangplank was hoisted free, a wild clamor of good-bys broke out, accompanied by a fluttering of white handkerchiefs, a flag or two, then the stertorous bellow of the great liner's whistle set the air trembling, and a fine vibration tickling the palm of Stan's hand as it rested on a brass railing told him that the big ship was under way.

Not until the next morning, when the steamer was nosing into frothy waves which broke now and then over her bows, deluging her forward deck, and when nothing could be seen through the gray mist but gray sky and the heaving billows of the gray sea, did Stan feel the tension of the past few weeks loosening its grip. With collar buttoned snugly about his neck, and the generous folds of his overcoat shutting out the gusts of air which caught at its skirt and whipped it against his knees, he trudged up and down the promenade deck, turning his face to meet every gust of spray which reached him through an open vent. Few passengers were about; steamer chairs were piled and lashed safely into corners; only one or two men besides himself braved the wet, rolling deck.

New York with its hurried pace was a thing of the past; a dreamless night's sleep had thoroughly rested him; he seemed to be himself again, and now, stealthily, out of the black corners of his mind, came stealing thoughts like tenuous tendrils of a nauseous vine, seeking to take hold.

He had meant to write Caddie before he sailed. He had planned a letter, rehearsed every word of it, and while realizing he could never tell her the truth, he had thought how to phrase it convincingly: company interests in the East had required immediate attention; his father had insisted upon his leaving at once; now that they had reached New York, his mother and sister were eager to see the coronation; Daisy, he intended to remind her, had been very ill, and her doctor had urged a sea voyage, and so on and so on. When he reached this part of the letter, the wording of it was not too clear to him; it was on the last page that he liked to think how he would express himself, for there he would tell her how dreadfully he missed her, how constantly he thought of her; her face and voice haunted him; her eyes, her big, friendly grin, her lovely expressive hands were always before him. He would tell her too that at night, when he concentrated very hard, he could smell that smell which clung to her, and it was incense to his nostrils! He would end by telling her— underscoring the words—that she was the only woman he had ever loved, would ever love!

On a sudden impulse he jerked back a heavy door leading to a stair- case, hurried down its steps to the deck below, and sought the writing salon. He did not write the letter he had so often composed in his mind. Instead, he told her briefly that this day was his first at sea, that it was blowing and raining, the ship rolled incessantly, but he didn't feel in the least bit sick. New York had been strenuous; he had hardly had time to think, none to write letters, and now London promised to be exciting and the coronation ought to be the spectacle of spectacles. "This king will be the last one ever crowned in history," he wrote, thinking the phrase might please her. "We go from London to Paris, and then maybe Italy. My sister steadily improves, and this trip ought to do her a world of good. If you should write, address me in care of the American Express at Rome."

At this point he paused, studied his words, biting the handle of the penholder; hastily he added, "I miss you very much." Then he quickly addressed the envelope, sealed it, handed it to the salon's steward with half a dollar, saying:

"Stamp and mail this as soon as we get to port, will you?" and went up on deck again to complete his promenade.

§ 6

The *Manhattan* rolled and plunged and now and then shuddered from stem to stern as her propellers rose free of the water and whirled in space. Frances and Daisy both were ill and hugged their berths, drinking soda and hot water and commiserating with each other. Stan roamed the ship, taking a lively interest in its arrangements, construction, and equipment, and one day secured permission to inspect the engine room. He made several acquaintances among his fellow passengers, bought chances in the five-dollar hat pools, and listened with nostalgic thoughts of Caddie as the orchestra in the lounge played sentimental music. On the second day he was happy to encounter Rodney Castaigne, whom he had met at the University Club luncheon. Castaigne was very British, and his rather distant manner at first did not encourage better acquaintance, but circumstances threw them together, and Stan, as he grew to know him, came to like him. While his mother and sister remained below, he invited Castaigne to have his meals at his table. The Englishman was pleased to accept, and Stan found him an interesting companion, surprisingly well informed, and while he talked most illuminatingly about the course of events in Spain, he was shy about answering questions regarding the Duke of Windsor or the probability of his marriage to Mrs. Wallis Simpson, whose divorce from Ernest Simpson was then pending.

They had sailed on Thursday, and after two days in their cabin Daisy and her mother decided they would brave the motion of the ship and appear for the gala dance on Saturday evening. Stan persuaded Castaigne to join them for dinner, thus making an even four at table. Daisy, appearing in a soft flowery dress of pale blue petals with forget-me-nots clustered at her shoulder, a fillet of the same flower in her bright hair, was as beautiful as her brother had ever seen her. Her slight indisposition since she had been on board had etherealized her; she suggested something unearthly—a breeze, a whisper, or a child on tiptoe—and was utterly bewitching. Castaigne promptly became enslaved.

From that time on, the Rutherfords and the Englishman made a congenial foursome, and Castaigne, handsome and well groomed, was ever in attendance on the girl. He danced with her constantly, they played deck tennis and shuffleboard together, and it was a joy to hear her silvery laugh running lightly up and down the scale to the accompaniment of his bass "haw—haw—haw."

The girl bloomed, and more than once her mother and brother exchanged looks as she floated by with her escort, making the rounds of the deck, or sat with him, sipping tea and nibbling cake in the late afternoon.

"Syd had better look to his laurels," Frances said to her son one day as they watched her across the lounge explaining the intricacies of a game of solitaire to her absorbed companion.

"Syd!" exclaimed Stan, sitting bolt upright and fixing his mother with amazed eyes.

"Oh yes," she said, nodding, "Syd's been very attentive of late."

"*Syd* has?"

"Didn't you know? Syd's a very modest fellow, and he keeps his own counsel. He used to come to visit Daisy at the sanitarium. He brought her some flowers one day, they chatted for a while, and after that he came two or three times a week. I finally began to suspect I was in the way. . . . Oh yes," she finished, "he's quite devoted."

Stan was dumfounded. Syd? Attentive to Daisy? The sly old fox had never given him so much as an inkling!

"I thought it was Eleanor," he said, still bewildered; "it used to be, didn't it?"

"That was just wishful thinking on poor Bessie's part. I guess she thought it would be nice to have Syd for a son-in-law. That was before that wretched Armitage fellow appeared on the scene."

"I'll be damned!" Stan murmured.

"He would be a good son-in-law, don't you think?" his mother commented.

"Syd's how old?"

"Oh, fortyish," she answered indifferently; "age doesn't matter. He'd make Daisy a good husband, gentle and kind and protective, and I know your father would be pleased."

Yes, the old man would be, Stan conceded. Shrewd old Syd would be marrying into the company as well as into the family. But that wasn't fair! There was nothing calculating about Syd. He was a fine, honest fellow—good and dependable.

"How does *she* feel about him?" he asked after a moment.

"Likes him well enough. I don't believe the thought of marrying him has crossed her mind, but she likes him. She feels 'comfy' with him, if you know what I mean."

"And this?" her son asked, indicating the couple on the other side of the lounge, where Castaigne's head was bent close to Daisy's.

His mother dismissed the thought his question implied with a wave of her hand. "Shipboard stuff; nothing serious; best thing for her. The more she sees of men, the more she'll appreciate Syd."

"Why, you wily old matchmaker!" Stan reproached her fondly.

His mother laughed, covering an ashamed face with a plump hand. "I'm only thinking of the girl's happiness," she said defensively.

Castaigne was still in attendance as they rode up to London on the boat train; he helped them claim their baggage, steered them through the crowded station, and even insisted upon accompanying them to the portals of the Savoy, where regretfully he said au revoir, promising to telephone within a few days.

The foyer of the famous caravansary was thronged as the Rutherfords entered. In the crowd were many distinguished-looking men—notables, diplomats already gathered for the approaching august ceremony. Uniforms—English and of other nationalities—were everywhere in evidence, and here and there in the slowly shifting assembly could be seen turbaned maharajas and maharanees, the latter with veils draped over heads and shoulders, some of the women with jewels embedded in a crevice of the nose, some with a round dark spot etched in the middle of their foreheads.

London was fascinating, and a tense excitement filled the air. Green Park, Hyde Park, every open area, was lined with tents of soldiers. Hundreds of policemen too—"bobbies," Daisy learned to her delight to call them—had been brought to London from other large English cities; tall men of serious mien they were, looking strange and just a trifle burlesque to the Americans in their chin-strapped stiff helmets and dark belted overcoats.

Even here, Stan discovered, there were labor troubles. The drivers of all busses were on strike, choosing the hour of the coronation to demand more pay; not one of the lumbering vehicles with their flamboyant advertising was to be seen in any of the streets. But strikes and industrial unrest were almost forgotten; what Rory O'Brien, Mat Swenson, and other labor agitators in San Francisco were doing and demanding now seemed of small importance. Strikes in England there might be, social unrest, and labor clamoring for recognition and higher wages, but the presence of soldiers and policemen spelled order and law-enforcement. There would be no rioting here, no soapbox oratory in the public squares. Strict precautions against any disturbance or demonstration were in evidence everywhere. There must be no mishap. Even the reviewing stands lining the streets, Stan noted, were built of steel rods, securely clamped together, so that there could be no possibility of an accident.

§7

In high feather they did the rounds, Frances and Daisy smothering their laughter whenever they saw something that seemed typically English and therefore strange. They visited the Tower, roamed Oxford Circle, Piccadilly, the West End, strolled along the Mall, dutifully attended the picture galleries, and inspected the treasures of the museums; they witnessed the thrilling ceremony of the changing of the guard before Buckingham Palace and in St. James's courtyard, and gazed in awe at the statuesque figures of the Horse Guards, brave in plumed helmets and shining breastplates as they motionlessly bestrode their black mounts on sentry duty before Whitehall Palace.

"Poor King Edward," Frances would sigh as she observed the gay throngs and the signs of military pomp, "he might have had all this."

"He didn't want it," Stan would remind her, "and he isn't king any more."

They motored to Oxford, and the next day visited Warwick Castle, walked in trepidation a little way into Marlborough's ducal estate at Blenheim, and peeped into Ann Hathaway's cottage at Stratford. On another occasion, when the murk of London had miraculously vanished and a spring sky was their good fortune, they took the train to Canterbury and stood in rapt contemplation of its great cathedral.

Frances was in a flutter of excitement when Lady Castaigne's cards were left at the hotel, and immediately thereafter arrived a note from her, written on coroneted stationery, in which she hoped that Rodney's fellow voyagers, of whom he spoke so enthusiastically, would come to Castaigne Manor for a buffet luncheon on the following Sunday.

A ponderous Rolls-Royce called for the Rutherfords at midmorning on the designated day, and they drove through villages with hedged lanes and over rolling country lush with green, church bells tolling

Sabbath services, and shortly after noon arrived at the manor house, a sprawling stone structure of turrets and gables set in acres of lawn, shrubbery, and formal gardens. The white-haired butler informed them that her ladyship was awaiting them on the Tudor Terrace and offered to conduct them there. Here they found a group of some twenty to thirty people beside a tennis court where a match was in progress. All the men, Stan noticed, were arrayed in outing attire, flannels and blazers which made him feel uncomfortably aware of his American business suit. Lady Castaigne, youngish and pretty, greeted them pleasantly, and Rodney, immediately taking them in charge, was profuse in his apologies for not having driven up to London to get them. Complete mental prostration came to Frances when the young man presented her to his grandfather and grandmother, the Earl and Countess of Athelstaine, a simple, gray-haired couple who acknowledged the presence of the Americans with polite smiles and said nothing. Frances could not wait until she had frankly asked Rodney if he would inherit the title someday.

"Oh, very prob'ly," he answered readily, "after the old man and the Pater pop off. This is my elder sister, Lady Crossley, Mrs. Rutherford, and this is Miss Rutherford and Mr. Rutherford, Rowena old dear. Rowena has had the bad taste to marry into the min'stry. Her husband's Home Secr't'ry."

He piloted them to some wicker basket chairs, made them comfortable, and established himself at Daisy's feet, explaining who was playing tennis, and said that they hoped for a cricket match in the afternoon.

"Moggridge—he's our local publican and a jolly fine bat. The last time we played on the village green he knocked up a hundred and fifty-two before getting out leg-before. An amazing fellow!"

Daisy said little; Stan could see she was ill at ease, but he thought she carried herself well and certainly looked beautiful. Rodney presently brought up some of his men friends and introduced them; all were young, mustached, British, and all spoke with their native languishing drawl which Stan could not decide whether he liked or not.

"Farnsby's a two-blue man," he overheard Rodney telling his sister as he presented a big blond giant, swathed in a loose coat and muffled to the ears, tennis racket beneath his arm.

Stan silently determined he hoped he would die without ever coming to know the meaning of a "two-blue man."

Luncheon was served by a procession of aproned maids who kept
passing an endless chain of hot-covered dishes, all very tempting.
Stan wondered what became of all the food; the assembled guests
could not account for a tenth of it, and even a domestic staff of fifty
would have been unable to consume what remained. His mother, to
whom he mentioned this on their drive back to London, observed:
"The parish gets it, don't you think? There's always a parish in every
English village, where they give away things they don't want."

The Rutherfords did not stay for the cricket. Rodney was going to
play, and he would no longer be able to shepherd them. They watched
the game for a few minutes, but, seeing that he was deeply engrossed, they found Lady Castaigne and took their leave, Frances
thanking her for the delightful day a little too profusely, Stan felt
uncomfortably.

§ 8

On the morning of Coronation Day, they rose at five o'clock, breakfasted in the Savoy grill amid haste and confusion, and joined the
throng hurrying along the Strand and heading for one narrow door
still open in the barricade which had been erected across the street.
Soon they were caught in the jam struggling toward this gate.
Crushed, panting a little, clinging tightly to the tickets for their seats
which must be shown in order to pass the entry, they inched forward
until at last they were vomited through it and found themselves in
Trafalgar Square, where had gathered one of the largest crowds Stan
had ever seen in his life. As far as he could see there was nothing but
people; windows, balconies, ledges, and roofs were black with them;
the crouching lions on the massive monument commemorating Nel-
son's great victory were hidden from view, men and boys clinging to
every vantage point. Lines of police fought to keep open a few passage lanes, and a loud-speaker hoarsely bellowed directions which
nobody could understand. Pushed into one of these lanes, Stan, his
mother, and his sister crossed the square with ease and came out at
the head of a wide street. It was more open here, but still the rivers of

people hurried on, fearing their places would be gone by the time they reached the reviewing stand in which they were located.

Eventually the Rutherfords found themselves in their rightful seats, bought by Stan at a staggering figure in New York before sailing. Certainly there were none better in all of London, for they were on a balcony of the Westminster Hospital directly facing the doors of the Abbey.

All the nobility of England and the Empire, all the royal visitors and foreign diplomats, all the maharajas and their maharanees, all the great personages of the world who had been bidden to the ceremony, were inside the church and in their allotted places by the time the Rutherfords settled themselves comfortably in theirs.

A long wait ensued, but toward midmorning gilt equipages emblazoned with coats of arms and bearing the members of the royal family began to arrive one by one—those of lesser kinship first, then the Duchesses of York, Kent, and Gloucester, the Queen Mother, the two little royal princesses, and after another long wait, martial music and shouting heralded the approach of the King and Queen.

The procession at last came in sight, honor guard after honor guard preceding the mammoth gold coach drawn by eight magnificent black horses. In front of the Abbey doors it stopped and the royal couple descended. As they mounted its steps the portals miraculously opened and from the archway, silhouetted against the dark interior, the glittering figure of the Duke of Norfolk, clad in ermine and crimson, starred and gartered and bejeweled, stepped forward to welcome their majesties.

This was no scene in a comic opera, no make-believe setting of a stage play, Stan kept reminding himself; this was real, authentic, true —an incident of history!

The booming of the bells followed, Big Ben's solemn chime distinguishable from the rest, and from the interior of the Abbey came the broadcast of the proceedings—the chanting of the boy choir, the faint intonations of the archbishop, the blurred responses of the principals, the murmur of the organ, and then, much later, the long roll of the snare drums and the distant booming of cannon. Long into the afternoon the ceremony lasted with interminable waits. Then as the newly crowned King and Queen reappeared and re-entered the royal coach, and, followed by their escort of titled cuirassiers, drove away, the rain began, a sprinkle at first, freshening into a downpour. Out from the Abbey streamed England's proud nobility, royal visitors, maharajas and maharanees, ambassadors and diplomats, and all crowded beneath a none too wide marquee above the entrances. Through some hitch, their equipages and motorcars failed to appear, and the distinguished grandees gathered up the skirts of their crimson robes, a few coronets awry, and huddled together like so many school children seeking shelter from a summer shower.

Unattended, Stan saw the tall, thin figure of the Archbishop of Canterbury marching off in the downpour without so much as an umbrella or a cloak to protect him, while the crowds, held back by the soldiers and police, gaped in consternation.

§9

Early in June they crossed the Channel. Until they left, Castaigne was constantly in Daisy's company; he called daily for her at the hotel, lunched her at swank restaurants, had her to tea, invited her, with her mother and brother, to dinner at the Embassy Club, took them to the theater. Sometimes Stan accepted these invitations; often he excused himself. The attentions of this well-meaning Englishman became something of a nuisance; neither his mother nor himself was in a position to compete with him in hospitality, although on Saturday nights—gala occasions at the Savoy—Stan dutifully donned tails and a white tie, and Castaigne dined with them and to Ray Noble's music danced every dance with Daisy.

Stan was glad therefore when the day of their departure arrived and was glad, too, to learn from his mother that his sister shared his feelings.

"They settled it last night," she told him; "apparently he took it very badly. Most American girls would have jumped at him; he'll inherit a great deal of money, so he says, and someday those ancestral estates will be his, and, of course, the title. She'd be the Countess of Athelstaine, but I'm glad she turned him down. Marrying a title is all very fine, and I'd have a lot of fun telling some of our friends in San Francisco that my daughter was going to marry an Englishman who would someday be an earl, but it would mean losing her completely, and I declare, I've been through too much, where that child's concerned, to give her up for the rest of my life and have her live over here with these haw-haws in a baronial castle and be addressed by servants for the rest of time as 'Meh Lady.' My guess is that Daisy sees it that way, too, because she gave Rodney a definite 'No.' I don't know, of course, but I suspect she gave him a hint, too, about Syd, and I shouldn't be surprised if she thinks about Syd a great deal. She gets a letter from him every mail, and I know she answers."

"Good," Stan commented, absent-mindedly. All this was welcome news, but his thoughts at the moment were of Caddie: he had not written as he had intended. He had sent her a couple of picture post-cards—one of a beefeater in his colorful regalia at the Tower, another of the royal jewels in their showcase. On the latter, he had penned: "These you might like to wear, but they wouldn't improve your looks the least bit as far as I'm concerned." He did not sign it; the English postmark would identify the sender.

Crossing the Channel, it began to rain, and the French country-side presented a dismal prospect from the train. Paris, too, was a blur of gray buildings, wet streets, shawled women, and burly workingmen in belted blue blouses and well-worn visored caps. Frances said she was sure she saw the Madeleine as they taxied past a columned building, but it was not until the Place de la Concorde, with its fountains and statues, burst into view that Stan could feel certain they had arrived in Paris.

The Crillon, where they had booked reservations, was none too prepossessing, he thought. Nothing he had seen so far in the way of hotels in Europe approached the elegance and imposing splendor of those in the United States. Perhaps these unpretentious-looking hostelries were in better taste, still . . .

He followed his mother through the revolving doors and found her at the reception desk, a cablegram in her hands.

"What do you make of *that?*" she wailed, giving it to him.

It was from Uncle Lloyd and read:

ELEANOR AND BYRON MACKEY MARRIED RENO YESTERDAY.

§ 10

"I don't know whether I'm glad or sorry," said Frances querulously when they had gone up to their rooms and she had collapsed into a chair.

"He's a good man," declared Stan.

"Grandmère will be wild," observed Daisy.

After the first confused and incredulous ejaculations, there followed an hour of excited talk. Frances wanted to know everything Stan had heard about the man. Daisy wondered where they would live. Stan finally left the women to their conjectures.

Frances wrote; Daisy wrote; Stan cabled his father, asking for further details, requesting an answer in care of the American Express in Rome.

Paris was not as amusing as London. Handicapped by his unfamiliarity with the language, there was little for Stan to do after sight-seeing tours and visiting tourists' points of interest. He took long walks and lunched at famous restaurants, where invariably he overate. The place to eat became the principal topic of discussion between himself, his mother, and his sister.

In the bar at the Crillon one afternoon he made the acquaintance of an American. The man had an engaging wirehair on leash; the dog made friendly overtures to Stan, and he and his owner exchanged pleasantries. It led to one drink and then another. Stan learned that his compatriot's name was Joseph Cavanaugh; he was a long resident of Paris and entertained an unflattering opinion of the French and a gloomy outlook for Europe. He was an interesting conversationalist, however, and on a subsequent day Stan encountered him at the Ritz. They became friendly and fell into the habit of meeting each other at the cocktail hour.

Stan told him something of his background, his interest in shipping, and this led to a brief summary of labor troubles in San Francisco. Cavanaugh wanted to hear the story of the general strike of three years before.

"I was in New York at the time," he said, "and was about to start for the Coast when the papers broke with the news. What caused the row and how was it settled?"

Stan warmed to the recital, and, Cavanaugh proving a good listener, he soon came to an account of the more recent waterfront troubles.

"We're a strike-ridden town, I fear," he told him; "it isn't only the shipowners who are the butt of the unions; labor is making trouble with every industry in the city and throughout the state, even in the agricultural districts. Workers demand higher wages and shorter hours. This is true not only of California but of the whole United States. Everywhere you go you hear nothing but 'strike.' I suppose we have to thank our President for it."

"Not necessarily," Cavanaugh returned; "democratic governments are obliged to make concessions to workers, or otherwise they'd be overthrown. Labor is insurgent throughout the world. Take France. This is the country where the sit-down strike originated. *Siège* is the word they use for it. At present we have a regime known as the 'Popular Front' with an old Socialist, Léon Blum, at its head. Just after the elections a year ago, sit-down strikes were the order of the day. Nearly a million workers were idle, and they tied up many essential services. When the Chamber convened in June, seventy-two members of it were Communists. In ten months after Blum took hold, sixty-five new laws were enacted; they provided for the forty-hour week, collective bargaining, paid vacations, anything to satisfy the workers. I doubt if Blum will last out this summer. The franc is steadily declining, and all the bolstering he can do cannot stop its fall. Over seven thousand million francs have been shipped out of France. The public debt is colossal, and the present budget indicates a deficit by the end of the fiscal year of from seven to eight billion. The French are demoralized. Charlatanism and corruption are rife; the people have lost all confidence in their leaders, most of whom are grafters and out for personal ambition. It's the devil take the hindmost.

"Consider the present Paris Exposition which was to have been ready to welcome coronation visitors. They opened it last month, but it is a shambles, and I very much doubt if it will ever be completed. Only two foreign buildings have so far been finished, and whose do you suppose they are? Russia's and Germany's. Why? Because Russia and Germany sent their own workmen here to do the job. The French? Their artisans spend a whole day driving in a few nails, and I honestly believe they come back at night and take them out. The Exposition in its present state is a litter of plaster and scaffolding, its grounds a trampled waste. The workmen do not care; they do not believe in anybody, not even in themselves. And while they quarrel and loaf, their arch enemy, Germany, is arming to the teeth."

"You think there will be trouble?"

"Every indication points to it."

"I can hardly believe it. Only last January Hitler, addressing the Reichstag said, 'There can be no humanly conceivable object of dispute whatsoever between Germany and France.'"

"That's just Hitler—a creature of lies and deception. It is no secret that he is arming, that he is building airplanes by the thousands, that his Krupp works are turning out tons of cannon, and that his 'Health Through Joy' program is nothing more than a scheme to build an army. But you don't find strikes in Germany; nor in Italy. Not one. Hitler eliminates unemployment by a stroke of the pen; he decrees that every man in the white-collar class who needs a job shall go to work for the State, and those who remain in offices shall foot the bills. It is as easy as that. A dictator decides who will work, at what, and how much he will be paid. Italy has shown the way. Mussolini abolished unions long ago, and a government agent sits in on every private business, reports its profits, and Benito then says how much the company shall be taxed. He makes fine roads, sees to it that trains run on schedule, and turns the Campagna—a malaria-infected swamp outside of Rome of which even Caesar complained—into a fertile area on which he builds hundreds of model farms. You see, you can do things like that if you have power."

"You're not suggesting, are you," Stan queried with a troubled frown, "that their way is better than ours?"

"Whose? Better than America's?"

"Everywhere in America there is trouble."

"Perhaps," conceded Cavanaugh, "but at least we get by without firing squads or concentration camps."

Stan shook his head. Forcing a smile, he said:

"Let's forget it and have another one of those sidecars. I find them exceedingly palatable."

§ 11

Walking in the gardens of the Tuileries one day, he had a startling experience. Sitting on a bench in charge of a small boy of four, he idly noticed a nursemaid in a blue-caped uniform and bonnet. The little boy, running toward him, fell and skinned one of his bare knees on the gravel. Stan picked him up and tried to comfort him, and the nursemaid, who he now saw was an English governess, came hurrying forward. As he was about to transfer the child to her care, a half-smothered exclamation burst from him. He was looking straight into a face so like Caddie's that the woman might have been her twin sister. She was about the same age; her brown curls turned up around the brim of her bonnet; there was the same wide space between her eyes; she had the same broad nose, the same big mouth, and double lines furrowed either cheek.

"He's always falling down," the governess said somewhat primly, brushing off the child's clothes. "Hush, Tommy; the gentleman's been very kind to you. I thank you, sir; he's a bit young to say so himself."

"Oh, it was nothing," Stan assured her; "I *do* hope he hasn't hurt his knee too badly."

He examined the bruise where a little blood was mixed with dirt. Turning again to the governess, he asked:

"Excuse me, but have you ever been to America?"

Suspicion darkened her face at once. She shook her head.

"Any relatives there?" he persisted. "I should explain," he continued, "that you resemble a friend of mine in San Francisco."

She was alarmed now, and disclaiming kinship with anyone in the United States, promptly bore away the still whimpering little boy.

He stood looking after her, hoping for another glimpse of her face, but she did not turn, and slowly and thoughtfully he made his way back to the Crillon, his heart in turmoil. He went to his room upon reaching the hotel and wrote Caddie a long letter, telling her about the incident and describing the coronation.

"We return in six weeks," he finished. "Chance encounters with unknown English governesses who look like you have a way of making me feel very homesick."

§ 12

A fortnight later they sent their trunks, now filled to overflowing, together with their keys, to a tourist agency to be shipped to Naples, and took the Simplon train for Italy, a long, dirty, tiresome trip, and in Milan they acquired a cumbersome and ancient Isotta, and Angelo. Angelo proved to be a treasure. He became their trusted friend, an ever-smiling and amiable chauffeur, who, although he failed to be the accomplished linguist he claimed he was, otherwise proved himself a most satisfactory cicerone. A week in Milan—one heavenly night when they dined at the Villa d'Este beside the limpid waters of Lake Como with mountains mirrored in its depths, a moon shining, and fishermen singing from a boat—then on to Venice and the sumptuous quarters at the Royal Danieli. Here Stan's mother became romantically enraptured with gondolas moving silently through the narrow canals and under age-old stone bridges, declaring it was a "sin and shame" to allow motorboats to pollute their waters. Stan's admiration of the city's medieval charm was somewhat mitigated by the refuse he saw floating in the canals—garbage, slops, even a dead cat.

Some days later they left for Florence, with the gentle and good-natured Angelo at the wheel of their enormous caravan, following paved and well-graded highways ever dipping and rising through olive orchards, vineyards, and between fields of brilliantly red wild poppies, stopping—cramped and a little weary—at the noon hour for a marvelous lunch of *gnocchi* and cheese, sour bread and red wine.

Everywhere Stan recognized the mailed fist of Il Duce—in the black-shirted boys at drill in the school compounds, in the prevalence of *Bersaglieri, carabinieri,* and bicycled police. On white-walled villas, barns, bridgeheads, and railway trestles, wherever there was a blank surface, appeared an inscription signed with the august name of the Dictator. The accommodating Angelo translated these in his faulty English. The uniformity of their character fascinated Stan: "Believe, Obey, Fight!"; "Italy's Great Hour Is at Hand"; "Fail Not Italy and

Italy Will Not Fail You," a hundred more, the magic name of "Mussolini" beneath each one. Stan marveled at the arrogance of the man, and marveled, too, at the labor all this involved, requiring, as it must, thousands of painters traveling the length and breadth of the land, daubing these mandates on fence and wall. No wonder there were no strikes! In the faces of the peasants and the workers, in towns and fields, in those of the attendants who came out of their small shops to pump petrol into Angelo's tank, in the demeanor of the proprietors and the *ragazzi* of small cafés where they stopped for refreshment, Stan saw no evidence of national pride. But there was fear! That was it—fear! Fear of Rome, fear of the police, fear of the *carabinieri* with their long rifles, the *Bersaglieri* with the arrogant swagger, fear of the black-shirts! A gracious, smiling country filled with an easygoing, happy-go-lucky, wine-drinking, sun-loving people, under a dictator's heel!

A few days in Florence with its sluggish Arno, Fiesoli with its warm terraces of vines and orchards, the Ponti Vecchio with its laces and corals, the Petti Palace with its treasures, then, at last, Rome. They planned to stay here but a few days; Naples was their point of embarkation, the *Conti di Savoia* was to sail the end of the month, and they wanted more time in *Bella Napoli*.

All the way from Milan, lumbering over the highways, weaving their way, with sporadic honking of their motor horn, through the narrow streets of small villages, passing vine-covered hills and poppy-carpeted fields, Stan, in the silences while his mother and sister dozed, reminded himself that if Caddie had written there should be a letter waiting for him in Rome.

Early the morning after their arrival there, Angelo drove him to the offices of the American Express.

Yes, said the young American clerk at the mail counter, there were quite a number of letters for "Rutherford." Stanley Rutherford, was it? And Mrs. John O. B. Rutherford and Miss Daisy Rutherford? An obliging fellow, this chap, affable and interested. Had they taken in the coronation on the way over? Must have been *some* spectacle!

Stan shuffled the sheaf of letters he handed to him. Yes; there was one from Caddie! . . . Two!

"Maybe there's some cables," the agreeable young man said. "I'll see."

Stan waited impatiently; he wanted to get back to the hotel before his mother and sister rose for breakfast, so as to be alone and feast on what Caddie had written.

"Yes," said the clerk, returning. "Here's one. Been here a week, our man says."

He offered the innocent-looking slip of folded gray paper. Stan burst its flap, read:

DEAR STANLEY: MY HEART IS HEAVY WITH SAD NEWS. YOUR DEAR FATHER HAD A STROKE YES-TERDAY. SUCCUMBED THIS MORNING. OUR DEEP-EST LOVE AND SYMPATHY TO YOUR MOTHER, SISTER, AND YOURSELF. LLOYD.

CHAPTER XVI

LLOYD AND SYD met them in Oakland when the Overland arrived. Frances burst into wild sobs at the sight of her brother-in-law; Stan grasped Syd's hand; they exchanged a look but no words; then his uncle took Daisy into an embrace, and Syd kissed her, too. She fluttered like a bird into Syd's arms and lifted her cheek unhesitatingly to his lips.

A sad home-coming, so different from the hilarious mood in which they had departed six months ago! The women now were in heavy mourning; Lloyd as well. Stan wore a black band about his arm. He was shocked by his uncle's appearance; the man seemed even frailer than when he had last seen him, was tremulous in his walk and movements and even a little uncertain in his speech. They drove across the Bridge and directly to Grandmère's house, and here there was another emotional scene, with Frances weeping uncontrollably, Daisy's eyes brimming in sympathy, Grandmère dabbing her own to keep the tears from leaving tracings on her withered, powdered cheeks.

"He was a fine man," she quavered, struggling for self-control; "and a good son, afraid of nothing."

"Oh, wasn't he!" sobbed Frances. "And—and always so k-kind."

"What about Eleanor?" Daisy asked.

Her grandmother flung up her head, biting her lips to still their trembling.

"Just one of those things," she said. "The man's an Indian—a treacherous Indian!"

"Where are they now?"

"At the moment, I think, in Geneva, Switzerland," Lloyd answered. "Mackey was sent over there to attend the International Labor Conference, so I read; Eleanor undoubtedly went with him. They took an apartment at the Shoreham when they first went to Washington. We haven't heard for—well, since we lost your father. She wrote a lovely letter then."

"Happy?"

"Yes, I believe so."

There was a short silence, broken only by Frances' quivering breaths.

"Did you suspect she was interested in him?"

"I think your father thought so," Lloyd replied; "he was very much upset at the time."

"She might have waited," Grandmère now said in a steadier voice, straightening herself. "She might have told me, at any rate."

Then, after a moment, she added testily: "An Indian!"

Lloyd lifted his hand; he wanted no criticisms. He turned to Frances, said kindly:

"We thought—Mother and I—that maybe you and Daisy would like to stay here for a while. Your own home can only have sad memories for you."

Frances bowed her head, struggling to stem a fresh rush of tears. There was another silence before she could continue.

"No, we think we'll go where we belong. Daisy and I talked it over. It's the only thing to do. We must go on, and I intend to be—to be *brave* about it. We'll have to resume living there sometime."

"It's all in readiness; I've been over there; Martha has it in good order," said Grandmère. Irrelevantly she stated:

"Charmion came up."

Stan understood. For the funeral, of course.

"How is she?" Frances asked.

"Oh, about the same." A note in the old lady's voice implied something wrong. They looked at her.

"Reggie's been sick," she stated.

"What's the matter with him?" Stan found this dreary family conference unendurable and fervently wished it were over.

"It's a long story," Grandmère answered, biting off the words, her teeth clicking; "we can discuss it later."

"Tell us more about Eleanor," Daisy said. She turned first to her grandmother, and then, noticing the old lady's acid expression, looked to her uncle.

"There's not much," he said, stilling his shaky fingers by clasping them together. "She telephoned from Reno, told me she and Mackey had been married by a justice of the peace, asked for my blessing, and said they were leaving that night for Washington. Then a letter came, and another some weeks ago—after your father went—wanting to know how to get in touch with you. I wired that you were due on the *Conti di Savoia* and would probably go to the Chatham in New York. Did you hear from her?"

"Not a word."

"They've probably left for Geneva."

"Do you think it's all right? The marriage, I mean."

Lloyd shrugged.

"I hope so. She seemed taken with him, and I think she'll like Washington life. She's very social, you know, and she'll enjoy meeting important people—friends of her husband. I understand he stands in high favor with the administration."

Stan rose. The strained atmosphere in the parlor was stifling. To Syd, who had sat silently through the talk, with occasional anxious looks at Daisy, he said:

"Come upstairs, will you? I've something I'd like to discuss with you. . . . May we, Grandmère?"

"Oh yes—surely. Use Eleanor's room. It's in order; I thought your mother and sister might be occupying it."

Stan waved Syd inside the bedroom when they had reached the upper floor and closed the door.

"Sit down," he said somewhat brusquely; "light yourself a cigarette. I want to know what happened; I want to know the details— how my father died. All that beating about the bush downstairs drove me crazy. They're so afraid to talk about it. Tell me—*everything*."

Syd settled himself and lighted the cigarette that Stan had suggested, frowned as he concentrated.

"It's rather complicated," he said. "Nothing about your father's collapse, but the circumstances that led up to it.

"We've been having a lot more strikes. Sixteen of our largest hotels have been closed, and the walkout has now spread to the smaller hotels. They're organizing the retail clerks, and the department stores will follow suit. It's one industry after another. Same all over the country. Last May police shot and killed sixteen striking steel workers in a battle outside the Republic Steel Corporation's plant in South Chicago. They had a free-for-all, with brickbats and bullets, and I don't know how many men were injured."

"I read about it in London. What about my father?"

"This CIO outfit which John L. Lewis has organized is causing a hell of a lot of trouble. The country faces not only the struggle between employers and unions, but is now being torn by jurisdictional disputes. Over a hundred and twenty thousand workers in eighteen states are at present in idleness for one reason or another. The fight between the rival unions is a fight for money and power. Unionism today is big business with an income of millions of dollars per year, affording a tremendous play for personal ambition. Lewis wants to be labor's czar. Only last month the United Mine Workers, of which he is head, purchased the University Club in Washington for a price of two hundred and seventy-five thousand dollars, and they intend to spend another two hundred and fifty thousand dollars in remodeling it. I ask you! All that for a labor union's headquarters!"

"What has all this got to do with my father?" Stan asked impatiently.

"It will help explain what's happened here. This summer Rory O'Brien led his Federation of the Pacific out of the A. F. of L. and joined the CIO. He had to receive the okay of the National Labor Relations Board before the charter was officially approved. The

Waterfront Employers' Association had a contract with the International Longshoremen's Association, which, at the time it was drawn, was an A. F. of L. outfit. O'Brien went to see Joe Halliday to ask if the shipowners would reword the contract, substituting 'CIO' for 'ILA.' Halliday pointed out that the employers could do nothing until the National Labor Relations Board certified the CIO was the proper bargaining agency.

"It just so happened that J.O.B. and I dropped into Halliday's office while they were having this talk. Percy Grant was with us. Of course, it was most unfortunate—your father's being there. What roused his anger was a statement O'Brien made in which he plainly said it was every man's right to join a union of his own choosing without intimidation or coercion, and in the next breath admitted that the men belonging to the original International Longshoremen's Association, who were still affiliated with A. F. of L., had been chased off the waterfront by his own goon squads. Your father demanded how O'Brien could square this admission with the principles he had just stated.

"O'Brien made some remark—nobody seems to have heard it except your father; he rose to his feet like a bull bursting with rage and roared: 'What's that?' O'Brien did not answer, but you know what a devilish face he has. He screwed it up into one of his nastiest sneers—mean and hateful and ugly. J.O.B. seemed to swell; his face turned purple and his whole frame shuddered. Even before he fell, I thought: 'My God, the man's going to have a stroke!' It was terrible to see him go down; it was like a monument toppling over. We stretched him out on the floor, and a doctor was there in fifteen minutes. Then the ambulance came; they got him onto a stretcher and took him to the St. Frances Hospital, the nearest. I suppose half a dozen medicos were summoned; Stewart, of course. The diagnosis was the same; all agreed on the treatment. Your uncle arrived—oh, I should say less than an hour after your father was brought in. He never regained consciousness and passed away about eight o'clock the next morning. That's all there is to it, Stan. He just let his temper get the best of him once too often."

"Cremated?" Stan asked, after a long silence.

"Yes. The question of the disposal of his remains was not raised.

Lloyd seemed to know his wishes. It was pretty tough on him and your grandmother, having you all away."

"I suppose so," Stan said, hardly conscious he spoke. He went to the window, pushed aside the lace curtain, and stood looking out upon the empty street. At an angle across the way he could see part of his home—his father's home—could see its gables and turrets, the heavy foliage and shrubbery surrounding it, the wrought-iron gates leading to the driveway. An empty mausoleum now, he thought. The old man had been so gratified by its ostentatiousness; he had mounted its steps, inserted his key in its massive front door, entered it always with a great pride of ownership. No place for his mother and sister to live, Stan reflected, or himself. Someday they'd move, and the old house would be pulled down. . . .

"Nate Jacobs filed his brief for Detrich, Dempsey, and Kerrigan early this month. It will be reviewed by the First District Court of Appeals," Syd remarked, breaking in upon his thoughts.

"Yeah?" Stan said indifferently. "Any chance of a new trial?"

"I doubt it; Sheridan made a tight case. Those fellows were guilty of conspiracy all right; they had every intention in the world of seeing that Vincent was beaten up. Perhaps they didn't plan to murder him, but they sent thugs after him."

"Did they ever locate Muscowitz?"

"No, he got away; went to Russia, they say. The unions are raising a new hullabaloo to get Mooney pardoned."

"Yeah?" Stan said again. It came to him, as he turned from the window and walked toward Syd, that here was a highly satisfactory friend, loyal to the family, devoted, dependable. He hoped his mother hadn't just imagined his interest in his sister. He laid a hand on his shoulder.

"What's all this I hear about you and Daisy?"

Syd's instant blush, mounting in a crimson wave to his temples, showed definitely that what Stan's mother had confided to him was not in the realm of fancy.

He patted Syd's shoulder.

"You don't have to tell me," he said; "I'd like to see it happen."

"If she'll have me," Syd stammered, his embarrassment as painful as a schoolboy's.

"I think she will; from what I hear, your chances are good."

Stan drew a long breath of weariness and turned back to the window again, staring out into the street, thinking how different his life was going to be from now on. His father had always been his boss—preceptor, rather—laying down codes and rules, acting as his judge, his court of appeal; the old man would like this, not like that, approve of such and such a procedure, disapprove of something different. Now, he was gone, and Stan must face the world and assume responsibilities without guidance. Uncle Lloyd was failing, and soon he would be the last male member of the Rutherford clan. Reggie?

The thought of him prompted Stan to ask:

"What's happened to my uncle down Visalia-way? Grandmère made a grimace when Charmion was mentioned. Anything wrong with him?"

"Yes," Syd admitted with a smile. "I heard the story from your father. Reggie likewise has been having his share of labor troubles. Various unions are at loggerheads with one another, have been trying to organize the pickers and farm workers. Reggie wouldn't have dealings with any of them and put guards along the highways bordering his property and around his help's quarters. One night, as I understand it, he was prowling around—I don't know what for, but he thought somebody was snooping around the camp where his 'cot pickers and cutters were tented—and one of his own guards shot him."

"Shot him!"

"Not seriously. It was a shotgun, but he was well peppered. He's been in the hospital ever since."

Stan's face darkened with a fresh scowl.

"Seems to me," he said, heavily, "everyone connected with this family is under a curse."

§2

He realized hard days lay ahead, but geared himself to meet them. His first concern was for his mother and sister, particularly the former, for she appeared broken and unable to rally. The big house, now barnlike and strangely empty, seemed to echo to the murmur of consoling friends and its mistress' tearful rejoinders. He was sorry for his mother, and even sorrier for his sister, who was at a loss to know how to cope with the situation and whose heart was not only torn with sympathy but heavy with its own loss. Stan appealed to Syd, urging him to get Daisy out, driving her to the park, the beach, over the newly opened Golden Gate Bridge. Syd was glad to comply, but the girl felt she should not desert her mother.

On Stan devolved the heart-rending task of disposing of his father's personal effects, and repeatedly he was compelled to turn to his mother to learn what she wanted done with them. Usually the articles were mementos of happier years, and the sight of them brought fresh floods of tears.

Lloyd came one evening when they were all present, broke the seal of the envelope containing J.O.B.'s will, and in a halting voice—a travesty of his old stentorian tones—read its contents. Frances inherited the house, some odds and ends of real estate, a few securities; his own stock in Wickwire, Rutherford & Company, J.O.B. divided between his two children. Frances had always owned a larger interest in the company than he, so that she was well provided for; he requested, however, that Stanley should be entrusted with the voting powers of both his wife's and daughter's holdings. This immediately brought up the choice of a new president. Stan was in favor of Syd, but his mother was doubtful.

"But why, Stan?" she asked; "you're a Rutherford, and among us —that is, between you and Daisy and me—we own the company. You ought to assume your father's place, don't you think?"

But he would not have it. He felt strongly that Syd deserved the position; he had been with Wickwire, Rutherford a score of years, had proved his loyalty and ability, whereas Stan had been associated with the company only since his Cambridge days. Syd knew more about the business than he or anyone else did, and Stan was aware that stepping aside in his favor would be popular with other officials in the company and in shipping circles as well. There was another reason of which he was almost wholly unconscious. Being president of W. R. & Co. would make him prominent; he would always be in the spotlight, always have to consider what others thought, always feel obliged to comport himself accordingly. He did not want to do that; he wanted to be free, to behave as he liked.

Syd protested vigorously at being promoted, but the matter was in Stan's hands; he was determined he should have the presidency, and at a special meeting of the stockholders Syd was duly elected.

Almost at once the waterfront was in a turmoil again, and there was a new tie-up of the docks. This time the trouble was caused by a jurisdictional dispute, one between rival unions, and in no wise involved the shipowners.

O'Brien and his lieutenants had sometime previously organized the inland warehousemen into a union closely affiliated with their own, but when the longshoremen went CIO, the teamsters, still A. F. of L., determined that the inland warehousemen belonged to them and not to John L. Lewis' organization. As long as the longshoremen stayed A. F. of L., the teamsters had been unwilling to start a war, but now they promptly threw down the gauntlet and established picket lines along the waterfront. Once more the Embarcadero was the scene of rioting, with docks and warehouses closed and ships moving in and out of port on greatly delayed schedules. Thousands of longshoremen and an equal number of teamsters gathered in opposing mobs, shouting and hurling insults at one another, with an occasional brickbat and a fist fight, while armed police stood guard. Loud-speakers simultaneously blasted conflicting arguments to the men, and the uproar was deafening. Shipment of all farm and dairy products came to a standstill, and ruin threatened thousands of farmers who were in no way parties to the controversy.

It was at this time that the "Committee of Forty-three" came into being. It originated in the minds of several leading merchants in the city, and its chief promoter was a public-spirited attorney. The Golden Gate International Exposition, due to open its gates on Treasure Island before very long, made it seem imperative—so it seemed to many—that labor troubles, which the city had known for so many years, should come to an end. The purpose of the committee was to serve in an advisory capacity and try to eliminate the continued controversies between employers and unions. It was organized on a few basic principles: that the public interest came first, that employers and employees should obey the law, that labor was entitled to fair wages, reasonable hours, and proper working conditions, that the use of force, coercion or intimidation should not be tolerated, that all parties involved in a labor dispute should co-operate to avoid strikes, and that agreements between employers and employees should be scrupulously observed. Businessmen had become increasingly conscious of the loss to the community from strikes. Since 1934 there had been 243 strikes in the San Francisco Bay area. In those strikes 154,968 men were engaged, the number of man workdays lost amounted to 1,613,721, and in wages something in excess of nine millions of dollars. As Syd pointed out, the figure representing the loss in wages did not include the losses suffered by employers, or by labor made idle as the result of strikes, or losses to the public in general.

"Besides," said he, "it is probable that every strike involves a loss in business of which only a part is regained."

"This city and the Bay area," Stan observed, nodding in agreement, "has gained a nation-wide reputation for labor trouble. I heard it everywhere when I was east. They all say San Francisco hasn't learned how to solve her labor problems."

"Outside of wages which the worker is out of pocket, and the profit the employer loses, there is another factor which I think most people fail to appreciate," Syd rejoined; "that is fear. The worker is less certain of his job; employers do not know whether they will be in business next week or next month; men who after years of industry and frugality believe themselves secure now have reason to doubt it; professional men, whose living comes from servicing their fellows, lack the old feeling of security. The future looks black. I wish you would serve on this committee, Stan. They asked me, but you are a Rutherford, and everybody respects the name. I can't spare the time."

"Okay," Stan agreed; "whatever you say goes, but I very much doubt if this group of forty-three worthy citizens will accomplish anything of importance."

"They don't aspire to accomplish much," Syd returned; "they hope to promote a discussion of labor disputes so that the public will learn what these are about and give the leaders of the contending factions a chance to cool off before declaring war."

§ 3

Stan had been home ten days when he received a letter from Caddie. It was addressed to the office. She said she was glad to hear he was back again; she had been terribly upset by the news of his father's death and knew what a sad home-coming he must have had; he had all her love and sympathy.

"I know," she wrote, "how involved you are just now with a thousand and one things, but when these are out of the way, and you have the time, remember there is someone very anxious to see you."

There were no amorous declarations, no mawkishness, no embarrassing endearments; the letter was sweet, simple, and understanding. It was the kind Caddie *would* write, Stan reflected.

She had been much in his thoughts on his way back from Europe, knowing that every mile was bringing him nearer to her, and again, after he was home, his mind frequently turned to her, but he could not bring himself to see her. Not for a while. Someday they would meet, someday he would telephone her and they would go to lunch together, or he would run up to her apartment for a chat and perhaps a drink. But he was not ready for that yet.

On a gusty October afternoon when the fog came in billowing from the Heads earlier than usual and a sharp trade wind, laden with salt and mist, had begun to blow fitfully around corners, whirling into eddies the chaff and dust of the streets, he found himself passing the Pitcairn Building. Without thinking and without a moment's hesitation, he pulled back one of the heavy doors and entered its drafty foyer, littered now with scurrying scraps of paper and trash. As he passed along the corridor, his heart began to beat. He stopped a moment before the opaque glass door of her office bearing its legend: "Catherine Welch. Life Insurance. Loans. Notary Public," and could feel the blood pulsing in his eardrums. Perhaps she wouldn't be in and the door locked! But it opened readily as he twisted the knob, and he saw her, standing at her desk, her face framed in its circle of brown curls which swept up and around the narrow brim of her small hat, her firm breasts outlined in the trim belted sweater he remembered so well. At sight of him, her eyes lighted, her big mouth widened, she cried: "Stan!" and held out both hands. He came in and took one of them, his own face reflecting her pleasure, his heart hammering.

"Well, Caddie . . ."

As he spoke, he was aware someone else was in the room. He turned and saw Rory O'Brien with his back to the window. The sudden apparition of the man stunned him. Their eyes met in an instant look of antagonism. Stan did not move; he felt his face grow rigid as he shut his teeth. Rory swept him with a glance, and Stan thought of the malevolent sneer which had enraged his father, and his hand fisted. The atmosphere in the small office was tense and charged with dynamite. The harsh scrape of a chair on the wooden floor broke the stillness as Rory shoved one aside. Then, measuring Stan with another contemptuous look, he nodded brusquely to Caddie, opened the office door, and went out.

Stan grasped the back of the chair Rory had moved, and held tightly to it. He felt a wind had passed over him, a wind of spleen and malice and death. The sense that the man who had just left was his adversary and his enemy rode him hard. He was unnerved, and the legs of the chair to which he clung chattered against the floor as it shook beneath his grip.

"I'm sorry, I'm sorry, Stan," Caddie kept repeating.

He stared at her, not hearing. She came to him and put her hand on his arm.

"I'm sorry," she said again; "I didn't know you were coming. He just dropped in a few minutes ago. I wouldn't have had you upset this way for anything in the world."

He continued to look at her, his face spasmodically twitching.

"Why do you associate with such a rat?" he asked then, teeth clenched.

She did not answer; she clung to his arm.

"Stan," she said tenderly, "you look badly; you've lost weight. I've been thinking about you every day since you got back," she went on, "oh, and before that! Always and always. I wanted so much to see you and talk to you—comfort you. I knew I couldn't, but I wanted to try just the same."

"Kind of you," he sneered.

"Oh, don't be that way!" she protested. "You've come to see me. That's all that matters. Just because you met him in my office is no reason why you should . . ."

She left the sentence unfinished and laid her other hand on his shoulder.

"I'm *so* glad to see you," she said.

He met her eyes, and some of the tightness around his head and heart seemed to lessen. He put his hand over hers.

"I didn't expect to meet him here," he growled.

"Of course you didn't."

"You know he . . . he's responsible for . . . my father."

"How, my dear?"

As if there were fog before his eyes, he brushed away his thought. He sat down in the chair and reached for his cigarette case and, with fingers that shook, took out one. Caddie scratched a match and held it to its tip. Then she too sat down—in the swivel chair behind her desk.

"You look good to me," she said after a moment, watching him as he inhaled. "Tell me about everything," she continued. "How was the coronation, and the trip, and how is your sister?"

He could not find the words to answer her. He made a motion with his hand and closed his eyes, thinking this was not how he had planned to meet her, this was not as he had imagined it. How was it possible that she—so affectionate and intelligent and desirable— could associate with such a blackguard! Fierce hatred for the man with his ragged red beard, misshapen jaw, and gutted eye welled up strong within him. He thought: *I'll go—I'll get out of here, and this Jezebel can consort with whom she pleases!*

She guessed what was passing in his mind, rose, came to him and put one hand on his neck, and then sank to her knee so that she could place both arms around him. He stiffened, but the touch of her and the smell of her overpowered him. Something started to break inside him—breaking, breaking, breaking—and then broke! He leaned toward her, and she caught him to her, kissing his hair, his ear, and a corner of his cheek, making little crooning noises as hungrily her lips caressed him. Suddenly a sob rose in his throat; he mastered it. This was the first affection, the first touch of tenderness he had had since his father's death. His head sank to her shoulder and his arm went round her, and he drew her close, breathing deeply of the incense she exhaled, her full breasts and warm body against his heart, while her lips continued to find his hair, his neck, and even his coat-covered shoulder, and she murmured soft sounds of endearment.

"Caddie," he whispered.

She raised his head, a hand beneath his chin, looked at him with glowing eyes, and kissed him tenderly.

"Well," she said then, sitting back on one heel, holding to him, her big smile lighting her face, "I guess it's that way between us!" And then, after a pause: "We need each other, don't we, my dear? I can't get along without you, and you can't without me. . . . I've been living for this moment. So have you."

He nodded and reached for her lips.

Oh, it was good, good, to be with her again! He hadn't realized how much she meant to him or how much he had missed her! She was an integral part of his life! As she said, they needed each other; they must never be separated.

She rose, flushed with excitement, and seized his head between her hands, her fingers clutching his hair.

"My darling darling!" she said, searching his eyes. She stood so for a long minute, then suddenly she sank again to the floor, her face buried in the crook of her elbow, her head across his knees, and cried brokenly:

"I love you so!"

§ 4

Laughing, talking, interrupting each other every minute or two, stopping to smother fresh laughter, they found their way to the street and followed its gentle ascent toward Caddie's apartment. Stan was not conscious of their direction. Only when they reached her doorway with its strip of shirred silk behind its glass and the row of brass-covered letter boxes and bells lining the narrow tiled entrance, did he pause. This was what he had fled from! He hesitated only a moment, then, with a flip of his finger, snapped the butt of his cigarette into the street and followed her as she unlocked the door.

§5

Christmas was upon the Rutherfords again. Only five members of the family gathered about Grandmère's breakfast table that morning, but today a sixth person—one soon to be added to their circle— was present: Syd Watterbury. Stan, studying him as he sat across the board and next to his pretty, birdlike sister, who, he hoped, would one day surrender to him her girlhood and fragile beauty, decided for the hundredth time that Syd would make Daisy a perfect husband, would always be gentle, kind, and protective. He was glad he was with them this Christmas; his presence spared them from melancholy sighs and doleful looks. All were conscious of the missing faces; next year their number might be even less. But today should be a day for rejoicing! Syd kept them cheerful.

There was much happy talk about the table regarding Eleanor. Her father had received a long Christmas letter from her, and Grandmère had had one too; both Frances and Daisy had heard from her, and weeks before she had written an affectionate note to Stan. Every line she penned indicated the success of her marriage. She and Byron were planning to spend the holidays in Connecticut with Byron's people—two aged aunts and an uncle who lived in rugged style on a New England farm. "I'm praying for snow," she wrote, "and Byron has promised to show me how to milk a cow!"

When this was quoted, Stan shouted joyously.

"I can just see my stately cousin tweaking a cow's teats and squirting the milk into a bucket with her head jammed into the animal's side, humming a lullaby so the beast will let down."

All joined the laugh.

"Just the same," Daisy whispered soberly to her brother when the mirth subsided, "I won't be married unless she's here—not if I have to wait a year!"

He patted her hand reassuringly.

Frances asked for news of Reggie and Charmion.

"Reggie seems to have recovered from his shotgun wounds," Lloyd answered her; "they weren't very serious, I take it, but now Charmion has had an accident."

"I wrote her early this month," supplemented Grandmère, surveying the plates of her guests to see if anyone could be persuaded
to have another helping. Wilbur stood respectfully at her elbow,
holding a large platterful of smoking waffles. "I wrote her early this
month," Grandmère repeated, "hoping they'd come up for Christmas, and Reggie answered. Poor Charmion—I declare I don't believe
my daughter has the sense she was born with! She must needs get
knocked down by a truck!"

"I'll bet it belonged to some union!" Stan interjected.

"It did," his uncle confirmed, acknowledging his guess with a nod.

"I don't know who it belonged to," Grandmère continued, "but
she got herself mixed up in a horrible fight. It seems to me . . ."

Her voice trailed off disconsolately, and Lloyd took up the story.

"A truck of freshly packed vegetables was standing at the curb in
Visalia close to Charmion, and it was about to pull out," he said;
"some malcontent threw an electric bulb filled with kerosene into
the truck. Police were present, and the man was promptly arrested; a
free-for-all followed. I don't know all the circumstances, but the
truck, backing up to make a getaway, backed into my sister, knocked
her down, and she broke three of her ribs. Later, when an ambulance
arrived and they lifted her, they found one of her lungs had been
punctured."

"Goodness me!" cried Frances, aghast.

"I fear it's pretty serious. She's in a hospital, and I'm going down
there again this coming week to see if there's anything more we can
do."

"I'll go with you," said Grandmère, one glistening white curl on
her silvery wig bobbing in emphasis. "I wish to heaven," she went
on after a moment, "Charmion would give up trying to live in such
a God-forsaken place where they know nothing about observing the
law. She'd be much wiser to make her home with me."

"Reggie?" Stan suggested, inquiringly.

"Reggie's an old stick-in-the-mud," his grandmother replied, shaking her curls; "he's forever getting himself into fights. I don't see
why he can't run his business without quarreling with everybody."

"Maybe the quarreling is forced on him; maybe he's a victim of
others' fights."

"Then he shouldn't entertain such grandiose agricultural ideas," Grandmère retorted. "He ought to come here and behave himself. I could put up with him if I had my daughter safely under my roof."

Stan caught Syd's eye. He twisted his mouth slyly, hunched a shoulder, said nothing.

"Well, children—what say? Presents now?"

The time-honored cue! They rose, brushing crumbs from their laps, drawing uncomfortable sighs after the too hearty breakfast, and —Grandmère on Lloyd's arm leading the way—crossed the hall to the parlor.

Here once more stood a resplendent tree. Daisy, her brother knew, had spent many hours during the past week hanging the colored balls and draping the tinsel. At the very top of the tree dangled a small angel bearing aloft a silvery star. From his earliest Christmases, Stan remembered seeing it there—Christmases when every one of the gaily wrapped packages piled around the base of the tree had set his boyish heart thumping in expectancy.

But there was no thumping now. These Christmas-morning gatherings were meaningless, significant only to those of the generation that was passing. Gifts no longer brought him pleasure. Only one that he had had this year was precious to him: a small medallion with a miniature painting of St. Christopher upon it.

"For your car," Caddie had said. "It will save you from smashups and keep people from running into you," she had told him, kissing the tip of his nose.

That morning he had awakened feeling that life was not worth the living. Syd had given him a hint some days ago that the business was not going any too well; the company had lost money; costs of operation were steadily mounting. But this had not been the cause of his dejection. It was Caddie! Caddie with all her charm and cantankerousness, her sweetness and perversity! The future held no promise of happiness. He was in love with her; he knew that beyond a doubt now. She was the only woman who had ever captured his heart. He remembered the letter he had planned to write her from New York, the letter he had never penned but whose phrases were indelibly etched upon his mind; he was to have ended it, he recalled, by telling her that she was the only woman he loved, and would *ever* love. How true it was!

So what? he had asked himself as he lay in bed this Christmas morning, the gray dawn struggling at his eastern windows, church bells sounding soft and hushed in the early fog. So what? He could not marry her. She would not consent to it, even if he were free. Nor could he go away with her; she would not agree to that either. And again—so what? Loving each other though they did, they quarreled. Each had convictions and opinions violently at variance with one another's. They thought differently about politics and society, about individual rights and individual freedom. She was a Communist; he, a capitalist. He had never stopped to consider whether he was one or not, but since he was opposed to everything she believed in, he must be a capitalist, even if owning a company employing a fleet of freighters and several thousand men did not make him so!

Christmas Eve they had gone to dinner together at a small restaurant near her apartment, and later to a movie, *Tovarich,* a poor screen adaptation of an excellent play he had seen that spring in London, and because it had been Russian in character, the picture had led them to a discussion of the Soviet way of government, Stan claiming that Stalin was a dictator, Caddie asserting that Russia was a democracy and the workers elected representatives of their own choosing under the new Soviet constitution. He had countered by reminding her of the scores of army officers that had been ruthlessly shot, the executions, arrests, and deportations of hundreds of others who had been accused of treason. Caddie finally had given way to tears, Stan had wrathfully sworn—at himself, at her, and their everlasting wrangling—and left in temper, walking angrily home, continuing his arguments mentally, pursuing them long after he was in bed and the pendulum clock in the hallway downstairs struck a sepulchral three. At times he decided they had reached the parting of the ways, and in the next moment realized that life without her was unthinkable. Happiness and contentment were not possible for him unless she shared them.

Now Daisy was calling to him to open Eleanor's box that had arrived by express from Washington. He went for a hammer, attacked its lid, tore off the boards. The crate was full of gifts, something for everyone: a velvet evening bag for Grandmère, gloves for Aunt Frances, a snakeskin wallet for Stan, one of her loveliest diamond brooches for "the bride-to-be," neckties of sober colors for sober Syd, and two heavy volumes for her beloved father—*Soviet Communism,* by Sidney and Beatrice Webb. There were gifts, too, for Reggie and Charmion and small remembrances for each of the servants.

"I declare," commented Grandmère, "she thought of everyone! I wonder if marrying that Indian has done the girl some good."

"Tough reading, I imagine," Stan observed, handing his uncle the bulky books.

"Pretty heavy to hold," the old man answered, examining their title pages.

"Seems to me we're getting an awful lot of Russia these days," Stan continued. "You'd think that Stalin and his crew of satellites had discovered a panacea for all the wrongs of the world. I'm getting fed up with all this propaganda, aren't you?"

"We-l-ll," drawled his uncle, fingering the pages of a volume, "there are always new messiahs who believe they know the right road. We've got quite a number of them now, what with Stalin, Hitler, Mussolini, and Roosevelt in the field. Takes strong men, I suppose, to keep the discontented from getting out of hand."

"I see the governor refused Mooney a pardon yesterday," Stan said.

"His case is up to the Supreme Court. Merriam won't do anything until they hand down a decision."

"Think Detrich, Dempsey, and Kerrigan will get a new trial?"

"Doubt it. I read the respondent's brief the other day. A sound job. Sheridan knows his stuff. I hear that persistent little whippersnapper —what's his name?—Jacobs proposes to carry the case to the California Supreme Court. He'll get nowhere."

"Those fellows surely connived at the murder!"

Lloyd glanced at Daisy over the rims of his pince-nez, lifted a warning hand. Stan noticed how white its skin was, with bulging blue veins and brown liver spots.

"Let's not talk quite so loud," his uncle cautioned, lowering his voice; "the child doesn't know a thing, does she?"

"I think Mother's very careful about that," Stan answered, matching his uncle's tone. "At any rate if she sees anything in the news-papers, she doesn't speak of it. I've never heard her mention Vince or the tragedy—once."

"Let's hope she's forgotten. When does she plan to be married?"

"Date's not set, but it will be some time next fall. Mother thinks Daisy ought to wait a year, you know. It will be very quiet; just the family."

His uncle nodded.

Stan was enjoying this chat. He had a great respect for the older man, and a deep-seated affection for him as well. Uncle Lloyd had been a magnificent figure in his day; all San Francisco respected him; Stan wished they had more of such talks.

"What about this fellow Rory O'Brien?" he asked now, anxious to continue their conversation. "Surely he's no messiah. Just plain dema-gogue, I'd say. An evil person. What right has he in this country? He's a rank Communist, isn't he?"

"If he is, it's no statutory crime," his uncle answered. "You can believe what you like in the United States, and go about preaching it, too. Think of our revered Pilgrim Fathers. Their beliefs would not find many converts today. They frowned on cards and dancing and almost any kind of innocent fun. If it was pleasure, then it was sin. Their Sunday laws were as strict and as uncompromising as any of the decrees of Hitler or Mussolini, and they did not hesitate to burn at the stake young girls suspected of witchcraft. Dealings in the black art did not have to be proved; denunciation was sufficient to drag the accused to the stake."

"But Rory O'Brien? A lot of people say he ought to be deported."

"I don't believe it's been proven he's an alien. He claims he was born here, but I don't think he's satisfied the authorities as yet. His name isn't Rory O'Brien, they tell me; it's something quite different."

"I never heard that!" Stan was genuinely surprised.

"Oh yes," his uncle affirmed. " 'Rory O'Brien' is assumed. That's Irish. The man's no more Irish than your grandmother. His real name, I understand, is quite a common American one—like Robin-son or Baker or Foster. . . . If he were an alien, the immigration au-thorities would have deported him long ago. He claims he's an

American citizen, and if he's right, he can preach all the iniquitous doctrines he pleases. That's his privilege under the Bill of Rights."

"What are you two gossiping about over there?" shrilled Grandmère. "This is Christmas, and you've got to get into the Christmas spirit. We're going to have some carols by and by. Anyway, it's time for the servants; you'd better call them."

Dutifully they filed in, sedate and solemn Wilbur heading the line as he had headed it—Stan computed—for sixteen years.

"All right, Lloyd; we'll have the story of the Nativity, now." Grandmère gestured to the others, indicating they were to arrange themselves and prepare for the reading.

Stan brought his uncle the Bible, and when the old man fumbled with its pages, found the passage for him. The book shook in his hands, and he had trouble adjusting his pince-nez. With eyes that began to water, he looked helplessly at his mother.

"I think," he quavered, "I think Stanley . . ."

"All right," said Grandmère, her white curls bobbing, "take the book, Stan, and read the passage." She looked severely at the servants and hard at Syd.

Stan felt his cheeks burning a little as he took the Bible from his uncle. So it was in the relay race when the baton was received from the hand of the spent runner and given to that of the fresh one.

He opened the book, moistened his lips, began:

"And there were in the same country shepherds abiding in the field, keeping watch over their flocks by night . . ."

CHAPTER XVII

"YOU CAN FIGURE IT OUT FOR YOURSELF," Syd said. "I've had our treasurer working on this report for weeks. It doesn't look so good, Stan."

It was February of the following year. The two men were in Syd's office—once J.O.B.'s—and against the gray-papered walls hung the photographs of clippers and sailing ships, and around the room stood the models of freighters with their brass plates and the dates of launching. Now whenever Stan was about to enter this room, he always experienced a qualm and, on a deep breath, stifled an emotion, slight though it was.

Today was Saturday. Syd had telephoned during the morning and asked him to save the afternoon for him.

"We'll be alone, nobody will interrupt us, and I must go over some figures with you," Syd had said.

For hours their heads had been bent over a large sheet of yellow paper, ruled and counterruled, and with long columns of figures and neat tabulations in red and black ink.

"I can't understand why your father didn't realize where we were heading," Syd was saying; "he must have suspected things weren't so good, but certainly he kept the information to himself. . . . I'm right about that, am I not?"

"He never said a word to me," Stan assured him.

"Well, look here. The cost of operating one of our boats averages $1,200 a day; there're twenty-six of them, so operating costs amount to twenty-six times $1,200, or $31,200 *per day*. When you take a strike which ended a year ago and lasted one hundred days, that means a hundred times $31,200, or $3,120,000! That's big money, Stan—and it spells *loss!* L-O-SS! You must add to this figure the overhead of keeping our organization intact, the cost of operating this building, meeting our pay rolls, maintaining our warehouses in Honolulu, New Orleans, Tacoma, Seattle—all of them. For one hundred days those warehouses stood empty or were piled high with stalled freight. Then there are our branch offices—in New York, Seattle, Los Angeles, and New Orleans. We spent $250,000 in improving crews' quarters. We have a shore staff of over five hundred persons and employ a seagoing personnel ranging from two thousand to twenty-five hundred persons, depending upon the time of the year. The wages and salaries we paid last year amounted to $4,815,450. Everything going out and damn little coming in! You can see where we come out. *In the soup!*

"Let's take our expenses and profits of four years ago. In spite of the general strike and tie-up in the summer of 1934, W. R. paid a dividend of three dollars a share. We won't be able to declare a cent this year! Costs have trebled, quadrupled. We can meet the boost in wages—we have to—but the unions won't give us our money's worth!

"See here. I received a report the other day from Captain Willard of the *San Fernando*——"

"Oh yes; I know him quite well. Nice guy," Stan supplied.

"The *San Fernando* was held up in New Orleans for six days," Syd continued; "she was due to sail on the tenth of December; she left on the sixteenth. Why was she delayed? Because her crew made certain demands, and unless these demands were granted, they refused to sail. I became interested and wanted to find out what their demands were, so I asked for a report. Here it is."

He fumbled in a basket of papers and brought out a typewritten sheet.

"Listen to this: First the sailors wanted fresh strawberries! Then they wanted Brussels sprouts, sixty pounds of tenderloin beef, ten cases of asparagus tips, a better brand of coffee, a finer-grade quality of soap than they had been getting, sixty additional pounds of turkey—they were to be on the Pacific Christmas week, and the turkey was for the holidays—fresh bottled milk, and a promise from the captain to stop at Panama and load up with more fresh vegetables; they also wanted twenty pounds of nuts, figs, and dates for Christmas. The port captain refused to okay such unreasonable demands, and so the crew went off to the town and got drunk. Willard was stuck. He couldn't hire another crew; the union wouldn't furnish him with one. There was nothing else for him to do but to give in.

"Now I ask you, how can you run ships under such circumstances? I have great sympathy for the sailors. They live a hard life; they're confined to small quarters; they have no diversions, so that what is dished up to them from the galley is the most important thing that happens to them day in and day out. Those are hard conditions, but that is a sailor's life. We alter our boats, knock out partitions, put four men in a cabin where we used to put eight, change the location of the crew's quarters so that the men will be cooler, provide them with showers and hot water, give them the best food we can buy, but when it comes to *strawberries* . . . ! Finding strawberries in New Orleans in the month of December is like finding daffodils in the Sahara. Willard told me that strawberries had never been heard of in New Orleans during that month, but the sailors insisted upon them. They would take no substitution. If they didn't get strawberries, they wouldn't sail. Willard had to wire for the fruit and got a hothouse variety at that!

"Y'understand what we're up against? Consider San Francisco. We are supposed to have an ironbound contract here with the sailors and longshoremen, signed a year ago. In that contract the unions agreed there should be no stoppages of work. None whatsoever. Do you know how many stoppages of work there have been during the last twelve months? Over three hundred! *Flagrant, unjustified stoppages of work!* When something doesn't quite suit their lordships, they just stop working, although they've contracted to submit any and all beefs to the port arbitrator.

"The longshoremen have insisted on the right to penalize their own members, but there is not *one single instance* when they have ever done so when men have been guilty of the slow-down.

"I was amazed the other day to find a man who had never heard of the slow-down. Zachariah Nugent took me to the Palace Hotel, and we were lunching at the round table, and a man near me asked what the slow-down was. I could hardly believe I heard straight. I came back to the office and ordered cards printed listing the kinds of slow-down there are. Here's one."

Stan glanced at it. It read:

THE SLOW-DOWN

Loafing.

Sleeping.

Drunkenness.

Holding men half working, half idling.

Leaving the ship and the dock to drink.

Gathering in the crew quarters for smoking and eating.

Setting illegally a 2100-pound all-over load limit.

Failure to meet the hook promptly.

Refusal to shift the work, freezing men in idleness.

Absence from the place of work.

Forcing use of unnecessary men.

Refusing to use the necessary trailers, or jitney drivers to unhook, and of longshoremen to pull loads at the hook.

Quitting early.
Arriving late.
Refusal to use the swing board.
Taking fixed turns on holds.
Rigid rotation of dock equipment to hook.

"I'm going to carry some of these cards with me," Syd said, "and I'm going to hand one of 'em to anybody who asks that question again.

"The contract between the Waterfront Employers and the unions comes up for renewal next September. Are we going to sign it? Are we going to continue this farce, allowing ourselves to be bulldozed, cheated, and made monkeys of?"

"I'm familiar with all that," Stan said wearily.

"I'm sorry," Syd continued; "this is old stuff to you—I realize that —but you represent your own, your sister's, and your mother's interests in this company now, and I feel responsible to you. You insisted upon my being president, and I'm doing my level best to do a conscientious job."

"I know, I know," Stan apologized. "I'm not sore—certainly not at you—but I *am* sore at these damn radicals who poison the men's minds and incite them to make trouble. Maybe we were at fault at the beginning—perhaps grievously so—but, by the Lord Harry, we're not at fault now!"

"There's more to it," continued Syd. "I'm sorry, pal, but you've got to know the score!

"Look at this list. There are *eighteen coastwise steamship services which have discontinued servicing the port of San Francisco owing to labor trouble.* In addition, there are five intercoastal lines no longer operating, and seven or eight foreign services—that is, companies operating ships to the Orient, to the South Seas, and to Europe; American lines, you understand. I say seven or eight because—this is the tip I got which started me on this investigation— I've learned on pretty sound authority that the Nickel Line is going to fold, the Lobenthal Company also, and—hold your hat!—Percy Grant is dickering with a South American outfit to sell his passenger steamers! If they quit, that will make *nine* companies in the ocean-to-ocean shipping business who will be out of the running or will do business from some other port than San Francisco. *Thirty lines all together!* No wonder the businessmen of this city are worried! No wonder they've organized a Committee of Forty-three! No wonder they call it a ghost town! . . . Next year San Francisco is going to open a world's fair—'A Pageant of the Pacific'—to show how wonderful we are! . . . It makes you sick!"

He paused and marched angrily up and down the room, while Stan sat scowling at the desk, his head in his hands.

"I want you to take these figures home with you," Syd resumed on a fresh breath. "I want you to take them home with you," he repeated, "and study them. You've *got* to, Stan. I can't carry the responsibility of running this company alone. If we can't make a go of it, the quicker we shut up shop, the better. Here are our operating costs, overhead, revenues, assets, bank loans, taxes. You'll have to analyze them. On this attached sheet I've written out a summary of what I think we may do this year and next. I don't know whether I'm right or not. It's pure guesswork. We may have a European war—looks that way if the British go on believing all the lies that Hitler tells them!—and a war isn't going to help matters. I see Eden resigned in disgust the other day, and this bombing of our gunboat the *Panay* in the Yangtze by the Japs last year doesn't indicate that our little brown brothers love us any too much. Suppose war comes, what becomes of the shipping business? No foreign trade; there'll be embargoes, restricted shipping zones, perhaps submarines! My guess is that the steamship business is about over unless something happens, and these testimonials of progress and achievement representing so many years of hard work of which your dad was so proud" —he waved his hand at the photographs on the walls and the ship models on their stands—"will be just so many interesting relics for a museum. I'm glad he isn't here to see the end of it!"

Stan rose and thumped the desk softly with a closed fist.

"Look here," he said with his jaw set, "I don't care a damn whether Wickwire & Rutherford makes a dime this year or next, or whether it *ever* makes a cent. I'm not going to quit. I'll go down in the ruins and take my mother and my sister with me, my uncle and my grandmother—everybody who will stick. I'm not going to lie down and let these sons of bitches walk all over me. I'll fight 'em with their own dirty underhanded methods, and I'll stab a knife in their backs without a moment's hesitation just the way they murdered Vincent Oliver."

§ 2

Stan walked gloomily up Market Street with a half-notion of catching the first taxi that passed and going up to his club.

His thoughts were too confused to think clearly; the long afternoon had tired him. Figures, figures, figures and dismal predictions! Syd, after all, was not the cheeriest person in the world; he was inclined to be pessimistic. Stan did not care whether the company liquidated or not, but he *would* like to square accounts with the unions and their damned incendiary leaders. He had no wish, however, to saddle himself with responsibility. He was different from his father, who had gloried in building the business; there was no satisfaction in carrying it on. If there were no profits, why continue? Taxes and high wages took them all! If only working hard and being a pack horse would bring him Caddie!

His spirits brightened at the thought of her. Perhaps she was home now. It would be far pleasanter to relax in her company over a scotch-and-soda than go to the club and risk running into Steve Gallagher or Tom Brophy at the bar. He quickened his pace.

But there was no response to his ring when he reached the apartment house where she lived. It had been arranged between them that he would always push the bell twice and follow with a short jingle. This afternoon there was no answering buzz to open the door. He rang four or five times and then walked to the middle of the street and looked up at her windows. Nothing. One window was raised a foot, and the lace hangings inside fluttered through the opening and seemed to be thumbing their nose at him.

Where was she? She should be at home at this hour. Frequently of late when he had telephoned she had been out. Even early in the morning. She told him she had an aunt in Berkeley who was sick, and said she had to see her two or three times a week. Was that the truth? Would she cook up such a cock-and-bull story to put him off? Was she running around with someone else? Jealousy roweled him, turning him a little sick. Caddie! . . . Why had he ever met her! Why had he ever stopped at her office to sign that affidavit! . . . Lord God, it was less than two years ago!

He went back to the apartment door and tried to look into the foyer, his hands cupped about his eyes. Ridiculous! He was behaving like a schoolboy! . . . He deliberated ringing one of the other tenants' bells, gaining admission to the building, mounting to the fifth floor, knocking at her door, finding out for sure if it was locked and she did not answer. He swore, deriding himself. Moody and angry, he ambled down the slight incline of the hill, waited for a taxi, and when none appeared, walked some blocks farther to a cable line, swung himself aboard a car, and rode disconsolately home.

There, beneath the garish light flooding the ornate drawing room with its polar-bear skins, its inlaid cabinets and heavy plush portieres, he found his black-robed mother and somberly dressed sister sitting at a card table, playing solitaire.

"Hello," he said.

"Hello, darling," they answered; "how's everything?"

Suppose he answered that everything was as bad as it could possibly be and that Wickwire, Rutherford & Co., which had provided them with all the comforts and luxuries they had ever known, might have to close its doors? It amused him to think of their consternation.

"Everything's fine," he assured them and, tucking the evening paper beneath his arm, began to ascend the broad, carpeted stairs, his hand on the carved balustrade.

"Stan," called his sister, "do you think it's all right if Syd takes me to the Opera House tonight? It's Lotte Lehmann in an all-Wagnerian program. Mother thinks maybe I oughtn't to go."

"Of course," he called back; "go by all means."

"He said he'd like to take me to dinner first—a quiet place, you know."

"Why not? You haven't been anywhere in weeks. Make her go, Mom."

He recommenced his climb, and it brought to mind his father

ponderously mounting these stairs, pulling himself upward with a heavy hand on the rail.

In his room he closed the door and tossed to the top of his bureau the bulky envelope containing all the charts and statements Syd wanted him to study. Then with a grateful sigh he sank into an armchair and opened the evening paper.

"Chancellor Hitler," he read, "in a speech in the Reichstag in Berlin, reiterated Germany's desire to co-operate in a peaceful solution of international problems. He said no differences except as to colonies existed between Germany and Great Britain."

A. E. Shaw, attorney and referee in the Tom Mooney hearing, was dead. His report, so the paper said, was used as the basis for the court's refusal three months ago to grant Mooney his freedom.

The President had named Rear-Admiral Emory S. Land as chairman of the Maritime Commission to succeed Joseph P. Kennedy, now headed for the Court of St. James's.

In London, Neville Chamberlain and Anthony Eden had reached a reported parting of the ways over Britain's policy toward Germany; Eden had resigned from the Cabinet.

An article giving an account of a hearing before the National Labor Relations Board interested him. The hearing was to determine the status of the Pacific Coast waterfront agreements and to establish the bargaining agency for longshoremen. Rory O'Brien had testified, so said the article, that membership in the longshoremen's union was in excess of eleven thousand.

Stan's lip curled. Half of those eleven thousand men had been bullied into joining O'Brien's union, now safe in the heart of Lewis' CIO. The handful of longshoremen who had had the temerity to refuse to join his band of gorillas and had tried to remain faithful to ILA had been run off the waterfront.

The attempt of the teamsters to obtain control of the inland warehouses had failed principally because the farmers in the state pleaded with them to lift their embargo, as otherwise they faced ruin; a second reason it had failed was that men who might have joined the teamsters were afraid to apply for enrollment at their headquarters, as in front of its doors were massed a hundred or more of O'Brien's toughs. The jurisdictional battle had lasted twenty-nine days, and O'Brien and his cohorts had triumphed. Stan was only too familiar with the way it was done.

"Look here, buddy, if you're wise, you'll scram. We know where you and your wife and kids are living. They'll have a fine time someday while you're working down at the docks, or they'll get a chance to shed a few salty tears when your body's brought home. Beat it—understand?"

It had been said so often, Stan could hear the ominous tone of the advice. He could see eight bruisers crowding around one man, thrusting out their truculent jaws, shaking their savage fists into his face, while their spokesman uttered the words of warning. An old story!

The last paragraph of the article was also of interest to him:

The recent disappearance of two complete files and the evidence of other papers having been disturbed at the headquarters of the Waterfront Employers' Association was revealed by A. E. Roth, its president.

That, too, was an old story!

He threw the paper aside, undressed, and for several minutes stood beneath the refreshing downpour of his shower, realizing his head was aching and the prospect of the evening before him was a dull one.

§ 3

"Well, Stanley, I believe we'll let our little bird out of her cage sometime this fall. It will be over a year since we lost your dear father. Long enough to wait, don't you think? Syd says September—of course he's impatient—but Eleanor cannot be here then; she writes that Byron's going to Europe to report to the President what all this trouble with Germany is about—and Daisy naturally wants her present. I can't blame her. Daisy was one of Eleanor's bridesmaids, and the girls were very close. Your sister wants just the family, and I quite agree. Poor Charmion's gone now. What a dreadful ending that was! Grandmère tells me she suffered terribly! I don't know as Reggie will feel like coming up, and I don't much care whether he does or not. After all, Reggie's no kin. But Daisy wants Eleanor, so that means December. We've set Saturday, the third, tentatively. Syd will make her a good husband, don't you think? It is such a relief to my mind whenever I think about them getting married that he knows all about that previous affair—about poor Vincent, I mean. It would be hard to explain to anybody else how attached she was to him. But Syd knows all about it, and he'll see to it that she never hears a word and that his name is never mentioned."

Stan's mother sat in her accustomed place at the dinner table, attempting to impale green peas on the prong of her fork. She was not thinking of what she was doing; she was lost in a cloud of speculation.

"Whenever they get married, I'd like to have as few present as possible," she proceeded. "If there's only a handful, so much the better. I don't want any kind of an affair which can remotely be construed by the press as a wedding ceremony or a reception. There will be you and me and Grandmère—three. Daisy tells me that Syd would like you as best man, but I say you're the only one—and the proper one—to give Daisy away, but since it will be such a small wedding, I don't suppose it will make much difference. Eleanor of course will be matron of honor, and I guess that will be all the attendants the poor bride will have. Then there will be Mr. Mackey— and Reggie if he comes. Eight or nine—and that seems about right, don't you think?

"Syd plans to take Daisy off to Honolulu for their honeymoon, and I don't see why not, do you? He's bent on sailing on the *Mauna Kea* and wants to engage one of those *lanai* suites. And I'm thinking, Stan, that after they're married we might as well break up here. Daisy wants one of those five-room apartments in the new Park Lane, and she has her own ideas of how she wants to furnish it. But this house will be far too big for just the two of us. I thought you and I might go to the Fairmont Hotel for a while and see how it feels living some other place. Of course, I love it here, but I'd be horribly lonesome after Daisy's married and you away at the office all day long. I'd be alone—frightfully alone—and of course I'd get blue and get thinking of bygone days. Do you think I'm selfish, Stan?"

He reached across the corner of the table and patted her bare forearm, plump and white, with the filigree of black lace from her elbow falling gracefully across it.

"No, no," he said, suppressing a yawn, "no, I don't think you're selfish in the least. We'll find some diggings of our own and be very happy. Martha will take good care of us."

"You're such a comfort to me, Stan. Then we'll set the wedding for December third, shall we?"

"Sure—any date. 'S all right with me. Suit yourself."

He yawned again, his chin quivering as he tried to smother it.

He thought: *Caddie may have come home by now!* The evening could hold no better entertainment for him than spending it with her. He'd telephone—but from a booth some place outside the house.

"I think I'll take a stroll tonight," he told his mother. "I like to prowl around the Presidio, and I love to walk out halfway across the Golden Gate Bridge. It's a wonderful sight from there at night—the Bay and the city and all the lights."

"Don't catch cold, and try to be home early," his mother urged.

§4

There was no answer to his call from the drugstore. He dropped another nickel in the telephone slot and dialed Caddie's number a second time. There was only a prolonged, repetitious buzzing. Forlornly he strolled out into the street. He was in no mood for a walk. Instead he wandered toward the bright lights of the city and presently —perhaps his feet unconsciously led him there!—found himself in the neighborhood of Caddie's home. He stood in front of her apartment house again and gazed up at her windows. No, she was not there. Where could she be? If only he knew the name of that aunt in Berkeley, he would telephone and suggest he come and get her in a taxicab.

Aimlessly he made his way toward winking neon signs and the murmur of Saturday night's merrymaking, watching enviously four rowdy youths, arms linked, pushing and jostling one another as they rollicked along the street, pleasure bound, and at a young couple in the shadow of a doorway, the man whispering to the girl, his head close to hers, his arm around her.

All the studying Syd wanted him to do would not alter his decision. The road was clear! If Syd wanted to quit, well and good; he'd take the presidency, run the company and crush the unions. . . .

Where in hell *was* Caddie?

The advertisement of a movie enticed him inside a theater; he was physically tired, was headachy again and sick of his own thoughts. He sat through a dismal picture and at eleven left, retracing his steps so as to pass Caddie's home. Her windows still were dark.

§5

He was shaving the next morning when there was a knock. He glanced at the clock as he went to answer it and noticed it was twenty minutes past eight.

Martha, the maid, was at the door.

"Mr. Stanley, Wilbur wants to speak to you. He's on the phone."

"Wilbur?"

"Yes, sir, the butler."

"You mean from my grandmother's house? Is there anything the matter?"

"He didn't say."

Stan slipped on a wrapper and ran downstairs to the telephone.

"Yes, Wilbur?"

"Mr. Stanley, sir, can you come over here right away?"

"Surely. What is it? My grandmother?"

"No, sir; it's Mr. Lloyd."

Stan jerked on an overcoat and in his slippers ran across the street. Wilbur opened the door.

"What is it?"

"Mr. Lloyd——" The muscles of the man's face twitched. "Mr. Lloyd's passed on."

"What do you mean? Dead?"

Wilbur nodded.

"I found him ten minutes ago. He's upstairs in his room all dressed just as if he laid down last night and made up his mind he wasn't to get up again."

"My grandmother know?"

"No, sir. She's in her room. I went right off to phone you. Nobody knows—Annabel nor nobody."

"Let's see."

They tiptoed upstairs.

Lloyd's bedroom door was closed. Wilbur opened it gently and stood aside as Stan entered. Lights were burning, shades drawn. Fully dressed, Lloyd lay on top of the bed. A glance and Stan knew that Wilbur was right; his uncle was dead. His skin was very white and shining and stretched tightly across his forehead, his nose, and cheekbones.

Stan drew nearer and stood looking down at him. He lifted his hand; it was cold and *rigor mortis* already had set in.

"Heart," he said, meeting the butler's eyes.

"Yes, sir."

Stan gently replaced the hand.

His uncle had had a peaceful death, he thought; he had relinquished life calmly, without protest. . . . Another Rutherford gone!

"When did you find him?" he asked.

"A little after eight o'clock this morning. I tell you, Mr. Stanley, there's something funny about all this. I'd like to tell you."

He went to the bedroom door and closed it noiselessly.

"Last night——" Wilbur began, but stopped to swallow.

"Last night," he resumed, "after the old lady went upstairs . Beg pardon, Mr. Stanley! Your grandmother, I mean!"

"Go on, go on!"

"Well, they had dinner as usual about seven o'clock, and then Mrs. Rutherford went upstairs 'bout nine. I was in the pantry, washing up, when Mr. Rutherford comes to the door and says he's expecting a visitor, and I'm not to wait up to let him in. He said he'd answer the door himself. So I said, 'Very good, sir,' and thought no more about the matter. But when I came downstairs this morning, I found the lights in the sitting room on and in the hall, too, and I could see where two chairs had been sat in. I thought it kind of strange that Mr. Rutherford should go to bed and leave the lights burning. After I had brushed up and set the table, I came up here to take a look round, and I saw a light under Mr. Rutherford's door. I waited, not knowing what to do, and so I knocked, and when there was no an-

swer I knocked again. Things didn't seem right somehow, so I opened
the door and found him lying where he is. I went right downstairs and
phoned you."

After a silence, Stan asked:

"You have no idea who his caller was?"

"No, sir."

"Nor what time he came in?"

"No, sir."

"Nor what time he left?"

"No, sir."

"Humph-h."

Stan gazed about the room, stepped toward the switch to extin-
guish the lights, thought better of it, and returned to the bed.

There *was* a mystery here!

"Did my uncle seem concerned or agitated in any way when he told
you he expected someone?" he asked.

"No, sir, not that I noticed."

"Was he in the habit of receiving late callers?"

"Never did before, sir—not since I've been here, now going on
seventeen years."

"You think there is some connection between the late visit and—
and this?" He indicated the body.

"Can't say, sir, but I thought you ought to know he *did* receive
somebody—quite late."

"How d'you know it was late?"

"I was in the kitchen talking to Annabel until after ten. I think I'd
of heard the bell if it had rung."

"Yes, of course."

"And sometimes I can hear it faintlike when I'm in my room."

"Your room's where?"

"On the third floor."

"You can hear it up *there?*"

"Yes, sir; there's a kind of hum. My ear's tuned to it, you might say.
But I didn't hear anything last night, and I wasn't asleep until after
eleven."

All this indeed was strange. Perhaps Luther Poltney, Lloyd's
partner, would know of some client who would want to talk to Stan's

uncle late at night, but why should he have been so mysterious about it? Why hadn't he simply told Wilbur he was expecting a caller and to wait up for him? It wasn't like him to answer the door himself.

Stan studied the shrunken features on the pillow, wondering what secret was locked behind their mask. The graven face with its crop of tight white curls was like that of a statue carved from marble. As he bent over, a square of cardboard near the dead man's right hand caught his eye.

"What's this?"

It was a cabinet-sized photograph of a small boy, wearing a caped overcoat, a round hat on the back of his head—a studio photograph with imitation grass about the subject's feet and a suggestion of a rustic gate and wooded landscape in the background. Written on its reverse side in faded ink were the words:

"Frank, *aetat* four, February, 1906."

"My God!" whispered Stan; "that's his son—Frank!"

He studied the features of the boy, but there was nothing about them to remind him of the small cousin he vaguely remembered. His glance moved to the waxen face upon the pillow. The sorrow of the scapegrace son had lain heavily upon his uncle's heart for many years. To his knowledge, Stan had never heard him refer to the boy except at the time the two longshoremen had been killed and he had accompanied Stan's father and himself to the undertaker's parlors in the Mission.

Had the late visitor last night any connection with the boy?

"Let's look around," Stan said, and as he spoke he saw the closet door directly behind him was open, and inside, the door of a small iron safe, imbedded in the wall, was open, too.

Stan knew about this safe. As children Eleanor had frequently shown it to him and his sister, telling them, with much mystery, that her father kept his "secret papers" there. The safe was not more than two feet in length and some ten to twelve inches in width. It had been built into the wall, bricks surrounding it, the door flush with the plaster. A bunch of keys now dangled from its lock. On a closet shelf near the safe stood a tin box, its lid raised. It contained, Stan found, a series of envelopes neatly arranged and labeled, bearing such inscriptions as: "Copy of Will," "Marriage Certificate," "List of

Stocks," "Diplomas," "Degrees," "Combination to Office Safe," "Private Papers," "Documents Relative to E.'s Divorce," one marked: "To Be Opened in Case of My Death." This Stan did not investigate; it would be best to wait, he decided, until his grandmother and mother were present before breaking its seal. Near by on the shelf lay a single, slightly larger envelope. It lay face down, its flap up, indicating it had been last touched by the dead man's hand. On the face of the envelope was written: "Birth Certificates," and inside was Eleanor's: "San Francisco; Dante Hospital; April 2nd, 1905." There was none other.

Stan fixed Wilbur with a look, but he was not thinking of the man, but of the contents of the tin box.

He turned again to it, examining its papers more carefully. All were in order; even the envelopes—numbered with a blue pencil—were arranged in sequence and corresponded to the list pasted on the inside of the lid. One only had been disturbed—the one which presumably had held the photograph and was labeled "Birth Certificates." Stan put the picture back into the envelope, filed it in its proper order, locked the box, returned it to the safe, locked this in turn, and put the keys on his uncle's dresser.

"You're right, Wilbur; there's something odd about all this," he said, rubbing his brow with a troubled hand. "There's something odd about all this," he repeated, "and I've got to clear it up." He paused, frowning. "I've been thinking," he continued, "that it would be a mistake to tell my mother and my grandmother about—well, about what seems to us both as unusual. Understand me?"

"Yes, sir."

"I see no good reason for agitating them unnecessarily, do you?"

"No, sir."

"They'll be terribly upset as it is. It would be a mistake—at least for the time being—to give them any hint about the photograph or the open safe. You and I know, but we must keep the matter between us. Get me?"

"Yes, sir."

"I mean nobody must know—that is, you must tell nobody, none of the other servants, not my grandmother—nor anybody. Is that clear?"

"Very good, sir."

"I shall inform Mr. Poltney what we found. Maybe he can throw some light on the situation. He ought to know, and he may think it best to have an autopsy. I presume it was my uncle's heart that failed him, but I'm no physician. I'll talk to him about that. . . . My cousin, Mrs. Mackey in Washington, must be informed too; I'll write her immediately. As for the others, I think they must be kept in the dark. You agree?"

"Oh, certainly, Mr. Stanley. Of course!—I won't breathe a word to a living soul."

"Good. Now, I suppose, I must break the news to my grandmother. Is she awake yet?"

"I think so, sir. Annabel usually brings her her glass of orange juice and tea at nine."

"Very well. Ask Annabel to tell her I'd like to see her and that the matter is urgent."

CHAPTER XVIII

SINCE IT HAD BEEN PLANNED from the beginning that Daisy's wedding should be quiet, it was decided not to postpone the event because of Lloyd's death.

"After all, it's been some months," Frances said to her mother-in-law. "If the papers mention it, naturally they'll say that on account of a recent bereavement in the family, only the immediate members of it will be present. Then, too, it seems to matter a great deal to Daisy to have Eleanor with her, and since Eleanor was unable to come west at the time of her dear father's funeral and since she writes she can positively be here in December, we ought to go ahead with our plans, don't you think?"

Grandmère stiffened perceptibly at this mention of her eldest son's last rites; her white curls trembled slightly, but that was as far as she permitted herself to betray emotion. One after another she had seen her three children laid to rest, and now sorrow had driven her into a silence of pride and a certain steeliness of manner had come to her which swathed her in protective armor.

She made no comment to Frances' proposal, and the latter construed her silence as consent.

A week before the wedding date, the Mackeys duly arrived from Washington and at Grandmère's invitation stayed at her house.

"Whatever sort of person he may be," she said to Frances, referring to her granddaughter's husband a day or so before they came, "my home is Eleanor's, the only real one the poor girl's ever known, for—as far as I can find out—when they are in Washington they live at a hotel! It's only right and proper the child should come to me, and I can put up with that Indian for the few days they are here, no matter how loud he trumpets and bellows. I declare, it will be a comfort to hear some noise about the house; it's pretty quiet most of the time. . . . How long do you expect they will be here?"

"I haven't an idea; probably until after Christmas."

Eleanor and Byron reached San Francisco the day after Thanksgiving; the wedding was set for the Saturday of the following week. On their first evening, they gathered with the rest of the Rutherfords at Frances' house for a bounteous repast. Syd, of course, was there—looking very sober and self-conscious—but not Reggie. Reggie had wired he would be unable to be present until the day of the ceremony.

"I'll be glad to see him," Frances commented to her mother-in-law when his message was repeated to her. "I haven't seen the poor fellow since Charmion's funeral."

Hilariously and with many kisses, Eleanor was welcomed to the family fold. Still tall, regal, and statuesquely beautiful, she had become increasingly sweeter and gentler; her face was given more readily to smiles, to expressions of tenderness and sympathy; a gray strand or two was not unbecoming.

From the first Stan had liked Byron; he admired the man's black hair which swept back so uncompromisingly from his forehead, liked the set of his square shoulders, his exaggerated stride. He too, it seemed to Stan, had grown in mental stature, adding to the strength of his personality if not to his height. Byron radiated purposefulness, carried force.

It was a garrulous group which found themselves seated around the dinner table—more garrulous and lighthearted, Stan thought, than he had seen any of them in many months. Even his grandmother betrayed some of her old-time dry criticism and indulged in acid observations as of yore. Stan glanced from her wrinkled, rouged, and powdered face to Daisy's, then to Byron's, his mother's, Syd's, and Eleanor's and thought how genuinely fond he was of them all; a vigorous, resolute people they were, every one of them; even shy, modest little Daisy, who could not easily be swayed once her mind was made up. .

All were interested to hear from Eleanor and Byron details of their trip abroad, but first Stan wanted the latter's opinion on the recent decision of the United States Supreme Court which refused to review the judgment of the California Supreme Court denying freedom to Tom Mooney.

"Yes, they voted against the petition," Byron told him; "six to two, Justices Black and Reed dissenting. No doubt your new governor will pardon him. Mooney's been a long time in jail."

"Don't you think there will be an awful unpleasant hubbub when they let him out?" Stan asked. "Labor will call him a martyr and kick up a row."

Byron smiled.

"Labor's been calling him a martyr for many years, and I don't believe they'll kick up more of a row than they've been doing in the past."

"I guess you're right there. We've had over fifty strikes in the Bay area already this year. The retail-department-store walkout was only settled the first of this month. Thirty-five stores have been strikebound since September seventh, and we're in for a lot of more tie-ups. This town is certainly a hotbed for labor trouble."

"Now look here," Grandmère interrupted sharply, rapping her rings on the edge of her plate, "if you're going to go on with any more of this strike talk, I shall put on my wrap and march home! I declare, I've heard nothing but strike for the last five years!"

Stan laid a placating hand over her gnarled and bejeweled fingers.

"Darling," he reassured her, "not another word."

"How's F.D.R.?" he asked, turning to Byron; "how did he take the recent elections?"

"They weren't as sweeping as we hoped," Mackey replied. "I'm surprised at the strength the Republicans showed; they nearly doubled their number in the House. But we still have a substantial majority."

"Sorry to hear it," Stan said with a dry smile.

"Come, let's move to the drawing room," Frances suggested; "Martha will serve our coffee in there. I'm anxious to hear all about Europe and about that dreadful man Hitler."

She led the way, and as they crossed the hall she slipped an affectionate arm about Eleanor's waist, gave her a hug, and Stan heard her say:

"It's good to have you back among us, my dear. We miss you. You've always been such a comfort to me."

§ 2

"I have no confidence in the success of Mr. Chamberlain's appeasement policy," Byron stated when they were all comfortably seated and had grouped themselves into a listening circle about him. "The partition of Czechoslovakia with England's and France's approval can only lead to further trouble. It was an atrocious crime, part and parcel of Hitler's misguided policy of liberating the German people through aggression. He began it with the annexation of Austria, and I truly believe his triumphant entry into Vienna affected his mind. If some of you haven't read *Mein Kampf,* you should. Everyone in the United States should read it. In it Hitler seriously declares that Germans are a super race and that the only hope of Europe lies in the complete dominance of the continent by the nazis. The man is mad, of course. He cries and screams and howls when thwarted like an uncontrollable child. But there is no question his propaganda machine has made him the idol of his countrymen."

Byron then gave a detailed account of recent European events, beginning with Chamberlain's visit to Hitler at the latter's summer home in Berchtesgaden, proceeding to the conference between the two at Godesberg, and ending with the meeting at Munich when the division of Czechoslovakia was decided upon by the four leaders with representatives of the Czech Government officially invited "onlookers."

"I am convinced war is inevitable," Byron continued. "Just what comfort Mussolini and Hitler find in each other's company is hard to explain except that each is the head of a fascist state and they recognize one another as natural allies. The struggle for survival between the totalitarian governments and the democracies has only begun."

"Spain?" queried Stan.

"Franco has conquered, and the heroic fight of the Loyalists is practically at an end. On October sixteenth the International brigades were disbanded. Franco could not have succeeded without the help of Germany and Italy, and, I may add, not without the assistance the United States contributed to his cause by our ridiculous embargo on arms and ammunition. On every count they deserved our sympathy and support. I very much regret that, at the insistence of the administration, the Senate Foreign Relations Committee laid aside the resolution of Senator Nye urging repeal of the embargo resolution. We have permitted another fascist state to join the ranks of the aggressors."

"What about Russia?" asked Syd.

"Russia so far is an unknown quantity, I mean of course as regards her foreign policy, but last March the Soviet Union asked for an immediate conference of powers—excluding Germany, Italy, and Japan—to deal with the menace to world peace. I fear that nothing came of the proposal and all of us may bitterly regret someday that nothing was done about it."

"You mention Japan. What is she up to?"

"Nothing good, I fear. In Geneva while I was there, I met Dr. V. K. W. Koo, who had just reported to the League of Nations Assembly that a million Chinese have been killed since the beginning of hostilities with Japan in 1937; he said thirty million others have been wounded or made homeless, and further, that there have been over two thousand air raids on civilian populations of China since the beginning of this year and that there are more than a million Japanese soldiers now operating on Chinese soil. Hankow has recently fallen and Chiang Kai-shek has fled to Chungking. Dr. Koo told me personally that the Japanese are secretly arming, building hundreds of submarines and thousands of airplanes. Last February, in a note to the United States, Great Britain, and France, Japan declined to give information as to her naval plans; she has always insisted on the right to build and maintain a navy as large as that of any other country in the world. I'm afraid there is mischief brewing in the Nipponese mind."

"Oh, goodness sakes alive," shrilled Grandmère in exasperated tones, brushing an imaginary fly from her lap with an impatient fillip of her fingers, "I won't listen to such gloomy talk any longer. Heaven knows we have enough troubles right here in our own country without bothering about what's happening in others."

"I wholly agree with you, Mrs. Rutherford," Byron Mackey said placidly. "I don't believe Europe's quarrels should be ours, and I earnestly hope we don't become embroiled in them—theirs or in the ones in the Far East—but I certainly think we should take drastic action immediately to be prepared."

"Prepared or not," snapped Grandmère, "there's going to be a wedding in this house a week from tomorrow and I'm going to be prepared for *that!*"

§3

Frances' hopes for a simple ceremony were fully gratified. At four o'clock Stan, waiting on a landing halfway up the stairs, saw Daisy, prettily veiled and arrayed in ivory satin, come to the head of the flight, accompanied by her mother and Eleanor. As she paused there, he ran down to the floor below and announced the bride was about to descend. Bishop Boggs, robed in vestments and stole, had taken up his position in front of the improvised altar in the drawing room. Syd was beside him, and near by stood Grandmère, Byron, and Reggie. Stan offered his arm to his sister as she reached the bottom step and escorted her to the smiling groom. The service began, the participants made their proper responses, the bishop in his well-modulated voice offered a prayer which invoked God's blessing on the newly married pair, and the ceremony was over. But not before several whimpers had escaped from Daisy's mother.

"I just couldn't help it," wept Frances, her cheeks drenched with tears as she embraced her daughter. "I just thought of all—of all—of all . . . It seemed to me I was losing my little girl forever, and I *did* miss some sort of music!

"I'm sure you'll take good care of her and always be kind and gentle," she told Syd; "she'll make a pretty nice wife, don't you think?"

There was a lavish wedding supper waiting in the dining room, lovely flowers, a mammoth wedding cake surmounted with two miniature figures of a bride and groom under a sugary bell; there was plenty of champagne and many toasts. Stan made a speech, Byron a most happily worded one, Reggie rose to his feet and murmured something unintelligible, Syd responded modestly, and the bride's health was drunk again and again.

Stan was shocked by the change in Reggie. He had always been a large man, full-stomached, cumbersome, and heavy; now he had lost some ninety pounds, his face was gray and seared with many crisscrossed wrinkles, only a suggestion of his former paunch remained, his hair had almost disappeared, his clothes bagged, and he looked sick and tired.

While Daisy was upstairs changing into her going-away costume, Stan had an opportunity for a few words with him. How were things going down at Visalia? How was he making out with his crops? Any more troubles with the unions?

Reggie shook his head in puzzled fashion and stared at his questioner as if trying to understand what he was being asked—an old habit, but Stan decided that what had been a mannerism had now become a necessity. His uncle's mind had definitely slowed down; he was obliged to ponder what was being asked before he understood the questions.

"Oh yes," he said, nodding, "lots of trouble. We farmers are trying to maintain the open shop, and we're having a tough time. Last year the State Federation of Labor attempted to organize the pickers and shed workers; then along came the Communists and started making trouble. Same thing happened down at Salinas; there's where most of the nation's lettuce comes from—you know that. The citizens burned down a Filipino settlement and drove the Googoos out. There were about eight hundred of them, and it created a riot. That brought in the organizers, and they demanded a closed shop. For three days there was a regular battle. Bricks and clubs were used, and tear- and emetic-gas shells. The mob tried to take over the town; they waylaid every truck that drove in from the fields. Some thirty-five trucks had all their glass broken, and some were overturned. In attacking the drivers, the strikers used apples and potatoes in which razor blades were imbedded; brickbats, pieces of iron, missiles of all sorts were thrown. The growers and shippers got about a hundred men from outside to come in and open the sheds. The strikers attacked these fellows with dynamite and homemade bombs. Well, the Highway Patrol, the chief of police, and the sheriff of the county got together, and every able-bodied citizen in Salinas was given a badge or some sort of insignia to show he represented the sheriff and was acting under his orders. Finally order was restored, but only temporarily. The Communists are at it again—stirring up trouble, demanding higher wages, insisting on the closed shop, and attempting to gain complete job control of all jobs in the industry.

"Same down our way. There have been lots of attempts by the CIO to organize the workers. The A. F. of L. has tried to come back into the picture, and there have been regular pitched battles. We farmers try to stand together; we want nothing to do with the unions; we offer work at top pay to any man or woman who wants work, regardless of whether they belong to a union or not. I'm sick of it all, Stanley. I've been fighting and fighting and I get no place. I'm about ready to quit. They can have my orchards and farm lands. I figure it this way: They want 'em, and I don't care enough about 'em to try and keep 'em, so let 'em have 'em."

There was laughter on the stairs, and Daisy appeared, clad in a blue hat and a blue gown, accompanied by her mother, grandmother, and cousin. Syd was waiting, overcoat on arm, hat in hand. Stan's car was at the curb outside. He had forgotten his duties, and now there was a scurrying as the trunk space at the back was opened and the luggage of the newlyweds stowed inside. There was a final round of kisses, a shower of rice, and with a farewell blast of the horn the bride and groom were off, Daisy fluttering her hand out of the window in a last gesture of good-by.

"She's married at last, and I'm happy about it," sobbed Frances, wiping her eyes.

"A sturdy fellow," commented Grandmère.

"They're a fine couple," contributed Eleanor; "they ought to be very happy."

Byron Mackey said nothing. Stan, glancing at him, noticed that his expression was set and stern.

"Why, what's the matter?" he involuntarily asked him. "Don't you think they'll be happy?"

"Oh yes, yes, yes," Byron hurried to assure him. "Oh yes, she's a lovely girl—sweet and charming and *very* pretty, and I have nothing but the friendliest feelings for him. They'll make a go of it, as Eleanor says, and no doubt will be happy—happier, I dare say, than most people. I was just thinking . . . well, I was just thinking that there are troublous times ahead, and it's too bad that they are running headlong into the midst of them. There's nothing to be done about it —nothing *they* can do about it—nothing that can save them. They're marrying just twenty years too late."

§4

Byron Mackey was calling on Rory O'Brien. Rory's office was on the fifth floor of the Balboa Building, where the headquarters of the Congress of Industrial Organization were located. It was a pleasant room, sparsely furnished with a polished flat-topped oak desk and a few round-backed oak chairs. A framed certificate or two hung upon the walls, and there were photographs of the Bay Bridge and another picture—a panorama of the Golden Gate International Exposition on Treasure Island, due to open the following year.

"Well, sir, I'm mighty glad to see you," Rory said, cordially greeting his caller in his harsh, rasping voice. He rose from his swivel chair and came around his desk to grasp the visitor's hand. "It's been almost two years, hasn't it?"

"I was in San Francisco a year ago last June, but I missed you. I came out here to get married."

Rory's smile waned.

"So I heard," he said shortly; "what brings you back *this* time?"

"Oh, another wedding in the family. My wife's cousin. She's marrying Sydney Watterbury—you know—of Wickwire, Rutherford & Company."

Rory nodded, a shadow darkening his disfigured, malevolent face.

"We've just returned from abroad, Mrs. Mackey and I," Byron

continued, taking the chair Rory indicated. "We've been to Germany, France, and England. Interesting trip. How're things in San Francisco? How you making out?"

The labor leader shrugged a bony shoulder and scratched the scar which plainly showed beneath the scraggy red beard.

"Still fighting," he said.

"With whom?"

"Oh, the employers are up to their old tricks. They conceived of a new dirty strategy; they don't call it a 'lockout' now, but it works just the same."

"What? Let's have it."

"Well, last August we had some trouble with the Woolworth Company. We called a strike and picketed their warehouse. Then Joe Halliday of the Industrial Association got the distributors together and pulled a fast one. They loaded a freight car with a few boxes of pencils, a couple dozen cartons of stationery, and some school stuff that Woolworth handles, shunted the car around on interurban tracks to the different warehouses, and expected the boys to unload it. Naturally they refused; the cargo was hot. So they closed the warehouses, claiming the union had broken its contract. They shut about a hundred warehouses, and thirty-seven more followed suit; that threw nearly five thousand men out of work!"

"And then?"

"The distributors kept their warehouses closed from the middle of last August until the twenty-fourth of October. What made it bad for us was that the A. F. of L. warehousemen signed a five-year blanket contract with the distributors on October sixth. That forced our hand as the damned employers knew it would; so did those bastards who like to kiss Green's ass. At any rate, we finally got together on terms which will run until June year after next; we conceded an industry-wide contract but kept everything we had gained—wages, hours, overtime, the closed shop, and agreed to ban strikes and lockouts. An arbitration board has been set up to settle beefs, and everything now is hunky-dory. We lost nothing! But what a lousy trick for those guys to try to get away with! Throwing five thousand men out of work to see if they could scare us!"

"They can't scare you any more. They're pretty scared themselves."

"*I'll* say they are!"

"What else?"

"Oh, it's been a rough-and-tumble year. We've made gains. We backed the A. F. of L. in their fight with the department stores, closed thirty-five of them for fifty-four days; the public supported us, lots of shoppers refusing to go through the picket lines, and God knows how much was lost in over-the-counter sales; the stores could make no deliveries, as the teamsters refused to transport merchandise. We intended to have a showdown with the shipowners last September, but the boys felt—and I guess they're right—that with the fair opening in February next year, it would be a bad time to start anything. But the next time we call a strike, believe you me, we'll get what's coming to us! I'd like to see every one of those lying, double-crossing bastards driven to the wall."

"I've told you before, Rory, and I've said it many times from the platform," Byron stated impressively; "once the workers connected with the transportation industries—the longshoremen, sailors, and teamsters—get together, you can dictate your own terms. Only I'd bide my time if I were you. Things overseas are pretty unsettled. We may be in for trouble——"

A knock on the door connecting with the waiting room interrupted him; both men looked up expectantly as a secretary entered and announced:

"Miss Welch and Mr. Jacobs."

"Oh, show them in, show them in, by all means!" Rory exclaimed, adding to Byron, "they'll certainly be surprised and glad to find you here.

"Hello, my dear," he went on, greeting the visitors and giving Caddie a peck on the cheek; "hello, Nate. See who's dropped in!"

Exclamations followed, a warm shaking of hands.

Caddie wore her jacket over her shoulders cape fashion; her cheeks were glowing. Nate, too, seemed to be in a gala mood, his bright blue eyes twinkling, his ruddy face ruddier than usual.

"What you two been up to?" Rory asked suspiciously.

Neither answered him immediately; all their attention was for the distinguished visitor.

"So nice to see you again, Mr. Mackey." Caddie took his proffered hand in both of hers. "You've certainly been a good friend to labor. Your Detroit speech was a wow."

"Glad you're back again, Mr. Mackey," said Nate; "we need you in this country."

" 'Byron,' please—to both of you," he said.

"Thanks—Byron."

Rory repeated his question as the newcomers found seats.

"You tell him, comrade," Caddie said and laughed gaily while she searched in her bag for a cigarette.

"Comrade, hey?" Byron elevated his eyebrows.

"We've been to a meeting," Nate explained. "It started out all right. We went there to choose delegates to the New York convention next year and attempted to draft some resolutions. Everything was fine until that fat little Russian, Rykov, got up and proposed a lot of ridiculous recommendations, one advocating the assassination of the President! We tried to boo him down, but he wouldn't be booed. The meeting broke up in a row, and Caddie and I left in hysterics. I don't know what they're going to do; some of them are fanatics, crackpots whose one idea is revolution."

"The revolution is under way already," Byron observed; "there's no need for violence."

"Of course not," Rory agreed; "all we need to do is to take our time."

"And get together," Byron stated.

"That may be difficult," Rory demurred.

"Yes, as long as self-interests and personal ambitions split your forces," Byron commented.

"I believe in our leader," Rory countered.

"And a number of others, equally as influential as you—who belong to rival organizations—believe in theirs.

"But I'm interested," he interrupted himself to say, turning to Caddie and Nate; "were any of those at the meeting in accord? Any principles acceptable to all?"

"Oh yes, a unanimous sentiment in favor of keeping this country out of war——"

"That may not be possible," Byron interrupted. He repeated what he had told the Rutherfords, and now, before a more interested audience, he enlarged on what he had seen and learned in Europe and spoke with more feeling.

"War, I believe, is inevitable," he concluded. "I cannot see how the United States can stay out of it."

Nate clamored for attention as Byron paused.

"Hitler ought to be castrated!" he cried passionately; "he ought to be made to pay again and again—a hundred times—for each one of his atrocities! Ah, listen! Do you know that just recently, following Von Rath's assassination in Paris by a poor kid of seventeen who had Jewish antecedents, anti-Jewish violence broke out all over Germany, and that in Berlin, Vienna, and other cities synagogues were set on fire and wrecked? Do you know that Jewish shops were robbed and Jews were beaten in the streets, and that then Hitler fined the Jews still left in Germany a billion marks to pay for all the damage that had been done—the wrecking and looting of homes and shops by his ruffian nazis? Do you know that after the first of next month all Jews will be barred from operating retail, mail-order, and handicraft establishments, and no Jew or anyone of Jewish extraction can be a shop leader, supervisor, or foreman in any shop or factory? Hitler's persecution is savage cruelty, far worse than the massacres in the pogroms of Russia by the Cossacks. There the poor devils were murdered; in Germany they are tortured!

"No!" he cried, knotting his thin hands together with such force that his knuckles whitened, "I'll not subscribe to any no-war program! We *must* get into this fight and clean the world of such fiendish maniacs!"

His passionate vehemence stilled the others, and for a few moments there was silence in the room.

"We've got other scores to settle with that skunk," Rory said at length; "what about his enslavement of children, his brutal treatment of labor, his burning of books, imprisonment of church leaders, and murdering of everyone opposed to him? Let's you and I stick around for a while, Nate, and see what happens to him. Somebody will knife him or send a bullet through his heart. I believe that right always catches up with wrong."

"What else was agreed to at your meeting?" Byron asked after another interval as Nate, overcome with emotion, jumped to his feet and walked to the window. When he came back he wiped away the taut lines from his flushed face, cleared his throat and, drawing breath, answered reasonably:

"Oh well, we were in accord about a number of things. We agreed about taxation—that the tax burden should be placed where it will least affect the standard of living—a real program of taxation based on the ability to pay; we agreed on the strengthening of trade unions, especially industrial unions; we were all for a militant leadership to gain shorter working hours and higher wages, and particularly in the unification of the labor movement into one democratically controlled center. Also nobody kicked about social security guaranteeing a minimum income of sixty dollars a month after sixty, or a permanent public-works program, through WPA and PWA, which would provide jobs for not less than three million workers, and—if I remember correctly—all were for some improved form of unemployment insurance, and of course, with that, a national health and a large-scale housing program—which seemed sensible to Caddie and me, and we were enthusiastic until that little fool of a Russian, Rykov, got up and began to shout about assassinations, concentration camps for the millionaires, and a national revolution. That started us laughing."

"I'm not so certain Rykov is very far off," Byron observed.

"What!" There was a chorus of startled exclamations.

All eyes focused on the speaker's face. They respected this man; they recognized him as a champion of labor; they knew he held an important position in Washington, enjoyed the President's confidence. What was he talking about? Assassination and concentration camps?

Byron smiled amiably and glanced about the circle of puzzled faces, amused at their consternation.

"You'll have to bear with me," he said apologetically, "if I treat you to a dissertation. Let me give you a glimpse into the future as I see it. The only hope of the world, I believe, is for labor to unite, not only in America, but in England, France, Germany, and Russia—all countries. Since we are particularly interested in the United States, let us first consider ourselves. Labor here must get together; personal ambitions, lust for power, jurisdictional disputes must be eliminated; all leaders must bow to one head. I heartily endorse what Nate says.

Am I quoting you correctly?" he asked, turning to the young attorney. "You said, I think, that your convention advocated 'the unification of the labor movement into one democratically controlled center.' Is that it?"

At Jacobs' eager nod, he continued:

"Well, I concur. Labor must form one party. Green and Lewis and Dubinsky and Murray, all must step aside and give place to *one* leader. The sooner this happens, the sooner we'll have a country we all will want to live in!"

He turned again to Nate.

"In principle, I'm in agreement with a no-war policy, but suppose Germany attacks the United States? It might easily happen. England is Hitler's adversary, and England—from my observations—is not in a position now to defend herself. All right, suppose Hitler forces England to her knees; will the United States stand aside and refuse to lend a helping hand? I doubt it. You may disagree with England's foreign policy, you may disapprove of her imperialistic ideas, her treatment of India. These will be forgotten. The English are our cousins; they are Anglo-Saxons, and whether we are wholly in sympathy with them or not, it will behoove us to aid her when war comes, if for no other reason than a selfish one. The Atlantic Ocean isn't as wide as it used to be.

"Let's concede for the sake of argument that we are involved in a world war within the next few years," he continued. "What then? We must presuppose that we win the war and maintain our independence. I hate to think of what our national debt will be when peace is restored; I hate to think of the crippled soldiers we will have to take care of. National debt is something vague, a digit with a long series of naughts after it; it will be colossal, too enormous for the human mind to encompass. But the interest on that debt is something far more tangible and something which every man can understand— *must* understand. After the close of the war in 1919, our national debt was over twenty-five billion dollars, the interest was a billion and some fifty-odd million dollars. If we are involved in another war, our national debt will probably be ten times as great, and the interest ten times as much. Just what are we going to do about paying that interest? We *must* pay it or go bankrupt. It will be too large to raise by taxation. Tax industry for every cent of profit and it will stop—and we will be faced with the greatest mass unemployment this country has ever known. There'll be starvation in America—and don't fool yourself!"

He paused, and there was a profound silence in the room.

"So what?" Rory asked at length.

"Turn over to the State the means of production; turn over the four vital instruments of production—the supply of capital and credit whether by banks, insurance, or building securities; the land; factories—durable-goods factories; import and export trade; transport, fuel and power. We can pay the interest then."

Caddie clapped her hands.

"Of course!" she cried.

"Not so fast," Byron stopped her. "How are you going to accomplish this? I don't believe that Mr. Rykov and his kind will get anywhere by violent methods. If he is going to attempt revolution, it will retard the goal of which I speak for fifty years—perhaps longer. He and his crowd will bring fascism to this country, and we'll have as rigid a dictatorship as now exists in Germany or Italy. No, that is not the way. It can only be achieved by a united—and I stress again the word *united*—labor party."

"Perhaps you're right," conceded Rory. "I just want to live long enough to smash these rascally employers here in San Francisco whom I *hate!*" He said this with such venom that even Caddie winced. "Then I'll hand over. Joe Curran is all right, and so's John Lewis; they'll carry on."

"Mr. Curran and Mr. Lewis won't be around at the time of which I'm speaking. If war doesn't come, it will take some years longer; if war *does* come, it may occur within ten years, perhaps after Mr. Roosevelt's next term of office. Of course he'll be elected President for a third time if we're involved—but I'm speaking of what may follow after he retires. I don't know of a man today who could take his place."

"He's been the great liberator," said Caddie.

"Yes, he's done a lot for labor, and labor should be ever grateful, but I fear labor won't be; not as long as there are selfish leaders seeking personal power. You've got to have a man at the head of labor's army who has only labor's interest at heart, and who will fight for that and nothing else."

"How about you?" Caddie asked.

Byron waved a deprecating hand, shook his head, but after a moment the smile left his face and, sobering, he said:

"Well, I might be the man—if I was wanted. I see clearly what must be done."

"What?" demanded Nate.

"For one thing we would have to be prepared—and *well* prepared—for revolt. You couldn't confiscate private property without violence—and perhaps armed resistance. I don't say it will come to that, but it might. That's what I meant when I said that assassinations and concentration camps might one day be possible. We should have to see to it that there were no riots, no assassinations, but concentration camps might be a necessity. Let us hope not. But labor coming to power on such a socialistic program would have to have a strong hand. First of all, we should have to have a President, a Senate, and a House of Representatives wholly devoted to labor's interests. One of the first measures I would advocate would be to curtail the power of the Supreme Court, which often nullifies acts of Congress. This might involve a constitutional amendment. I am not quite certain how far we would have to go in striking down the First Amendment and State Rights. That perhaps is looking too far ahead."

"Explain," demanded Caddie.

"Well," Byron smiled again and smoothed back his wing of black hair; "it's all guesswork, but for some years I've been thinking of some such socialist program as a cure-all for most of our present ills. The press—the power of free speech—would have to be muzzled until our experiment in socialism proved a success. We couldn't have columnists and editorial writers thundering denunciations, inflaming the public mind. Consider: newspapers and magazines are privately owned, some by powerful individuals, some by companies with many stockholders. Big advertisers, who furnish the bulk of their revenue, would most certainly be against us. The press would not think kindly of our experiment, and it would be imperative that some form of supervision be employed so that riots and rebellion would be avoided. That might require an armed force—and we should be accused of dictatorship. We would have to accept the accusation and hope to prove that our objectives were justified. But imagine the indignation of many of our worthy citizens!"

Rory laughed and slapped his knee.

"I'd like to be around to see their faces!" he exclaimed.

"You may be if war comes as fast as I think it will. We must be prepared, and—frankly I will tell you three friends—I am touring the country now, preaching what I believe. The FBI may catch up with me, trump up some absurd charge and clap me into jail, but I think I could prove to any impartial judge or jury that my motives are sincerely and wholly patriotic."

"No question about that," observed Nate.

"Then there are other things I would propose. For instance, I would advocate representatives, like senators, holding office for six years, a third of each body to retire at the end of every two years; none would be eligible for re-election. Six years for the President as well, and he, too, could not be a candidate a second time.

"I would urge legislation permitting the President to eliminate certain portions of bills of which he did not approve, veto what he did not like. Today all sorts of outrageous riders are tacked onto otherwise wise and necessary laws. At present he has to accept the bad with the good."

"What about ceilings on income?" Nate asked.

"Naturally," Byron approved. "We'd start off with—oh, say twenty-five thousand a year, subject to adjustment, for no one can foretell what the value of the dollar may be one day. Income should be in proportion to what the workers receive."

"What about 'dated money'?"

Byron frowned as he considered his answer, and as he paused Caddie asked:

"What do you mean by 'dated money'?"

"Oh, something like what Dr. Townsend preaches," Nate explained; "say two hundred dollars a month for everybody, the amount to be spent within a specified time—say thirty days."

"That wouldn't be necessary when the means of production are owned by the State," Byron countered; "the only reason I have considered it is that it might be offered as a bait to voters. I mean, if there was a plank in the Labor Party's platform promising a monthly stipend to every citizen—and it might be as much as two hundred a month—it would influence a lot of people. After labor was in the saddle, Congress could make up its mind whether to pass such legislation or not. However, I would be for labor taking over with clean hands and with no false promises. We'll have our problem in censoring the press!"

"Yes, that'll be a job," Rory agreed. "There'll be a terrific howl at first about modifying the Bill of Rights. Personally, I'm sick of what the Bill of Rights is supposed to guarantee. It's been infringed and disregarded and flagrantly ignored in countless instances."

"True, and it may be necessary to clarify those rights—define them, I mean. They would have to have new meanings under a socialistic government. We would be obliged to rewrite them.

"I should prefer," he went on, warming to his subject, "that labor's platform should confine itself to promising no more unemployment, no more hunger, no more want, and of course obligate itself to old-age pensions, health insurance, and unemployment insurance; I would advocate the initiation of a widespread health, education, and reclamation program which would eliminate from society such scandals as illiteracy and venereal disease; we would have to take care of the farmers, too, but since all land would be owned by the State, farmers would be tenants and their interests safeguarded. There would be no need for them to worry.

"I want to digress here for a minute," he interrupted himself to say, "to make an observation about a matter which has always interested me. Thomas Jefferson, one of the greatest statesmen that ever lived, is credited with the phrasing of our Declaration of Independence. It states, as you all know, 'We hold these truths to be self-evident, that all men are created equal . . .' Now, to my thinking, there never was a more outrageous misstatement of fact. Men are *not* created equal, and everybody knows it. What Jefferson should have said, and what he *meant* to say, was: 'All men are born worthy of an equal chance.'"

"Bravo!" cried Caddie.

"Let me rehearse what I said or meant to say at the beginning of this harangue," Byron pursued; "I began by presupposing a colossal national debt in case of another war. If the State owns all the means of production, we need not worry about the debt or the interest. The worker will be rewarded in proportion to his ability to produce, and for the shirker or the bum or the drunkard we will have labor camps to which they will be sent until they justify their release. I can see a time coming when a man need work for only thirty hours a week, when he will have ample time to loaf in the sunshine, play with his children, tend his garden, enjoy the theater or a movie, read a good book, listen to good music. Honor will spur men to labor diligently; fellow workers will look upon a shirker with scorn. To the man of intelligence and industry will come power and authority; the more he contributes to the commonwealth, the more the commonwealth will place its trust in him. I believe and I reiterate, and I think this should be stamped in every man's brain and engraven on his heart: when the system by which we propose to live is geared to production instead of to profit, the more who work, the more wealth will be produced for all.

"One more observation and I am through," Byron said with a sudden frown of deep concentration; "it should be clear that before us lies the century of the common man, and if this is so, there must be a partnership between those who work with their heads and those who work with their hands. We must all insist on a common interest because we will be workers of the world, and the workers must control their governments in order to have a chance to build a better life in every nation upon the earth.

"I feel"—he drew breath, moistening his lips—"as if I were making a speech. Well, suppose I am! I'll try to remember what I'm saying now so I can repeat myself next time I'm on a platform." He swept his listeners with a smile. "There is no real cleavage between intellectual and manual contributions if in both cases the dignity of work well done is the badge of glory. There is no reason why workers as a whole cannot join hands in every nation, understand each other, and make the future a time of greater opportunity. Yet even though we achieve socialism, we must be on our guard. Human liberty is not something that can ever become automatic. No matter what social-economic system governs this country or governs the world, men will need to exert titanic efforts to maintain the freedom already won and to win others still unknown. . . . I'm through!"

He smiled once more and, drawing a handkerchief from his breast pocket, mopped his forehead.

Caddie leaped to her feet and threw her arms about him.

"Byron Mackey for President!" she cried.

CHAPTER XIX

"I'm TIRED OF LIVING, Caddie; it's too much for me."

"What's the matter, my dear?"

"You wouldn't understand, and if you did you wouldn't care!"

"Why not? What's on your mind?"

"Oh-h . . ."

Stan sighed wearily.

"Come," she urged; "what's troubling you?"

He passed a hand over his furrowed brow.

She came to where he was sitting on the sofa and smoothed his hair, her fingers gentle and caressing.

"It's the company," he said heavily.

"*Your* company?"

"Yes."

"Troubles?"

"Plenty. We've lost a lot of money, and I don't see how we can go on. . . . Labor's doing," he added bitterly.

She made no response for a moment, then:

"It couldn't be possible, could it, that labor is only demanding a share of your profits?"

He roused instantly.

"There aren't any profits! Unions have taken them! They've demanded more and more, and now we'll have to quit or go broke."

"I think you'll manage to get along," Caddie said dryly, and then on a different note: "If you can't, labor'll take over."

"What do you mean?"

"Labor will run your ships and run everything else."

"I don't understand you!"

"Well-l . . ." She shrugged.

"I'd like to know exactly what you're driving at."

"Labor will become the State; labor will control the means of production, and everybody will have enough, everybody'll be happy. Including *you*," she ended with a smile.

He was angry now.

" 'Re you talking communism to me?"

"Communism or socialism, does it matter which? Listen and try to be open-minded—*please*." She began to quote some of Byron's words, but he stopped her before she had gone very far.

"Who told you such hogwash?"

"A friend."

"Who?" he insisted.

"Oh, a friend," she answered evasively. "Don't be so cantankerous, Stan; be generous and hear me out. Don't interrupt me for a couple of minutes, and then you can have *your* say. Is that a go?"

"Okay," he agreed.

She sketched Byron's plan of a future socialistic state as she remembered it.

"There," she said, "that's it. When our way of living depends on production instead of on profit, the more people who work, the more everybody will have. Those who work with their heads and those who work with their hands should have a common interest. There should be centralized government controlling all means of production."

She stopped, drawing breath, and reached for a cigarette.

"Now is it my turn?" he asked.

She nodded.

He fisted his hands.

"Well, listen to me. Society proceeds in a vicious circle. When there is a depression on, able individuals are encouraged; they create new enterprises and create work for those who are incapable of contributing anything. The clever guys earn their reward, and nobody begrudges it to them. My father started out with a small shipping company forty years ago, and he created a business that gave employment to thousands. Everybody thought J. O. B. Rutherford a clearheaded, upstanding, fine American. But presently a lot of people commenced to envy him; then they began to slander him and after a time came to hate him merely because he was rich and successful.

Eventually the dumb clucks and the envious ones destroy men of his kind and the enterprises they build. Then the wolves settle down to squalor and poverty, and the cycle begins over again.

"We Americans must choose between individual freedom and state control, and I maintain that you radicals who claim that the people can collectively direct their own industrial efforts are just plain fools. Your criticism of men like my father is always based upon the alleged exploitation of the workers he employs. You say that the workers are deprived of the fruits of their labor. The cold facts show that eighty-five per cent of all national income is paid out in wages and salaries and that capital seldom keeps enough profit to do much better than break even. Did you ever stop to think, Caddie, that if it weren't for the inventors and the industrialists, you'd never have automobiles, sewing machines, washing machines, electric irons, or radios? The men who invented and manufactured these contrivances for general use could have made more profit investing their money in government bonds than putting it into their businesses. As long as the inventor and manufacturer, the shipowner and industrialist are able to serve the consumer at comparatively little cost, the consumer is better off to accept the benefits of the system and let the capitalists continue to risk their money competing with one another for public patronage.

"Wait a moment," he said, his hand uplifted, "I'm not through yet by a long shot!

"In any society there is always a large percentage of people who contribute nothing or very little to the national wealth. Some of them are even unable to make their own living, so since they cannot be allowed to starve, the only way to make up the deficit between what they need and what they earn is to take it away from those able to produce *more* than they need.

"If the State persists in subsidizing and pampering the useless citizen at the expense of the useful, one of two things—as I see it— will happen: either the useful citizen will rise up in his wrath and control the State, or, lacking that power, he will lose his initiative and sink toward the level of the group he is being made to support. There are three stages to this tragic process: first the manufacturer loses his initiative because his profits are taken from him; next fol-

lows a gradual shrinkage in national wealth as a result of less manu-
facturing; lastly the wealth of a country dwindles until there is no
surplus to feed the poor, the sick, or the natural bum. Putting it
another way, the State that allows the creative individual free play
never has much trouble collecting taxes needed to support the un-
productive citizen at a reasonable living standard. The more millionaires a society can produce, the less suffering there will be, because
there are greater tax sources through which to support the needy.

"Private enterprise must make money or it goes out of business.
That's what I'm worried about right now—Wickwire, Rutherford &
Company may have to close its doors. But suppose the State takes
over? The company doesn't have to make money then, because if it
doesn't under state management the taxpayer will make up the deficit.
But if *we* lose money our stockholders are out of pocket and they are
assessed to make good the loss. The only way we can make money is
to operate an efficient business and serve the public——"

"Or fill your pockets with fat dividends!" Caddie broke in.

"Please!" Stan urged. "A state-owned industry," he continued,
"not having any competitors, serves the public only as well as its
politically appointed management and its politically controlled workers decide that it should.

"I believe in freedom—the freedom of the individual, the freedom
to develop one's own productive abilities, sell them to the highest
bidder and retain a fair share of the profits. The Government takes
most of our profits now, and my guess is that as long as the present
pump-primers and subsidy-granters are in office our profits will grow
less and less. But I claim that when you Communists take this freedom away, the entire democratic structure goes with it, and in its
place you will have fascism and a dictatorship. I don't want to be
here then. You can have America, and I'll go down to the Marquesas
and live there with the natives—and take you with me, by God!"

He caught her about the waist and pulled her to him, roughly
handling her until she lay in his arms, her face with a tolerant, indul-
gent smile just below his. But he did not return the smile. He glow-
ered at her, then kissed her savagely. She struggled to free herself,
but he held her firmly and continued to scowl at her, his eyes moving
somberly from one feature to another.

"Listen," he said, "there's just one more thing I want to say to you. You talk about a united labor party; you talk about labor running this nation. Never! Not in a blue moon! Take it from me. There has never been a labor leader from Samuel Gompers down the line who hasn't exploited labor for his own benefit or for his own personal power. That's why there are so many factions today. Some shrewd old boy discovered it was a lucrative racket. Start a union, collect dues on the promise of higher wages. Don't overlook the dues! The annual dues of most of our major labor organizations run into millions. It's a fact. The American Federation of Labor began this year with a cash balance of $580,000—had an annual income of almost two million; the Congress of Industrial Organizations presented a financial report for three years at the Pittsburgh convention in which they showed total receipts of three and a half million! Quite a sockful! When the suckers pungle up with their dues and it begins to roll up into something sizable, then you get jurisdictional disputes and labor leaders calling each other names and fighting like the dogs they are. Everybody wants some of the glue, and so, my dear cockeyed little radical, your dream of a labor-controlled United States will never, never come to pass.

"Why don't you go away with me?" he demanded suddenly. "Why don't we get out of this city where we're both so well known, rid ourselves of friends and acquaintances, and begin life over again in Honduras or Jamaica or Majorca? To hell with unions and employers, squabbling and backbiting! Let's you and I run away together— always *be* together, never having *anyone* say or do anything to affect our lives or our communion?"

"Where's Majorca?" she asked. He saw she was laughing at him.

"It's one of the Balearic Islands in the Mediterranean. . . . You devil!"

Her smile was all affection now, and she played with a hanging lock of his hair, then tweaked the end of his nose.

"What you need, my darling," she said, straightening herself, "is a drink! I'm going out to get some ice and a bottle."

"No, no," he protested; "you've been very generous listening to me——"

"A lot of nonsense," she observed airily.

"I'll go," he volunteered, ignoring her remark, but he did not make the offer in a very convincing tone; he had no desire to drink this evening. Caddie, however, took him up promptly.

"All right," she said; "run along. I'm dying for a scotch-and-soda myself, and one will do you good. We don't get angry with each other over our liquor. Go along; down at the corner grocery; and don't forget some fizz water and the ice. Twenty-five pounds if you can manage it. Give the boy a quarter and he'll carry it for you. I'll see what I've got to eat, but I know there's something. I expected you last Saturday; where were you? I waited until five o'clock."

"I was tied up with Syd at the office, but I telephoned as soon as I was through and got no answer. Where were *you?*"

"Oh, you run along and get the scotch, and I'll tell you when you get back."

She waved him off with a gesture, but his first words upon returning were to repeat the question.

With arms akimbo, she surveyed him head and foot, screwing up the corners of her mouth in affected exasperation.

"When I got no word from you, I thought you had forgotten the date, and I went to a meeting."

"What kind of a meeting?"

"Wouldn't you like to know! . . . Seriously, Stan, you don't think for a moment, do you, that my life is confined to the notary-public business in the Pitcairn Building? I've got work to do—committee work, planning and organizing work."

"You mean for the Party?"

"What if I do? I don't try to proselytize you, do I?"

"The hell you don't! You've just been sounding off with a lot of rubbish about labor running this country."

"Well, if I believe that would be a good thing, what's it to you?

"Oh, I don't mean to be rude, my dear," she hurried to add. "You and I think differently, that's all. But my life is my life, and I've got to live it. I really try my best not to say things that distress you, and I think you ought to be as considerate of me. Isn't that fair?"

He sank back against the sofa, scowling and angry.

The Party, the Party! Communism certainly had caused him a lot of trouble! Rory O'Brien and his gang of thugs! He had a score to settle with that rascal! All that smug talk of his about the rights of the underprivileged! If Wickwire, Rutherford & Company had to close its doors and the Mission Fleet had to be broken up, it would be *his* handiwork! He thought how dearly he would love to punch his ugly face.

Caddie brought him a scotch-and-soda and ruffled his hair.

"Here, my darling, drink this. It's medicine, and will do you good. . . . Oh, Stan, Stan, why do we have to quarrel? I see you so seldom these days, and I don't want any more fighting. Let's be happy and have a good time. . . . Here's a go!"

She lifted her glass, and he half emptied his. The whisky felt warm and soothing as it went down. He *had* needed the drink!

He smiled up at her, and she stooped and answered it with a kiss.

"Old Crosspatch," she said reproachfully; "if I didn't love you so much, I'd get awfully mad at you sometimes."

"Oh, don't do that! *Ever.* If I sounded off tonight, forget it."

"You're spoiled, Stan; that's what's the matter with you. You only see things your own way, and you want everything your own way."

"I want *you* my own way!"

"You have me—any way you want me. I adore you, Stan, and you know it."

"Do you?"

"Of course! Don't be foolish. . . . Now, what would you like for dinner? I've got some canned tamales, a couple of alligator pears, and a head of lettuce. I have in mind making you the best salad you ever ate."

"Perfect!" he cried. "Gee," he went on boyishly, his spirits brightening, "it's so much more fun eating up here with you than going to some hot, noisy restaurant where you can't hear yourself think! We have good talks even if we do disagree."

She waved him silent.

"Hush, now, and let me think," she said. "If you leave me alone in the kitchen for twenty minutes I'll have everything ready; I've even got a bottle of *vino rougo!*"

"You darling! You say 'scat' to my blues, and fooey, they're gone!"

"You're such a baby!"

"Say," he said as she turned kitchenward, "I ran into a friend of yours while I was out."

"Yeah? Who?"

"That red-headed shyster, Nate Jacobs."

She wheeled instantly, alert and alarmed.

"Where did you see him?"

"Down at the corner, just as I was leaving the grocery with the bottles and the ice."

"Did he see you?"

"Sure; we said hello to each other. I haven't clapped eyes on the guy since the trial in Oakland. He didn't get his men out of San Quentin, did he?"

She fixed him with a frown.

"Did he see where you were going?"

"Sure, I guess so. We walked up the hill together and parted as I turned in here. What's the matter? What difference does it make?"

"Oh, nothing," she said carelessly, "but I don't relish his knowing I'm such a friend of yours. You can understand that, can't you? He regards you as a horrible ogre who preys upon the poor, down-trodden workingman, and naturally he would think it funny if I had you here."

"He can go jump in the lake as far as I'm concerned."

"Yeah, but Nate has a trick of jumping in and jumping out again. He's a shrewd little son of a bitch, if you'll excuse my French."

"What's it to him if I come to see you?"

He was aroused; he wanted to argue the matter.

"Oh, don't be tiresome," she sighed; "I told you Nate's got a chip on his shoulder, and the next time I see him he'll rib me for having you here. That's all. Calm down and finish your drink. I'll fix you another soon's I get things started."

§ 2

"Where do you get this French bread? We never have it at home."

"There's a bakery down here a couple of blocks. They bake it every day. I love it when it's fresh and smelly, don't you?"

"It's fragrant; I wouldn't call it 'smelly.'"

"You're susceptible to odors, aren't you?"

She smiled at him, and he smiled back.

"There's only one perfume in the world for me," he said, "and that's you."

He enjoyed the food, praised the salad, the wine and the *rhum babas* with which she surprised him at the end of the meal.

"You're a wonder," he told her; "you've a knack in making a man feel contented and comfy. I wonder you didn't marry. You never did, did you?"

"Sure I did."

"You *did?*"

"Certainly."

"Why, I never knew that!"

"It was a long time ago."

"Tell me about it?"

She hesitated, firming her lips as if at some unpleasant memory.

"Is he still alive?"

"Oh, gracious no!"

She freed herself from whatever thought had troubled her and gave him an easy smile.

"Pete's been dead a long time," she said. "His name was Aloysius Xavier Welch, and he was a nice person—a swell guy. Everybody called him 'Pete.' . . . You'll be interested to know he was a longshoreman!" she added and paused, her grin disarming.

"Yes," she continued, "he was a longshoreman. He got into a row one night in a saloon down on the waterfront, and somebody pulled a knife on him. Poor chap, he didn't live more than a day or two. I was married to him less than a year, but I was very fond of him. I never learned what the row was about, but somebody told me he butted into a scrap in which a buddy of his was getting the worst of it. It's all of ten years ago. But I'm *Mrs.* Welch, if you should ever write me formally."

"Well, I'll be damned!" he said wonderingly. "Mrs. Welch, hey? Glad to know you, Mrs. Welch."

It was very pleasant sitting at the white enameled table in the warm kitchen. Stan leaned back in his chair, his legs crossed, and inhaled luxuriously on his cigarette, squinting contentedly at Caddie through the smoke. This was something like it, he reflected. This was comfort and peace and—and love!

Presently she went into the sitting room, drew the shades, turned out the electric lights.

"No use advertising I've got company," she said when she returned; "we might have the ubiquitous Mr. Jacobs sticking his red head in here to find out what's going on."

Questions came to Stan—questions about Jacobs, about the trio of his convicted clients now serving sentences in San Quentin, questions about Rory and Mat and the latest beef along the waterfront; he wanted to ask how it served the Party to stir up dissension between employers and their employees; he wanted to ask why this was Moscow's policy. But he did not voice his thoughts. Nothing must disturb the felicity of this hour. Dear Caddie. A wonderful, vital, beautiful woman. If only in some way he could control her, dominate her, so that nothing distasteful to him would influence her! Why couldn't she be his—all his?

"Come on; I'll help you," he said, bringing his chair to the floor and rising as she stood to attack the cluttered sink.

"Don't be foolish. It's too small in here for more than one person to work, and I like to wash dishes. You sit there and smoke your cigarette and let me do the job. *Please,* Stan."

"I feel like a bum."

"Nothing of the kind. We can talk while I fuss."

"Caddie," he said after a moment, considering her as she stood at the sink, "why can't you and I go away together? What's the use of our way of living? I love you, and I believe—I really think—you love me. Well, we both have our own lives to live, and they're pulling us apart. Is there anything in this world so important as love?"

She did not answer immediately.

"Yes, I think there is," she said then. "A person's work is more important. If you're working at a job you like and you're doing it well, that's the greatest happiness there is. I truly believe that."

"And you enjoy your work?"

"No, because I do it very badly."

He did not ask how or why. He thought about his own work and decided it brought him no happiness whatever. While his father had been alive, there had been some object in reporting at the office in the mornings, plugging away at his desk until six at night. He had done this to please the old man, but there was no satisfaction in doing it for Syd. It would be wonderful to have something to do which absorbed him. And around in the cycle of his thoughts came Caddie again, and he marveled at his love for her, and how dear her face was with its cap of brown curls, her laughing eyes, her big friendly mouth with the two parallel creases on either side made by her ready smiles.

He tossed the butt of his cigarette into an open pail, rose and went to her, putting his arms about her. She smelled of kitchen smoke and of cooking now, but as always the fragrance of her was a delight to him.

She sloshed out the bottom of the sink with a mop, rinsing the white enameled dishpan.

"Go away," she said; "you'll get yourself all wet."

"I love you," he said, his lips in her hair.

She dried her hands and faced him, smiling at his look, and held him at arm's length.

"You're such a big booby," she said fondly.

"You've accused me of being a lot of things this evening."

"You're all of them. I never knew a man so many-sided. . . . Let me alone," she protested as he tried to kiss her; "I reek of the kitchen. Let me go and powder my nose and rid myself of some of this stench."

She pushed him aside and went into the bedroom. He followed, and as she stood at the dresser he put his arms around her again and kissed her neck, her hair, and the lobe of her ear.

"Go away," she insisted; "you're like a clumsy, bumbling puppy."

"Something new, now."

"Well, what do you want?"

"You."

She regarded him soberly, placing both arms around his neck.

"What am I going to do with you?" she asked at length.

"Marry me."

"No, I won't do that."

"Love me, then."

"I do already."

"Go away with me."

"I can't do that, and *you* can't."

"What do you suggest?"

"That's what I'd like to know."

His arms went round her, and hers encircled him; he pulled her to him gently and strongly and kissed her.

"Love is love," he whispered, and drew her to the bed beside him. "Wait a moment," she said; "we'd better undress first." She switched off the lights.

§3

Half an hour later—perhaps it was longer—he was dozing with his cheek upon her breast, an arm around her. They had lain so for a long time, neither moving nor speaking.

Suddenly there was a noise, an earsplitting crash. Crash upon crash upon crash! Ax blows! Splintering wood! The harsh clamor sprang upon them from the darkness. They sat up, gripping each other in terror. Something terrible was happening—was going to happen! Stan's one instinct was to protect Caddie. But he could not move. Then their bedroom door burst open; the lights blazed. In the doorway, overcoated and hatless, stood Rory O'Brien, scowling hate. In the tense silence, he said slowly, snarlingly to Caddie:

"You dirty whore!"

Naked as he was, Stan leaped for him.

The first bullet pierced Stan's heart; the next stopped Caddie's wild scream of terror. Rory swayed a little as the smoke swirled in scarves about his head, the reek of powder filling the room, the bedclothes growing red and ever redder.

His lip curled as he surveyed the two bodies—one in the bed, the other at his feet. Then, with slow deliberation, he placed the muzzle of the gun inside his mouth and pulled the trigger. He slumped where he stood, his head sliding along the floor to meet Stan's hand.

CHAPTER XX

"Byron? This is Nate Jacobs speaking."

"Yes, I know; the butler told me."

"You've seen the papers?"

"The coroner called last night. I've been down there."

"To the morgue?"

"Yes. They telephoned his house, got his mother. We went down together—with Mrs. Mackey."

Silence.

"My God, Byron, this is a hell of a mess!"

"Yes, it's pretty terrible."

Another interval.

"Byron, I got to see you. She's still alive, you know."

"Where is she?"

"At the City and County. They called the nearest emergency hospital, and when the steward of the ambulance found she had a pulse they took her to the City and County."

"Is she badly hurt? Is she going to live?"

"I don't know. They wouldn't tell me. . . . Listen, Byron, I got to see you; I got to see *some*body!"

"What's the matter?"

"I'm responsible for the whole thing!"

"What do you mean? You had nothing to do with the shooting, did you?"

"No-o, but I tipped Rory off."

Byron could hear Nate gulp.

"How you mean?"

"Oh, I saw him—I saw Stan go in to where she lives, and I guessed where he was headed. Then I ran into Rory about nine or nine-thirty; we happened to meet at a bar—that McAllister Street place—and like a damn fool I mentioned it. I didn't know he was going to be so mad; he didn't show anything. We had a drink, and then he went out. He didn't say anything; he just went out!"

Byron waited for Nate to speak again.

"Say, listen, Byron, you got to help me. I'm nearly out of my mind. She's living yet. I've just been out to the hospital. The bullet went through the neck, cut the spinal cord. I tried to see her. They wouldn't let me! She told them she didn't want to see me! Y'understand? I talked to the superintendent; he wouldn't let me go up. He said Caddie was conscious and wasn't suffering, but that's all. Byron, *I got to do something.* I want her to have the best medical care that can be had. Won't you do something? You see how it is? She thinks I blabbed on her, and that's why she won't see me, but she told them she'd like to see *you*. Guess it's all up with her, but maybe it isn't— maybe something can be done. Perhaps a specialist. Won't you help me out? . . . Oh, God, if I had only kept my mouth shut!"

He stopped, and Byron could hear him gulping again.

"What do you want me to do?"

"Oh, I don't know! Go see her anyway, and do everything you can for her. I'll pay the bills. I'll pay anything!"

"Where are you now?"

"In my office. Could you come down? I'll tell you the whole story. I got to talk to somebody. If there's anything I can do for the poor girl, I want to do it—and you're the only person that can help me— or her. Won't you come down and see me?"

Byron glanced across the room at Eleanor, who sat watching him from eyes swollen with tears. She did not speak.

"All right, I'll be down. Where's your office?"

Nate told him.

"Expect me in half an hour."

He hung up.

§2

"Oh, I don't know," the superintendent of the hospital said doubtfully, shaking his head; "you're not a reporter, are you?"

"No, no; just a friend," Byron reassured him.

"What was it you wanted to see her about? Our rules are very strict."

"I have a pass from the chief of police." He presented it.

Dr. Haggard examined it carefully, pulling at his underlip, his brows puckered.

"You're Byron Mackey?"

"Yes."

"I've heard of you, haven't I?"

"Perhaps."

"You understand that Miss Welch is very ill?"

"Is she going to die?"

"Oh, I hope not; we always proceed on the supposition that our patients are going to get well. Dr. Christopher is the surgeon in charge; he will know more about the case than I. When I came on duty this morning I was informed Miss Welch had been brought here, and of course I've seen the papers. It's a pretty messy case, isn't it? I asked about her when I came in and was told that when the steward of the ambulance found she had a pulse he gave her artificial respiration and, because we have better equipment, told the driver to bring her to the City and County; as soon as she got here they put her into a respirator. Dr. Schultz, our nerve specialist, saw her this morning, but there's nothing to be done for the present. You understand, of course, that her spinal cord has been severed; she's paralyzed from the neck down; her whole system has had a very terrible shock. But of course people who have been as badly hurt as she has been frequently make a complete recovery."

"Is she suffering?"

"I doubt it. You see, she can't feel anything. She has considerable difficulty in breathing and swallowing, but I don't think there is any pain."

"Can she talk?"

"Oh yes, and hear—quite clearly. Dr. Christopher is better qualified to answer your questions than I. He's on his rounds right now."

"I understand Miss Welch is anxious to see me."

"Since you have police permission, I'm sure there won't be any difficulty. I think, however, I'd better ascertain if it's advisable just now—or convenient; you understand about that? I'll go upstairs and find Dr. Christopher; I must consult him, of course. He's busy at the moment, and I hate to call him to the telephone when he's on his rounds. You don't mind waiting, do you?"

"Oh no, but while I have your attention I'd like to have it understood that Miss Welch is to have the best of care, a private room, and as many nurses as necessary. I'll see to the expenses. When Dr. Christopher is free, I'd be happy to talk to him, and I would also like your permission to have Dr. Stewart see Miss Welch. Dr. Stewart was Mr. Rutherford's physician—the family's physician."

"Dr. Wilson Stewart?"

"Yes."

"Dr. Stewart is a member of our staff. We'll be glad to have his opinion. Now—if you'll excuse me—I'll find out if it's all right for you to see her."

Dr. Haggard departed, and while he waited Byron studied the floor, shaking his head slowly and sadly, a deep frown contracting his black brows. The tragic circumstances of Stan's death rode him hard. Stan's mother was prostrated; Grandmère as well. Either might die. Probably the old lady, whose pride had been crushed and who was frail as well. Eleanor had taken the shocking news with the fortitude which was characteristic of her. Only Daisy, off on her honeymoon, lighthearted and skylarking with Syd somewhere in Honolulu, had yet to be told. Sooner or later the terrible tidings would catch up with her, for the nation's press would blazon the story—*had* blazoned it!—from coast to coast, many of them sparing none of the sordid details.

"Yes, you can go up," Dr. Haggard said, re-entering his office; "Ward J."

"Good God, she isn't in a ward, is she?"

"Well," he said, smiling at the visitor's consternation, "she's in a room adjacent to Ward J; that's on the fifth floor. There's police supervision—naturally—so we put her into a room that was unoccupied. She's pretty sick, the head nurse tells me, but she's been asking for you constantly. You won't stay too long? She needs all the strength she has. Take the elevator to the fifth floor. The head nurse is expecting you, and I'll get word to Dr. Christopher that you'd like to see him."

§ 3

A policeman sat in front of Caddie's door, his chair tilted against the wall, a newspaper in his hands. He rose as Byron approached and examined his pass carefully. Then he eyed him critically.

"You're Mr. Mackey?"

Byron nodded and showed him letters which identified him.

"Okay," said the officer, "but I got strict orders to allow no reporters or snoopers inside. . . . Go ahead."

Caddie lay very straight and pillowless in a high hospital cot, its head raised on square blocks so that her body was inclined at a slight angle; bedclothes covered her to the chin, and her hair was bound back from her forehead and ears by a circlet of gauze. She looked ghastly—like a skeleton—her face drained of color, her cheekbones sharply defined, but she smiled wanly as she recognized her visitor, and her eyes showed pleasure.

"Hello, Byron. So nice of you to come."

Her voice was weak; there was a plaintive huskiness to it, and she spoke with difficulty.

"Sorry I can't shake hands," she whispered and closed her eyes.

"Sit down," she went on after a moment, and then to the hovering nurse she said: "Won't you go, please? I have to see Mr. Mackey alone. . . . *Please,*" she urged as the woman hesitated.

"I'll call you if she wants you," Byron offered. The nurse reluctantly departed, closing the door softly behind her.

Caddie smiled again and held the smile for a moment before she spoke.

"Guess I'm a goner," she said. "I heard them talking last night when I was in that iron-lung thing. But I don't want to live like this. . . . Oh, don't worry about me," she went on with a frown; "I had it coming to me—all the way. Don't be sorry—not for me." Then on a quivering breath she added: "There're the others . . ."

She stopped, and her eyes closed once more while she pressed her lips together as she struggled for self-control.

"Is there anything I can do?" Byron asked. "Anything you want?"

"Wait," she whispered. There was a long moment of silence.

"Just listen and try not to interrupt," she presently continued; "I don't know how long I'm going to be this way, and I don't much care, but now that I can think and talk, there's something I've got to get off my chest. . . . But, damn it, it's so hard to breathe."

She swallowed painfully, trying to smile.

"Don't worry about me," she repeated, "not if I die right here and now. I got something to tell you—something others ought to know, or at least *you* ought to know." A pause. Then with an effort she said:

"Rory was Frank Rutherford."

Byron stared at her.

"Rory was who?"

"Rory was Frank Rutherford," she said again, her eyes shut. "He was your brother-in-law, Lloyd Rutherford's son. Listen—and remember what I'm going to tell you. I'll do the best I can, but you see how it is."

She panted like a spent runner.

"My name was Catherine Slovak; my mother and father died when I was quite little; then I went to live with my aunt in Berkeley. When I was fifteen, I started out to make my own living and got a job in a laundry on Polk Street; I worked there for over five years. I grew tired of the job after a while and got another as a nursemaid with the Stoval family; they lived just a block below the Rutherfords. That's when I met Frank. You should have seen him then, Byron; he was one of God's handsomest men, and I fell for him hard. He was young and a daredevil and—and beautiful, not the way Stan was, but almost as attractive. We went together for about a year; I was crazy about him all right, and then I found I was going to have a baby. . . . Please," she begged, swallowing with obvious pain and struggling for breath as Byron half rose to call the nurse.

"Let me finish," she gasped, "even if it kills me. Sometimes I can't breathe . . . but I'll be all right."

She rested a minute before continuing, and Byron waited.

"Frank wanted to marry me, but I didn't want him to," Caddie went on. "He asked his father, and old Lloyd was furious. I wasn't the right kind of girl to marry Frank Rutherford; I knew that. I was a slovenly nursemaid who took care of a kid down the block, and I knew how his father would feel. I told Frank again and again I wouldn't marry him; all I wanted was enough money to take care of me and the baby when the baby came. I could go to my aunt in Berkeley, but she was rheumatic and couldn't do much for me. I swear to God, Byron, I didn't want to marry Frank. But he thought he wanted to marry *me* and asked his father. They had a terrible row. I don't know what happened, but they used some pretty strong language to each other, and Frank left the house and swore he'd never return. Then he came to me and wanted me to marry him. I wouldn't. I ran away to the country—to a girl friend's house down near Gilroy. He couldn't find me, got sore, went down to the docks and signed up as a sailor on board a Swedish tramp bound for Australia."

Suddenly she gagged; a spasm contorted her face, but her frown stopped him as he reached for the call bell.

When she recaptured her breath, she attempted a smile, panting a little, and whispered:

"Water—there—please."

She sucked at the tube in the glass and then lay with her eyes closed for some moments, waiting for her strength to gather.

"Well, he went away and I had my baby, but the baby died. A little boy. I wasn't sorry. I didn't want Frank to feel I had a hold on him or that there was a living tie between us. 'Bout a year or two later I married a man named Welch. Everybody called him Pete. He was a good guy, and I liked him well enough, but our marriage didn't last very long. He was a stevedore, and one night he got into a row in a barroom down along the waterfront and somebody knifed him. It wasn't *his* row; it was a friend's. Anyway, that's what they told me, but I felt badly when Pete died. He was all right.

"After that I decided to better myself, so I went to night school and studied shorthand and typing. While I was doing that I supported myself by doing chamber work in a rooming house where sailors and longshoremen went, and I made a lot of good friends there. 'Port o' Storm,' old Mrs. Peterson called it, and sometimes it was all of that. It was down on Clay Street, but Ma Peterson was a fine sort. The men swore by her; and she was good to me, too. . . . Water, please."

She drained at the tube again and rested as before. Byron watched her with concern, fully realizing that the recital was exhausting her, but he was afraid to interrupt.

"After I graduated from night school," she resumed, "I set myself up as a notary public, and I began to write a lot of life insurance for some of the fellows I had learned to know at the rooming house.

I made a great many friends—friends I like to remember. Swell bunch of fellows, most of 'em, and I was pretty popular. Anyway, along comes '34 and I got interested in the strike, and advised and helped with the Strike Committee. Then one day I met Rory O'Brien. He'd come back to the States and turned out to be a firebrand! Of course, I didn't know he was Frank Rutherford. He'd changed his name and had been badly burned, had grown a beard. He claimed the accident had happened on a Wickwire, Rutherford freighter—but I don't know about that. They never made the South Pacific run. A boiler burst, and he was scalded terribly—the whole left side of his body, his face and eyes. He always said it was something defective with the machinery and that the owners knew it, but as I say, I don't know how true it was. Rory was a little screwy.

"Well, they got him to a hospital in Melbourne, and he was there for several months. They tried to save his eyes, but they only succeeded with one, and they did all sorts of things to his face, grafted skin and I don't know what all. At any rate, when he was able to get about again, he went to work for the Camperdown Stevedoring Company—I think it was. He grew a beard, and when he decided to return to the States he changed his name. I don't know what for, but he hated the Rutherfords—all of them; he hated them worse than I've ever known a man to hate anything or anybody. I always thought that burn twisted his mind somehow. He was just poisoned by hate. He would have been a big man if it hadn't been for his hate. Deep down inside him, he was a great human being. Almost as much as he hated the Rutherfords, he loved his friends—his pals among the longshoremen and sailors. You never got to know Rory, but beneath that sneering, sarcastic way of his he had a heart of gold. He'd hand out his last nickel to a stevedore if he needed it, and he was always broke because he gave away everything he had. He knew all about the tough deal the longshoremen and sailors were having, and he dedicated his life to helping them.

"Of course I didn't know who he was when we first met, but after a few weeks, when we got to know each other, he told me, and then we started living together again, both working for the cause. Later on it was my idea to form the Maritime Federation of the Pacific, and Rory put it over. I was all for labor—I'm *still* for labor—

but it was the only interest I had in life then. . . . That was before I met Stan."

She closed her eyes, and as Byron bent closer two tears slowly formed beneath their lids and trickled down her cheeks. He could see she was suffering. He held the tube in the glass to her lips, and she drained the water eagerly and looked up through swimming eyes to thank him with a tremulous smile.

"Let me go on," she said after another moment or two, when she lay spent and panting. "I want someone—*you*—to know the whole story and then I'm done; I won't care.

"I loved Stan. He was the only man I ever really loved, and I loved him with every fiber of my being. . . . And I killed him; I was the cause of his death. It might just as well have been my hand that fired that shot!"

The eyes closed, the tears reappeared again, and presently she was gasping for air. Before he could call the nurse, she recovered and stopped him.

"Wipe these damn things away," she begged. "I don't want anything else. Use your handkerchief, but don't call that damned nurse. There's just a little more."

When he had dried her cheeks and gently mopped her eyes, he gave her another sip of water.

"Thanks," she whispered; "I'm sorry I'm so helpless," she added, with one of her characteristic big smiles. "Wait a few minutes, please. After I'm sure you know, it will be easier—truly.

"Oh, I loved Stan all right; I loved him better than he ever suspected. I was afraid to tell Rory about him, although of course Rory knew who he was, but he never guessed we were intimate. I made a mess of things, but you see how it was: I couldn't tell Rory about Stan, and I couldn't tell Stan about Rory. And they were first cousins, too! Rory hated Stan at sight, and if he had thought we were fond of each other he would have killed him—just as he did!"

She had to stop now and gasp, but the paroxysm was not as bad as before, and when breath returned she continued more easily.

"When they accused Rory of being an alien and threatened him with deportation, he had to prove he was an American citizen. You see, when he had shipped out of Melbourne, he registered as a

British subject and faked a seaman's passport. That's all he had to show, so he needed his birth certificate and I guess a statement from his father that he was his son. One night he went to see him—round midnight, I heard. I don't know what happened—nobody does—but I guess the shock of seeing his son again after so many years and identifying him as Rory O'Brien was too much for old Lloyd, and he just snuffed out. Rory never said anything to me. I put two and two together from what Stan told me, but I couldn't give Stan a hint of what I suspected. I swore I'd never tell anyone who Rory was, and I never did. It wouldn't have done any good, anyhow.

"That's about all there is, Byron. Rory O'Brien was your wife's brother, and you can tell her or not just as you see fit. I just don't want to die with that secret inside me. Now it's told and I'm happier—lots happier. Nobody else knows it but you and me—not even that dirty rat who squealed on me!"

She had to stop again and fight for breath.

"I've been thinking, Byron, that in a funny way Rory and Stan represented labor and capital. Rory was labor; Stan was capital—employee and employer, the worker and the businessman. When they fight, see what happens? They destroy each other! If they could be friends . . . however . . . It will always be that way, I guess.

"I've been through hell, Byron; guess you can understand that. The more I loved Stan, the harder it was for me. I knew that if Rory suspected about Stan and me, there'd be trouble, and of course I should have run away, dropped out of sight—or gone the way I'm going now. I deserve what's happening to me; I deserve every bit of it. I wish there was more physical pain; perhaps I'd mind the mental pain less. I loved Stan and he loved me. He wanted me to marry him, but there were a million more reasons why I couldn't marry him than there were for not marrying Rory. Stan begged me to run away with him, and I couldn't do that either. I'd have ruined his life; I knew that. Perhaps it would have been better if I had . . . for now he's dead."

The tears began sliding down her cheeks again, and Byron rose to wipe them away.

Then there was a long silence in the little room. Caddie rested, only now and then struggling for breath. Byron sat on, thinking over the story she had told, thinking of the tragedy of it all—hers and Stan's and Rory's—wondering too if there was some question he should ask which would clear up a detail, clear it up while yet there was time!

The nurse came in and, after lingering a minute, stole away. Caddie remained motionless and seemed to be in no pain—only that little gasp for air once in a while. Next came the doctor—Dr. Christopher; he nodded to Byron and stood by the bed, slightly frowning as he looked down at its occupant. Caddie did not move; she did not open her eyes; she lay serene and calm, reaching now and then for that needed breath. Then, without a word, the physician too went out, and Byron remained alone. And presently, as he watched, it seemed to him that some new quality of peace had come to the dying woman's face. It was as if a gentle hand had passed its fingers over it and smoothed away its lines of pain and anguish, and in its place he seemed to see the features of a younger Caddie—a vigorous, vital, eager girl, the handsome nursemaid who had once attracted Frank Rutherford's roving glance—a woman in her early twenties, strong-limbed, robust, seeking life, welcoming it with out-stretched arms, kind, loving, overgenerous.

Presently she opened her eyes and smiled at him, and he saw resignation and tranquillity in her gaze. Her strength was ebbing, and he realized the physician should be warned. He rose and, since he could not touch her hand, he bent over the bed and gently kissed her cheek.

The tears began to flow again, but the smile was broad and big and confident.

"Byron Mackey for President," she whispered.